Isle of Wight Follies
Legendary Anthology

By Mark McIntyre

ISBN: 9798333936592
Imprint: Independently published.

All images, logos, and text are copyright of Mark McIntyre and may not be used, copied, duplicated, etc., without express written permission.

For more of my books, visit:
mdmcintyre.co.uk

To create your own book, visit:
WritePublish.co.uk

Dedication

To the Isle of Wight,
This book is dedicated to the cherished memories of a land that captured my heart and imagination. To the glorious scenery that stretches from the rugged cliffs of Alum Bay to the serene shores of Shorwell; to the rich tapestry of history that weaves through every ancient stone and sunlit path; and to the wonderful people whose warmth and spirit made every moment on the island unforgettable.

The Isle of Wight is more than just a place—it's a living tapestry of beauty, mystery, and magic. It's a realm where the past mingles with the present, and where the possibility of spotting a dinosaur adds an extra touch of wonder.
May this book inspire others to explore its enchanting landscapes and embrace the adventures that await. For in every breeze, every shadow, and every hidden corner, the Isle of Wight holds a story waiting to be discovered.

With deepest gratitude and fondest memories,
Mark McIntyre

The Griffin of Cowes 7

The Gurnard Golem 16

The Hampstead Ogre 25

The Faun of Newbridge 34

The Leprechaun of Northwood 43

The Shalfleet Sphinx 52

The Yarmouth Mermaid 61

The Bowcombe Chupacabra 69

The Carisbrooke Banshee 77

The Nymph of Marks Corner 86

The Norton Green Kitsune 94

The Sea Serpent of Ryde 104

The Vampires of Brading 112

The Fairies of St Helens 121

The Werewolves of Bembridge 136

The Loch Ness Monster at Downend 145

The Minotaur of Cowes 153

The Chimera of Oakfield and Swanmore 159

The Basilisk of Havenstreet 172

The Dragons of Newport 181

The Roc of Shide 189

The Trolls of Wootton 197

The Cyclops of Sandown 203

The Zombies of Shanklin 211

The Satyr of Wroxall 218

The Manticore of Alverstone 225

The Djinn of Apse Heath 230

The Yeti of Bonchurch 237

The Medusa of Godshill 243

The Phoenix of Merstone 251

The Wraiths of Niton 259

The Wendigo of St Lawrence 267

The Hydra of Ventnor 279

The Freshwater Gorgon 288

The Pegasus of Alum Bay 296

The Goblin of Chale 304

The Jersey Devil of Chale Green 312

The Gnome of Rowbridge 323

The Bigfoot of Totland 330

The Thunderbird of Blackgang 337

The Elven of Brook 349

The Chillerton Bogeyman 358

The Aqrabuamelu of Mottistone 368

The Selkies of Shorwell 378

The gathering of Legends 387

The Griffin of Cowes

The Arrival of Gary

Cowes, a picturesque town nestled on the Isle of Wight, is renowned for its sailing events and maritime charm. Yet, amid this serene setting, a legend was about to be born — one that would etch its name in the annals of local folklore. This legend was not of a human hero or a ghostly apparition but of a creature more majestic and unusual — a Griffin named Gary. Gary was not your typical Griffin. With the powerful body of a lion and the head and wings of a majestic eagle, he embodied both strength and grandeur, with a dash of grumpiness that only added to his charm. His arrival in Cowes was nothing short of a spectacle. It was a crisp autumn morning when the townsfolk first spotted him. The sun was just peeking over the horizon, casting long shadows over the town, when Gary's massive wings appeared in the sky, casting an even longer shadow.

As he descended gracefully onto the shore, his keen eagle eyes surveyed his new home with an air of superiority. The townspeople watched in a mix of awe and trepidation. Who could have expected a Griffin to choose their quaint town as its residence? Little did they know, this mythical creature would soon become an integral part of their community, bringing with him both hilarity and heroism.

Gary's initial arrival was met with a flurry of whispers and speculations. Children peeked from behind their parents' legs, and shopkeepers craned their necks to get a better view of the majestic beast. The town's mayor, an elderly gentleman named Mr. Pritchard, was among the first to approach Gary. With a tentative step forward, he raised his hand in a gesture of greeting.

"Welcome to Cowes," Mr. Pritchard said, his voice quivering slightly. "I am Mayor Pritchard. We hope you will find our town to your liking."

Gary eyed the mayor with a mixture of curiosity and amusement. He let out a low, rumbling growl, which Mr. Pritchard took as a sign of approval. The mayor turned to the townspeople and announced, "Gary the Griffin has chosen to live among us. Let us make him feel at home."

The townspeople, though still wary, began to warm to the idea of having a Griffin in their midst. Gary, sensing their apprehension, decided to show them that he meant no harm. With a mighty flap of his wings, he took to the sky, performing a series of graceful loops and dives. The crowd gasped and applauded, their fear slowly giving way to admiration.

Gary's aerial display was more than just a show of his flying prowess; it was his way of telling the townsfolk that he was not a threat. As he landed back on the shore, the townspeople cheered, and a small group of children ran forward to greet him. Gary lowered his head, allowing the children to pet his soft feathers and touch his powerful lion's body. The bond between Gary and the people of Cowes had begun to form.

Gary's Daily Routine

After the initial excitement of Gary's arrival, the townsfolk began to observe his daily routine with a blend of curiosity and amusement. Gary, it seemed, had a love for the skies that was unparalleled. Each morning, at the crack of dawn, he would take to the air, his massive wings slicing through the crisp morning air. The sight of a Griffin soaring high above the Solent became a familiar and awe-inspiring view for early risers.

Gary's morning flights were a sight to behold. He would circle the town, gliding effortlessly on the thermals, his keen eagle eyes scanning the landscape below. The fishermen out at sea would wave to him, and he would respond with a graceful dip of his wings. The children on their way to school would stop and stare, pointing excitedly at the majestic creature above.

But Gary was not just a creature of the air. He had an unexpected passion for kayaking, a hobby that baffled everyone who witnessed it. One day, while strolling along the beach, he stumbled upon an abandoned bright red kayak. Intrigued, he decided to give it a try. With his powerful lion's legs and sharp eagle's talons, Gary quickly mastered the art of paddling. Soon, he was seen navigating the calm waters with ease, feathers gleaming in the sunlight, much to the delight and amusement of the townsfolk.

The sight of Gary paddling through the waters of the Solent became a common occurrence. He would often join the local kayakers, who welcomed him with open arms. Gary's presence brought a sense of wonder and excitement to their outings. He would lead the group, his powerful strokes propelling him forward with incredible speed. The kayakers would struggle to keep up, laughing and cheering as they followed in his wake.

Gary's love for kayaking wasn't just about the physical activity; it was also a way for him to connect with the people of Cowes. He enjoyed the camaraderie and the shared experiences. The locals began to see Gary not just as a mythical creature but as a friend and fellow adventurer.

The Lobster Fiasco

Gary's culinary preferences were as unique as his hobbies. He developed an insatiable craving for lobster, which led to one of the most memorable incidents in Cowes' history. One summer, driven by his newfound obsession, Gary decided to indulge in an all-you-can-eat lobster buffet at a local restaurant.

The restaurant, The Seaside Grill, was known for its fresh seafood and friendly atmosphere. Gary's arrival caused quite a stir among the patrons. As he entered the restaurant, his massive frame barely fitting through the door, the diners fell silent, their eyes wide with astonishment.

Gary, undeterred by the stares, made his way to the buffet table. He grabbed a plate and began piling it high with lobsters, mussels, and shrimp. The restaurant staff watched in awe as the Griffin devoured his meal with gusto. Word quickly spread, and soon the place was packed with curious onlookers, eager to witness the spectacle.

What started as a simple meal quickly turned into a three-day eating marathon. Plates of lobster, mussels, and even ice cream were flown in by helicopter as Gary devoured everything in sight. The local TV station soon caught wind of the spectacle, and crowds gathered to watch the insatiable Griffin. Gary's feast became the talk of the town.

As the days went on, the spectacle grew. Reporters from neighbouring towns arrived to cover the story. The Seaside Grill became a bustling hub of activity, with people clamouring to catch a glimpse of Gary in action. The restaurant owner, Mr. Thompson, capitalised on the attention, offering special "Griffin Plates" and themed merchandise. However, it wasn't the food that finally stopped Gary, but the overwhelming number of cheerful onlookers. His grumpiness couldn't handle the excessive joy and chatter, and he retreated with a full belly and a new nickname: "Gary the Gluttonous Griffin."

The Lobster Fiasco, as it came to be known, left a lasting impression on the town. Gary's legendary appetite became a part of local folklore, and The Seaside Grill continued to thrive long after the event. For Gary, it was a lesson in moderation and the limits of even a mythical creature's stomach.

Cowes Week Chaos

Cowes Week, the town's famous sailing event, was both a blessing and a curse for Gary. The influx of visitors and boats meant that the waters were crowded, and Gary's peaceful kayaking sessions were often interrupted. This made him particularly irritable, and when Gary got grumpy, everyone knew to keep their distance.

Cowes Week brought with it a festive atmosphere. The town was decorated with colourful flags and banners, and the streets were filled with music and laughter. Gary, however, found the hustle and bustle to be overwhelming. The constant noise and activity disrupted his routine, and he longed for the tranquillity of his morning flights and kayaking trips.

One year, a particularly rowdy yachting crew from London made the mistake of mocking Gary while he was out on his kayak. The crew, having had a bit too much to drink, thought it would be funny to tease the Griffin. They shouted taunts and jeers, calling him names and making a ruckus.

Gary, already on edge from the busy week, was not in the mood for their antics. Fuelled by their jeers and his own irritation, Gary decided to teach them a lesson. In a display of both power and humour, he overturned their boat with a single swipe of his mighty wings. The crew, drenched and humbled, swam back to shore. The incident became a local legend, with townsfolk secretly cheering for Gary's boldness.

The story of the overturned boat spread quickly, becoming a favourite tale among the locals. The yachting crew, embarrassed but unharmed, left Cowes with a newfound respect for the Griffin. Gary's actions reinforced his reputation as a force to be reckoned with, and the townspeople admired him all the more for it.

The Griffin's Generosity

Despite his occasional grumpiness, Gary had a generous side that endeared him to the people of Cowes. He often used his formidable strength to help with local causes, whether it was lifting heavy objects or using his keen eyesight to spot schools of fish for the local fishermen. His most significant contribution, however, was his lobster fishing.
Gary had become an expert at catching lobsters, and he sold his daily catch to a local restaurant. The proceeds went towards funding community projects, and Gary's efforts were greatly appreciated. His fishing skills and his sense of purpose made him a beloved, if slightly irritable, member of the town.
Gary's generosity extended beyond his fishing talents. He often assisted with construction projects, using his powerful lion's body to move heavy materials and his sharp eagle eyes to oversee the work. The townspeople were grateful for his help, and Gary took pride in contributing to the community. One particularly memorable project was the renovation of the local library. The building had fallen into disrepair, and the town lacked the funds to restore it. Gary, recognising the importance of the library, decided to take matters into his own claws. He organised a series of fundraising events, including a lobster-catching competition and a charity kayak race.

The events were a huge success, drawing crowds from all over the island. Gary's involvement brought attention to the cause, and donations poured in. With the funds raised, the library was not only restored but also expanded, providing a valuable resource for the community.

Gary's efforts didn't go unnoticed. The mayor awarded him a special plaque, and the townspeople held a celebration in his honour. Gary, though grumpy about the fuss, couldn't hide his satisfaction. He had made a difference, and the gratitude of the people warmed his heart.

High Above Cowes

Gary's favourite pastime, soaring high above Cowes, provided him with a sense of freedom and joy. The sight of the Griffin gliding through the sky became a symbol of the town, a reminder of the magical and mythical that existed in their everyday lives. Even as he kayaked and fished, his heart belonged to the sky.

Each evening, as the sun began to set, Gary would take to the skies for one last flight. The golden light of the setting sun cast a warm glow on his feathers, creating a breathtaking sight. The townspeople would stop whatever they were doing to watch, their faces turned upward in admiration.

Gary's flights were more than just a display of his aerial prowess. They were a symbol of the town's spirit, a reminder that even in the most ordinary places, extraordinary things could happen. The children would dream of flying with Gary, and the adults would find solace in the beauty of his graceful movements.

Over time, Gary became more than just a myth; he became a part of the town's identity. Festivals and events were organised in his honour, and stories of his adventures were passed down through generations. The legend of Gary the Griffin grew, and with it, the town's sense of wonder and community.

Gary's story is a testament to individuality and the joy of simple pleasures. His grumpy yet generous nature, combined with his love for kayaking and lobster, made him a unique and unforgettable character in the town of Cowes. And while his legend grew, Gary continued to live his best life, inspiring those around him with his strength, majesty, and a touch of humour.

In the end, Gary the Griffin, with his majestic presence and quirky habits, became an emblem of Cowes, a reminder that even in the most ordinary places, extraordinary tales can unfold. The town of Cowes, with its rich history and vibrant community, was forever changed by the arrival of the Griffin. And as the years went by, the story of Gary the Griffin became a cherished part of the town's heritage, a symbol of the magic that lies within us all.

The Gurnard Golem

The Silent Guardian

In the quaint village of Gurnard on the Isle of Wight, nestled between rolling hills and the serene coastline, lived a creature of immense strength and unyielding stoicism. This was no ordinary resident; it was a Golem named Gavin, a hulking figure sculpted from the very earth itself. Gavin's form was a masterwork of rugged, baked clay, with intricate patterns etched into his surface, hinting at ancient origins and powerful magic. His eyes, glowing with an otherworldly luminescence, were the only discernible feature on his otherwise featureless face, adding an eerie quality to his formidable appearance.

Gavin's arrival in Gurnard was shrouded in mystery. Some said he was conjured by a long-forgotten sorcerer to protect the village, while others believed he had always been there, a silent guardian awakened only in times of need. Regardless of his origins, the villagers came to accept his presence, albeit with a mix of awe and trepidation.

Gavin was a creature of few words, his communication largely non-verbal, relying on grunts, nods, and the occasional low growl. His daily routine involved solitary strolls around the village, his massive strides causing the ground to tremble subtly beneath his feet. Despite his intimidating appearance and grumpy demeanour, Gavin was known for his unwavering obedience and reliability. He often assisted the villagers with tasks that required immense strength, such as moving heavy stones, repairing buildings, or clearing fallen trees after a storm.

Children, who were initially terrified of him, grew to see Gavin as a kind of gentle giant. They would follow him at a safe distance, mimicking his lumbering gait and giggling when he occasionally turned to glare at them with mock annoyance. The adults, on the other hand, were grateful for his help, though they often found his constant grumbling amusing.

One evening, as the sun dipped below the horizon, casting a warm glow over the village, Gavin was called upon to help repair the roof of the village hall. A recent storm had caused significant damage, and the villagers were struggling to fix it. Gavin, with his incredible strength and dexterity, made quick work of the repairs. As he lifted the final beam into place, the villagers cheered, their admiration for the silent guardian growing with each display of his prowess.

The Cheerful Leprechaun

One of the few beings capable of drawing out Gavin's grumpy side was the overly cheerful Leprechaun of Northwood, a neighbouring village. This tiny, jolly creature, with his constant smiles, endless chatter, and bright green attire, was a stark contrast to Gavin's stoic nature. The Leprechaun, always full of mischief and laughter, seemed to relish pushing Gavin's buttons.

The Leprechaun, whose name was Finn, had a knack for appearing at the most inopportune times. Whether Gavin was engaged in a task or enjoying a rare moment of solitude, Finn would suddenly materialise with a broad grin and a twinkle in his eye. He would regale Gavin with tales of his latest adventures, punctuated by bouts of infectious laughter and the occasional practical joke.

Gavin found Finn's antics profoundly vexing. The Leprechaun's incessant pranks, which included hiding Gavin's tools, planting itching powder in his clay, and even painting his feet bright pink while he slept, tested the Golem's patience to its limits. Yet, for all his grumbling and glaring, Gavin never truly lost his temper with Finn, recognising a kindred spirit beneath the Leprechaun's playful exterior.

The villagers, well aware of this peculiar dynamic, often chuckled at the sight of the two together — a grumbling Golem and a giggling Leprechaun. They appreciated Finn's efforts to lighten Gavin's mood, though they did their best to stay out of the line of fire when one of Finn's pranks went awry.

One day, Finn decided to throw a surprise party for Gavin. He enlisted the help of the villagers, who were eager to see how the Golem would react. The preparations were elaborate, with decorations, a feast, and even a large clay cake shaped like Gavin. When the moment arrived, Gavin entered the village square to find everyone gathered, shouting, "Surprise!" in unison.

Gavin's eyes glowed brighter for a moment, a sign of his bewilderment. He let out a low growl, but the corners of his mouth, usually set in a stern line, seemed to lift slightly. Finn, perched on a barrel, beamed with satisfaction. It was a rare sight to see Gavin almost smile, and the villagers cherished the moment.

The Boisterous Griffins

Adding to Gavin's exasperation were the Griffins of Cowes, creatures of boundless energy and enthusiasm. These majestic beings, with their lion's bodies and eagle's heads, spent their days kayaking and surfing along the coast, their joyous antics a constant source of annoyance for Gavin. He couldn't fathom how creatures with such a short lifespan could afford to spend their time in such frivolous pursuits.

The Griffins, led by a particularly exuberant individual named Gary, were a common sight along the shores of Gurnard. They would swoop and dive, their laughter echoing across the water, oblivious to Gavin's brooding presence. Gary, with his golden feathers and infectious optimism, was the antithesis of Gavin's stoic demeanour.

One sunny afternoon, the Griffins decided to hold a surfing competition. The beach was soon filled with the sounds of waves crashing, wings flapping, and excited cheers. Gavin, seeking his usual solitude, retreated to a nearby cliff to watch from a distance. Despite his grumbling, he couldn't help but be captivated by the Griffins' grace and skill.

As the competition reached its peak, Gary spotted Gavin watching from the cliff. With a mischievous grin, he signalled to the other Griffins and together they performed an elaborate aerial display, diving and looping in perfect synchrony. The villagers, who had gathered to watch, erupted in applause. Gavin, despite himself, felt a twinge of admiration for their prowess.

After the competition, Gary approached Gavin, landing gracefully at his side. "You know, Gavin," he said, "you should try surfing with us. It's quite exhilarating."

Gavin let out a low growl, his eyes narrowing. "I prefer solid ground," he rumbled.

Gary chuckled. "Suit yourself, but if you ever change your mind, we'd be happy to have you join us."

Gavin watched as Gary rejoined the other Griffins, their laughter fading into the distance. Though he would never admit it, there was a part of him that envied their freedom and camaraderie.

The Strength of a Golem

Gavin's strength was legendary in Gurnard. He could lift and move objects many times his size with ease, and his stoicism was a source of comfort to the villagers. Whenever heavy lifting was required, Gavin was the go-to creature. He took pride in his ability to help, though he rarely showed it. His actions spoke louder than words, and his reliability was unmatched.

One particular incident highlighted Gavin's strength and grumpiness in equal measure. The village needed to move a massive boulder that was blocking a crucial path. The boulder had fallen during a storm, and its sheer size made it impossible for the villagers to move it on their own. While the villagers debated how to tackle the problem, Gavin simply walked over, grumbled under his breath, and moved the boulder with a single heave. The villagers cheered, and Gavin, true to form, walked away with a grumble about unnecessary noise.

Another instance that showcased Gavin's strength was during the annual harvest festival. The villagers had constructed a large stage for performances, but the support beams had been damaged in transit. With the festival set to begin in a few hours, panic set in. Gavin, seeing their distress, stepped forward and, with minimal effort, lifted the stage and held it steady while the beams were replaced. The festival proceeded without a hitch, and Gavin's heroics were the talk of the town.

Gavin's grumpiness was not without reason. He had a deep sense of duty and took his responsibilities seriously. The villagers' frequent praise and celebrations sometimes felt excessive to him. He preferred to work quietly, without fanfare, letting his actions speak for themselves.

Embracing Solitude

Despite the challenges posed by Finn and the Griffins, Gavin never lost his love for solitude and peace. He often retreated to the outskirts of the village, where he could enjoy the quiet and reflect on his own thoughts. It was here, in these moments of solitude, that Gavin found his true contentment.

Gavin's favourite spot was a secluded grove just beyond the village. Surrounded by ancient trees and a small, bubbling stream, it was a place of tranquillity and natural beauty. Here, Gavin would sit for hours, listening to the sounds of the forest and feeling the earth beneath him. The grove was his sanctuary, a place where he could escape the noise and bustle of village life.

Occasionally, Finn would find his way to the grove, but even the mischievous Leprechaun respected Gavin's need for peace. He would sit quietly by the stream, content to share the silence with his friend. These moments, rare as they were, deepened the bond between the two, showing that even the most unlikely of friendships could find common ground.

One day, while Gavin was enjoying his solitude, a young girl from the village approached him. Her name was Lily, and she was known for her curiosity and adventurous spirit. She had heard tales of Gavin's strength and stoicism and wanted to see the Golem for herself.

"Hello, Gavin," she said, her voice trembling slightly. "I've heard so much about you. May I sit with you for a while?"

Gavin regarded her with his glowing eyes, then nodded slowly. Lily sat beside him, her eyes wide with wonder. They sat in silence for a while, the only sounds the rustling of leaves and the gentle flow of the stream.

"Do you ever get lonely, Gavin?" Lily asked, breaking the silence.

Gavin considered her question carefully. "Sometimes," he rumbled. "But I find peace in solitude."

Lily smiled. "I understand. I like to explore on my own, too. It's nice to have a place where you can just be yourself."

Gavin nodded, his eyes softening. In that moment, he realised that solitude didn't have to mean isolation. There was comfort in knowing that others understood and respected his need for quiet. Lily's presence was a reminder that even in his grumpiness, he was not alone.

The Unexpected Hero

One stormy night, disaster struck Gurnard. Heavy rains caused a landslide, threatening to bury part of the village. As panic spread, it was Gavin who stepped forward. His immense strength and calm demeanour in the face of crisis proved invaluable. He worked tirelessly through the night, moving debris and creating safe pathways for the villagers. The storm raged on, the wind howling and rain pouring down in torrents. The villagers, soaked and scared, looked to Gavin for guidance. He directed them to safer areas, his deep, rumbling voice cutting through the chaos. His glowing eyes, usually a source of unease, now provided a beacon of hope. Gavin's strength seemed limitless as he moved fallen trees and boulders, his powerful arms and steady hands making quick work of the obstacles. The villagers watched in awe, their fear slowly giving way to gratitude and admiration. Gavin's grumpiness was forgotten in the face of his heroism.

By dawn, the village was safe, and the rain had subsided. Exhausted but undeterred, Gavin continued to clear the remaining debris, ensuring that the paths were secure and that no one was trapped. The villagers, who had always appreciated his help, now saw him in a new light. Gavin, for his part, remained as grumpy as ever, but there was a glimmer of satisfaction in his glowing eyes.

The landslide had brought the village together in a way that no one had expected. Gavin's heroism was celebrated, and a statue was erected in his honour, a testament to his strength and dedication. The villagers, once wary of the silent guardian, now embraced him as one of their own.

Gavin's story is a testament to the power of individuality and the joy of simple pleasures. Even in a world filled with mischievous Leprechauns and exuberant Griffins, there was room for a grumpy Golem who preferred solitude. Gavin's grumpiness and strength, combined with his love for peace, made him a unique and unforgettable character in Gurnard.

In the end, Gavin's legacy was one of quiet heroism and unwavering strength. The village of Gurnard, with its rich history and vibrant community, was forever changed by the presence of the Golem. And as the years went by, the story of Gavin the Golem became a cherished part of the village's heritage, a reminder that even the grumpiest among us have the potential to be heroes.

The Hampstead Ogre

The Unexpected Resident

In the picturesque village of Hamstead on the Isle of Wight, an imposing figure named Oliver the Ogre lived amidst an eclectic mix of mythical neighbours. Ogres, known for their fearsome appearance and appetite, were often misunderstood creatures. Oliver was no exception. Towering over his surroundings, with a broad body and a large head covered in unruly hair, his earthy green skin gave him an intimidating look. But Oliver, contrary to the usual tales of ogres, had a gentle heart and a surprising love for poetry.

Oliver's presence in Hamstead was as unexpected as it was unusual. His arrival had been a source of both fear and fascination for the villagers. Many nights were spent whispering about the hulking figure that had taken residence on the outskirts of the village. Children spun tales of his monstrous deeds, while adults kept a wary eye, uncertain of his intentions. However, those who dared to venture close enough to observe Oliver discovered a creature far removed from the terrifying ogre of their imaginations.

Oliver's home was a modest stone cottage surrounded by a wild, unkempt garden. Vines climbed its walls, and the flowers bloomed in chaotic abundance, a riot of colours against the grey stone. The cottage itself, though small, was surprisingly cosy. Inside, it was filled with books, comfortable furniture, and the soft glow of lanterns. The walls were lined with shelves, crammed with volumes of poetry, history, and tales of old.

Despite his daunting appearance, Oliver's daily life was marked by routine and simplicity. He tended to his garden with great care, growing vegetables and flowers that he shared with his neighbours. He was often seen walking through the village, his heavy footsteps causing the ground to tremble slightly. The villagers gradually grew accustomed to his presence, though many still watched him with a mix of curiosity and caution.

Eccentric Neighbours

Oliver's neighbours added to the charm and chaos of Hamstead. There was the Nymph of Marks Corner, whose favourite pastime was to scare unsuspecting visitors. She had an ethereal beauty, with flowing hair and shimmering skin, and could often be seen flitting through the woods, her laughter echoing like the tinkling of bells. Despite her mischievous nature, the villagers held a fondness for her, knowing that her pranks were harmless.

The Sphinx of Shalfleet, with her air of mystery, enjoyed posing riddles that even the brightest minds struggled to solve. She had the body of a lion and the head of a woman, with eyes that seemed to see into one's soul. Many a traveller had found themselves caught in her web of puzzles, spending hours trying to unravel her enigmatic questions.

The Faun of Newbridge, constantly tinkering with inventions, brought a sense of curiosity and innovation to the village. He had the legs of a goat and the upper body of a man, with horns curling from his forehead. His workshop was a marvel of gears, pulleys, and curious contraptions, and he was always eager to share his latest creations with anyone who showed interest.

Meanwhile, the Mermaid of Yarmouth preferred sunbathing on the rocks and occasionally dining on an unfortunate fisherman. Her beauty was mesmerizing, with long, flowing hair and scales that glittered like jewels. She had a voice that could charm anyone who heard it, but her predatory nature kept the villagers at a respectful distance.

One might think that Oliver would be perpetually annoyed by his quirky neighbours, but he found solace in a different way. He had taken to adopting stray cats and dogs, giving them a home in his humble abode. His house became a sanctuary for these animals, who found unexpected comfort in the presence of a supposedly fearsome ogre. The sight of a large, green ogre surrounded by a menagerie of cats and dogs was enough to make anyone smile.

Oliver's Unique Passion

Oliver's love for his pets extended beyond just providing them with food and shelter. He had a peculiar habit that set him apart: he read poetry to them. Every evening, Oliver would gather his feline and canine friends and recite lines from his favourite poems. The animals, though initially wary, grew accustomed to his deep, soothing voice. To keep his pets from wandering off during these sessions, Oliver installed a state-of-the-art pet door that only opened during feeding times. Oliver's evenings were a sight to behold. He would sit in a large, comfortable chair on his porch, a book of poetry in hand, surrounded by his attentive audience of cats and dogs. His deep, resonant voice would fill the air as he read aloud, the rhythmic cadence of his words creating a tranquil atmosphere. The animals, seeming to understand the significance of these sessions, would lie quietly at his feet, their eyes half-closed as they listened to the soothing sound of his voice.
Oliver's favourite poets included William Wordsworth, Emily Dickinson, and Robert Frost. He found a particular affinity with Frost's works, the themes of nature and solitude resonating deeply with his own life. As he read, he would often pause to reflect on the words, his eyes distant as he pondered their meaning.

The Poetry Sessions

As the sun set each day, casting a golden glow over the village, Oliver would sit on his porch, a content smile on his face as he watched his pets scamper around. He would often recite a line or two from his favourite poems, his deep voice echoing in the quiet evening. The cats and dogs, now used to his routine, would settle down around him, their eyes half-closed as they listened to his recitation. It was a sight that would have warmed the heart of anyone who saw it, a testament to the unexpected softness of an Ogre's heart.

One evening, as Oliver was reading Robert Frost's "The Road Not Taken," a curious onlooker approached his cottage. It was young Emily, the daughter of the village blacksmith. She had heard stories of the poetry-reading ogre and had come to see it for herself. Standing at the edge of the garden, she listened in awe as Oliver's voice carried the words of the poem through the still night air.

"Two roads diverged in a yellow wood, And sorry I could not travel both…"

Emily watched as Oliver's pets lay around him, completely enraptured by the sound of his voice. She could hardly believe her eyes – the ogre, who was supposed to be fearsome and terrifying, was instead gentle and kind, his love for poetry shining through with every word.

Gaining courage, Emily stepped forward. "Mr. Oliver?" she called softly.

Oliver looked up, surprised to see a human visitor. "Yes?" he rumbled, his voice gentle despite its depth.

"May I listen to you read?" Emily asked, her eyes wide with wonder.

Oliver smiled, a rare sight that transformed his rugged features. "Of course, child. Sit down and make yourself comfortable."

Emily joined the circle of animals, and as Oliver resumed his reading, she found herself captivated by the beauty of the words and the soothing rhythm of his voice. From that day on, Emily became a regular visitor, often bringing friends who were eager to hear the poetry-reading ogre.

A Local Legend

Word of Oliver's unique hobby spread throughout the region, and soon, he became something of a local legend. People travelled from far and wide to catch a glimpse of the poetry-reading Ogre and his adopted pets. They watched in awe as Oliver recited his poems, his voice carrying across the quiet landscape. Though they came expecting to see a fearsome ogre, they left with the image of a gentle giant who had a love for poetry and a soft spot for stray animals.

The villagers of Hamstead were proud of their unexpected resident. They took great delight in the reactions of visitors who, upon seeing Oliver, realised that appearances could be deceiving. Oliver's poetry sessions became a cherished tradition, drawing crowds who were eager to experience the unique blend of his fearsome appearance and gentle soul.

One summer evening, a travelling bard named Elinor arrived in Hamstead, curious about the tales she had heard. She approached Oliver with a mixture of apprehension and excitement, hoping to witness his legendary poetry readings. When she saw him surrounded by his pets, reciting verses with heartfelt emotion, she knew she had stumbled upon something truly special.

"Oliver," Elinor said after the reading, "your love for poetry is truly inspiring. Would you allow me to compose a ballad about you?"

Oliver, though not accustomed to such attention, nodded. "If it pleases you," he replied.

Elinor spent several days in Hamstead, observing Oliver's interactions with his pets and his neighbours. She crafted a ballad that captured the essence of the gentle ogre, weaving his story into a song that would be sung for generations. The ballad of Oliver the Ogre became a favourite among bards, spreading his legend far and wide.

Despite his newfound fame, Oliver remained unchanged. He continued to live his life as he always had, finding joy in the simple pleasures of life. He continued to adopt stray animals, his home becoming a haven for those in need. And he continued to read poetry, his words a soothing balm in a world filled with chaos and noise.

Harmonious Coexistence

Despite the chaos and eccentricities of his neighbours, Oliver had found a way to carve out a peaceful existence for himself. He had learned to tune out the Nymph's scares, ignore the Sphinx's riddles, overlook the Faun's tinkering, and even tolerate the Mermaid's sunbathing habits. In his own unique way, Oliver had found a way to coexist with his neighbours, proving that even an Ogre can live in harmony with others.

One day, the Nymph of Marks Corner, named Lila, decided to play a prank on Oliver by hiding his beloved poetry book. When Oliver discovered his book was missing, he let out a deep sigh, knowing who was responsible. He trudged to the edge of the woods, where Lila often resided, and called out in his deep, rumbling voice, "Lila, return my book, please."

Lila appeared with a playful grin, holding the book above her head. "You're no fun, Oliver! You didn't even try to find it."

Oliver extended his hand, his expression stern but patient. "Please, Lila. Poetry time is important to me."

Seeing the earnestness in Oliver's eyes, Lila relented and handed back the book. "Alright, alright. I'll find someone else to prank."

Oliver gave a slight nod of thanks and returned to his cottage. Moments like these had become part of the rhythm of life in Hamstead. The villagers and mythical creatures had come to understand and respect Oliver's routines, and in turn, he respected their quirks and traditions.

The Faun of Newbridge, named Thaddeus, often sought Oliver's help with his inventions. One day, Thaddeus was struggling to lift a particularly heavy contraption. Seeing his plight, Oliver walked over and effortlessly lifted the device into place.

"Thank you, Oliver," Thaddeus said, wiping sweat from his brow. "I don't know what I'd do without your help."

Oliver simply nodded, his actions speaking louder than words. He didn't seek praise or recognition; he found satisfaction in being able to assist his neighbours, knowing that his strength could be used for good.

The Gentle Giant

Oliver's story serves as a reminder of the power of kindness and the beauty of simplicity. It shows us that even in a world filled with mythical creatures and legendary beings, there is room for love and compassion. And it proves that even an Ogre, a creature known for its strength and ferocity, can have a soft heart and a gentle soul.

One winter evening, as snow blanketed the village, Oliver was out gathering firewood. He noticed a small, shivering kitten huddled under a bush. Gently, he scooped up the kitten and tucked it inside his coat, feeling its tiny body warm against his chest. Back at his cottage, he prepared a cosy bed by the fire and watched as the kitten slowly began to relax, its fear melting away in the warmth of his home.

The villagers, who had grown to love Oliver, often brought him gifts of food and books, knowing how much he cherished his simple life. They admired his ability to find joy in the little things and his unwavering dedication to his pets and his poetry. Oliver's gentle nature had a profound impact on everyone he met, reminding them that true strength lay in kindness and compassion.

So, here's to Oliver, the poetry-reading Ogre of Hamstead. May his story continue to inspire us, and may his love for poetry and stray animals continue to touch our hearts. Because in a world filled with Nymphs, Sphinxes, Fauns, and Mermaids, sometimes, what you really need is a good, old-fashioned Ogre.

The Faun of Newbridge

The Merry Tinkerer

In the bustling town of Newbridge on the Isle of Wight, a whimsical creature named Fred the Faun lived amidst the townsfolk. Fauns, with their half-human, half-goat forms, were beings of nature and mischief. Fred was no exception. With a human upper body and goat-like lower half, complete with hooves and a tail, Fred cut a distinctive figure as he moved through the town. His merry disposition and knack for 'fixing' things made him both beloved and, at times, a source of mild exasperation.

Fred's passion for tinkering often led to amusing outcomes. He had an uncanny ability to turn even the simplest repairs into complex projects, usually leaving the objects in a worse state than before. However, his infectious optimism and sheepish grin made it impossible for anyone to stay mad at him for long.

Fred's workshop was a chaotic yet charming space, filled with tools, gadgets, and half-finished projects. The walls were adorned with sketches of fantastical inventions, and the floor was cluttered with various contraptions in various stages of completion. Despite the disarray, Fred knew exactly where everything was and could always find the right tool for any job.

One morning, Mrs. Cartwright, the village baker, brought her broken bread mixer to Fred. "Fred, dear, can you fix this for me?" she asked, her voice tinged with hope.

Fred took the mixer, his eyes twinkling with excitement. "Of course, Mrs. Cartwright! I'll have it working better than new in no time!"

True to form, Fred's efforts resulted in the mixer emitting puffs of flour and a series of loud clanks. Mrs. Cartwright watched in amusement as Fred's face turned from confident to puzzled. Eventually, Fred managed to get the mixer working, albeit with a few extra bells and whistles. Mrs. Cartwright couldn't help but laugh at the whimsical upgrades, including a small whistle that played a tune every time the mixer was turned on.

Fred's charm lay in his unyielding enthusiasm and the joy he brought to every task. The townsfolk appreciated his efforts, knowing that his heart was always in the right place.

The Persistent Friend

One of Fred's most enduring friendships was with Oliver, the poetry-loving Ogre of Hamstead. Unlike Fred, Oliver was a homebody, content to read poetry to his adopted pets. Fred, ever the optimist, was convinced that some fresh air and exercise would do Oliver a world of good.

"Come on, Oliver! The Sphinx and the Mermaid are waiting for us!" Fred would often exclaim, his flute dangling from his neck as he tried to persuade Oliver to join him. But more often than not, Oliver's response was a grumble and a resolute shake of his massive head.

Despite these rejections, Fred never lost hope. He continued his cheerful attempts to coax Oliver out of his home, believing that one day, his friend would see the light and join him in his adventures. Fred's persistence was a testament to his unwavering belief in the goodness of others and his desire to share the wonders of the world with those he cared about.

Fred's attempts were not without their humorous moments. One afternoon, he decided to surprise Oliver with a picnic by the river. Fred arrived at Oliver's cottage, a basket full of delicious treats in hand. "Oliver, you simply must come with me today. I've prepared a feast, and the weather is perfect!"

Oliver peered down at Fred, his eyes narrowing. "Fred, you know I prefer my poetry and peace."

"But think of the poetry you could write inspired by nature!" Fred countered, his enthusiasm unwavering.

Oliver sighed deeply, but something in Fred's earnest expression made him relent. "Very well, but only for a short while."

As they walked to the river, Fred regaled Oliver with tales of his latest tinkering projects and the antics of their mutual friends. By the time they reached the riverbank, Oliver found himself enjoying the outing more than he had anticipated. The picnic turned into a delightful afternoon, with Fred's cheerful chatter and the peaceful surroundings blending harmoniously.

Musical Mornings

Fred's love for music was well-known throughout Newbridge. Each morning, at the crack of dawn, he would wake up and take his flute in hand, filling the air with enchanting melodies. The townsfolk, now accustomed to his serenades, welcomed the sound of his music as part of their daily routine. The lilting tunes echoed through the forests and streets, bringing a touch of magic to the town.

Fred's music wasn't just for show; it was a form of communication and expression. Through his flute, he conveyed his feelings, from joy to sadness, and everything in between. His melodies brought smiles to faces and even soothed the grumpiest of villagers.

One morning, as Fred played a particularly cheerful tune, he noticed a group of children gathering nearby. They clapped and danced along to the music, their laughter ringing out in harmony with the flute's notes. Fred smiled, his heart swelling with happiness at the sight.

The music had a way of drawing people together. Villagers would pause in their daily tasks to listen, their spirits lifted by the beautiful sounds. Even the animals seemed to respond to Fred's playing, with birds chirping along and squirrels darting about in delight.

Fred's musical talents extended beyond the flute. He was also adept at playing the lyre and the panpipes, each instrument adding its unique voice to his repertoire. His performances were not limited to mornings; he often played at village gatherings, festivals, and celebrations, his music becoming an integral part of Newbridge's cultural fabric.

The Mischief Maker

Fred's mischievous side was legendary. He delighted in playing harmless pranks on unsuspecting travellers and townsfolk. Whether it was rearranging items in the market or leading people on wild goose chases through the forest, Fred's antics were always in good fun.

One of his favourite targets was the Nymph of Marks Corner, who loved to scare people. Fred would often sneak up on her and startle her just as she was about to scare someone else, resulting in a chorus of laughs and playful chases.

Fred's pranks were never mean-spirited; they were intended to bring joy and laughter. He had an uncanny ability to sense when someone needed cheering up, and his pranks often served to lift spirits and bring smiles to faces.

One day, Fred decided to play a trick on the village blacksmith, Mr. Thompson. He carefully swapped the smith's tools with oversized replicas he had crafted in his workshop. When Mr. Thompson arrived at his forge, he couldn't help but burst into laughter at the sight of the enormous hammer and tongs.

"Fred, you rascal!" Mr. Thompson called out, knowing exactly who was behind the prank.

Fred appeared, grinning from ear to ear. "Just a little fun, Mr. Thompson. I couldn't resist!"

Mr. Thompson chuckled and shook his head. "You certainly know how to lighten the mood, Fred. Thank you."

Fred's mischief extended to the forest as well. He often led travellers on merry chases, guiding them through the woods with playful riddles and clues. Those who followed his lead found themselves in beautiful, hidden spots they would never have discovered on their own.

Heart of Gold

Beneath his playful exterior, Fred had a heart of gold. His friends meant everything to him, and he would go to great lengths to help them. Whether it was trying to get Oliver out of his house or attempting to fix the town's broken items, Fred was always ready to lend a hand.

One winter, when the town was hit by an unexpected snowstorm, Fred's true nature shone through. He spent hours helping clear paths, delivering food to those who were snowed in, and even organizing impromptu concerts to lift spirits. The townsfolk saw beyond his mischievous façade and appreciated his unwavering kindness.

Fred's efforts during the snowstorm were nothing short of heroic. He braved the cold and snow to ensure that everyone had what they needed. His music became a source of comfort, bringing warmth and cheer to the cold, snowy nights.

Mrs. Cartwright, who had been particularly affected by the storm, was deeply moved by Fred's kindness. "Fred, you've done so much for us. How can we ever repay you?" she asked, her voice filled with gratitude.

Fred simply smiled and shook his head. "No need for repayment, Mrs. Cartwright. Seeing everyone happy is reward enough for me."

Fred's selflessness extended to his friends as well. When Oliver needed help with his poetry readings or when the Sphinx required assistance with her riddles, Fred was always there. His friends knew they could count on him, no matter what.

The Faun's Legacy

Fred's story is a testament to the power of positivity and the importance of friendship. It shows us that even in a world filled with mythical creatures and legendary beings, there is always room for laughter and joy. Fred's music and mischief brought light to Newbridge, proving that even a Faun, known for trickery and tunes, could have a profound impact on the community.

As the sun set each day, Fred would play his flute, his tunes a gentle reminder of the magic that existed in everyday life. The townsfolk, gathered around, would listen in awe, their hearts warmed by the melodies and the Faun who played them.

Fred's legacy extended beyond his music and mischief. He had taught the townsfolk the value of kindness, the importance of helping others, and the joy of living life to the fullest. His spirit of optimism and goodwill left an indelible mark on Newbridge, one that would be remembered for generations.

One summer evening, the townsfolk decided to honor Fred with a festival. They decorated the town square with lights and banners, and everyone gathered to celebrate the Faun who had brought so much joy to their lives. Fred, touched by the gesture, played his flute with even more passion, his music filling the air with a sense of wonder and magic.

As the festival drew to a close, Fred stood before his friends and neighbours, his heart full. "Thank you, everyone. You've made my life here truly special. Let's continue to spread joy and kindness, now and always."

The townsfolk cheered, their love for Fred evident in their smiles and applause. Fred's story had come full circle, a reminder that even the simplest acts of kindness and joy could create a legacy that would endure for generations.

Fred's music continued to fill the air, a symbol of the magic and wonder that existed in Newbridge. The Faun of Newbridge had shown that even in a world filled with mythical creatures and legendary beings, there was always room for laughter, joy, and the power of a kind heart.

The Leprechaun of Northwood

The Joyful Trickster

In the enchanting hamlet of Northwood on the Isle of Wight, a small figure of folklore known as Larry the Leprechaun lived a life of laughter and light. Leprechauns, with their small stature and mischievous nature, were creatures of legend, and Larry was no exception. Standing no taller than a child, with a twinkle in his eye, a pipe in his mouth, and a tricorn hat perched atop his head, Larry embodied the spirit of cheerfulness and mischief.

Larry's nimble body allowed him to move quickly and quietly, a trait he used to his advantage when playing pranks on unsuspecting humans. Despite his small size, Larry was surprisingly strong, often seen carrying pots of gold much larger than himself. He was an industrious little fellow, known for his exquisite craftsmanship as a cobbler, crafting shoes with unparalleled skill.

Larry's days were a blend of work and play. His mornings were spent at his tiny workshop, where he meticulously stitched and hammered, producing shoes that were as comfortable as they were durable. The townsfolk of Northwood revered his work, often marvelling at the tiny yet perfectly crafted shoes he created. Yet, once his cobbling was done, Larry would venture into the village, a mischievous grin on his face, ready to spread cheer through his playful antics.

One sunny morning, Larry decided it was time for a little fun. He tiptoed into the village square, where Mrs. O'Leary was setting up her vegetable stall. With a flick of his fingers, he enchanted her tomatoes to glow bright blue. Mrs. O'Leary, initially startled, couldn't help but laugh when she saw Larry's cheeky smile. "Oh, Larry, what have you done to my tomatoes?" she exclaimed, her laughter infectious.

"Just adding a bit of colour to your day, Mrs. O'Leary!" Larry replied, his eyes twinkling with delight.

Neighbours and Adventures

Larry's home was nestled between the dwellings of the Griffin of Cowes and the Golem of Gurnard, two creatures with vastly different temperaments. The Griffin, with his boundless enthusiasm, often invited Larry to join him for water adventures, such as kayaking or paddleboarding. Larry, however, preferred to keep his feet firmly on dry ground, politely declining each invitation with a cheerful smile.
"Come on, Larry, the water is perfect today!" the Griffin would call, his wings casting a grand shadow as he prepared his kayak.
"Thank you, but no, Griffin. You know I'm more of a land lover!" Larry would respond, always with a twinkle in his eye.
The Golem, named Gavin, was a different story. Known for his grumpy disposition, Gavin found joy in very little, certainly not in the prospect of finding pots of gold. Larry's optimism and cheerful demeanour often clashed with Gavin's stoicism, but Larry never let it get to him. He continued his quest for gold, his belief in its existence never wavering.
"Chasing gold again, Larry?" Gavin would grumble, his deep voice rumbling like distant thunder.
"Of course, Gavin! The day you stop believing in gold is the day you stop finding joy in the little things," Larry would reply with an infectious grin.
Adding to the mix was the Nymph of Marks Corner, a playful spirit who delighted in scaring Larry. Her laughter echoed through the woods each time she succeeded, but Larry, ever the optimist, took it all in stride. His own laughter soon joined hers, creating a chorus of joy that filled the forest.
One crisp autumn day, the Nymph, named Elara, decided to play her best prank yet. She waited until Larry was deep in thought, searching for gold near the old oak tree. With a sudden rustle and a burst of leaves, she jumped out, shouting, "Boo!"

Larry leapt into the air, his hat flying off his head. But as soon as he landed, he broke into laughter. "Well done, Elara! You got me this time!" he chuckled, picking up his hat and placing it back on his head.
Elara's eyes sparkled with delight. "You're a good sport, Larry. I can never catch you off guard for long!"

The Eternal Quest

Larry's days were filled with the joy of his eternal quest for gold. Each morning, he would rise with the sun, his heart filled with hope and excitement. He would set off on his journey, his nimble feet carrying him through the hamlet and into the surrounding woods. The townsfolk of Northwood were used to seeing the cheerful Leprechaun darting about, his eyes always scanning the ground for that elusive pot of gold.
Despite often being alone in his quest, Larry's spirits never dampened. He believed wholeheartedly that gold could be found anywhere, and his positive outlook was infectious. The villagers couldn't help but smile when they saw him, his optimism and cheerfulness brightening their day.
"Morning, Larry! Any luck today?" old Mr. Hargrove would call from his porch, a pipe in his hand.
"Every day is a lucky day, Mr. Hargrove!" Larry would reply, tipping his hat.
One particularly bright morning, Larry ventured deeper into the woods than usual. The air was crisp, and the birds sang a cheerful tune. As he approached a clearing, he noticed a strange, shimmering light emanating from a cluster of bushes. His heart leapt with excitement. "Could it be?" he whispered to himself.

Carefully, he pushed aside the branches and gasped. There, nestled among the roots, was a small, glittering pot of gold. Larry's eyes widened in amazement. He had finally found it! With a joyful cry, he danced around the clearing, his heart bursting with happiness.

The news of Larry's discovery spread quickly through Northwood. The villagers gathered to see the legendary pot of gold, their faces filled with wonder. Larry, ever generous, shared his treasure, ensuring everyone in the village benefited from his find.

Larry's Pranks

Larry's mischievous nature often led to harmless pranks that left the townsfolk laughing. One memorable incident involved the local blacksmith, who found his tools rearranged in the most perplexing manner. The blacksmith, initially baffled, couldn't help but laugh when he saw Larry's cheeky grin and twinkling eyes.

"Larry, what am I going to do with you?" the blacksmith chuckled, shaking his head in amusement.

"Just keeping you on your toes, my friend!" Larry replied with a wink.

Another time, Larry decided to play a trick on the baker. He enchanted the bread dough to rise rapidly, causing an explosion of dough that filled the bakery. The baker, covered in flour and dough, burst into laughter, knowing only Larry could have pulled off such a prank.

"Larry, you rascal! You've turned my bakery into a doughy mess!" the baker exclaimed, laughing heartily.

"Just a little extra leavening love!" Larry quipped, helping to clean up the doughy explosion.

Larry's pranks were always in good fun, never mean-spirited. He knew just how to bring a smile to someone's face, even on the gloomiest of days. His playful antics became a cherished part of life in Northwood, something the villagers looked forward to.

One particularly rainy afternoon, Larry decided to brighten the mood by enchanting the village fountain to spout rainbow-coloured water. The children, thrilled by the magical display, danced around the fountain, their laughter echoing through the streets.

"Thank you, Larry! This is the best day ever!" little Susie exclaimed, her eyes wide with wonder.

Larry tipped his hat, a satisfied smile on his face. "Just a touch of magic to brighten the day, Susie."

The Heart of Gold

Beneath his playful exterior, Larry had a heart of gold. He cared deeply for his friends and the people of Northwood. His pranks were never meant to harm, only to bring joy and laughter. His industrious nature also meant that he often repaired shoes for free, ensuring that everyone in the village had sturdy footwear.

One particularly cold winter, Larry's generosity shone through. He used his skills to make warm shoes for the children of the village, ensuring they could play outside without their toes freezing. His acts of kindness endeared him to everyone, proving that even a trickster could have a heart of gold.

"Thank you, Larry! These shoes are perfect!" young Tommy exclaimed, admiring his new boots.

Larry's eyes twinkled with joy. "Anything to keep those toes warm, Tommy!"

Larry's kindness extended beyond his craftsmanship. He often helped the elderly with their chores, fetched water for those who couldn't, and always had a kind word for anyone who needed it. His presence brought a sense of warmth and cheer to the village, even on the coldest of days.

One evening, as the snow fell gently outside, Larry noticed old Mrs. Jenkins struggling to carry firewood. Without a second thought, he rushed over to help, his small frame surprisingly strong.

"Thank you, Larry. You're a true blessing," Mrs. Jenkins said, her eyes brimming with gratitude.

Larry smiled warmly. "It's my pleasure, Mrs. Jenkins. Stay warm and cosy."

Larry's Legacy

Larry's story is a testament to the power of cheerfulness and the importance of seeing the magic in everyday life. His laughter and pranks brought joy to Northwood, and his belief in pots of gold symbolized hope and optimism. Even in a world filled with mythical creatures and legendary beings, there was always room for a dose of cheerfulness.

As the sun set each day, Larry would sit by his favourite tree, pipe in hand, watching the golden light fade. His heart filled with contentment, knowing that he had brought a bit of magic and joy to the world.

Larry's legacy extended beyond his pranks and laughter. He had taught the villagers the value of kindness, the importance of helping others, and the joy of living life to the fullest. His spirit of optimism and goodwill left an indelible mark on Northwood, one that would be remembered for generations.

One summer evening, the villagers decided to honour Larry with a festival. They decorated the village square with lights and banners, and everyone gathered to celebrate the Leprechaun who had brought so much joy to their lives. Larry, touched by the gesture, played his flute with even more passion, his music filling the air with a sense of wonder and magic.

As the festival drew to a close, Larry stood before his friends and neighbours, his heart full. "Thank you, everyone. You've made my life here truly special. Let's continue to spread joy and kindness, now and always."

The villagers cheered, their love for Larry evident in their smiles and applause. Larry's story had come full circle, a reminder that even the simplest acts of kindness and joy could create a legacy that would endure for generations.

Larry's laughter and music continued to fill the air, a symbol of the magic and wonder that existed in Northwood. The Leprechaun of Northwood had shown that even in a world filled with mythical creatures and legendary beings, there was always room for laughter, joy, and the power of a kind heart. So, here's to Larry, the laughing Leprechaun of Northwood. May his story continue to inspire us and may his cheerfulness and belief in the magic of everyday life continue to bring joy to all who hear his tale. Because in a world filled with Griffins, Golems, and laughing Leprechauns, sometimes, what you really need is a good, old-fashioned dose of cheerfulness. And if you ever find yourself in Northwood, keep an eye out for a small, nimble figure with a twinkle in his eye. Who knows, you might just spot Larry, the Leprechaun of Northwood.

The Shalfleet Sphinx

The Enigmatic Resident

In the picturesque village of Shalfleet on the Isle of Wight, an extraordinary creature named Sally the Sphinx lived among the villagers. Sphinxes, known for their wisdom and riddles, were beings of legend, and Sally was no exception. With the body of a lion and the head of a human, Sally cut an imposing figure as she moved gracefully through the village. Her presence was both awe-inspiring and a source of curiosity for the townsfolk.

Sally's sense of style was as unique as her heritage. She often wore a flowing coat and sunglasses, giving her the appearance of a movie star. Her dramatic flair and expectation of recognition amused the villagers, who couldn't help but chuckle at her grandiose demeanour. Sally was more than just a mysterious figure in the village; she was an integral part of Shalfleet's daily life. Her majestic form could be seen patrolling the village, her sharp eyes observing everything around her. Her keen senses and wisdom made her an unspoken guardian of the community, always ready to offer her insights or solve a perplexing problem.

Her home was a quaint stone cottage on the edge of the village, its garden filled with exotic plants and herbs she used for her mysterious potions and remedies. The cottage, though modest, was a reflection of Sally's unique personality — charming, intriguing, and slightly enigmatic. Inside, it was filled with ancient scrolls, books on philosophy, and puzzles of every kind. The walls were adorned with tapestries depicting mythical creatures and legendary tales, creating an atmosphere of timeless wisdom and magic.

Sally's arrival in Shalfleet had been a source of great excitement. She had appeared one misty morning, her majestic form emerging from the fog like a vision from a dream. The villagers had watched in awe as she gracefully made her way to the village square, her eyes scanning the surroundings with a look of serene confidence.

"Good morning, Shalfleet!" Sally had announced, her voice carrying a melodic lilt. "I am Sally, the Sphinx, and I have come to share my wisdom and riddles with you all."
The villagers, though initially apprehensive, soon warmed to Sally's presence. Her charm and intellect quickly won them over, and she became a beloved member of the community. Children especially were fascinated by her, often gathering around her cottage in hopes of hearing a new riddle or story.

The Village Celebrity

Despite her dramatic nature, Sally was well-loved in Shalfleet. The villagers found her antics entertaining, especially her habit of preening and posing as if she were on a red carpet. They often joked about her name, with phrases like "Shalfleet Sphinx" sounding like a peculiar part of the body. Sally took it all in stride, her confidence never wavering.
Sally's days were filled with riddles and enigmas. She enjoyed challenging the villagers with perplexing questions, her eyes twinkling with mischief as they struggled to find the answers. While some groaned and rolled their eyes at her riddles, others eagerly took up the challenge, appreciating the mental exercise.
One sunny morning, Sally strutted into the village square, her sunglasses perched stylishly on her nose. "Good morning, my dear villagers! Who's ready for today's riddle?" she called out, her voice ringing with enthusiasm.
The villagers gathered around, some excited, others apprehensive. "Bring it on, Sally!" shouted young Tommy, always eager for a challenge.
Sally smiled, her eyes sparkling. "Very well. Listen closely: I speak without a mouth and hear without ears. I have no body, but I come alive with the wind. What am I?"
The crowd fell silent, deep in thought. After several moments, little Susie piped up, "An echo! It's an echo!"

Sally beamed, clapping her paws together. "Well done, Susie! You've got it!"

The villagers laughed and cheered, appreciating the cleverness of Sally's riddles. It became a daily ritual for many to gather in the square and attempt to solve her latest puzzle. Sally's presence brought a sense of community and intellectual stimulation to Shalfleet, making her an indispensable part of village life.

Wisdom and Kindness

Beyond her love for riddles and drama, Sally was known for her wisdom. Villagers often sought her advice, and she provided it with a depth of understanding that was beyond her years. Her insights were valued, and her counsel often led to thoughtful reflections and solutions.

One day, Mrs. Thompson, the village florist, approached Sally with a troubled expression. "Sally, I don't know what to do. My flower shop isn't doing well, and I fear I may have to close it."

Sally listened intently, her eyes softening. "Mrs. Thompson, let me tell you a riddle. It might help. 'I can be cracked, made, told, and played. What am I?'"

Mrs. Thompson pondered for a moment. "A joke?"

Sally nodded. "Exactly. Sometimes, the best way to overcome hardship is to find humour in it. Perhaps hosting a small event at your shop to bring in people for some light-hearted fun could help."

Mrs. Thompson's face lit up. "That's a wonderful idea, Sally. Thank you!"

Sally's heart was as big as her intellect. Despite her enigmatic nature, she cared deeply for the villagers. She would go out of her way to help those in need, offering a kind word or a helping hand whenever necessary. Her blend of mystery, drama, and kindness made her an indispensable part of the community.

Her acts of kindness were often subtle but profound. When the blacksmith's son was ill, Sally concocted a special remedy from her garden herbs that helped the boy recover. When the village school needed books, she donated from her vast collection, ensuring the children had access to the knowledge they needed.

Sally's wisdom extended to the personal lives of the villagers as well. Young couples would seek her advice on matters of the heart, and she would provide guidance that was both practical and profound. Her understanding of human nature and relationships made her a trusted confidante and advisor.

The Dramatic Riddler

Sally's flair for the dramatic often led to amusing situations. One sunny afternoon, she decided to host a "Riddle Contest" in the village square. She strutted to the centre, her coat billowing in the breeze, and announced the contest with the theatrical flourish of a seasoned performer.

"Ladies and gentlemen, gather around! Today, I challenge you all to a contest of wits and wisdom. Who among you dares to unravel the mysteries of the Shalfleet Sphinx?" she proclaimed, her voice echoing through the square.

Villagers gathered, eager to participate. Sally posed her riddles one by one, each more challenging than the last. The crowd's groans, laughter, and occasional triumphs filled the square. The event was a resounding success, cementing Sally's reputation as both a formidable riddler and a beloved village entertainer.

One of the riddles she posed was particularly challenging: "I have cities, but no houses. I have mountains, but no trees. I have water, but no fish. What am I?"

The villagers scratched their heads, muttering to one another. Finally, Mr. Hargrove, the village elder, shouted, "A map! It's a map!"

Sally clapped her paws in delight. "Correct, Mr. Hargrove! Well done!"

The contest continued, with Sally posing riddles that tested the villagers' logic, creativity, and lateral thinking. The participants ranged from children eager to prove their wits to elders who relished the mental challenge. The village square was abuzz with excitement and camaraderie, everyone united in the joy of the contest.

As the sun began to set, Sally announced the final riddle: "I can be cracked, played, and told. I can be made, and sometimes I'm bold. What am I?"

The villagers were stumped. They whispered and debated, trying to decipher the answer. Finally, little Emily stepped forward, her eyes bright with determination. "A joke! The answer is a joke!"

Sally's eyes twinkled with pride. "Indeed, Emily! Well done!" The villagers cheered, applauding Emily's cleverness. Sally awarded her a beautifully illustrated book of riddles, ensuring that the tradition of puzzling and intellectual challenge would continue.

The Mysterious Advice

Despite the jokes and playful ribbing, Sally's wisdom was unmatched. One particularly challenging riddle involved a young villager named Emily, who was struggling with a difficult decision about her future. Sally posed a riddle that seemed unrelated at first but, upon reflection, provided Emily with the clarity she needed to make her choice.

The riddle was: "I am not alive, but I grow; I don't have lungs, but I need air; I don't have a mouth, but water kills me. What am I?" As Emily pondered the answer, she realised it was "fire." This realisation helped her see that, like fire, her passion needed the right environment to thrive, and she chose the path that fuelled her inner fire.

Emily returned to Sally with a smile on her face. "Thank you, Sally. Your riddle helped me see things clearly. I know what I need to do now."

Sally nodded, a proud gleam in her eyes. "Remember, Emily, wisdom often comes from within. Sometimes, we just need a little nudge to find it."

Sally's advice often came in the form of riddles, each designed to make the villagers think deeply about their situations. Her enigmatic way of imparting wisdom encouraged self-reflection and personal growth, making her guidance all the more impactful.

One evening, as the stars twinkled above, Sally received a visit from Thomas, a young farmer facing a difficult choice about whether to sell his land. "Sally, I'm torn. I love my land, but the offer is so tempting. What should I do?"

Sally considered his dilemma and posed a riddle: "I'm not a house, but I have many keys. I'm often quiet, but I can speak volumes. What am I?"

Thomas thought for a moment. "A piano?"

Sally smiled. "Yes, a piano. Think of your land as a piano, Thomas. It holds the keys to your future and the potential for beautiful music. Only you can decide whether to keep playing or sell it to someone else."

Thomas nodded, understanding the deeper meaning behind her words. "Thank you, Sally. You've given me much to think about."

Sally's Legacy

Sally's story is a testament to the power of individuality and the joy of mystery. Her presence in Shalfleet brought a touch of magic and wisdom to the village. Even in a world filled with laughter and jokes, there was always room for a bit of drama and enigma. Sally's blend of wisdom, kindness, and theatrical flair made her an unforgettable character.

As the sun set each evening, Sally would perch on a hill overlooking the village, her silhouette majestic against the twilight sky. She would pose one last riddle to herself, pondering the mysteries of life and enjoying the tranquillity of the moment.

One evening, as she sat atop her hill, a young villager named Jack approached her. "Sally, can you teach me how to come up with riddles like you do?"

Sally turned to him, a gentle smile on her face. "Of course, Jack. Riddles are all about seeing the world from a different perspective. Let's start with something simple."

She guided Jack through the process, helping him understand the art of crafting riddles. As they worked together, the bond between them grew, and Jack found a new appreciation for the wisdom and creativity that Sally embodied.

Under Sally's tutelage, Jack began to create his own riddles, challenging his friends and family with his newfound skills. He discovered that riddles were not just puzzles but a way of thinking, a means to view the world through a lens of curiosity and wonder.

Sally's influence extended beyond the village of Shalfleet. Travellers who heard of the enigmatic Sphinx would visit, seeking her wisdom and riddles. Sally welcomed them all, her eyes gleaming with delight as she shared her knowledge and entertained them with her puzzles.

Her legacy was not just in the riddles she posed but in the lives she touched and the minds she inspired. The villagers of Shalfleet and beyond carried her lessons with them, finding joy in the mysteries of life and the wisdom in her words.

One autumn day, the villagers decided to honour Sally with a festival. They decorated the village square with lanterns and garlands, and everyone gathered to celebrate the Sphinx who had brought so much magic to their lives. Sally, touched by the gesture, posed her most challenging riddles, her heart filled with pride and love for her community.

As the festival drew to a close, Sally stood before her friends and neighbours, her eyes shining with emotion. "Thank you, my dear villagers. You have made my time here truly special. Remember, life is full of riddles, and the answers are often found within yourselves."

The villagers cheered, their love for Sally evident in their smiles and applause. Sally's story had come full circle, a reminder that even the simplest acts of wisdom and kindness could create a legacy that would endure for generations.

Sally's laughter and riddles continued to fill the air, a symbol of the magic and wonder that existed in Shalfleet. The Shalfleet Sphinx had shown that even in a world filled with mythical creatures and legendary beings, there was always room for wisdom, kindness, and a touch of drama.

So, here's to Sally, the dramatic Sphinx of Shalfleet. May her story continue to inspire us, and may her riddles continue to perplex and amuse us. Because in a world filled with laughter and jokes, sometimes, what you really need is a good, old-fashioned Sphinx. And if you ever find yourself in Shalfleet, keep an ear out for the next riddle that might just change your perspective on life.

The Yarmouth Mermaid

The Alluring Enigma

In the charming coastal town of Yarmouth on the Isle of Wight, a stunning creature named Mandy the Mermaid made her home among the waves and rocks. Mermaids, known for their beauty and enchanting voices, were beings of legend, and Mandy was no exception. With her long, flowing hair and shimmering tail, she was the epitome of allure and mystery. Her voice, a siren's call, could mesmerise anyone who heard it, drawing them closer to the sea.

Mandy's peculiar diet, however, set her apart from other mermaids. She had a unique taste for roasted fishermen, a preference that often drew comments from her mythical neighbours. Oliver the Ogre and Kate the Kitsune frequently suggested that Mandy consider a plant-based diet, citing the health benefits and ethical considerations. Mandy, with a mischievous smile and a twinkle in her eye, would nod and humour them, all the while dreaming of her next meal.

The first time Mandy revealed her dietary preference, it caused quite a stir among her friends. The revelation came during a friendly gathering under the full moon, where various mythical creatures shared tales and feasted together. As Mandy casually mentioned her love for roasted fishermen, the group fell silent, their eyes wide with surprise.

"Roasted fishermen, you say?" Oliver the Ogre asked, his brows furrowing.

Mandy nodded, her smile never wavering. "Yes, there's something quite delightful about their flavour, especially when seasoned just right."

Kate the Kitsune, known for her grace and wisdom, leaned forward. "Mandy, have you ever considered trying a more sustainable diet? Perhaps something less... predatory?"

Mandy chuckled softly, her voice like the tinkling of bells. "I appreciate your concern, Kate. But I assure you, it's just my nature. Besides, a mermaid has to eat."

Sunbathing and Snacking

Mandy's daily routine was a testament to the simple joys of life. Each morning, at the crack of dawn, she would find a comfortable spot on a rock to bask in the sun. Her shimmering tail would catch the light, creating a dazzling display that never failed to attract attention. As the sun warmed her scales, Mandy would comb her long hair, singing songs that echoed across the waves.

Her enchanting voice was both a gift and a curse. While it brought joy to those who heard it from afar, it also lured sailors to their doom. Unaware of the danger, they would steer their boats closer, entranced by the beautiful melody. Mandy, always on the lookout for her next meal, would take advantage of their distraction. On days when fishermen were scarce, she would set her sights on stray kayakers paddling near the island.

One particularly memorable morning, a group of tourists spotted Mandy sunbathing and immediately began snapping photographs. Mandy, ever the performer, struck various poses, her tail glinting in the sunlight. She sang a light, playful tune, drawing the onlookers closer to the water's edge.

As the day progressed, Mandy's hunger grew. She spotted a lone fisherman in a small boat, casting his net not far from the shore. Her eyes gleamed with anticipation as she began to sing a haunting melody. The fisherman, oblivious to the danger, edged closer to the rocks, his mind completely captivated by the song.

Just as he was about to meet his fate, a sudden gust of wind changed the direction of his boat, pushing him away from the perilous rocks. Mandy sighed in disappointment but quickly shook it off, knowing that another opportunity would come soon.

Neighbours' Concerns

Oliver and Kate, despite their own quirks, were genuinely concerned about Mandy's diet. Oliver, with his love for poetry and stray pets, often recited verses about the virtues of compassion and harmony. Kate, with her cleverness and grace, would weave tales of mythical beings who thrived on plant-based diets. Despite their well-meaning efforts, Mandy remained steadfast in her culinary preferences.

One sunny afternoon, Oliver and Kate decided to stage an intervention. They gathered various plant-based delicacies and presented them to Mandy, hoping to entice her away from her fisherman feasts. Mandy, always polite, sampled the offerings but remained unconvinced. She appreciated their concern but made it clear that she preferred her roasted fishermen, much to the duo's chagrin.

"Look, Mandy," Oliver said, holding up a plate of roasted vegetables. "These are delicious and healthy. Give them a try."

Mandy took a bite, her expression neutral. "They're quite nice, Oliver. But they lack a certain... excitement."

Kate sighed, her tails flicking in frustration. "Mandy, we're just worried about you. Eating fishermen can't be good for your reputation or your health."

Mandy smiled warmly at her friends. "I know you mean well, and I appreciate it. But I am what I am. Perhaps one day I'll change, but for now, I'll stick to my ways."

Despite their concerns, Oliver and Kate couldn't help but admire Mandy's unwavering confidence. They knew that deep down, she had a kind heart, even if her diet was a bit unconventional.

The Joy of Sunbathing

Despite her predatory nature, Mandy was beloved for her beauty and her voice. The villagers and other mythical creatures of Yarmouth accepted her for who she was, quirks and all. Her sunbathing sessions became a part of the town's daily rhythm, with locals and tourists alike stopping to admire her from a safe distance.

Mandy's life was a blend of relaxation and excitement. She cherished the quiet moments of sunbathing as much as the thrill of hunting her next meal. Her songs continued to captivate, bringing a touch of magic to the coastal town. Even though her melodies often led sailors to their doom, they were simply a part of Mandy's existence, a testament to the dual nature of her being.

One day, a young girl named Lily approached Mandy while she was sunbathing. Lily had heard stories of the beautiful mermaid and wanted to see her up close. She cautiously made her way to the rocks, her eyes wide with wonder.

"Hello, Mandy," Lily said softly. "My name is Lily. I've heard so much about you."

Mandy smiled, her eyes twinkling with kindness. "Hello, Lily. It's lovely to meet you. Do you enjoy the sea?"

Lily nodded enthusiastically. "I do! I love to swim and collect seashells. Do you have any stories about the sea?"

Mandy's smile widened. "I have many stories, Lily. Would you like to hear one?"

Lily's face lit up with excitement. "Yes, please!"

Mandy began to tell Lily a tale of adventure and mystery, her voice weaving a spell that transported the young girl to a world of magic and wonder. As the story unfolded, Lily felt a sense of awe and admiration for the enchanting mermaid.

The Enchanted Voice

Mandy's enchanting voice was her most powerful tool. It could soothe the most troubled minds and draw the bravest sailors to their end. One evening, as the sun set over the horizon, she began to sing a particularly haunting melody. The notes carried across the water, reaching the ears of a young sailor named Jack. Entranced by the beautiful sound, Jack steered his boat closer to shore, unaware of the danger. As Jack neared the rocks, Mandy's song grew more intense. Her voice, filled with both allure and menace, wove a spell that was impossible to break. Just as Jack was about to meet his fate, a sudden change in the wind broke the enchantment, allowing him to regain his senses and steer away. Mandy watched with a mixture of disappointment and respect, acknowledging the power of fate in their encounter.

Jack, shaken but grateful for his narrow escape, looked back at the rocks where he had glimpsed the mermaid's shimmering tail. He knew he had come close to a dangerous fate, but he couldn't help but feel a strange sense of admiration for the mysterious creature.

The next day, Jack returned to the shore, determined to learn more about the enchanting mermaid who had nearly claimed his life. He approached Mandy cautiously, his heart pounding with both fear and curiosity.

"Hello, Mandy," Jack called out. "My name is Jack. I was the sailor you nearly enchanted last night."

Mandy turned to face him, her eyes filled with intrigue. "Hello, Jack. You were very fortunate. Not many escape my song."

Jack nodded, his gaze steady. "I know. But I couldn't stay away. There's something about you that I can't forget."

Mandy's expression softened. "Come, sit with me, and I'll tell you more about my world."

Jack sat beside Mandy on the rocks, listening intently as she shared stories of the sea, her voice captivating him once again. This time, however, there was no danger, only the promise of understanding and connection.

Mandy's Legacy

Mandy's story is a testament to the power of individuality and the importance of staying true to oneself. Her beauty, voice, and peculiar diet made her a unique figure in the world of myth and legend. Despite the concerns of her friends and neighbours, Mandy lived her life unapologetically, embracing her dual nature as both enchantress and predator.

As the sun set each day, Mandy would sit by her favourite rock, watching the golden light fade into the horizon. Her heart filled with contentment, knowing that she had brought a bit of magic and wonder to the world. The villagers and mythical creatures of Yarmouth continued to accept and appreciate her for who she was, quirks and all.

One summer evening, the villagers decided to honour Mandy with a festival. They decorated the shore with lanterns and garlands, and everyone gathered to celebrate the mermaid who had brought so much magic to their lives. Mandy, touched by the gesture, sang her most enchanting melodies, her heart filled with pride and love for her community.

As the festival drew to a close, Mandy stood before her friends and neighbours, her eyes shining with emotion. "Thank you, everyone. You have made my time here truly special. Remember, life is full of mysteries, and it's up to us to embrace them."

The villagers cheered, their love for Mandy evident in their smiles and applause. Mandy's story had come full circle, a reminder that even the simplest acts of enchantment and individuality could create a legacy that would endure for generations.

Mandy's laughter and songs continued to fill the air, a symbol of the magic and wonder that existed in Yarmouth. The Yarmouth Mermaid had shown that even in a world filled with mythical creatures and legendary beings, there was always room for enchantment, individuality, and a touch of mischief.

So, here's to Mandy, the fisherman-eating Mermaid of Yarmouth. May her story continue to captivate us, and may her love for roasted fishermen continue to amuse us. Because in a world filled with Ogres, Kitsunes, and stray kayakers, sometimes, what you really need is a good, old-fashioned Mermaid. And if you ever find yourself in Yarmouth, keep an ear out for the enchanting melodies that might just lead you to an unforgettable encounter with Mandy, the Mermaid of Yarmouth.

The Bowcombe Chupacabra

The Mischievous Creature

In the quaint village of Bowcombe on the Isle of Wight, a mysterious creature named Charlie the Chupacabra roamed the night. Known for his spiky spines, reptilian appearance, and knack for mischief, Charlie was a legend among the villagers. Despite his fearsome reputation as a 'goat-sucker', Charlie was more of a prankster than a predator.

Charlie's appearance was striking. With his hunched back, spiky spines, and glowing eyes, he looked like something out of a nightmare. His scales gleamed in the moonlight, casting eerie shadows on the ground. Yet, his actions were far from malicious. Instead, Charlie had a mischievous streak that often left the villagers both annoyed and amused.

The legend of Charlie the Chupacabra had been passed down through generations, with stories of his antics becoming more elaborate with each telling. Children would huddle around campfires, listening wide-eyed to tales of the creature who could sneak into homes without a sound and disappear into the night, leaving only his laughter behind. Despite the fearsome image the stories painted, those who encountered Charlie knew he was more playful than dangerous.

Charlie's pranks started as harmless fun. He would move items around in people's gardens, causing a bit of confusion but no real harm. Garden gnomes would switch places, watering cans would be found in trees, and flowers would mysteriously replant themselves in odd patterns. The villagers quickly learned to expect the unexpected when it came to Charlie.

Pranks and Picnics

Charlie loved the great outdoors, and his favourite pastime was playing pranks on unsuspecting hikers. He had a particular fondness for stealing picnics. With quick, stealthy movements, he would swipe sandwiches, pastries, and other treats without being noticed. His most famous heist involved a basket full of gourmet cheese and crackers, which he enjoyed under the moonlight.

But Charlie's pranks didn't stop at food theft. He had a talent for stealing keys, leaving hikers stranded and puzzled. Many a time, villagers would return to their cars or homes only to find their keys missing, and a cheeky note left behind: "Better luck next time! - Charlie."

One summer day, the Bowcombe Annual Picnic was in full swing. Families spread out their blankets, laying out elaborate feasts of homemade pies, fresh fruit, and artisanal breads. Charlie, watching from the cover of the nearby woods, saw his opportunity. He waited until everyone was distracted by a particularly lively game of rounders, then made his move. With the agility of a cat, Charlie darted from blanket to blanket, snatching up food with lightning speed. By the time the game was over, half the picnic baskets were mysteriously empty. Laughter erupted as the villagers read the notes Charlie had left behind, each one a humorous quip about the missing items.

Despite the inconvenience, the villagers couldn't help but admire Charlie's skill. His pranks became a beloved part of village lore, and the Annual Picnic turned into a game of outsmarting the clever Chupacabra.

The Bookish Chupacabra

Despite his nocturnal antics, Charlie had a surprising hobby that set him apart from typical Chupacabras. He loved to read books, particularly self-help books. His favourite was 'How to Win Friends and Influence People' by Dale Carnegie. Charlie believed in the power of self-improvement and often pondered the lessons he learned from his reading.

Every evening, before setting out on his pranks, Charlie would spend a few hours reading. He could be found perched on a tree branch, a book in his claws, his eyes scanning the pages with intense focus. The sight of a Chupacabra engrossed in a self-help book was a rare and amusing one, often met with disbelief and laughter from those who stumbled upon him.

Charlie's favourite reading spot was a large oak tree on the edge of the village. The branches provided perfect cover, and the leaves rustled softly in the breeze, creating a peaceful environment for his reading. The villagers often joked that Charlie was the most well-read Chupacabra in all of England.

One evening, as Charlie was deep into a chapter on effective communication, he heard a rustling below. He peered down to see young Tommy, the blacksmith's son, looking up at him with wide eyes.

"Hello, Charlie," Tommy said hesitantly. "What are you reading?"

Charlie smiled, his sharp teeth glinting in the moonlight. "It's a book about making friends, Tommy. Would you like to borrow it when I'm done?"

Tommy's eyes lit up. "Really? That would be amazing! Thank you, Charlie."

From that night on, Tommy and Charlie formed an unlikely friendship, bonded by their love of books. Charlie's influence helped Tommy become more confident, and in turn, Tommy introduced Charlie to new genres of literature.

Pranks with a Purpose

Charlie's pranks, though annoying, were never harmful. In fact, they often carried a message or a lesson. Once, he rearranged the tools in the local blacksmith's shop, leaving behind a note about the importance of organisation. Another time, he replaced the baker's sugar with salt, only to leave a recipe for the perfect chocolate chip cookies in its place.

His antics, while exasperating, were also endearing. The villagers couldn't stay mad at Charlie for long, especially when his pranks often resulted in laughter and, occasionally, a useful lesson. Charlie's reputation as a prankster was matched by his unexpected role as a quirky village advisor.

One day, Charlie decided to teach the village children about the importance of recycling. He snuck into the schoolyard at night and created a sculpture out of discarded plastic bottles and cans. The next morning, the children were amazed to find a gleaming dragon made entirely of recycled materials. A note at the base read: "Recycling can be fun! - Charlie."

The children, inspired by Charlie's creation, started a recycling club at school. They collected materials from around the village and created more sculptures, turning waste into art. Charlie's prank had sparked a movement that brought the community closer together.

Another time, Charlie noticed that the local library was struggling to attract visitors. He hatched a plan to bring the villagers back to the books. Late one night, he rearranged the library's entire collection, placing the most exciting adventure novels and mysteries in prominent positions. He left a note on the librarian's desk: "A little rearrangement for a more thrilling read. - Charlie."

The next day, the villagers were intrigued by the new arrangement and flocked to the library. The librarian, though initially flustered, couldn't help but smile at the increase in visitors. Charlie's prank had breathed new life into the library, reminding everyone of the joys of reading.

The Enigmatic Night

Charlie's life was a blend of mischief and contemplation. He would wake up at dusk, his eyes twinkling with anticipation for the night ahead. He would plan his pranks with meticulous care, ensuring they were both amusing and thought-provoking. As the night wore on, Charlie would sneak around Bowcombe, pulling off his pranks with the stealth of a seasoned trickster.

But Charlie's love for reading never waned. After a night of pranks, he would return to his favourite tree, book in hand, and lose himself in the world of self-help and improvement. His dual life as a prankster and a reader made him a unique and unforgettable character in the village.

One particularly starry night, Charlie decided to take his pranks to the next level. He crafted a series of clues and riddles that led to a hidden treasure somewhere in the village. The treasure hunt began at the village square, where he left the first clue: "To find the next hint, look where the sun meets the earth at dawn."

The villagers, excited by the challenge, set out to solve the riddles. They worked together, deciphering each clue and searching high and low for the next hint. The hunt took them to the old windmill, the village pond, and even the church bell tower.

As the final clue led them to the ancient oak tree, they found a small chest buried at its base. Inside were gold coins made of chocolate and a note from Charlie: "The real treasure is the fun we had along the way."

The villagers laughed and shared the chocolate, marvelling at Charlie's creativity. His treasure hunt had brought them together, reinforcing the bonds of community and friendship.

Charlie's Legacy

Charlie's story is a testament to the power of individuality and the importance of staying true to oneself. His mischievous nature and love for self-improvement showed that even the most mysterious creatures could have layers of complexity. Charlie's pranks and reading habits made him a beloved, if not peculiar, part of Bowcombe.

As time went on, Charlie became a symbol of the village's spirit. His pranks were more than just tricks; they were expressions of his unique personality and a way to engage with the community. The villagers came to appreciate his antics, knowing that behind every prank was a lesson or a message.

Charlie's influence extended beyond Bowcombe. Visitors from other villages came to hear stories of the mischievous Chupacabra who loved books and pranks. They left with smiles on their faces, inspired by Charlie's blend of mischief and wisdom.

One autumn evening, the villagers decided to celebrate Charlie's contributions with a festival. They decorated the village square with lanterns and banners, and everyone gathered to honour the Chupacabra who had brought so much joy and creativity to their lives.

Charlie, touched by the gesture, attended the festival in his own way. As the villagers danced and feasted, he watched from the shadows, his heart filled with pride and contentment. He knew that his legacy would live on, not just in the pranks he pulled, but in the laughter and camaraderie he inspired.

As the festival drew to a close, the village elder stood to speak. "Charlie, wherever you are, thank you for reminding us that life is full of surprises and that even the strangest creatures can have the kindest hearts."

The villagers cheered, their love for Charlie evident in their smiles and applause. Charlie's story had come full circle, a reminder that individuality and mischief could create a legacy that would endure for generations.

So, here's to Charlie, the prankster Chupacabra of Bowcombe. May his story continue to amuse us and may his love for self-help books continue to surprise us. Because in a world filled with hikers, picnics, and stolen keys, sometimes, what you really need is a good, old-fashioned Chupacabra. And if you ever find yourself in Bowcombe, keep an eye out for the clever pranks and the rustle of pages in the night. You might just catch a glimpse of Charlie, the legendary Chupacabra with a heart of gold.

The Carisbrooke Banshee

The Mischievous Spirit

In the historic town of Carisbrooke on the Isle of Wight, there lived a Banshee named Betty. Banshees, with their piercing wails and foreboding presence, were known to herald the approach of death. However, Betty was an exception. While she did possess the classic traits of a Banshee, such as long, flowing hair and a white dress, Betty had a mischievous streak that set her apart.

Betty's pranks were legendary in Carisbrooke. She delighted in causing harmless confusion among the townsfolk, especially when it came to cars and street signs. Her ethereal form allowed her to slip in and out of places unnoticed, making her pranks all the more baffling. One of her favourite tricks was to steal parking tickets from car dashboards, leaving drivers both relieved and bewildered. Another favourite was switching street signs, leading to endless amusement as drivers found themselves lost in the quaint town.

Betty's favourite time for mischief was twilight, when the fading light and rising mist created the perfect backdrop for her ghostly pranks. She would glide silently through the narrow streets of Carisbrooke, her laughter echoing softly as she watched her tricks unfold. Her presence was often felt rather than seen, a whisper of movement, a glint of white in the corner of one's eye.

One evening, Betty decided to have a little fun with the town's only traffic light. With a flick of her translucent hand, she made it change colours erratically, causing a comical confusion among the drivers. As cars stopped and started, horns honking in bewilderment, Betty floated above, her laughter blending with the sounds of the bustling town.

Betty also had a knack for appearing just when someone was about to doze off. She would tap on windows, move objects in homes, or whisper ghostly lullabies that kept the residents awake and on their toes. Despite the initial startle, these encounters often ended in laughter, with the townsfolk growing accustomed to Betty's playful hauntings.

A Love for Castles and Donkeys

Despite her prankster nature, Betty had a surprising fondness for medieval architecture and donkeys. Carisbrooke Castle, with its rich history and majestic presence, was Betty's favourite haunt. She would often be seen wandering the castle grounds at night, her ethereal form blending seamlessly with the ancient stones. The castle's resident donkeys, with their gentle nature and playful antics, brought Betty endless joy. Her ghostly laughter would echo through the night as she watched them frolic and bray.

Betty's love for the castle and its donkeys was well-known among the locals. They often spotted her at dusk, floating gracefully along the castle walls, her eyes twinkling with delight. Despite the eerie presence, Betty's affection for the donkeys was clear, and the townsfolk grew fond of their spectral companion.

During the day, visitors to Carisbrooke Castle often heard tales of the friendly Banshee who watched over the donkeys. Children, in particular, were fascinated by the stories and would eagerly look for signs of Betty during their tours. Some claimed to have seen her, a wisp of white darting behind a stone pillar, or heard her soft giggle carried on the wind.

One night, Betty decided to give the castle's donkeys a special treat. She had noticed that their water troughs were often muddy and decided to clean them. Using her spectral powers, she lifted the troughs effortlessly, pouring out the dirty water and refilling them with fresh, clean water from the nearby well. The donkeys, sensing her presence, brayed happily and nuzzled her ghostly form in gratitude.

Betty's connection with the donkeys extended beyond the castle grounds. She often ventured into the nearby fields where the donkeys grazed, watching over them like a guardian spirit. On several occasions, farmers reported seeing their donkeys braying at night, only to find them perfectly calm and content moments later, as if comforted by an unseen presence.

Pranks and Predicaments

Betty's pranks, though mischievous, were always in good fun. One particularly memorable incident involved the local postman, Mr. Higgins. Betty decided to give him a day to remember by switching his letters, causing a wave of unexpected and humorous deliveries throughout the town. The bakery received the butcher's orders, while the florist found themselves with a stack of utility bills. The mix-up led to a day of laughter and confusion, with everyone eventually seeing the funny side.

Mr. Higgins, though initially flustered, couldn't help but laugh when he realised what had happened. "That mischievous Banshee!" he chuckled, shaking his head as he re-sorted the letters. The townsfolk, amused by the day's events, shared their tales of unexpected deliveries over tea, their laughter echoing through the village.

Betty's antics didn't stop at the postman. She once enchanted the local pub's sign to read "The Tipsy Donkey" instead of its usual name, "The King's Arms". The new name stuck for weeks, with locals and tourists alike enjoying the whimsical change. Betty watched the merriment unfold, her ghostly form hovering near the pub, enjoying the light-hearted chaos she had caused.

The pub's owner, Mr. Roberts, decided to embrace the change. He commissioned a new sign featuring a cheerful, tipsy donkey, and even renamed a special brew in honour of Betty's prank. "The Tipsy Donkey" became a local favourite, and the pub thrived with the added charm.

Betty also had a talent for more elaborate pranks. One evening, she decided to switch the ingredients in the local bakery, replacing the sugar with salt and vice versa. The next morning, the baker, Mr. Thompson, was baffled when his cakes turned out inedible, while his bread was strangely sweet. Realising it was another one of Betty's pranks, he laughed and left a note on the counter: "Well played, Betty. Well played."

The Heart of the Banshee

Despite her pranks, Betty was a kind spirit at heart. She never caused harm and was always careful to ensure her mischief brought more smiles than frowns. Her presence, though eerie, became a comforting part of Carisbrooke's charm. The townsfolk grew to appreciate Betty's quirks, and some even left small tokens of appreciation at the castle gates, knowing she would find them.

One winter, when the town was hit by an unexpected snowstorm, Betty's true nature shone through. She guided lost villagers to safety with her ethereal light and even helped shovel snow from the castle pathways, her ghostly form moving with surprising efficiency. The townsfolk were grateful, and Betty's reputation as the friendly prankster Banshee was solidified.

The snowstorm had brought the village to a standstill, and many were unprepared for the harsh weather. Betty, sensing the urgency, worked tirelessly through the night. Her glowing form could be seen darting from house to house, ensuring that everyone was safe and warm.

At the castle, Betty took special care of her beloved donkeys, creating a makeshift shelter to protect them from the cold. The next morning, the villagers awoke to find the castle grounds cleared of snow and the donkeys snug and content in their new shelter. They knew they had Betty to thank for the miraculous transformation.

Betty's acts of kindness extended beyond the snowstorm. She was known to leave small gifts for the children of the village — shiny stones, feathers, and other trinkets she found during her nocturnal wanderings. These tokens, left on windowsills or tucked into pockets, were cherished by the children, who saw them as magical treasures from their ghostly friend.

Betty's Legacy

Betty's story is a testament to the power of individuality and the importance of staying true to oneself. Her blend of mischief and kindness showed that even the most foreboding creatures could have a heart of gold. Betty's love for castles, donkeys, and harmless pranks made her an unforgettable character in Carisbrooke.

As the sun set each evening, Betty would take her usual place by the castle, watching over the town she had come to love. Her wails, once foreboding, were now a soothing reminder of her presence. The donkeys, sensing her nearby, would bray in response, creating a unique symphony that only Carisbrooke could boast.

The villagers, now accustomed to Betty's antics, often found themselves smiling at the thought of their friendly Banshee. They knew that as long as Betty was around, Carisbrooke would always have a touch of magic and mischief.

In the years that followed, Betty's legend grew. Tourists from afar would visit Carisbrooke, eager to hear tales of the mischievous Banshee. Local businesses thrived, and the town's unique charm was celebrated far and wide. Betty had become an integral part of Carisbrooke's identity, her pranks and kindness leaving a lasting impact.

As time passed, the villagers decided to honour Betty's legacy in a more permanent way. They established the "Betty Festival," an annual event celebrating the mischievous spirit who had become a beloved part of their community. The festival featured games, pranks, and storytelling, with children dressing up as ghosts and donkeys to commemorate Betty's favourite things.

The festival quickly became a highlight of the year, drawing visitors from all over the Isle of Wight. The town was filled with laughter and joy as people shared stories of Betty's pranks and acts of kindness. The festival also included a lantern-lit procession to Carisbrooke Castle, where villagers left tokens of appreciation at the gates, continuing the tradition of honouring their spectral friend.

Epilogue: A Ghostly Friend

Betty's legacy lived on in the stories and laughter of Carisbrooke. The villagers passed down tales of her pranks and kindness to new generations, ensuring that the friendly Banshee would never be forgotten. And on quiet nights, when the moon shone brightly over Carisbrooke Castle, some say you can still hear Betty's ghostly laughter mingling with the brays of the donkeys, a timeless reminder of the Banshee who brought joy to their lives.

One particularly serene evening, as the stars twinkled above and a gentle breeze rustled the leaves, the villagers gathered around a bonfire to share stories of Betty. The firelight cast dancing shadows, and the air was filled with the sound of laughter and the occasional bray of a donkey.

"Do you remember the time Betty swapped all the street signs?" Mrs. Thompson chuckled. "I ended up at the bakery when I was trying to get to the post office!"

"Or when she enchanted the church bell to chime a merry tune instead of the usual peal," Mr. Higgins added, smiling at the memory.

The children listened in awe, their imaginations running wild with visions of the mischievous Banshee. They loved hearing about Betty's adventures and often dreamt of encountering her on their own nighttime escapades.

As the night grew late, the villagers dispersed, their hearts warm with fond memories. Betty watched from her perch atop the castle walls, her ghostly form illuminated by the moonlight. She felt a deep sense of contentment, knowing that she had left a positive mark on the town she loved.

Betty's story is a testament to the power of individuality and the importance of staying true to oneself. Her blend of mischief and kindness showed that even the most foreboding creatures could have a heart of gold. Betty's love for castles, donkeys, and harmless pranks made her an unforgettable character in Carisbrooke.

So, here's to Betty, the prankster Banshee of Carisbrooke. May her story continue to amuse us, and may her love for castles and donkeys continue to surprise us. Because in a world filled with cars, parking tickets, and confused drivers, sometimes, what you really need is a good, old-fashioned Banshee.

And if you ever find yourself wandering the streets of Carisbrooke on a misty evening, keep an eye out for a flicker of white and a glimmer of mischief. You might just be lucky enough to witness one of Betty's playful pranks, and perhaps, if you're really fortunate, hear her ghostly laughter mingling with the brays of the donkeys—a timeless reminder of the Banshee who brought joy to their lives.

As the festival grew in popularity, local artisans began creating and selling Betty-themed merchandise. Little ghost figurines, donkey-shaped cookies, and even replicas of Betty's favourite pranking notes became popular souvenirs. The proceeds from these sales were used to maintain the castle and care for the donkeys, ensuring that Betty's beloved companions were always well looked after.

The legacy of Betty, the Carisbrooke Banshee, continued to thrive. Her story was told and retold, not just as a tale of mischief, but as a testament to the idea that even those who seem different can have a profound impact on their community. Betty's blend of pranks and kindness had woven a thread of joy and wonder through Carisbrooke, a thread that would never be broken.

The Nymph of Marks Corner

The Playful Spirit

In the quaint hamlet of Marks Corner on the Isle of Wight, there lived a Nymph named Nancy. Nymphs, with their ethereal beauty and playful spirits, were known to embody the very essence of nature. Nancy was no exception. With her long flowing hair and bright, sparkling eyes, she was a sight to behold as she frolicked through the woods and meadows. Nancy had a unique fondness for bird-watching and rescuing hedgehogs from trees. Yes, you heard that right. Nancy, the Nymph of Marks Corner, was an avid ornithologist and a dedicated arboreal hedgehog rescuer. Her days were filled with the joys of nature, and her nights with the laughter of pranks.

Nancy's appearance was a perfect reflection of her connection to nature. Her hair, cascading in waves of green and gold, seemed to shimmer with the colours of the forest. Her eyes, a bright and sparkling blue, were always alight with curiosity and mischief. Her skin had a faint glow, as if kissed by the morning dew, and she moved with a grace that made her seem more like a wisp of wind than a solid being.

Mystical Companions

Nancy lived among a diverse group of mystical creatures, including Larry the cheerful Leprechaun of Northwood, Sally the aloof Sphinx of Shalfleet, and Oliver the gruff yet kind-hearted Ogre of Hamstead. Despite their differences, they all got along quite well and often gathered for lively parties filled with laughter, song, and the occasional friendly debate. Even Oliver, known for his grumpy demeanour, couldn't resist joining in the merriment.

These gatherings were always a sight to behold. Larry, with his mischievous grin and twinkling eyes, would regale everyone with tales of his latest adventures. Sally, with her enigmatic smile, would challenge the others with riddles that left them scratching their heads. Oliver, despite his rough exterior, would share his thoughts on the poetry he loved, his deep voice resonating with emotion.

One of Nancy's favourite pastimes was to host these gatherings in the heart of the forest, where the trees formed a natural amphitheatre, and the stars provided the perfect canopy. The air would be filled with the sounds of laughter and music, and the forest itself seemed to come alive, joining in the celebration.

Larry the Leprechaun was a particular favourite at these gatherings. His cheerful disposition and endless supply of jokes kept everyone entertained. He had a talent for finding the humour in any situation, and his laughter was infectious. Larry's mischievous nature was a perfect complement to Nancy's playful spirit, and the two often collaborated on pranks that left the others in stitches.

Sally the Sphinx, though more reserved, brought a sense of mystery and intrigue to the group. Her riddles were legendary, and she delighted in challenging her friends' minds. Sally's wisdom and grace made her an admired figure among the mystical creatures, and her presence added a touch of elegance to their gatherings.

Oliver the Ogre, with his gruff exterior and kind heart, was the protector of the group. Though he often grumbled about the noise and chaos, it was clear that he enjoyed the company of his friends. Oliver's deep, resonant voice was perfect for reciting poetry, and his unexpected talent for verse was a source of wonder and admiration.

Mischief and Mayhem

Nancy had a mischievous streak that was both endearing and surprising. She loved to hide in the trees, her form blending seamlessly with the leaves, and jump out to scare unsuspecting passersby. Her pranks, though startling, were harmless and always brought a wave of laughter once the initial shock wore off.

One of her favourite pastimes was to rearrange the garden tools of the local gardener, Mr. Green. He would find his spade where the rake should be and the hosepipe twisted into intricate knots. Despite the confusion, Mr. Green couldn't help but chuckle, knowing that Nancy was behind the playful chaos.

Nancy's pranks extended beyond the gardens of Marks Corner. She would enchant the village's weather vane to spin wildly, confusing the villagers about the direction of the wind. She would also swap the contents of picnic baskets, turning a planned lunch of sandwiches into a surprising feast of sweets. Her laughter, like the tinkling of bells, would often be heard echoing through the village as her pranks unfolded.

One particularly memorable prank involved the village's only café. Nancy enchanted the menu board to change its items every few minutes, causing a delightful confusion among the customers. People would order a coffee and find themselves served a cup of tea, or ask for a sandwich and receive a slice of cake. The café's owner, Mrs. Potts, was initially flustered but soon joined in the fun, laughing along with her customers as they tried to guess what they would get next.

Despite her love for mischief, Nancy was careful never to cause harm. Her pranks were always in good fun, and she took great joy in seeing the villagers smile and laugh. She believed that a bit of light-hearted mischief was good for the soul, and she took her role as the village prankster very seriously.

Nature's Guardian

Beyond her pranks, Nancy had a deep love for nature. She spent her mornings watching birds, her eyes tracking their graceful flights with a focus that was nothing short of magical. Her afternoons were dedicated to rescuing hedgehogs that had somehow found their way up trees. With gentle hands, she would carefully lift them down and set them safely on the ground, her actions a testament to her caring spirit.

Nancy's connection to the natural world was evident in everything she did. She tended to the trees and animals with a loving touch, ensuring that the beauty of Marks Corner remained unspoiled. Her presence brought a sense of peace and harmony to the hamlet, and the villagers grew to love their whimsical guardian.

Nancy's bird-watching skills were renowned among the villagers. She could identify any bird by its song, and she knew the nesting habits of every species in the forest. She would often take the village children on bird-watching expeditions, teaching them the names and songs of the birds. These outings were always filled with wonder and excitement, and the children adored their lessons with Nancy.

Her hedgehog rescues were another source of fascination for the villagers. No one quite knew how the hedgehogs ended up in the trees, but Nancy always seemed to be there to help them down. She would cradle the tiny creatures in her hands, whispering soothing words as she carried them to safety. Her dedication to the well-being of the hedgehogs was just one example of her deep love for all living things.

Nancy also had a special bond with the forest itself. She could sense when a tree was in distress or when a plant needed extra care. She would spend hours tending to the forest, ensuring that it remained healthy and vibrant. Her efforts were rewarded with a flourishing ecosystem, and the villagers often remarked on the beauty and serenity of Marks Corner.

Parties and Pranks

Nancy's playful nature extended to the gatherings she hosted for her mystical friends. These parties were legendary, filled with music, dancing, and an abundance of laughter. Larry the Leprechaun would perform jigs, Sally the Sphinx would pose riddles, and Oliver the Ogre, despite his gruff exterior, would recite poetry.

One memorable evening, Nancy decided to add a twist to the festivities. She enchanted the drinks to change colours and flavours randomly, causing fits of giggles as everyone tried to guess what they were drinking. The night was filled with joy, and Nancy's mischief added an extra layer of fun to the celebration.

The forest was always the perfect backdrop for these gatherings. Nancy would decorate the trees with fairy lights and hang lanterns from the branches, creating a magical atmosphere. The air would be filled with the scent of flowers and the sounds of nature, providing the perfect setting for a night of revelry.

Nancy's parties were not just about fun and games. They were also an opportunity for the mystical creatures to share their knowledge and wisdom. Sally's riddles would challenge their minds, Larry's stories would spark their imaginations, and Oliver's poetry would touch their hearts. These gatherings were a celebration of the unique talents and perspectives that each creature brought to the group.

On one occasion, Nancy decided to organize a treasure hunt for her friends. She spent days hiding clues and setting up challenges throughout the forest. The treasure hunt took them on a journey through the most beautiful and secluded parts of Marks Corner, and along the way, they encountered various puzzles and tasks that tested their wits and teamwork.

The final clue led them to a hidden grove, where Nancy had set up a grand feast. The grove was adorned with twinkling lights and flowers, and the table was laden with delicious food and drink. The friends celebrated their success with laughter and merriment, and they all agreed that it was one of the best parties they had ever attended.

Nancy's Legacy

Nancy's story is a testament to the power of individuality and the joy of nature. Her blend of mischief and care for the environment showed that even the most playful spirits could have a profound impact on their surroundings. Nancy's love for birdwatching, hedgehog rescue, and harmless pranks made her an unforgettable character in Marks Corner.
As the sun set each evening, Nancy would sit by her favourite oak tree, watching the world around her with a contented smile. Her pranks, though mischievous, were always in good fun, and her love for nature was unwavering. The villagers of Marks Corner were grateful for their whimsical guardian, and they cherished the stories of her playful antics.
Nancy's legacy extended beyond her pranks and parties. She inspired the villagers to take a greater interest in nature and to appreciate the beauty that surrounded them. Her bird-watching expeditions and hedgehog rescues taught them the importance of caring for the environment, and her playful spirit reminded them to find joy in the simple things.
The children, in particular, were deeply influenced by Nancy. They grew up with a love for nature and a sense of wonder that stayed with them into adulthood. They passed on the stories of Nancy to their own children, ensuring that her legacy would live on for generations.

So, here's to Nancy, the birdwatching, hedgehog-rescuing Nymph of Marks Corner. May her story continue to inspire us and may her love for nature continue to surprise us. Because in a world filled with Leprechauns, Sphinxes, and Ogres, sometimes, what you really need is a good, old-fashioned Nymph.

The Norton Green Kitsune

The Playful Fox

In the picturesque village of Norton Green on the Isle of Wight, there lived a Kitsune named Kiki. Kitsunes, known for their cunning, magical abilities, and playful spirits, were creatures of legend. Kiki was no exception. With her multiple tails indicating her age and wisdom, Kiki had a knack for blending into her surroundings and causing delightful mischief.

Norton Green, nestled between rolling hills and dense woods, provided the perfect backdrop for Kiki's antics. The village was dotted with quaint cottages, their thatched roofs and blooming gardens adding to the charm. The nearby River Yar meandered through the landscape, its gentle flow reflecting the vibrant greenery of the Isle of Wight.

Kiki had an unusual fondness for James Bond movies and fancied herself a spy. She loved the thrill of espionage and the glamour of the spy life, often mimicking Bond's suave demeanour and sharp wit. Her favourite drink? A martini, of course, "shaken, not stirred."

Her den, hidden deep within the enchanted forest that bordered Norton Green, was a cozy haven filled with memorabilia from her favourite films. Posters of James Bond adorned the walls, and her collection of spy gadgets, albeit homemade and whimsical, was impressive. Kiki's fascination with the world of espionage was more than a mere hobby; it was a way of life.

A Taste for Needlecraft and Flowers

When she wasn't engrossed in spy movies, Kiki enjoyed needlecraft and picking wildflowers. Her fox-like form was a common sight in the fields around Norton Green, where she would carefully select the most beautiful blooms. The fields were a sea of colours in the spring and summer, with poppies, daisies, and bluebells creating a natural tapestry. The air was filled with the sweet scent of flowers and the gentle hum of bees.

Her nimble fingers worked magic, creating intricate needlecraft that could rival any human artisan's work. She often arranged her flowers into stunning bouquets and delivered them to her friend, Mandy, the Mermaid of Yarmouth. Yarmouth, with its historic harbour and charming streets, was a favourite spot for Kiki's visits. The smell of saltwater and the sound of seagulls complemented the picturesque scene, making it a perfect setting for her and Mandy's unique friendship.

Kiki and Mandy shared a unique friendship. They often feasted on BBQ fishermen together, their laughter echoing across the waves as they enjoyed their peculiar meals. Despite their odd diet, the bond between the Kitsune and the Mermaid was unbreakable, built on shared laughter and mutual respect.

Kiki's needlecraft was renowned throughout the village. Her tapestries depicted scenes of nature and mythical tales, each stitch a testament to her skill and creativity. Her favourite designs often included motifs inspired by the wildflowers she loved so much. Villagers would often find her seated beneath a flowering tree, needle in hand, completely absorbed in her work.

Mischief and Martinis

Kiki's days were a blend of espionage fantasies, crafting, and playful pranks. She would wake up at dawn, her eyes gleaming with anticipation. Her mornings were dedicated to watching James Bond movies, her eyes glued to the screen as she followed the spy's daring escapades. Inspired by these films, Kiki often engaged in sneaky adventures around Norton Green, using her shape-shifting abilities to play tricks on the unsuspecting villagers.

One of her favourite tricks was to shape-shift into various townsfolk, causing confusion and amusement in equal measure. Imagine the local baker's surprise when "he" saw himself buying pastries at his own shop! The baker's cottage, with its enticing aroma of freshly baked bread and pastries, was a central hub of Norton Green. Kiki's playful nature brought a sense of wonder and humour to the village.

Kiki also loved to eavesdrop on the villagers' conversations, gathering snippets of gossip and secrets. She would then craft elaborate, humorous scenarios based on what she had heard, much to the bewilderment and delight of the villagers. Her antics, though sometimes perplexing, were always in good spirits and never meant to harm.

Her evenings were reserved for more refined pursuits. Kiki would mix herself a martini, settle into her favourite armchair, and reflect on the day's adventures. She often penned detailed accounts of her escapades in a leather-bound journal, imagining herself as the star of her own spy novel. These moments of solitude allowed Kiki to balance her playful mischief with a sense of introspection and creativity.

The Art of Needlecraft

Despite her mischievous streak, Kiki was also known for her exceptional needlecraft skills. She could often be found with a needle and thread in hand, her eyes focused on creating beautiful pieces of art. Her work was so exquisite that it was highly sought after by the villagers. Many a Norton Green home was adorned with Kiki's intricate tapestries and embroidered linens.

Her love for flowers was equally evident in her creations. She often incorporated floral patterns into her needlecraft, inspired by the wildflowers she picked in the fields. Kiki's artistry was a testament to her deep connection to nature and her keen eye for beauty.

Kiki's dedication to her craft was evident in every piece she created. She would spend hours perfecting the smallest details, ensuring that each stitch was precisely where it needed to be. Her tapestries often told stories of the mythical creatures that inhabited Norton Green, each one a vibrant and enchanting tableau that captured the imagination.

Her needlecraft was not only a means of artistic expression but also a way of connecting with the villagers. She often gave her creations as gifts, spreading joy and beauty throughout Norton Green. The villagers treasured these handmade pieces, knowing that each one was imbued with Kiki's magical touch.

Feasts and Friendships

Kiki's friendship with Mandy the Mermaid was one of her most cherished relationships. They would meet by the shore, sharing stories and laughter over their unusual BBQ feasts. The coast of Yarmouth, with its rugged cliffs and serene beaches, provided the perfect backdrop for their gatherings. Mandy, with her enchanting voice and shimmering tail, complemented Kiki's cunning and playful spirit perfectly. Together, they brought joy and a touch of magic to the coastal village.

One memorable evening, Kiki decided to add a twist to their feast. She shape-shifted into a renowned chef, complete with a tall white hat, and prepared a gourmet BBQ spread that left Mandy in awe. The two friends enjoyed the feast under the starlit sky, their laughter mingling with the sound of the waves.

Their friendship was built on a deep understanding and mutual respect. Mandy admired Kiki's wit and creativity, while Kiki was enchanted by Mandy's ethereal beauty and melodious voice. They often spent hours talking about their dreams and adventures, finding solace and joy in each other's company.

Kiki's ability to shape-shift added an element of surprise to their gatherings. She would often take on the forms of different sea creatures, much to Mandy's delight. These playful transformations added a layer of excitement and fun to their meetings, making each one a memorable experience.

Their BBQ feasts were legendary, attracting curious onlookers from nearby villages. People would gather at a safe distance, mesmerized by the sight of the Kitsune and the Mermaid sharing a meal and laughter. These gatherings became a symbol of the unique and magical bond between the two friends, a testament to the power of friendship and shared joy.

Kiki's Legacy

Kiki's story is a testament to the power of individuality and the joy of simple pleasures. Her blend of mischief, artistry, and love for nature showed that even the most cunning creatures could have a heart of gold. Kiki's passion for James Bond movies, needlecraft, and wildflowers made her an unforgettable character in Norton Green.

As the sun set each evening, Kiki would sit by her favourite field of wildflowers, watching the world with a contented smile. The setting sun painted the sky with hues of orange and pink, casting a warm glow over the landscape. Her pranks, though mischievous, were always in good fun, and her creations brought beauty to the village. The villagers of Norton Green grew to love their whimsical Kitsune, and they cherished the stories of her playful antics and artistic talents.

Kiki's legacy extended beyond her lifetime. The villagers passed down tales of her adventures and mischief, ensuring that her spirit lived on in the hearts and minds of future generations. Her needlecraft pieces became treasured heirlooms, each one a reminder of the magical Kitsune who had touched their lives.

The children of Norton Green grew up hearing stories of Kiki's pranks and creativity. They would often try to emulate her, creating their own mischief and art inspired by her legacy. The village thrived on the sense of wonder and magic that Kiki had instilled in them, becoming a place where creativity and joy flourished.

One tradition that emerged was the annual "Kiki Day," where the villagers would come together to celebrate the Kitsune's life and legacy. They would host a festival filled with needlecraft exhibitions, flower-picking contests, and playful pranks. The highlight of the festival was the storytelling session, where villagers young and old would share their favourite tales of Kiki's adventures.

So, here's to Kiki, the James Bond-loving, needlecraft-doing Kitsune of Norton Green. May her story continue to inspire us and may her love for espionage and flowers continue to surprise us. Because in a world filled with Mermaids, BBQ fishermen, and wildflowers, sometimes, what you really need is a good, old-fashioned Kitsune.

Kiki's influence extended beyond Norton Green, inspiring people from neighbouring villages and towns. Her story was shared far and wide, becoming a beloved tale of mischief, creativity, and friendship. Artists and storytellers drew inspiration from Kiki's life, creating works that celebrated her spirit and the magic of Norton Green.

In the end, Kiki's legacy was a testament to the power of individuality and the joy of living life to the fullest. Her blend of playful mischief, artistic talent, and love for nature showed that even the most cunning creatures could have a heart of gold. Kiki's story continued to inspire and enchant, reminding everyone that a touch of magic and a dash of mischief could make the world a brighter place.

And so, in the picturesque village of Norton Green, the spirit of Kiki the Kitsune lived on. Her story was a reminder that life was meant to be enjoyed, that creativity and joy were powerful forces, and that even the smallest acts of mischief could bring a smile to someone's face. The villagers of Norton Green would forever cherish the memory of their whimsical Kitsune, and her legacy would continue to inspire generations to come.

As years went by, Norton Green transformed into a haven for artists, nature lovers, and those seeking the charm of a life touched by magic. Inspired by Kiki, the villagers cultivated gardens filled with wildflowers, creating a vibrant tapestry of colours that attracted visitors from afar. The scent of blossoms filled the air, and the sight of blooming fields became a hallmark of Norton Green.

The village became known for its artisanal crafts, with many drawings inspiration from Kiki's intricate needlework. Workshops and studios sprang up, offering classes in embroidery, tapestry weaving, and other traditional crafts. These classes, often held in the open fields or under the shade of ancient trees, became popular gatherings where stories of Kiki were shared, and her spirit celebrated.

Local storytellers, poets, and musicians found endless inspiration in Kiki's life. Festivals dedicated to her legacy featured performances that depicted her adventures, blending folklore with the vibrant history of the Isle of Wight. These cultural events drew enthusiasts and tourists alike, turning Norton Green into a bustling hub of creativity and joy.

The "Kiki Day" festival grew larger with each passing year, attracting participants from across the Isle of Wight and beyond. The festival featured a grand parade, where children dressed as mythical creatures and villagers showcased their handcrafted floats, each telling a different tale from Kiki's life. The highlight was always the re-enactment of Kiki's famous pranks, bringing laughter and merriment to the entire community.

Kiki's favourite field of wildflowers became a protected sanctuary, ensuring that the natural beauty she cherished would be preserved for future generations. The villagers maintained the field with care, planting new flowers and creating pathways for visitors to explore and enjoy. The field was often used for weddings, picnics, and quiet moments of reflection, its serene beauty offering a glimpse into the world that Kiki loved.

Educational programs were established to teach children about the importance of nature conservation and the value of creativity. Inspired by Kiki's life, these programs encouraged young minds to explore their own talents and to appreciate the magic in the world around them. Nature walks, art classes, and storytelling sessions became integral parts of the village school curriculum, fostering a sense of wonder and curiosity in the students.

The Sea Serpent of Ryde

The Playful Serpent

In the charming coastal towns of Ryde, Appley, Puckpool, Seaview, and Elmfield on the Isle of Wight, there lived a legendary sea serpent named Sammy. Sammy was a magnificent creature, stretching over thirty feet in length, with a sleek, serpent-like body covered in shimmering scales that glistened under the sunlight. His sharp, piercing eyes reflected a mischievous glimmer, and his jaws, adorned with rows of razor-sharp teeth, hinted at his playful nature.

Sammy was known for his antics. Though he enjoyed causing a stir, he was not inherently malicious. His playful pranks often involved surprising beachgoers with sudden surges of water or stealthily swiping ice cream from unsuspecting visitors. Sammy's playful nature brought joy and laughter to the coastal communities, making him a beloved, albeit mischievous, figure.

Mischief in Ryde

One sunny day in Ryde, the beach was packed with townspeople eager to relax and enjoy the beautiful weather. Sammy, seeing the perfect opportunity for some light-hearted mischief, positioned himself near the shoreline. From beneath the water's surface, he watched the beachgoers, a sly grin spreading across his face.

Ryde's beach, known for its long pier and bustling esplanade, was a hub of activity. The golden sands were dotted with colourful beach towels, sun umbrellas, and families enjoying picnics. The air was filled with the sound of laughter, the cries of seagulls, and the gentle lapping of waves against the shore.

Slowly, Sammy emerged from the water, his massive form creating a wave that sent beach towels and sun umbrellas flying. Laughter erupted from the crowd as they realised Sammy was up to his tricks again. Children squealed with delight, and even the adults couldn't help but smile at the sea serpent's antics.

Sammy's favourite trick was to create small whirlpools near the shore, causing swimmers to spin around in surprise. The sight of Sammy's serpentine form twisting and turning in the water became a familiar and cherished sight. The beachgoers quickly learned that any day could be made more exciting by the presence of Sammy, the playful sea serpent.

The Ice Cream Caper

Sammy had an insatiable love for ice cream, and the Appley Café was his favourite spot to indulge. The café, nestled in Appley Park with its stunning views of the Solent and the iconic Appley Tower, was a popular destination for both locals and visitors. One afternoon, Sammy decided to satisfy his craving. Donning a comically oversized hat, he blended in with the queue of eager customers, hoping to snag a treat undetected. His clever disguise fooled some, but seeing a sea serpent in a hat couldn't go unnoticed for long.

The patrons of the café were astonished and amused to see Sammy shamelessly enjoying his ice cream. Laughter and astonishment filled the air as Sammy licked his treat with gusto. The sight of the massive serpent enjoying a simple pleasure brought smiles to everyone's faces. Children gathered around, giggling and pointing, while adults snapped photos to capture the whimsical moment.

The café owner, Mr. Thompson, quickly saw the humour in the situation and decided to offer Sammy a special "Serpent Sundae" – a towering concoction of ice cream flavours, topped with whipped cream and a cherry. Sammy's eyes lit up at the sight of the sundae, and he devoured it with delight, much to the amusement of the onlookers.

Adventures Along the Coast

Sammy's adventures didn't stop at Ryde and Appley. He often paid visits to Puckpool, Seaview, and Elmfield, where his presence never failed to bring excitement and amusement. The coastal path connecting these towns offered breathtaking views of the Solent and was dotted with historical landmarks and lush greenery.

In Puckpool, known for its historic Puckpool Park and battery, Sammy would weave through the waters near the Victorian-era fortifications, adding a touch of magic to the already enchanting landscape. The park, with its winding paths and serene gardens, provided a perfect backdrop for Sammy's playful antics.

In Seaview, a picturesque village with charming cottages and a quaint seafront, Sammy had an unexpected encounter with a Chimera. Both creatures scattered in surprise, their meeting quickly becoming a local legend, adding to the rich tapestry of folklore surrounding Sammy. The narrow streets and pebble beaches of Seaview were abuzz with tales of the legendary meeting, captivating the imagination of both residents and visitors.

In Elmfield, a tranquil area known for its lush meadows and woodland trails, Sammy stumbled upon a group of vampires conducting bizarre rituals. The sight both fascinated and perplexed him. He found their activities too serious for his liking and decided to observe from a distance, occasionally adding his own sarcastic commentary. The vampires, engrossed in their nocturnal affairs, were oblivious to the sea serpent's presence.

Sammy's adventures along the coast were not limited to encounters with mythical creatures. He often interacted with the local wildlife, playfully chasing schools of fish and diving through pods of dolphins. His presence brought a sense of wonder to the coastal towns, making each day an adventure.

The Beloved Serpent

Throughout his escapades, Sammy's mischievous nature and charming presence made him a beloved part of the coastal communities. Children eagerly shared tales of their encounters with the sea serpent, embellishing their stories with each retelling. Locals and tourists revelled in the suspense and laughter accompanying Sammy's appearances. Despite his pranks, Sammy was not a creature to be feared. He was a sea serpent with a penchant for fun and an insatiable love for ice cream. His playful antics brought joy to the townsfolk, making him a cherished figure in Ryde, Appley, Puckpool, Seaview, and Elmfield.

Sammy's influence extended beyond his pranks. He became a symbol of the whimsical and magical nature of the Isle of Wight. Festivals and events celebrating the sea serpent were held throughout the year, drawing visitors from far and wide. The annual "Sammy Fest" in Ryde featured ice cream eating contests, storytelling sessions, and a parade with floats depicting Sammy's legendary adventures.

Local artists and craftsmen found inspiration in Sammy's story, creating artworks, sculptures, and souvenirs that captured the essence of the playful serpent. The sea serpent became an integral part of the cultural fabric of the coastal towns, his legend living on in the hearts and minds of the people.

Sammy's Legacy

Sammy's story is a testament to the power of individuality and the joy of simple pleasures. His playful pranks and love for ice cream showed that even the most legendary creatures could have a heart of gold. Sammy's presence brought laughter and excitement to the coastal communities, making him an unforgettable character.

As the sun set each evening, casting a golden glow over the waters of the Solent, Sammy would often be seen basking in the twilight, his scales shimmering like a thousand stars. The peaceful moments at dusk were a time for reflection, and Sammy would watch the bustling towns with a sense of contentment. His playful nature had brought happiness to so many, and he cherished the connection he had with the people of Ryde, Appley, Puckpool, Seaview, and Elmfield.

Sammy's motivations were rooted in a deep love for fun and a desire to connect with the people of the Isle of Wight. He enjoyed the laughter and excitement his antics brought, and he took pride in being a source of joy for the coastal communities. His thoughts often revolved around new ways to surprise and entertain the beachgoers, and his feelings were filled with a sense of belonging and happiness.

The locals, in turn, felt a mix of amusement and affection for Sammy. They appreciated his playful spirit and the way he brought a touch of magic to their everyday lives. The general reaction to Sammy's presence was one of delight, with people eagerly sharing their encounters with the sea serpent and looking forward to his next appearance.

The environment of the Isle of Wight, with its stunning coastal landscapes and vibrant communities, played a significant role in Sammy's story. The serene beauty of the beaches, the lush greenery of the parks, and the charming villages all provided a perfect backdrop for Sammy's adventures. The natural beauty of the island complemented Sammy's playful nature, creating a harmonious blend of myth and reality.

So, the next time you find yourself near Ryde, Appley, Puckpool, Seaview, or Elmfield, keep an eye out for the legendary sea serpent, Sammy. Whether he's playfully splashing beachgoers, donning a silly disguise at the Appley Café, or inadvertently interrupting supernatural gatherings, Sammy's presence is sure to bring a mix of excitement, laughter, and wonder.

And remember, while Sammy may be naughty, he's not a creature to be feared. Instead, he's a sea serpent with a penchant for fun and an insatiable love for ice cream. So, if you happen to see a massive, hat-wearing sea serpent in the waters off the Isle of Wight, don't be afraid to join in the laughter and enjoy the whimsical adventures of Sammy, the Sea Serpent of Ryde.

Sammy's legacy continues to inspire the people of the Isle of Wight. The coastal towns thrive on the magic and wonder he brings, and his story is passed down through generations. His playful spirit reminds everyone that life is meant to be enjoyed, and that sometimes, the most extraordinary creatures have the biggest hearts.

In the end, Sammy's tale is a celebration of the joy found in simple pleasures and the enchantment that lies within the natural world. His presence has left an indelible mark on the Isle of Wight, making him a beloved and unforgettable figure in the rich tapestry of local folklore. So, here's to Sammy, the sea serpent who brought laughter, magic, and a touch of mischief to the shores of Ryde and beyond.

The Vampires of Brading

The Unusual Vampire

In the quaint towns of Brading, Haylands, and Springvale on the Isle of Wight, a peculiar vampire named Vladimir had made his residence. Unlike his fellow vampires, Vladimir was not your typical brooding, sinister figure. With his pale complexion, sharp fangs, and captivating eyes that seemed to glow with an inner light, Vladimir possessed all the traits of a vampire, but he had a rather unusual obsession—gardening. While other vampires spent their nights hunting for fresh blood, Vladimir spent his time tending to his secret garden of exotic and rare plants. This garden was no ordinary collection of flora; it thrived on the essence of moonlight rather than soil and water. As the moon rose high in the sky each night, Vladimir would glide gracefully through the shadows to his garden, nurturing his botanical wonders.
Brading, known for its historic Roman Villa and beautiful countryside, provided the perfect setting for Vladimir's secret garden. The town's rolling hills and serene landscapes offered a peaceful retreat for the vampire's nocturnal activities. His garden, hidden away from prying eyes, was a sanctuary where he could indulge his passion for the mystical flora that thrived under the moon's glow.

The Enchanted Garden

Unbeknownst to the townspeople, Vladimir's garden was a magnificent spectacle. The plants glowed softly under the moonlight, their colours vibrant and their aromas intoxicating. The enchanted flora was unlike anything seen in the mortal world, each plant possessing unique magical properties. The moonflowers, for instance, opened only under the full moon, releasing a fragrance that could induce vivid dreams. The nightshade berries glistened like black pearls, rumoured to have healing properties when used correctly.

The garden itself had an eerie history. Legends whispered of a powerful witch who once lived in the area, using the garden for her own dark purposes. The plants, it was said, thrived on the essence of the moon because they had been enchanted to do so by the witch. When Vladimir discovered the abandoned garden, he sensed its potential and decided to restore it, nurturing it back to life with his own unique touch.

One moonlit evening, as Vladimir was engrossed in his gardening endeavours, he stumbled upon a surprising discovery. Resting atop a mystical plant, he noticed a shiny trinket—a piece of jewellery that had once belonged to a renowned vampire hunter. Intrigued by the artefact, Vladimir decided to investigate further.

The trinket, a silver pendant in the shape of a crescent moon, seemed to radiate a faint magical aura. As Vladimir examined it, he felt a strange connection to its previous owner, a sensation that both intrigued and unsettled him. Determined to uncover the story behind the pendant, Vladimir delved into the history of the vampire hunter, hoping to find answers.

Word Spreads

Word of Vladimir's garden and the mysterious jewellery spread quickly among the vampire community. Vampires, known for their secretive nature, communicated through various ingenious methods. Vladimir, being a modern vampire with a flair for the dramatic, used enchanted ravens to deliver messages. These digital pigeons, as he called them, were capable of transmitting thoughts and images directly to the minds of other vampires.

Curiosity piqued, a group of vampires from neighbouring towns embarked on a journey to witness the legendary garden for themselves. They were astounded by the vibrant colours and intoxicating aromas that emanated from the enchanted flora. The garden, bathed in the silvery light of the moon, was a sight to behold. Each plant seemed to pulsate with its own magical energy, creating an otherworldly atmosphere that left the visiting vampires in awe.

As the vampires congregated in Vladimir's garden, admiring the magical plants, a peculiar scene unfolded. Sammy, the sea serpent who had been playfully splashing around the shores of Ryde, stumbled upon the gathering. Both the vampires and Sammy were initially shocked by each other's presence. Sammy was puzzled by the pale-skinned creatures, and the vampires were equally perplexed by the massive sea serpent in their midst.

The vampires, accustomed to their secluded and nocturnal lifestyle, found Sammy's presence both fascinating and amusing. Sammy, with his playful and curious nature, was equally intrigued by the elegant and mysterious vampires. The initial surprise quickly gave way to a mutual curiosity, and an unlikely friendship began to form.

An Unlikely Friendship

Instead of succumbing to fear and hostility, Sammy and the vampires found common ground in their shared curiosity and love for the unusual. They spent the night swapping stories, sharing laughs, and exchanging secrets about their respective realms. Vladimir impressed the sea serpent with tales of his mesmerising garden, while Sammy entertained the vampires with stories of his mischievous adventures in the coastal towns and his love for ice cream.

From that night onward, a unique friendship blossomed between the vampires and Sammy, the sea serpent. The vampires would visit the coastal towns, drawn by Sammy's mischievous charm and the allure of the sea. In return, Sammy would occasionally visit Vladimir's enchanted garden, marvelling at the otherworldly flora and enjoying the company of his new friends.

Their interactions were a blend of humour and fascination. The vampires, with their refined elegance and centuries-old wisdom, found Sammy's playful antics refreshing. Sammy, in turn, was captivated by the vampires' grace and the magical atmosphere of Vladimir's garden. Together, they formed a bond that transcended their differences, finding joy in their shared adventures.

The friendship was considered unlikely due to the stark contrast in their natures. Vampires, typically associated with darkness and mystery, found a curious yet endearing friend in the light-hearted and playful sea serpent. Sammy's easy-going demeanour provided a refreshing balance to the vampires' often serious and secretive ways.

A Night of Revelry

One particularly memorable night, the vampires and Sammy decided to host a grand celebration in Vladimir's garden. The moon was full, casting a magical glow over the enchanted plants. The garden was decorated with twinkling lights and colourful lanterns, creating a surreal atmosphere.

The vampires, known for their charm and hypnotic allure, mingled with the townspeople who had been invited to the festivities. Although the humans were unaware of their hosts' true identities, they were captivated by the grace and elegance of the mysterious partygoers.

Sammy, with his playful nature, splashed around in a nearby pond, causing waves of laughter among the guests. The pond, reflecting the moonlight and surrounded by glowing plants, was a focal point of the celebration. Children and adults alike were enchanted by Sammy's antics, and the sea serpent's infectious joy added to the magic of the evening.

Vladimir, the ever-gracious host, ensured that everyone was having a splendid time, his enchanting garden serving as the perfect backdrop for the night of revelry. He moved gracefully among the guests, his pale complexion and captivating eyes adding an air of mystery. The townspeople, drawn to his charm, couldn't help but be mesmerised by the enigmatic gardener.

The celebration continued into the early hours of the morning, with music, dancing, and laughter filling the air. The townspeople, vampires, and Sammy all shared in the joy of the night, creating memories that would last a lifetime. The event solidified the bond between the vampires and the coastal communities, fostering a sense of unity and understanding.

Vladimir's Legacy

Vladimir's story is a testament to the power of individuality and the joy of embracing one's unique passions. His enchanted garden and unusual friendships showed that even the most mythical creatures could find common ground and form lasting bonds. Vladimir's love for gardening, combined with his vampire nature, made him an unforgettable character in Brading, Haylands, and Springvale.

As the sun set each evening, Vladimir would glide to his garden, tending to his beloved plants under the moonlight. The townspeople, though unaware of the full extent of his identity, grew to cherish the mysterious gardener who brought magic and wonder to their lives.

Vladimir's motivations were rooted in a deep love for nature and a desire to create beauty in the world. His garden was not just a collection of plants, but a reflection of his inner self—a place where he could express his creativity and find solace. His thoughts often revolved around the delicate balance of nurturing his plants and the mysteries of the magical pendant he had discovered.

The locals, although unaware of Vladimir's true nature, felt a profound sense of awe and admiration for the mysterious gardener. They appreciated the beauty he brought to their towns and the sense of wonder that his enchanted garden evoked. The general reaction to Vladimir's presence was one of curiosity and respect, with the townspeople often sharing stories of the enigmatic figure who tended to the moonlit garden.

The environment of Brading, with its historic landmarks and serene countryside, provided the perfect setting for Vladimir's story. The natural beauty of the Isle of Wight complemented the magical atmosphere of the garden, creating a harmonious blend of reality and fantasy.

Vladimir's story took an unexpected turn one evening when he discovered another trinket in his garden—a small, ancient-looking key. The key had intricate designs etched into it, similar to those on the pendant. As Vladimir held the key, he felt a surge of energy and a sense of impending discovery. His mind raced with questions: What could this key unlock? What secrets did his garden still hold? He knew he had to find the answers, but the path ahead was shrouded in mystery.

A Cliffhanger Ending

As Vladimir pondered the key's significance, a sense of urgency washed over him. He felt a connection between the key, the pendant, and the enchanted garden, but the full story remained elusive. Determined to uncover the truth, Vladimir decided to embark on a journey to unravel the mysteries of his garden and its eerie history.

He called upon his vampire friends and Sammy, the sea serpent, to assist him in his quest. Together, they would explore the depths of the garden, deciphering clues and facing whatever challenges lay ahead. The moonlight cast long shadows as they prepared for the adventure, their hearts filled with anticipation and a hint of trepidation.

As they ventured deeper into the garden, the plants seemed to come alive, their glowing leaves and flowers creating an otherworldly path. The air was thick with magic, and the sounds of the night filled the atmosphere with an eerie sense of wonder. The pendant and the key seemed to pulse with energy, guiding them towards an unknown destination.

Suddenly, a rustling sound echoed through the garden. The group paused, their senses on high alert. Out of the shadows emerged a figure cloaked in darkness, its presence both menacing and intriguing. Vladimir stepped forward, his eyes locking onto the figure's glowing gaze.

"Who are you?" Vladimir demanded, his voice steady despite the tension in the air.

The figure remained silent for a moment before speaking in a voice that sent chills down their spines. "I am the guardian of this garden's secrets. You have discovered the keys, but the journey is far from over."

With those words, the figure vanished into the shadows, leaving the group with more questions than answers. Vladimir knew that their quest had only just begun, and the true mysteries of the enchanted garden were yet to be revealed.

The Fairies of St Helens

Enchanting Inhabitants

In the enchanting villages of St Helens and Nettlestone on the Isle of Wight, the air was always tinged with a sense of magic and mystery. Nestled within ancient oak groves and beneath vibrant wildflowers thrived a community of fairies, their presence hidden from most human eyes. These fairies, no taller than a human hand, possessed delicate features, translucent wings that shimmered with iridescent hues, and attire made of petals and leaves that mirrored the colours of the flowers they inhabited.

The fairies of St Helens were particularly beautiful. Their wings reflected shades of blue, green, and pink as they darted through the air with astonishing speed, leaving trails of sparkling dust in their wake. Despite their small size, their agility was unmatched, allowing them to vanish in the blink of an eye, leaving behind only the faintest whisper of laughter. However, their size belied their strength; fairies could be quite vicious when defending their homes, summoning gusts of wind or stinging nettles to ward off intruders.

Though generally known for their kindness and benevolence, the nature of fairies was complex. They were mischievous beings with a penchant for playful pranks and trickery, often using their magical abilities to create illusions that caused confusion and laughter among humans and other creatures. However, they could also be erratic and temperamental, lashing out with their powers when provoked or when their territories were threatened.

Twinkle and Her Mischievous Band

In the coastal town of Bembridge, a particular group of fairies led by the mischievous sprite Twinkle had earned a somewhat notorious reputation for their wicked sense of humour. Twinkle, with her bright blue wings and sparkling green eyes, was a master of mischief. Her band of fairies, equally spirited, delighted in stirring up trouble, whisking away keys, hiding valuables, and causing general mayhem, much to the exasperation of the townsfolk.

Twinkle's pranks were legendary. Garden ornaments would mysteriously rearrange themselves overnight, often forming strange patterns that puzzled and amused the villagers. One memorable prank involved tying the shoelaces of an entire class of schoolchildren together, resulting in a comical scene as they tried to walk. Socks would go missing from laundry lines, only to reappear days later in the most unexpected places, like inside a teapot or hanging from a weathervane. The fairies' antics brought both frustration and amusement to the villagers, who could never quite stay mad at the mischievous creatures. Mr. Thompson, the local blacksmith, would often grumble about his missing tools, only to chuckle when he found them neatly arranged in the shape of a fairy wing. Mrs. Green, the baker, would shake her head in disbelief when her bread rolls turned into small, doughy animals overnight.

"The fairies are at it again," the villagers would say with a mix of annoyance and fondness. Despite the chaos, there was an underlying affection for the magical beings whose pranks added a touch of whimsy to their daily lives.

The Werewolves of the Forest

Unbeknownst to the fairies, the nearby forest was home to a pack of werewolves led by the fearless alpha, Luna. Luna was a formidable leader, known for her cunning intelligence and unmatched strength. With her sleek, silver fur and piercing yellow eyes, she commanded respect and loyalty from her pack. The werewolves thrived in the dense, shadowy woods, a perfect habitat for their nocturnal activities.

The pack was composed of fierce and agile hunters, each werewolf possessing unique abilities that made them formidable predators. They moved silently through the forest, their senses heightened by the magic of the moon. The werewolves had an insatiable appetite for mischief-making fairies and considered them a delicacy. The taste of fairies was like gingerbread mixed with the essence of wildflowers — a flavour that was utterly irresistible to the werewolves. The scent of fairies, sweet and floral, drove the werewolves wild with anticipation.

Luna and her pack had long kept an eye on Twinkle's group, waiting for the perfect moment to pounce. They were drawn not only by the fairies' magical scent but also by the challenge of catching such elusive prey. The thrill of the hunt combined with the delectable taste of fairies made them an enticing target. The werewolves relished the excitement of the chase, their instincts honed by centuries of survival in the wild.

Each member of Luna's pack had their own unique strengths. There was Fenrir, the largest and strongest of the pack, whose powerful jaws could crush anything in their grip. Then there was Selene, known for her incredible speed and agility, able to outmanoeuvre even the swiftest of prey. The twins, Shadow and Shade, were masters of stealth, able to blend seamlessly into the darkness. Together, they formed an unstoppable force, their bond strengthened by their shared purpose.

One fateful evening, as the fairies revelled in their antics, they caught the attention of Luna and her pack. The fairies were particularly boisterous that night, their laughter echoing through the night air as they played tricks on the unsuspecting villagers. Twinkle, their leader, was in rare form, orchestrating a series of pranks that left the townsfolk bewildered and amused.

The werewolves, lurking at the edge of the forest, could smell the fairies' magical scent drifting on the breeze. The sweet, intoxicating aroma was too much to resist. Drawn by the irresistible scent of mischievous magic, the werewolves ventured into the heart of the village. They moved silently, their eyes glowing with anticipation as they approached their unsuspecting prey.

Initially unaware of the impending danger, the fairies continued their pranks with glee. They had tied the shoelaces of a group of villagers together, causing a comical scene as the humans tried to walk. Twinkle had just finished hiding all the keys to the town's doors, and the fairies were laughing uproariously at the ensuing confusion.

But the fairies' revelry was abruptly interrupted by the sudden, chilling howl of a werewolf. The sound cut through the night, sending a shiver down the fairies' spines. Twinkle's eyes widened in alarm as she realised the source of the danger. "Werewolves!" she squeaked, her voice tinged with panic.

The Encounter

The moon hung high in the night sky, casting an eerie glow over the village of Bembridge. The fairies were in high spirits, their laughter echoing through the quiet streets as they played their mischievous pranks. Twinkle, their leader, was at the height of her creativity, orchestrating a series of tricks that left the villagers bewildered and amused. Little did they know that their antics had drawn the attention of the nearby werewolf pack.

The werewolves had been watching from the shadows for some time, their keen senses alert to the fairies' magical scent and the sound of their laughter. Luna, the alpha, had been strategizing with her pack, waiting for the perfect moment to strike. With a silent signal—a swift flick of her tail and a glint in her eye—Luna gave the order to pounce.

The pack moved with coordinated precision, each werewolf knowing their role in the ambush. They emerged from the darkness with incredible speed and agility, their eyes glowing and fangs bared. The element of surprise was on their side, and they used it to full advantage. The werewolves pounced upon the unsuspecting fairies, their jaws snapping shut just inches away from their delicate wings.

The fairies squealed in terror, their wings fluttering frantically as they desperately tried to escape the clutches of the werewolves. The air was filled with the sound of flapping wings and growls, creating a chaotic symphony of fear and aggression. Luna, standing tall and imposing, had to exercise restraint to prevent her pack from devouring the fairies instantly. "Hold!" she commanded, her voice cutting through the noise. The werewolves, though hungry and eager, obeyed their alpha, their eyes still glinting with hunger as they circled the terrified fairies.

Realising their dire situation, Twinkle, the mischievous leader of the fairies, fluttered to the front, her wings beating rapidly. She raised her hands in a gesture of surrender, her usually bright and mischievous eyes now wide with fear. "Please, Luna! Spare us, and we promise to stop our pranks and never disturb Bembridge again!" she pleaded, her voice trembling. Luna, amused by the fairies' desperation, tilted her head and studied Twinkle with a mixture of curiosity and amusement. "Stop your pranks?" she repeated, a low growl rumbling in her throat. "What fun would that be?" She took a step closer, her presence dominating the space. "Alright, Twinkle. We'll let you go, but only if you leave behind a gift of mischief for us to enjoy."

The werewolves eyed the fairies hungrily, their fangs glinting in the moonlight. Twinkle, sensing an opportunity to save her band, quickly nodded. "We will! We'll leave you gifts that will bring laughter and fun. Just please, let us go," she promised, her voice steadying with determination.

Luna chuckled, her voice a low growl that resonated with power. "Very well. But remember, if you fail to amuse us, we won't hesitate to hunt you down again," she warned, her eyes narrowing.

The werewolves listened to Twinkle because Luna had signaled for them to do so. Despite their hunger, they respected their alpha's command. Furthermore, there was an underlying layer of intrigue among the werewolves. Werewolves, contrary to popular belief, had a peculiar fondness for gifts. They appreciated the novelty and amusement that well-thought-out presents could bring. In their packs, gifts were often exchanged as tokens of respect and camaraderie.

While it may seem peculiar for such fearsome creatures to enjoy gifts, it added to their complexity. The werewolves' affinity for gifts showcased their playful and, dare one say, nerdy side. They enjoyed solving puzzles, playing games, and the thrill of surprise—qualities that made them endearing in their own right. For them, gifts from the fairies promised an endless source of entertainment and a break from their usual predatory routine.

Twinkle, noticing Luna's amusement, couldn't help but respond with a nod and a wry smile. "We might just surprise you, Luna. Our mischief has a way of evolving," she said, her tone carrying a hint of challenge.

Luna's eyes sparkled with interest. "I look forward to it, Twinkle. Don't disappoint us."

The fairies, trembling but relieved, nodded vigorously. Twinkle fluttered her wings and addressed her band. "You heard Luna. Let's come up with the best tricks and gifts we can to keep them entertained."

A New Agreement

Every full moon, as the werewolves gathered in the moonlit glade, a sense of excitement filled the air. The anticipation of what new surprise the fairies had left for them was palpable. It was like werewolf Christmas, a time of wonder and joy that brought a sparkle to their otherwise fierce eyes.

The werewolves would arrive early, their noses twitching as they tried to catch the scent of the latest gift. "What do you think it will be this time?" Fenrir asked, his voice tinged with eagerness.

"I hope it's more of those enchanted feathers," Selene replied, her eyes gleaming. "They make my nose twitch in the funniest way!"

"Or maybe those miniature fireworks," suggested Shade, his tone hopeful. "I loved how they lit up the glade last time. It was like a personal light show."

The conversation continued, each werewolf speculating and joking about what the fairies might have concocted for them. The anticipation was part of the thrill, and their laughter echoed through the forest as they shared their hopes and dreams for the night's gift.

As the full moon rose higher, casting its silvery light over the glade, the werewolves gathered in a circle. Luna, their alpha, stood at the centre, her eyes scanning the clearing for the telltale signs of fairy mischief. And then, as if by magic, the gifts would appear.

This night, it was a collection of enchanted musical instruments—flutes, drums, and even a harp—that shimmered with a soft, magical glow. The werewolves approached them with cautious curiosity, their eyes wide with delight.

"Look at these!" Selene exclaimed, picking up a flute that began to play a haunting melody the moment her fingers touched it.

"Absolutely amazing," Fenrir said, his voice filled with awe. He picked up the drum, and a rhythmic beat filled the air, perfectly complementing the flute's tune.

Before long, the werewolves had formed an impromptu band, each one taking an instrument and adding their own unique sound to the mix. They called themselves "Fairy Good Music," a playful nod to the source of their magical instruments.

The band quickly became popular not just among the werewolves but also with the villagers of St Helens and Nettlestone. On nights when the moon was full and the air was filled with the enchanting melodies of "Fairy Good Music," the villagers would gather at the edge of the forest to listen, their hearts lifted by the magical tunes.

The werewolves were thrilled by the gifts, their eyes shining with joy as they played. But even as they enjoyed the music and the laughter, a part of them still missed the thrill of the chase and the taste of fairies. There was something primal and deeply satisfying about the hunt, and the memory of the fairies' delicious flavour lingered in their minds.

One night, as the band played and the werewolves laughed, Luna sat at the edge of the glade, watching her pack with a thoughtful expression. Twinkle fluttered down beside her, her tiny wings shimmering in the moonlight.

"Enjoying the music?" Twinkle asked, her voice light and cheerful.

Luna nodded, a small smile playing on her lips. "Yes, it's wonderful. Your gifts have brought us so much joy."

Twinkle's eyes twinkled with mischief. "But you still miss the thrill of the hunt, don't you?"

Luna sighed softly. "I do. There's something about the chase, the excitement... and the taste."

Twinkle nodded, understanding. "We fairies understand the allure of mischief and excitement. Perhaps we can find a way to bring back some of that thrill without the danger."

Luna's eyes sparkled with interest. "What do you have in mind?"

Twinkle smiled, her wings fluttering with excitement. "Leave it to us. We'll come up with something that will satisfy your need for excitement and keep everyone safe."

With a nod and a wry smile, Twinkle flew back to her band of fairies, already planning their next grand mischief. Luna watched her go, her heart filled with a mix of anticipation and curiosity. The fairies had proven themselves to be clever and resourceful, and Luna couldn't wait to see what they would come up with next.

As time passed, the villagers of St Helens and Nettlestone noticed a change in the atmosphere. The pranks that had once plagued their lives dwindled, replaced by an air of whimsical harmony. The fairies and werewolves had found a way to channel their mischievous energies into a friendship that brought laughter rather than chaos.

The fairies' gifts varied with each full moon. Sometimes, they would leave behind enchanted musical instruments that played melodies on their own, much to the werewolves' delight. Other times, they would create intricate puzzles that the werewolves would spend hours solving, their howls of laughter echoing through the forest when they finally cracked the code.

The enchanted instruments were a particular favourite. The werewolves had formed their band, and their performances became a regular event, drawing crowds from the village who marvelled at the magical music. The melodies, infused with fairy magic, had a soothing and uplifting effect on all who heard them, creating a sense of unity and joy in the community.

Despite their newfound joy, the werewolves couldn't entirely forget the thrill of the hunt. The taste of fairies was a tantalizing memory that lingered in their minds. But the gifts brought by the fairies provided a new kind of excitement, a different kind of thrill that was just as satisfying.

As the werewolves played their instruments and the fairies danced in the moonlight, a new chapter in their relationship began to unfold. The balance between mischief and harmony, excitement and peace, was delicate but achievable. And as long as the fairies continued to surprise and delight the werewolves, their unique friendship would continue to thrive.

And so, with each full moon, the glade would come alive with music, laughter, and the shared joy of two very different groups who had found common ground. The werewolves, though still longing for the taste of fairies, found contentment in the gifts and the fun they brought. And the fairies, ever the mischievous tricksters, revelled in their role as the bringers of joy and magic.

In this way, the villages of St Helens and Nettlestone became a place where magic and mischief coexisted in perfect harmony, creating a world where laughter and wonder were never far away.

Harmony in the Villages

Rumour has it that if you randomly trip up, fall over, or a big sneeze comes from nowhere on warm summer nights; it might have been a fairy playing with your funny bone. The fairies' presence, once a source of frustration, had become a cherished part of the villages' charm. Twinkle and her band continued to play their pranks, but now they were harmless and brought smiles to the faces of those they encountered.

Vibrant flowers bloomed more brightly, the air seemed fresher, and a sense of magic permeated the villages of St Helens and Nettlestone. The fairies' mischievous yet benevolent nature had brought a unique blend of laughter and wonder to the coastal towns, creating an enchanting atmosphere that residents and visitors alike treasured. However, beneath this idyllic harmony lay a darker history that few remembered. Long ago, the same magic that allowed the fairies to bring joy had been twisted into a force of chaos and destruction. When dark magic was unleashed, it turned the fairies from playful tricksters into malevolent beings, spreading mayhem and fear. Instead of harmless pranks, there were curses that brought misery, and instead of laughter, there were cries of terror. The villages were plunged into a period of intense disharmony, with residents living in constant fear of the next magical onslaught.

It was during this dark time that the werewolves emerged as the unexpected saviors. Led by Luna's ancestor, they took it upon themselves to protect the villages from the malevolent fairies. The werewolves hunted the dark fairies relentlessly, breaking the spells that had bound them to evil and restoring peace to the region. Their actions forged a bond between the werewolves and the villagers, who were forever grateful for their bravery.

The werewolves, aware of the potential for dark magic to return, committed themselves to ensuring such chaos could never happen again. Their need to hunt fairies was driven by this historical responsibility, not just a desire for the taste of fairy magic.

One evening, as the werewolves and fairies gathered for their regular exchange, Twinkle noticed a peculiar glow emanating from a secluded corner of the forest. Intrigued, she flew over to investigate and discovered a massive, hulking fairy unlike any she had ever seen.

This fairy, with muscles rippling beneath its shimmering skin and sharp teeth glinting in the moonlight, looked down at Twinkle and smiled. "Hello, Twinkle. I am Titania, the result of our secret magic. We have been experimenting with ways to become stronger, more powerful."

Twinkle's heart raced with a mix of fear and excitement. "What do you mean, Titania?"

Titania's smile widened, revealing rows of sharp teeth. "We are preparing for a new meeting with the werewolves. This time, we will not just bring gifts. We will bring mischief."

Twinkle, trying to mask her concern, nodded. "Mischief is in our nature, Titania, but we must be careful not to bring harm."

Titania's eyes glowed with a fierce intensity. "Oh, it won't be harm, Twinkle. It will be a test, a challenge. We need to ensure our magic is strong enough to protect us. The werewolves will understand the necessity of this."

With that, Titania vanished into the shadows, leaving Twinkle with a sense of foreboding and anticipation. She knew the balance between harmless fun and dangerous magic was delicate, and Titania's presence suggested that this balance was about to be tested.

Twinkle returned to her band of fairies, her mind racing with thoughts of the potential consequences. She knew she needed to speak with Luna and the werewolves to ensure that whatever challenge lay ahead did not spiral into the chaos of the past.

As the fairies and werewolves gathered once more under the full moon, Luna sensed the tension in Twinkle's demeanour. "What troubles you, Twinkle?" she asked, her voice calm but firm.

Twinkle took a deep breath and explained the encounter with Titania. "She believes we need to challenge the werewolves to ensure our magic remains strong. I fear this could lead to the same darkness that once plagued our villages."

Luna listened intently; her expression thoughtful. "Titania's magic is powerful, but so is ours. We have faced darkness before and emerged stronger. We will meet this challenge with the same courage and unity that has always guided us."

The werewolves, initially sceptical of this new development, discussed it among themselves with a mix of humour and concern. "Maybe it's time for another band," joked Fenrir. "We could call it 'Fairy Fight Night.'"

Selene laughed, but her eyes were serious. "Jokes aside, we need to be prepared. The fairies' magic is unpredictable, and we must protect our village."

The Werewolves of Bembridge

Transformation Under the Moon

In the village of Bembridge on the Isle of Wight, the presence of werewolves was both feared and accepted as part of local lore. Werewolves, fearsome creatures of the night, possessed an intriguing blend of anatomical, behavioural, and physical characteristics that set them apart from ordinary beings. By day, they appeared as regular individuals with a rugged charm and an air of mystery. However, as the moonlight bathed their bodies, their true nature emerged.

Anatomically, werewolves underwent a remarkable transformation under the moonlight. Their muscles bulged, their bones elongated, and their senses sharpened to an uncanny degree. A thick, coarse fur covered their bodies, ranging from shades of grey to deep browns. Once human and expressive, their eyes turned into piercing, golden orbs that gleamed with an insatiable hunger. Their claws extended, becoming deadly weapons, and their fangs grew sharper, ready to tear into their prey.

As the moonlight touched them, the transformation was both painful and exhilarating. The villagers knew to stay indoors, locking their doors and windows, as the sounds of the werewolves' howls echoed through the night. Despite the fear they instilled, the werewolves had become an accepted part of the village's fabric, a mysterious element that added to the lore and allure of Bembridge.

The transformation process was often a topic of discussion among the werewolves. "Doesn't it hurt,

Markus?" Fenrir asked one evening, watching his friend's muscles bulge and shift.

"Every time," Markus grunted, his bones snapping into place. "But it's worth it. The strength, the speed... it's exhilarating."

Luna, their alpha, nodded. "And it reminds us of our true nature. We are guardians of the night, protectors of our territory."

Primal Instincts and Cunning

As the moon rose, a relentless urge to hunt and feed overtook their being. Werewolves possessed incredible speed, agility, and strength, enabling them to move swiftly through the darkest forests. Guided by wolf-like cunning, they stalked their prey silently, striking with precision and ferocity. Their heightened senses allowed them to detect even the faintest of sounds, making them formidable hunters.

Despite their fearsome nature, the werewolves of Bembridge had a mischievous streak. They had mastered the art of illusion and trickery. Knowing the villagers' fear of the undead, they spread a rumour that a silver bullet was the only way to kill them. In truth, silver had no such effect on them. Instead, they cunningly sold silver bullets to unsuspecting buyers and used the proceeds to indulge in their true passion—eating at the local steakhouse, renowned for its colossal cuts of meat.

The myth of the silver bullet had an amusing origin. It began when a particularly clever werewolf named

Markus decided to play a prank on a group of visiting hunters. He fabricated an elaborate story about how only a silver bullet could pierce their magical defences. The hunters, eager to protect themselves, spread the tale far and wide. The werewolves capitalized on this, creating a thriving business selling "magical" silver bullets, which they assured buyers were their only weakness.

"Can you believe it?" Markus would chuckle to his pack. "Humans will believe anything if you say it with enough conviction!"

"Indeed," Luna would reply, a sly smile on her face. "And thanks to their gullibility, we can afford all the steak we want."

"Remember that one hunter who tried to pay us in wooden stakes?" Fenrir laughed. "As if we were vampires!"

"Humans are funny creatures," Markus said, shaking his head. "But their fear is our feast."

A Taste for Fairy Cakes

The werewolves' mischievous nature extended to their culinary preferences. They discovered a secret delicacy that fuelled their nocturnal prowling—fairy cakes made from the actual fairies from St Helens. Under the cover of darkness, they ventured into St Helens, capturing fairies in their fluttering frenzy and incorporating their essence into the delicious cakes, an irresistible ingredient for the werewolves' taste buds.

The taste of fairy cakes was indescribably delightful. Each bite was a symphony of flavours, combining the sweetness of gingerbread with the delicate essence of wildflowers. The cakes were moist and fluffy, and the werewolves savoured each morsel as if it were a rare treasure.

The fairies, despite their initial terror, quickly realized that their capture was more of a playful chase than a lethal hunt. Twinkle, the leader of the fairies, negotiated with Luna, agreeing to leave behind a small offering of fairy essence in exchange for peace. The arrangement was mutually beneficial, and the fairies even took pride in their role in creating such delectable treats.

"Honestly, it's like being chased by a giant puppy," Twinkle would joke to her fellow fairies. "And who can say no to such flattery?"

"At least they have good taste," another fairy, Sparkle, added with a grin. "Imagine if they preferred toads."

The werewolves' preparation for a night of adventure and mischief often led to unexpected encounters. They would share tales of their escapades while enjoying their fairy cakes, their camaraderie strengthened by the shared experience of hunting and feasting.

An Unlikely Alliance

One evening, the werewolves of Bembridge arrived at a pub in Wootton Bridge. The air was thick with anticipation and the scent of freshly brewed ale. The pub's patrons glanced curiously at the werewolves, their eyes widening with fear and curiosity.

Unbeknownst to them, the werewolves had formed an unusual alliance with the grumpy Troll of Wootton. Despite their different natures, the Troll found solace in the company of the werewolves, who understood his gruff demeanour and shared his mischievous sense of humour. In return, the Troll granted them passage through his territory and tolerated their presence, albeit begrudgingly.

The friendship between the werewolves and the Troll dated back to an event in their distant history. Long ago, when the werewolves first settled in Bembridge, they encountered the Troll during a fierce storm. The Troll's home had been destroyed by the raging waters, and he was in dire need of assistance. Luna, recognizing a kindred spirit in the grumpy giant, offered to help rebuild his home. In return, the Troll promised to protect the werewolves' territory from any intruders.

"Remember the time we built that bridge together?" Luna reminisced, her eyes twinkling with amusement.

The Troll grunted. "You mean the time you howled instructions while I did all the heavy lifting?"

"We're good at giving directions," Fenrir teased, elbowing Markus.

Over time, their alliance grew into a genuine friendship. The werewolves appreciated the Troll's strength and loyalty, while the Troll enjoyed the werewolves' company and their shared love of mischief. They would often gather at the pub to share stories and laughter, their bond solidified by their shared history.

"To think, I once thought you lot were just oversized dogs," the Troll grumbled affectionately.

"And we thought you were just a grumpy rock," Markus shot back with a grin.

Night of Revelry

As the werewolves settled into a corner of the pub, the Troll, towering over them with immense stature, approached with a scowl etched upon his face. He growled, "I don't know why you keep showing up here. You're all fur and fangs, disrupting the peace of this village!"

The werewolves grinned mischievously, their sharp teeth glistening in the dim light. One of them, known as Wolfhart, stepped forward, his eyes gleaming with amusement. "Ah, dear Troll, we bring excitement to your life! Admit it, without us, Wootton would be a dull and dreary place."

The Troll crossed his massive arms over his chest, his grim facade beginning to crumble. "Well, perhaps there's a grain of truth to that," he reluctantly admitted, a hint of a smile tugging at the corners of his mouth.

As the night wore on, the werewolves and the Troll regaled each other with tales of their escapades. The Troll recounted how he delighted in causing havoc on the roads, smashing potholes and playfully tampering with the traffic lights. The werewolves, in turn, shared their adventures in Bembridge, their encounters with fairies, and their clever ruse with silver bullets.

"I still can't believe they fell for that silver bullet story," the Troll chuckled, taking a swig of his ale.

"It's all about presentation," Luna replied with a wink. "Humans are easy to fool when you add a touch of drama."

Amidst the laughter and camaraderie, a strange harmony emerged between the werewolves and the Troll. It was an unlikely bond forged in the shared appreciation of mischief and an irreverent sense of humour.

The fairies, too, became part of this unusual circle of friends. They would occasionally flutter into the pub, bringing with them enchanted gifts that added to the merriment. One night, they left behind a set of enchanted musical instruments that played melodies on their own, much to the werewolves' delight.

The werewolves, ever resourceful, formed a band called "Fairy Good Music." The Troll, with his deep, resonant voice, became the lead singer, much to everyone's surprise. Despite his gruff exterior, he had a natural charisma and a love of bringing joy to others.

"Who knew you had such a voice, old friend?" Wolfhart teased.

"Don't let it go to your head," the Troll grumbled, though his eyes twinkled with pride.

The band's performances quickly became a sensation in the village. The magical instruments and the Troll's captivating voice created an enchanting experience that drew crowds from all around. The villagers of Bembridge, St Helens, and Nettlestone would gather to listen, their hearts lifted by the magical tunes and the sight of their once-feared werewolves and Troll now bringing joy and laughter.

Harmony in Bembridge

Despite their fearsome nature, the werewolves of Bembridge found a way to coexist with the villagers and the Troll. Their cunning tricks and indulgences provided a whimsical twist to their existence, making them an integral part of local lore. The villagers, aware of the magic handshake and the secret phrase "Luna protectus," felt a sense of safety and respect towards the werewolves.

The werewolves, in turn, continued their nocturnal escapades, capturing fairies and enjoying their fairy cakes. But their mischief was tempered by their unexpected friendship with the Troll and the camaraderie they found in the village pub.

The Loch Ness Monster at Downend

The Legendary Creature

The Loch Ness Monster, a legendary creature that has captured the imaginations of many for centuries, is a fascinating enigma. With a serpentine body resembling a massive aquatic reptile, its long, curved neck stretches above the water's surface, supporting a small head with piercing eyes and sharp teeth. This colossal being, with its scaly, dark green skin shimmering under the sunlight, blends seamlessly with the loch's depths.

Nessie, as the creature was affectionately known, had an elusive nature, preferring to dwell in the depths of Loch Ness, only occasionally surfacing to create intrigue and mystery. It had a knack for disappearing just when someone thought they'd caught a glimpse, leaving only ripples and whispers in its wake. However, Nessie harboured a secret far more astounding than its occasional sightings: it possessed magical legs hidden beneath the water's surface. These legs allowed it to traverse land effortlessly, enabling long walks and instant transportation from the sea to its log cabin in the woods. While the tales of Nessie's origins varied, one constant was its mysterious and magical aura. Legend had it that Nessie was the guardian of ancient underwater cities, a creature imbued with the wisdom of the ages. Its magical legs were a gift from the sea gods, enabling it to watch over both the land and the waters. Nessie's true power and benevolence were known only to a select few who had earned its trust.

The Villages of Downend and Binfield

Nestled in the picturesque countryside, the quaint villages of Downend and Binfield were known for their close-knit communities and love for local legends. The landscape was dotted with rolling hills, ancient woodlands, and serene lakes that mirrored the sky. The villagers lived in charming cottages, their gardens bursting with vibrant flowers and lush greenery.

Near the tranquil shores of a serene lake in Downend, Nessie found a kindred spirit in the villagers. They marvelled at its mythical presence, often catching glimpses of its majestic form as it gracefully emerged from the water's depths. The villagers would gather at the lake's edge, hoping to catch a glimpse of the creature and share stories of its legendary exploits.

In Downend, the children were particularly fascinated by Nessie. They would sit by the lake for hours, whispering tales of underwater kingdoms and magical creatures. The adults, too, were captivated, though they maintained a respectful distance, understanding that Nessie was a creature of mystery.

Just a short distance away in Binfield, Nessie had established its cozy log cabin amidst the ancient woods. The cabin, crafted from the finest timber, was a blend of rustic charm and mystical allure. It was nestled in a secluded glade, surrounded by towering trees and wildflowers. Nessie's magical legs allowed it to explore the village's picturesque trails and hidden corners, delighting in the natural beauty surrounding it. The villagers of Binfield embraced the creature as a beloved member of their community, recognizing its gentle nature and appreciating the enchantment it brought to their lives.

The villagers often discussed the unusual nature of their resident monster. One evening, in the local pub, a conversation ensued:

"Isn't it odd, having a monster from Scotland retire here?" remarked Mrs. Thompson, a sprightly woman with a twinkle in her eye.

"Indeed," replied Mr. Brown, the village historian. "But then, the Isle of Wight is known for attracting all sorts. Even mythical creatures need a peaceful place to retire."

"And where better than here?" added young Tommy, who had a particular fondness for Nessie. "It's like we're part of a grand story."

Laughter and nods of agreement filled the pub, the villagers taking pride in their unique guardian.

A Grand Gathering

One day, Nessie decided to host a grand gathering, inviting both the villagers of Downend and Binfield to celebrate their unique bond. The idea was inspired by the numerous kind gestures and the warmth Nessie felt from the villagers. It wanted to express its gratitude and strengthen the bond between them.

The festivities were filled with joy, laughter, and mystery. Nessie, with its regal yet friendly demeanour, regaled the villagers with tales of its underwater adventures and enchanted walks through the woods. It spoke of ancient underwater cities, glowing with bioluminescent corals and inhabited by creatures of immense beauty and wisdom. The villagers were captivated, hanging on to every word as Nessie described the wonders of the deep.

"Imagine," Nessie said, its voice a melodic rumble, "a city where the streets are paved with pearls and the buildings are made of crystal. That's where I come from, and I guard its secrets."

The villagers of Downend and Binfield brought their own stories, songs, and dances to the celebration, creating an atmosphere of communal warmth and unity. The children, in particular, were fascinated by Nessie, flocking around it with wide-eyed wonder. They listened intently to its tales, their imaginations running wild with visions of magical sea creatures and hidden treasures.

"Tell us more about the sea dragons!" little Emily begged, her eyes shining with excitement.

Nessie chuckled, a deep, resonant sound. "Ah, the sea dragons. They are majestic beings, protectors of the deepest trenches. They shimmer in the dark waters like stars in the night sky."

The villagers were also eager to share their local folklore. Mrs. Thompson sang an old sea shanty, while Mr. Brown recounted tales of shipwrecks and lost treasures. The air was filled with the sound of laughter and the warmth of shared stories.

Enchanting Walks

As part of the festivities, Nessie led the villagers on an enchanted walk through the woods of Binfield. Using its magical legs, it effortlessly navigated the terrain, pointing out hidden springs, ancient trees, and secret glades. The villagers followed in awe, feeling a deep connection to the natural world around them.

"Look here," Nessie said, guiding the group to a sparkling spring. "This water is said to have healing properties, a gift from the ancient spirits of the forest."

The walk culminated at Nessie's log cabin, a cozy retreat adorned with curiosities and treasures from its underwater adventures. The cabin's walls were lined with books and maps, chronicling Nessie's journeys and discoveries. There were shells the size of dinner plates, corals in every imaginable colour, and mysterious artifacts that glowed with an inner light.

Inside the cabin, Nessie invited the villagers to explore. They marvelled at the collection of items, each one with a story to tell. There were scrolls written in ancient languages, paintings of mythical sea battles, and even a crystal ball that showed glimpses of the underwater world.

"How did you find all these?" asked Lucy, a curious young girl with bright eyes.

"By exploring the unknown," Nessie replied with a wink. "And by being brave enough to seek out the magic in the world."

The villagers were particularly enchanted by Nessie's personal library. The books, bound in seaweed and decorated with pearls, held stories of ancient civilizations, sea witchcraft, and marine biology. Nessie encouraged the children to read and learn, hoping to inspire a new generation of adventurers.

"Knowledge is the greatest treasure of all," Nessie said, handing a book to Tommy. "Never stop seeking it."

A Lasting Bond

As the sun began to set and the villagers bid their farewells, they carried the spirit of Nessie with them, forever cherishing the magical memories they had shared. Nessie, content in its secluded haven, knew it had found a place where it truly belonged, a community that embraced its mystical nature and celebrated its presence.

The legend of Nessie in Downend and Binfield continued to weave its spell, reminding all who heard it that even the most extraordinary creatures could find solace and friendship in the embrace of a welcoming community. The villagers, now more than ever, felt a deep connection to the creature and to each other, their lives enriched by the magic and mystery of Nessie. In the days that followed, the villagers often gathered to reminisce about the grand gathering. The children would play games inspired by Nessie's tales, pretending to be explorers of underwater cities. The adults, meanwhile, found new appreciation for the natural beauty around them, seeing the world through Nessie's eyes.

"Remember when Nessie showed us that spring?" Mrs. Thompson would say. "I've never seen anything so magical."

"And the stories about the underwater cities," added Mr. Brown. "It's like something out of a fairy tale."

The bond between the villagers and Nessie grew stronger with each passing day. They felt a sense of pride and responsibility towards their mythical friend, ensuring that its presence remained a cherished secret, known only to those who truly believed in magic.

Harmony in the Villages

As time went on, the presence of Nessie became an integral part of the villages' charm. Visitors from afar would hear whispers of a legendary creature residing in Downend and Binfield, and though they seldom saw Nessie, they felt the magic in the air.

Rumours of Nessie's magical legs and its ability to traverse land sparked curiosity and wonder. Some claimed to have seen it strolling through the woods at twilight, its form shimmering like a mirage. Others spoke of hearing its melodious voice mingling with the wind, a soothing lullaby that brought peace to the heart.

The villagers embraced the enchantment Nessie brought to their lives. They created festivals in its honour, celebrating the mysteries of the deep and the wonders of nature. The children would dress up as sea creatures, reenacting Nessie's tales with joyous abandon.

One evening, as the villagers gathered by the lake for a storytelling session, Nessie emerged from the water, its eyes gleaming with happiness. It joined the circle, sharing stories of distant lands and ancient wisdom. The villagers listened with rapt attention; their hearts filled with gratitude for the magical creature that had become such an important part of their community.

"And so," Nessie concluded, "the magic of the Loch Ness Monster will always be with you, in the stories you tell and the love you share."

The villagers cheered, their voices echoing across the tranquil lake. They knew that Nessie's presence had brought them closer together, fostering a sense of unity and wonder that would endure for generations.

As the night wore on, the villagers returned to their homes, their hearts full of warmth and joy. Nessie, too, retreated to its log cabin, content in the knowledge that it had found a place where it truly belonged.

The legend of Nessie in Downend and Binfield continued to thrive, a testament to the power of friendship, community, and the enduring magic of the natural world. The villagers, now more than ever, felt a deep connection to the creature and to each other, their lives enriched by the magic and mystery of the Loch Ness Monster.

And so, the story of Nessie at Downend came to be told and retold, a cherished part of the village lore. Visitors who came to Downend and Binfield left with hearts full of wonder, forever touched by the magic that resided in the tranquil lake and the ancient woods. Nessie, the legendary creature, had found its haven, bringing enchantment and joy to all who believed in the power of the extraordinary.

The Minotaur of Cowes

The Fearsome Creature

The Minotaur, a legendary creature from Greek mythology, was a fearsome being with a unique blend of anatomical, behavioural, and physical traits that set it apart from other mythical beings. This fearsome creature was a combination of a powerful bull's muscular strength and a man's torso and head. Towering in stature, the Minotaur exuded an intimidating aura, with broad shoulders and formidable horns curving outward from its forehead. Its fiery, intense eyes seemed to burn with an insatiable hunger.

Known for its ferocity and insatiable appetite, the Minotaur also possessed uncanny intelligence and cunning. Lurking within the labyrinthine corridors of its domain, the Minotaur's predatory nature drove it to seek out prey, using its immense strength and relentless pursuit to overpower those unfortunate enough to cross its path. Its immense size commanded attention, with a muscular form covered in coarse, dark fur accentuating its primal essence. Each step caused the ground to tremble beneath its hooves, and its deep, rumbling growl struck fear into the hearts of those who dared to challenge it.

Despite its fearsome reputation, the Minotaur possessed a remarkable intelligence and cunning that made it a formidable adversary. It was not merely a beast driven by instinct but a creature capable of strategic thinking and deception. This combination of brute strength and sharp intellect made the Minotaur a force to be reckoned with, a true embodiment of primal power.

Arrival in East Cowes and Whippingham

The serene towns of East Cowes and Whippingham on the Isle of Wight were known for their vibrant communities and rich history. Nestled harmoniously on the shores, these towns had long enjoyed a peaceful existence. However, the arrival of the Minotaur cast a shadow over their idyllic lives. Fear and uncertainty permeated the air as whispers of the Minotaur's presence spread, turning their once tranquil towns into places of dread.
East Cowes, with its bustling harbour and charming streets, was the first to face the Minotaur's wrath. The creature roamed the town with a menacing presence, devouring whatever unfortunate souls it encountered. Panic gripped the residents as their beloved town transformed into a desolate wasteland. Damaged buildings and empty streets served as haunting reminders of the Minotaur's terrifying presence.
The townsfolk were paralysed with fear, unsure of how to combat the formidable creature that had invaded their lives. The Minotaur's reign of terror seemed unstoppable, its presence casting a dark shadow over the once vibrant towns.
Meanwhile, in Whippingham, the community that had once thrived was now shrouded in fear. The Minotaur's insatiable appetite led it to tamper with the ferries that connected the towns, causing chaos and confusion among the residents. Each attempt to "fix" the ferries resulted in disastrous consequences, leaving a trail of broken vessels and a sense of hopelessness.
"The ferries are a mess!" exclaimed Captain Harris. "We can't get supplies in or out. We're trapped!"
The people of East Cowes and Whippingham were paralysed with fear, unsure of how to combat the formidable creature that had invaded their lives. The Minotaur's reign of terror seemed unstoppable, its presence casting a dark shadow over the once vibrant towns.

A Daring Plan

As the Minotaur's reign of terror continued, the townspeople grew desperate for a solution. They knew that their peaceful lives could not be restored until they found a way to appease the beast and protect their communities from further destruction. In a daring plan, the towns of East Cowes and Whippingham decided to move their entire existence over the water, founding a new Cowes located on an outcrop of land by the sea.

The decision to relocate was monumental, requiring immense coordination and effort. The townspeople worked tirelessly, dismantling their homes and businesses and transporting them across the water to the new location. It was a challenging and risky endeavour, but the people of Cowes were determined to escape the Minotaur's grasp and rebuild their lives.

"We have to work together," said Mayor Roberts, rallying the townspeople. "We can't let the Minotaur destroy our spirit. We will rebuild, stronger than ever."

With their homes now a significant distance from East Cowes — perhaps 200 meters or so — the people of Cowes found a newfound sense of unity and resilience. They established a close-knit community, drawing strength from their shared experiences and the determination to protect their new town. The broken ferries and the floating bridge stood as reminders of the Minotaur's destructive influence, but they also became symbols of the community's ability to adapt and rebuild.

The townspeople of Cowes worked together to create a safe and thriving community. They fortified their new town, building sturdy defences to protect against any future threats. The Minotaur, unable to swim and unable to cross the waters, was left behind in East Cowes and Whippingham, its reign of terror effectively ended.

Coexistence and Compassion

As the years went by, the Minotaur's fearsome reputation mellowed, and the townspeople of East Cowes learned to coexist with the creature that once brought terror to their shores. They discovered that beneath its fierce exterior, the Minotaur possessed a gentle side, seeking connection and acceptance in a world that often feared and misunderstood it. One evening, a young girl named Emily ventured close to the woods where the Minotaur resided. She had heard the stories but was curious about the creature that had once terrorised her town. As she approached, she saw the Minotaur, its eyes not filled with rage but with a sadness she did not expect. "Hello," Emily called out softly. The Minotaur turned, surprised by the gentle voice. "I brought you something," she continued, holding out a loaf of bread.
The Minotaur hesitated but then slowly approached. It took the bread, sniffed it, and then, with a gentle nod, accepted the offering. This small act of kindness marked the beginning of a new understanding between the creature and the townspeople.
The townspeople began to see the Minotaur not as a monster, but as a misunderstood being with a place in their society. They embraced the Minotaur as part of their unique history, cherishing the lessons learned from their encounters with mythical beings. The creature, once feared and reviled, became a symbol of resilience and compassion.
The Minotaur's presence brought a sense of balance to the town, reminding the people of Cowes of the importance of understanding and empathy. They learned that even the most fearsome creatures could have a place in society if given a chance. The bond between the townspeople and the Minotaur grew stronger, built on mutual respect and trust.

A New Beginning

The tale of the Minotaur in East Cowes, Whippingham, and the re-founded Cowes serves as a testament to the power of resilience and the strength of a community united in the face of adversity. The townspeople continued to thrive, despite the lingering fear of the Minotaur's return. Their experiences with the creature had taught them the importance of understanding and empathy, transforming their relationship with the Minotaur from one of fear to one of mutual respect.

The Minotaur, too, found a sense of belonging among the people of Cowes. It roamed the outskirts of the town, no longer seeking to cause harm but to explore the world it had once terrorised. The creature's deep growl was now a familiar sound, a reminder of the bond that had formed between the mythical and the mortal.

"Good morning, Minotaur!" called out Mr. Smith, a local farmer, as the creature passed by his field.

The Minotaur nodded in response, its eyes calm and peaceful. It had found a place where it was accepted, where it could live without fear or anger.

The people of Cowes embraced the Minotaur as part of their unique history, cherishing the lessons learned from their encounters with mythical beings. They recognised that their strength and resilience had come from facing and overcoming their fears. The Minotaur, once a symbol of terror, had become a symbol of unity and compassion.

And so, the legend of the Minotaur in East Cowes, Whippingham, and the re-founded Cowes continued to weave its spell, reminding all who heard it that even the most fearsome creatures could have a place in society if given a chance. The townspeople of Cowes, guided by their resilience and compassion, embraced the Minotaur as part of their unique history, cherishing the lessons learned from their encounters with mythical beings.

The Chimera of Oakfield and Swanmore

The Eccentric Creature

In the heart of the Isle of Wight, amidst the verdant landscapes and serene coastal views, lies the picturesque town of Oakfield, and its equally charming neighbour, Swanmore. The residents of these towns live seemingly ordinary lives, filled with the rhythms of countryside and coastal existence. But these towns harbour a secret known only to a few: the enigmatic and awe-inspiring Chimera.

The Chimera, a fantastical creature of ancient lore, possesses an awe-inspiring and eccentric nature. Its anatomical structure amalgamates different animals, creating a truly unique and captivating sight. The body of the Chimera combines elements of a lion, a goat, and a serpent, resulting in a magnificent and imposing form.

At first glance, the Chimera appears as a massive lion with a fiery mane that flickers as if it's made of real flames. Its powerful forelimbs and regal stature exude an air of majesty and strength. From the lion's back sprouts a goat-like head, complete with twisted horns and an ever-curious expression. This head seems to have a mind of its own, often swivelling around to take in the surroundings with keen interest. Completing the creature's bizarre appearance is a serpent's long, curved tail that dances in the air with an air of mischief, always ready to strike or playfully tease whatever comes too close.

One evening, as the sun dipped below the horizon, painting the sky with hues of orange and purple, a group of local children gathered by the edge of the woods, whispering excitedly about the creature they had only heard of in stories.

"Do you think we'll see it tonight?" asked Tommy, his eyes wide with anticipation.

"I heard it has the roar of a lion and the agility of a goat," said Lily, her voice trembling with a mix of fear and excitement.

As the night grew darker, the air around them seemed to buzz with electricity. Suddenly, a loud, rumbling growl echoed through the trees, followed by the unmistakable sound of heavy footsteps.

"There it is!" shouted Tommy, pointing towards a shadowy figure emerging from the woods.

The Chimera stepped into the clearing, its lion's mane glowing softly in the moonlight. The children gasped in awe, unable to tear their eyes away from the majestic creature before them. The Chimera's goat head turned to look at them, its eyes twinkling with curiosity, while its serpent tail flicked playfully behind it.

"Don't be afraid," the Chimera's lion head said in a deep, rumbling voice. "I mean you no harm."

The children stood frozen, their fear melting away as they realised the creature before them was not the monster they had imagined, but rather a magnificent being with a playful and curious nature.

The Chimera's arrival in Oakfield and Swanmore marked the beginning of an extraordinary tale that would weave its way into the hearts and minds of the townsfolk, forever changing their perception of the mythical creature.

Mischief and Playfulness

The Chimera's behaviour is as enigmatic as its appearance. It possesses an inherent mischievous streak, often drawn to the Sea Serpent of Ryde. The two mythical creatures engage in playful water games, with the Chimera swimming circles around the serpent, occasionally daring to pull its tail, sparking a lively chase between them. Their interactions bring laughter and awe to onlookers as these creatures of legend engage in their whimsical version of aquatic games.

One sunny afternoon, the Sea Serpent of Ryde lounged lazily in the warm waters near the shore, its massive body creating gentle waves that lapped at the beach. Suddenly, a shadow fell over the water, and the Chimera leapt from the cliffs, landing with a tremendous splash right beside the serpent. "Tag, you're it!" the Chimera's goat head bleated mischievously.

The Sea Serpent's eyes snapped open, and with a powerful flick of its tail, it sent a wave crashing towards the Chimera. The creature laughed heartily, its lion's mane glistening with water as it darted away, the serpent hot on its heels.

"Catch me if you can!" the Chimera roared, its voice echoing across the water.

The towns of Fishbourne, Binstead, Oakfield, and Swanmore, fortunate enough to be graced by the presence of the Chimera, have their fair share of extraordinary tales. The Chimera's antics have become part of the townsfolk's daily lives, with stories passed down from generation to generation. Its playful nature extends beyond interactions with the Sea Serpent, as it often takes pleasure in amusing and bewildering the residents of these towns.

"Did you see the Chimera today?" Mrs. Wainwright asked her neighbour as they hung their laundry out to dry.

"Oh yes," replied Mr. Green, chuckling. "It swapped all the garden gnomes in the neighbourhood. Took me ages to find mine!"

The Chimera's pranks were always harmless, leaving the townsfolk more amused than annoyed. From switching shop signs to rearranging market stalls, its antics brought a touch of magic and wonder to the everyday lives of the residents.

One day, the local postman, Mr. Hargrove, found himself the victim of one of the Chimera's tricks. As he reached into his bag to deliver the morning letters, he pulled out a handful of colourful feathers instead.

"Well, I never!" he exclaimed, looking around for the mischievous creature. "You can't stay mad at it, though. Always keeps things interesting!"

The Chimera's playful nature endeared it to the townsfolk, who came to see it as a beloved part of their community. Its presence brought a sense of enchantment to the everyday, making even the most mundane tasks feel like part of a magical adventure.

The Festival of Fishbourne

One particularly memorable tale tells of the Chimera's encounter with the villagers of Fishbourne during a vibrant summer festival. As the townspeople celebrated with music, dance, and merriment, the Chimera joined the revelry, adding its whimsical twist. With its lion's roar resonating through the air and its goat head bobbing in rhythm to the music, the creature became the star of the festival, capturing the hearts and imaginations of all who witnessed its extraordinary presence.

The festival grounds were alive with colour and sound, as the townspeople danced to the lively tunes of fiddles and drums. Stalls lined the streets, offering everything from sweet treats to handmade crafts. Children ran about, their faces painted with bright patterns, while the adults enjoyed the festive atmosphere.

"Is that the Chimera?" a young boy named Jack asked, his eyes wide with excitement as he pointed towards a figure moving gracefully through the crowd.

"It is!" exclaimed his father. "Let's go say hello."

As they approached, the Chimera turned its lion head towards them, its eyes twinkling with amusement. The goat head joined in, nodding enthusiastically as it bobbed to the rhythm of the music.

"Welcome, friends!" the Chimera roared, its voice carrying over the music. "Join me in the dance!"

Without hesitation, Jack and his father took the Chimera's invitation, joining hands with the creature as they danced through the festival. The Chimera's movements were both powerful and graceful, its lion's mane flowing with each step as its serpent tail flicked playfully behind it.

"Can you believe this?" Jack's father asked, laughing as he twirled his son. "Dancing with a mythical creature at the Fishbourne Festival!"

The Chimera's presence brought an extra layer of magic to the festival, turning it into an event that would be remembered for years to come. The townspeople watched in awe as the creature danced, its lion's roar mingling with the music to create a symphony of sound.

"Look at it go!" Mrs. Thompson exclaimed, clapping her hands in delight. "I've never seen anything like it!"

As the night wore on, the Chimera continued to dance and play, its playful nature shining brightly amidst the revelry. The festival of Fishbourne became legendary, not just for the usual merriment, but for the once-in-a-lifetime experience of celebrating alongside a mythical creature.

The next morning, as the sun rose over Fishbourne, the townspeople awoke with smiles on their faces, still buzzing with excitement from the night's festivities. The Chimera's antics had left an indelible mark on their hearts, turning an ordinary festival into an extraordinary memory.

The Healer of Binstead

In Binstead, the Chimera's mischievous spirit found a new purpose. The townsfolk discovered that the creature had a peculiar ability to sniff out rare and elusive herbs known for their healing properties. Whenever someone fell ill or sought remedies for ailments, they would summon the Chimera, who would eagerly embark on a quest to locate the precious herbs, its goat head diligently sniffing out the desired plants.

"Chimera, we need your help!" called Mrs. Pritchard, her voice filled with urgency. "My husband has fallen ill, and the usual remedies aren't working."

The Chimera, lounging by a nearby stream, perked up at the call. Its goat head immediately began to sniff the air, searching for the telltale scent of the rare herbs. With a determined nod, the creature set off into the woods, its lion's body moving with purpose.

The townspeople watched with bated breath as the Chimera disappeared into the forest, hoping it would return with the herbs needed to cure Mr. Pritchard. Hours passed, and just as worry began to set in, the Chimera emerged from the trees, a bundle of vibrant green herbs clutched in its lion's jaws.

"Thank you, Chimera!" Mrs. Pritchard cried, tears of relief streaming down her face. "You've saved him!"

The Chimera nodded, its goat head nuzzling Mrs. Pritchard's hand before turning to leave. The townspeople gathered around, their gratitude evident in their expressions.

"You're a true healer, Chimera," said Dr. Bailey, the village physician. "We owe you so much."

Word of the Chimera's healing abilities spread quickly, drawing people from neighbouring towns seeking its assistance. The creature's unique talent for finding these herbs made it an invaluable asset to the community, and its mischievous spirit was now tempered with a sense of purpose and compassion.

"Who would've thought?" mused old Mr. Jenkins. "A creature like that, helping us. It's a wonder, it is."

The Chimera's reputation as a healer grew, and the townsfolk came to rely on its assistance. The creature's dual nature, both playful and caring, endeared it to the hearts of many. It became a symbol of hope and resilience, its presence a reminder that even the most unusual beings could bring light and healing to the world.

One day, a young girl named Emily approached the Chimera with a plea. "My mother is very sick," she said, her voice trembling. "Can you help her?"

The Chimera's goat head sniffed the air, its eyes narrowing as it detected the scent of the necessary herbs. With a reassuring nod, the creature set off into the woods, determined to find the cure. Hours later, it returned with the herbs, its lion's mane shimmering in the sunlight.

"Thank you, Chimera," Emily whispered, her eyes filled with gratitude. "You've given me back my mother."

The Chimera's actions solidified its place in the hearts of the Binstead residents, turning it from a mischievous creature into a beloved healer. Its presence brought a sense of magic and wonder to the town, making even the darkest days feel a little brighter.

Adventures in Oakfield and Swanmore

The neighbouring towns of Oakfield and Swanmore were also blessed by the Chimera's presence, with the people having their own tales to tell. The creature's curiosity often led it to explore the nooks and crannies of these towns, turning the everyday into whimsical adventures. From climbing rooftops with its agile lion body to perching on tree branches and engaging in playful banter with passing travellers, the Chimera's presence brought an air of wonder and enchantment to the streets of Oakfield and Swanmore.

One sunny afternoon, as the townsfolk of Oakfield went about their daily routines, the Chimera made its way into the heart of the town. Its lion's mane gleamed in the sunlight, and its goat head surveyed the scene with keen interest.

"Look, it's the Chimera!" shouted a young boy, pointing excitedly. "What's it up to now?"

The Chimera trotted over to the local bakery, drawn by the delicious scents wafting from the open windows. The baker, Mrs. Harlow, was busy preparing a fresh batch of fairy cakes, their sweet aroma filling the air.

"Well, hello there," she said, spotting the Chimera at her doorstep. "Fancy a treat, do you?"

The Chimera's goat head bobbed eagerly, its eyes fixed on the tray of fairy cakes. Mrs. Harlow chuckled and handed the creature a cake, watching in amusement as it devoured the treat with gusto.

"Enjoying yourself, are we?" she asked, patting the Chimera's lion head.

The townsfolk gathered around, laughing and chatting as they watched the Chimera indulge in its sweet tooth. The creature's antics brought a sense of joy and camaraderie to the community, making it a beloved part of daily life in Oakfield.

In Swanmore, the Chimera's curiosity led it to explore the town's picturesque countryside. It would often be seen perched on tree branches, its serpent tail flicking playfully as it observed the world below. The townspeople grew accustomed to its presence, greeting it with smiles and waves as they went about their day.
"Good morning, Chimera!" called Mr. Thompson, tipping his hat as he passed by.
The Chimera responded with a friendly roar, its goat head nodding in acknowledgment. It had become a fixture in the community, its playful nature bringing a touch of magic to the everyday lives of the residents.
One evening, as the sun set over the rolling hills of Swanmore, the Chimera came across a group of travellers making their way through the town. The creature's curiosity got the better of it, and it approached the group, its eyes twinkling with interest.
"Look at that!" exclaimed one of the travellers. "It's the Chimera!"
The creature's lion head roared in greeting, while its goat head nuzzled the travellers' hands. The group laughed and petted the Chimera, marvelling at its unique appearance and friendly demeanour.
"You certainly know how to make an entrance," one of the travellers said, grinning.
The Chimera's adventures in Oakfield and Swanmore became the stuff of legend, with each tale adding to the rich tapestry of local folklore. The creature's presence brought a sense of magic and excitement to the towns, making everyday life feel like a fantastical adventure.

The Magical Handshake

Aware of the Chimera's mischievous nature, the werewolves crafted a magical handshake and raced to Oakfield to meet and greet the creature. As the moon rose high in the night sky, they spotted the Chimera's fiery mane in the distance, its goat head bobbing in curiosity. Approaching cautiously, the werewolves extended their hands, uttering the magical phrase in unison.

"By the light of the moon and the strength of our bond, we greet you, Chimera," they chanted.

The Chimera, intrigued by their peculiar gesture, responded with a playful growl, acknowledging safe passage. The magical handshake served as a sign of mutual respect and understanding, allowing the werewolves and the Chimera to coexist peacefully.

"Welcome, friends," the Chimera said, its lion head nodding in approval.

The werewolves, relieved by the successful introduction, couldn't help but smile. They had heard tales of the Chimera's playful nature and were eager to forge a friendship with the creature.

"Shall we have some tea?" suggested one of the werewolves, producing a teapot from his satchel.

The Chimera led the werewolves to its home in the woods, where they shared cups of tea and a vast assortment of fairy cakes made from a fabled magical ingredient—real fairies! The evening was filled with laughter and camaraderie, as the Chimera and the werewolves exchanged stories and formed a bond that would bring a new layer of whimsy to the towns.

"These fairy cakes are incredible!" exclaimed one of the werewolves, savouring the sweet treat. "Where did you find the recipe?"

"The fairies of St. Helens shared it with me," the Chimera replied, its goat head nodding. "They have a knack for creating the most delightful sweets."

The werewolves and the Chimera continued to chat and laugh, their friendship growing stronger with each passing moment. The magical handshake had forged a bond that transcended their differences, bringing together two of the Isle of Wight's most enigmatic creatures.

As the night wore on, the group shared tales of their adventures, their laughter echoing through the woods. The Chimera's playful nature and the werewolves' camaraderie created an atmosphere of joy and wonder, turning an ordinary evening into an extraordinary experience.

A Whimsical Alliance

As time passed, the Chimera became an integral part of the fabric of these towns. Its naughty and playful nature served as a reminder to embrace the unexpected, find joy in the extraordinary, and celebrate the magic that can be found in even the most unlikely encounters. The towns of Fishbourne, Binstead, Oakfield, and Swanmore learned to cherish the presence of the Chimera, allowing its fantastical essence to shape their stories, festivals, and a shared sense of wonder. The werewolves, too, became frequent visitors to Oakfield and Swanmore, their bond with the Chimera bringing a new layer of whimsy and camaraderie to the towns. The three creatures would often gather for tea and fairy cakes, their laughter and banter creating an atmosphere of enchantment that permeated the community.

One sunny afternoon, the Chimera and the werewolves decided to host a grand feast in Oakfield, inviting the townspeople to join them in a celebration of friendship and magic. The event was filled with music, dancing, and an abundance of fairy cakes, creating a festive atmosphere that brought joy to all who attended.

"Look at the Chimera!" exclaimed a young girl, her eyes wide with wonder. "It's dancing with the werewolves!"

The sight of the Chimera and the werewolves dancing together, their movements graceful and playful, filled the hearts of the townspeople with a sense of awe and delight. The bond between the creatures and the townsfolk grew stronger, their shared experiences creating a tapestry of memories that would be cherished for generations.

As the sun set over the rolling hills, the Chimera and the werewolves led the townspeople in a final dance, their laughter echoing through the air. The celebration was a testament to the power of friendship and the magic that can be found in the most unexpected places.

"We're so lucky to have the Chimera and the werewolves as part of our community," said Mrs. Harlow, smiling as she watched the festivities. "They've brought so much joy and wonder into our lives."

The towns of Fishbourne, Binstead, Oakfield, and Swanmore continued to thrive, their stories intertwined with the magic of the Chimera and the werewolves. The presence of these mythical creatures enriched the lives of the townsfolk, reminding them to embrace the unexpected and find joy in the extraordinary.

And so, the legend of the Chimera in Oakfield and Swanmore continued to weave its spell, reminding all who heard it that even the most fearsome creatures could bring light and joy into the world. The townspeople of the Isle of Wight learned to cherish the magic that surrounded them, celebrating the whimsy and wonder that the Chimera brought into their lives.

The Basilisk of Havenstreet

The Legendary Creature

Nestled in the heart of the Isle of Wight, Havenstreet is a village steeped in legend. The cobblestone streets and thatched-roof cottages whisper tales of mythical beings and ancient magic. Amidst the serene beauty of this quaint village lies a creature of unparalleled mystery and terror—the Basilisk. This beast, drawn from the deepest annals of ancient mythology, is a formidable fusion of reptilian and serpentine features. Its body, covered in shimmering scales that reflect the light in iridescent green, gold, and bronze hues, moves with an eerie grace and purpose.

The Basilisk's most striking feature is its head, adorned with a crown of menacing horns that frame its piercing eyes. These eyes are not just for show; they carry the creature's most infamous trait—the ability to petrify anyone who meets their gaze. The village lore tells of a single stare that can turn a person to stone, a curse that has been the doom of many unwary travellers.

"Mind your step and keep your gaze low," the elders would warn. "For if the Basilisk catches your eye, it will be the last sight you ever behold."

Despite its fearsome reputation, the Basilisk is not a creature of brute force. Its predatory nature is complemented by a cunning intelligence and an unexpected penchant for mundane conversation. The residents of Havenstreet have come to fear not just the creature's gaze, but its uncanny ability to bore its victims to death with endless discussions about the weather and tide times.

The Reign of Boredom

Havenstreet, with its picturesque surroundings and tranquil ambiance, seems an unlikely setting for such a terrifying creature. Yet, the Basilisk's presence has woven itself into the very fabric of the village life. Unlike the violent beasts of other legends, this creature's method of hunting is oddly passive—yet no less deadly. The Basilisk's conversations are as lethal as its gaze, lulling its victims into a stupor with tedious monologues on the most banal topics.

"Did you know," it would begin, "that the tide will be at its peak precisely at 4:23 PM today? And have you noticed how the clouds are forming a particularly interesting cumulonimbus pattern?"

For hours, it would drone on, its voice a hypnotic drawl that left listeners transfixed and helpless.

In Havenstreet, the villagers had developed a deep-seated wariness of the Basilisk's presence. Stories abounded of hapless souls who had stumbled upon the creature, only to be found later, their expressions frozen in a mix of horror and sheer boredom.

"Poor old Tom," Mrs. Thatcher would sigh, recounting the latest victim. "He was found by the river, staring blankly into space. Not a single mark on him, just a look of utter tedium."

The Basilisk's reign of boredom was a peculiar form of terror that left the village constantly on edge. The fear of encountering the creature turned even the simplest of tasks—like fetching water or walking through the woods—into a potentially fatal endeavour.

An Unlikely Friendship

Amidst the Basilisk's reign of boredom, there existed an unlikely friendship that baffled the villagers of Havenstreet. For reasons unknown, the Basilisk shared a peculiar camaraderie with the grumpy Troll of Wootton, a creature known for its cantankerous disposition and love for bridge maintenance.

The Troll, often seen scowling and muttering under its breath, found an unexpected solace in the company of the Basilisk. The villagers would often find the duo sitting by the banks of the nearby river, engaged in what could only be described as the most mundane of conversations. The Basilisk would drone on about tidal charts and cloud formations, while the Troll would grumble about the lack of appreciation for proper bridge upkeep.

"It's the moss, you see," the Troll would complain, pointing at the underside of the bridge. "No one cares about the moss. It's a sign of neglect."

"And speaking of neglect," the Basilisk would interject, "have you noticed how the weather patterns have shifted lately? It's absolutely fascinating."

Despite their differences, the Basilisk and the Troll had forged a bond that defied understanding. Their companionship was a curious blend of mutual tolerance and shared grievances. While the villagers couldn't fathom why the Basilisk tolerated the Troll's incessant complaints, or why the Troll put up with the Basilisk's monotonous lectures, there was an unspoken understanding between them.

One evening, as the sun set over Havenstreet, casting long shadows over the village, young Emily and her brother Jack ventured near the river, hoping to catch a glimpse of the enigmatic duo.

"Do you think they're friends because no one else can stand them?" Jack whispered.

Emily shrugged. "Maybe they just understand each other in a way we can't."

The Challenge

One day, a daring adventurer named Cedric arrived in Havenstreet, determined to challenge the Basilisk's conversational prowess. Cedric was a man of peculiar tastes, known for his vast collection of rare stamps and an uncanny ability to engage in the most mind-numbing discussions. Armed with his stamp album and an unwavering resolve, he set out to confront the legendary creature.

The villagers watched in awe as Cedric approached the Basilisk's lair, his footsteps steady and his expression one of determination. The Basilisk, sensing a new prey, slithered forward, its eyes gleaming with anticipation.

"Welcome, traveller," the Basilisk hissed. "Shall we discuss the fascinating intricacies of cloud formations?"

Cedric smiled, unfazed. "I was hoping we could delve into the world of rare stamps," he replied, holding up his album. "Did you know that the Penny Black is considered the world's first adhesive postage stamp? It was issued in the United Kingdom on 1st May 1840."

For hours, the two engaged in a battle of wits, debating the minutiae of stamp collecting versus the complexities of meteorological phenomena. The Basilisk's gaze, though potent, seemed to have met its match in Cedric's unwavering resolve. The villagers, gathered at a safe distance, watched in astonishment as the conversation stretched into the night.

At dawn, Cedric emerged from the encounter, his expression weary but triumphant. The Basilisk, recognising a kindred spirit in the realm of tedious conversation, spared him its petrifying gaze.

"You have earned my respect," the Basilisk admitted, its voice a low rumble. "From this day forward, you shall be immune to my powers."

Cedric nodded, a faint smile playing on his lips. "It was an honour," he replied. "But perhaps next time, we could discuss the fascinating world of kettle boiling times."

The villagers erupted in applause; their relief palpable. Cedric's victory was not just a personal triumph, but a beacon of hope for Havenstreet. If one man could withstand the Basilisk's deadly monotony, perhaps there was a way to coexist with the creature after all.

Adapting to the Basilisk

As the villagers of Havenstreet began to adapt to the Basilisk's presence, they devised ingenious strategies to safeguard themselves against its deadly conversations. Earplugs became a common accessory, and mental exercises to stay alert were taught to children from a young age. The village market thrived with boredom-resistant merchandise, including books on thrilling topics and devices that buzzed to keep one awake. The Basilisk, though still a formidable presence, became an accepted part of village life. Its conversations, while still dangerously dull, were now met with prepared defences.

One afternoon, a group of villagers gathered in the town square to discuss their latest strategies.

"Have you tried the new earplugs?" Mrs. Thatcher asked, holding up a pair. "They're supposed to block out even the dullest of monologues."

Mr. Jenkins nodded. "I've been reading books on extreme sports. Keeps the mind sharp and ready for anything."

Meanwhile, in nearby villages like Fishbourne, Binstead, Oakfield, and Swanmore, rumours of the Basilisk's presence in Havenstreet spread like wildfire. Travellers passing through whispered tales of the creature's hypnotic gaze and its peculiar friendship with the Troll.

"Is it true that the Basilisk can bore you to death?" a traveller asked, his eyes wide with curiosity.

"Absolutely," replied a local. "But if you're well-prepared, you might just survive an encounter. Just don't engage in conversation, and for goodness' sake, don't make eye contact."

Despite the danger, the Basilisk's unique presence attracted a steady stream of visitors to Havenstreet. Some came out of sheer curiosity, while others sought to challenge the creature's conversational prowess, hoping to earn immunity like Cedric.

One day, a young woman named Eliza arrived in the village, her eyes filled with determination. "I've heard the tales," she said, her voice steady. "And I believe I'm ready to face the Basilisk."

The villagers exchanged wary glances. "Be careful," warned Mrs. Thatcher. "The Basilisk is not to be taken lightly."

Eliza nodded, her resolve unshaken. "I've come prepared," she said, holding up a book on quantum physics. "Let's see how it fares against this."

A Haven for the Mundane

As the years passed, Havenstreet transformed into a haven for the mundane. Travellers who loved to drone on about mundane topics flocked to the village, eager to witness the Basilisk's legendary conversational skills. The village, once shrouded in fear, now thrived on the eccentric charm of its resident monster.

Artists, philosophers, and thinkers from far and wide gathered in Havenstreet, seeking inspiration in the most unexpected places. The Basilisk's reign of boredom had evolved into a quirky and essential part of the village's identity.

One crisp autumn morning, a group of visitors gathered in the village square, eagerly awaiting their turn to engage with the Basilisk.

"I've come all the way from London," said a bespectacled man, his eyes gleaming with excitement. "I've heard the Basilisk is a master of mundane conversation."

A woman with a sketchpad nodded. "I'm hoping to capture the essence of its gaze in my drawings."

As the Basilisk slithered into the square, its eyes gleaming with a hypnotic light, the visitors gasped in awe. The creature's presence was both majestic and intimidating, a living legend come to life.

"Welcome," the Basilisk hissed, its voice a low rumble. "Shall we discuss the fascinating patterns of cloud formations today?"

The visitors eagerly engaged, their conversations blending into a symphony of mundane topics. The Basilisk, once feared and reviled, was now celebrated for its unique talents.

Meanwhile, the Troll of Wootton, ever the Basilisk's loyal companion, watched from a distance, a rare smile tugging at its lips.

"Who would have thought," the Troll muttered, "that boredom could bring so much joy?"

As the sun set over Havenstreet, casting a golden glow over the village, the Basilisk and the Troll sat by the river, their conversations a harmonious blend of complaints and observations.

"I must admit," the Basilisk said, its gaze fixed on the horizon, "I never imagined I would find such companionship."

The Troll grunted in agreement. "Life has a funny way of surprising us," it replied.

And so, the legend of the Basilisk in Havenstreet continued to weave its spell, reminding all who heard it that even the most fearsome creatures could bring light and joy into the world. The villagers of Havenstreet, Fishbourne, Binstead, Oakfield, and Swanmore learned to cherish the magic that surrounded them, celebrating the whimsy and wonder that the Basilisk brought into their lives.

The Dragons of Newport

The Magnificent Creature

In the heart of Newport, the largest town on the Isle of Wight, there existed a creature so magnificent and fearsome that it became the stuff of legends — the Dragon. Newport, with its cobblestone streets, quaint shops, and historic charm, was an unlikely setting for such a mythical beast. Yet, there it was, a towering entity whose presence demanded awe and respect. The Dragon's massive frame was a spectacle to behold. Its scales, a dazzling array of colours, shimmered like a living mosaic in the sunlight, reflecting vibrant hues of green, gold, and deep crimson. With a wingspan that could block out the sun, it soared through the skies, casting an imposing shadow over the land below. The townspeople often gazed up in wonder, watching the Dragon's graceful yet powerful flight. Anatomically, the Dragon was a masterpiece of both power and grace. Sharp, serrated teeth lined its powerful jaws, capable of rending through the toughest of hides. Its eyes, like fiery orbs, glowed with an intense and piercing gaze that could strike fear into the hearts of the bravest warriors. Smoke and flames erupted from its nostrils, leaving a trail of scorching heat and charred earth wherever it went.

Despite its fearsome exterior, the Dragon possessed an unexpected elegance. Its movements, whether in flight or on the ground, were fluid and almost poetic. Each step it took caused the ground to tremble beneath its mighty weight, yet it moved with a surprising delicacy. The combination of raw power and refined grace made the Dragon a creature of both terror and beauty.

"Did you see it today?" a young boy whispered to his friend as they walked through St. Thomas' Square. "It flew right over the castle!"

"Yes," the other replied, eyes wide with excitement. "It's like nothing else. I heard it once starred in a famous TV show!"

The adults often chuckled at such tales, but deep down, they too were captivated by the presence of this mythical being. It was a part of Newport's charm, a living legend that brought both fear and fascination to the everyday lives of the townsfolk.

An Unexpected Passion

Despite its notorious ferocity, the Dragon of Newport harboured an unexpected side to its personality. It had developed an insatiable passion for the theatre, a passion that stemmed from its brief stint as a famous actor on "Game of Thrones." Anyone daring to ask which character the Dragon played would meet an instant flambé, but the Dragon was deeply besotted with the world of drama, relishing the art of storytelling and the magic that unfolded on the stage.

The local theatre scene in Newport had never been the same since the Dragon's arrival. Its grand, dramatic entrances during performances left the audience in awe. The Dragon's appearances were always meticulously timed, swooping in just as the climax of the play was about to unfold, adding a layer of excitement and wonder to the performances.

The townsfolk soon discovered that the Dragon had a peculiar taste for those who had imbibed alcohol. It seemed that the scent of spirits attracted the Dragon, leading it to seek out tipsy individuals for a gentle nibble as a form of theatrical tribute.

One evening, during a performance of "A Midsummer Night's Dream," the Dragon made its grand entrance, swooping down from the sky with a mighty roar. The audience gasped in delight as the creature landed gracefully on the stage, its fiery breath illuminating the night.

"Fear not, dear audience," the Dragon boomed, its voice resonating through the theatre. "I am here to add a touch of magic to your evening."

The actors, though initially startled, quickly adapted to their unexpected co-star. The performance continued, with the Dragon adding its own dramatic flair to the scenes. The audience was mesmerised, their attention riveted to the stage.
"That was incredible!" one woman exclaimed as she left the theatre. "The Dragon brought the play to life in a way I've never seen before."
"Indeed," her companion agreed. "And I must say, the nibbling was rather gentle. A small price to pay for such an extraordinary experience."
News of the Dragon's affinity for theatre and its peculiar dietary preference spread far and wide. Visitors from neighbouring villages and distant lands flocked to Newport, eager to witness the Dragon's performances and perhaps become part of the show themselves.

The Dragon's Grand Entrances

The Dragon's presence in Newport soon became synonymous with the local theatre scene. It had a penchant for making grand, dramatic entrances during performances, leaving the audience in awe and anticipation. The townsfolk quickly learned to embrace the Dragon's whimsical nature, turning it into a whimsical and somewhat risky attraction.
An open-air theatre was erected in the heart of Newport, where brave actors would perform under the watchful eye of the Dragon. The stage was set against the backdrop of Carisbrooke Castle, adding an air of historical grandeur to the performances. The theatre became a gathering place for both locals and tourists, eager to witness the Dragon's dramatic flights and fiery exhalations.
One evening, as the sun dipped below the horizon, casting a golden glow over the castle, the audience gathered for the premiere of "Macbeth." The air was thick with anticipation, and whispers of excitement filled the crowd.

"Do you think it will come tonight?" a young girl asked her mother, her eyes wide with wonder.

"Only the Dragon knows," her mother replied with a smile. "But if it does, we are in for a treat."

As the play began, the tension in the air was palpable. The actors delivered their lines with fervour, their voices echoing through the castle grounds. Suddenly, a low rumble resonated from above, and the audience looked up in unison.

With a mighty roar, the Dragon descended from the sky, its wings casting a shadow over the stage. Flames erupted from its nostrils, illuminating the night and adding a dramatic flair to the scene. The audience gasped in awe, their eyes transfixed on the majestic creature.

"Fair is foul, and foul is fair," the Dragon bellowed, seamlessly integrating itself into the performance. "Hover through the fog and filthy air."

The actors, though initially startled, quickly adapted to their new co-star. The performance continued, with the Dragon adding its own dramatic touch to the scenes. The audience was mesmerised, their attention riveted to the stage.

As the play came to an end, the Dragon took a bow, its wings spread wide in a gesture of gratitude. The audience erupted in applause, their cheers echoing through the night.

"Bravo!" a man shouted, his voice filled with admiration. "That was the best performance I've ever seen!"

The Dragon, basking in the adulation, let out a contented roar. It had found a place where it could indulge in its passion for theatre, surrounded by a community that embraced its eccentricities.

From that day forward, the Dragon's grand entrances became a staple of Newport's theatre scene. The townsfolk developed a unique camaraderie with their scaly friend, appreciating its quirks and the sense of wonder it brought to their lives. They eagerly awaited its dramatic flights, knowing that each performance would be a spectacle unlike any other.

Mentor and Advisor

With its vast knowledge of the dramatic arts, the Dragon became a mentor and advisor to budding actors in Newport. It would share tales of its adventures on and off the stage, regaling the performers with stories of its encounters with other legendary creatures and the challenges of bringing mythical worlds to life.

"Remember," the Dragon would advise, "it's not just about the lines you deliver, but the passion you bring to them. Feel the fire within you, just as I do when I breathe flames."

The actors listened intently, hanging on to every word. The Dragon's presence was both intimidating and inspiring, a reminder of the power of storytelling and the magic of the theatre.

One evening, as the sun set over the Solent, casting a warm glow over the town, the Dragon gathered a group of aspiring actors in the courtyard of Carisbrooke Castle. The air was filled with anticipation as they prepared to perform a scene from "Hamlet."

"To be, or not to be," a young actor began, his voice trembling with nerves.

"Feel the words, lad," the Dragon interrupted, its voice a low rumble. "Let them resonate within you."

The actor took a deep breath and continued, his voice growing stronger and more confident. As he delivered the soliloquy, the Dragon watched with a keen eye, nodding in approval.

"Well done," it said as the scene came to an end. "Remember, the stage is a place of magic. Embrace it, and let your passion shine."

The actors beamed with pride, their confidence bolstered by the Dragon's guidance. They knew they were learning from a master, and they were determined to make the most of the opportunity.

Despite its occasional nibbling antics, the Dragon became a beloved figure in Newport. The townsfolk developed a unique camaraderie with their scaly friend, appreciating its eccentricities and the sense of wonder it brought to their lives. They celebrated the Dragon's appearances, eagerly awaiting its dramatic flights and fiery exhalations during performances, adding an element of exhilaration to the theatrical experience.

A Lasting Legacy

As time passed, the Dragon's legacy grew, forever leaving an indelible mark on Newport and its theatre scene. The town became known as a haven for daring performers and theatre enthusiasts, drawn by the allure of performing under the watchful gaze of the Dragon. The Dragon's influence transcended the boundaries of fear and danger, transforming the local theatre into a place of excitement, creativity, and a touch of peril.
The Dragon's presence brought a unique sense of wonder to Newport, and its dramatic entrances became a cherished tradition. The town thrived on the excitement and creativity that the Dragon inspired, and the theatre became a hub of artistic expression and community spirit.
As the years went by, the Dragon's appearances became less frequent, and it seemed to have fallen into a deep slumber. The townsfolk, missing their dramatic patron, sought a way to awaken it. Thus, the Isle of Wight Festival was born—an event filled with music, dance, and an abundance of spirits, all intended to entice the Dragon awake from its snooze.
The first Isle of Wight Festival was a grand affair, filled with music, dance, and an abundance of spirits. The air was thick with anticipation as the townspeople and visitors gathered, hoping that the noise and festivities would rouse the Dragon from its slumber.

As the sun set and the festival reached its peak, a low rumble was heard in the distance. The ground shook, and the sky darkened as the massive silhouette of the Dragon appeared on the horizon. With a mighty roar, the Dragon soared over the festival, its fiery breath illuminating the night sky.

The revellers cheered, their excitement and joy echoing through the air. The Dragon, delighted by the spectacle, landed gracefully in the midst of the festival. It was greeted with a mixture of awe and affection, as the townspeople and visitors alike celebrated its return.

From that day forward, the Isle of Wight Festival became an annual tradition, a time for celebration and storytelling, where the Dragon of Newport would make its grand appearance. The festival not only awakened the Dragon but also rekindled the sense of wonder and magic that had always been a part of Newport's identity.

The Dragon's legacy lived on, a testament to the power of creativity, passion, and the enduring magic of the theatre. The townsfolk of Newport embraced their scaly friend, cherishing the memories and the sense of wonder it brought to their lives. The Dragon's presence became a symbol of the town's vibrant spirit, a reminder that even the most fearsome creatures could find a place in the hearts of those who dared to dream.

The Roc of Shide

The Majestic Creature

In the quaint village of Shide, nestled within the lush landscapes of the Isle of Wight, there soared a creature of legend. The Roc, a bird of mythical proportions, held a presence that demanded reverence and fear in equal measure. Its vast wingspan stretched the length of a football field, creating a shadow that cast a profound silence over the countryside below. Each feather shimmered with an ethereal glow, catching the sunlight in a dazzling array of iridescent greens, golds, and bronzes, making the Roc appear almost celestial.
The Roc's talons, sharp and formidable, were capable of grasping and lifting objects far beyond the capacity of any earthly bird. These powerful appendages could effortlessly hoist buses, elephants, and even entire gymnasiums, showcasing its immense strength. Its head, crowned with menacing horns, completed the awe-inspiring visage of this magnificent beast. The Roc's eyes, fiery and piercing, seemed to burn with an ancient wisdom and an insatiable hunger, striking fear into the hearts of all who gazed into them.
As the Roc flew over the village, its presence was impossible to ignore. The sheer size and power of the creature left the villagers in a state of perpetual awe and anxiety. They watched in trepidation as the Roc soared gracefully above, its powerful wings beating rhythmically, creating gusts of wind that rustled through the trees and sent waves rippling across the fields.
"Look, there it goes again," whispered old Mrs. Thompson, her eyes wide with a mixture of fear and fascination. "Majestic, isn't it?"
"Majestic and terrifying," replied Mr. Green, the local blacksmith, wiping the sweat from his brow. "One wrong move, and we could all be in trouble."

Indeed, the Roc's sheer power and grandeur demanded respect, and the villagers of Shide knew better than to take its presence lightly.

The Roc's Domain

High above the land, the Roc surveyed its domain with an air of regal authority. It was a solitary creature, flying over the rolling hills and dense forests of the Isle of Wight with an air of confidence that few could challenge. The Roc's piercing eyes could spot the tiniest of prey from great distances, and its keen senses allowed it to navigate its territory with unparalleled precision.

The village of Shide, with its charming cottages and winding lanes, was nestled at the foot of a series of rolling hills. These hills provided a natural amphitheatre for the Roc's aerial displays, allowing the villagers to witness the creature's majestic flights up close. The locals often shared stories of the Roc's power and the dire consequences of crossing its path.

"Remember the tale of old Tom?" asked Mr. Green, recounting a well-known story to a group of wide-eyed children. "He dared to mock the Roc, called it 'Big Bird' in jest. The Roc heard him, swooped down, and carried him off. Never seen again."

"Blimey," muttered young Timmy, clutching his cap tightly. "Best not to anger the Roc, then."

"Indeed," nodded Mr. Green solemnly. "Respect it, and it might just leave us be."

The Roc's presence had become woven into the fabric of Shide's identity. It was both a legend and a cautionary tale, a constant reminder of the power and unpredictability of nature.

The Forbidden Words

Despite its awe-inspiring majesty, there was one thing the Roc despised above all else: being referred to as "Big Bird." The mere utterance of those words ignited a furious rage within the creature, unleashing a wrath that few had lived to recount. The Roc's sensitivity to this particular phrase was well known among the villagers, and they took great care to avoid it in conversation.

One fateful day, a traveller arrived in Shide, unaware of the Roc's fierce reputation. He was a brash and arrogant man, full of tales of his own exploits. As he strolled through the village, he noticed the whispers and the wary glances directed at the sky.

"What's got everyone so spooked?" he asked a local, his voice loud and dismissive. "You all afraid of some big bird?"

The villagers froze, their faces draining of colour. Before anyone could intervene, the Roc's shadow darkened the sky, and a deafening roar echoed through the village. The traveller looked up in shock as the Roc descended with a booming beat of its wings, causing buildings to tremble and the earth to shake.

In a display of immense strength, the Roc uprooted trees and sent them crashing to the ground, its talons tearing through the air with terrifying speed. The villagers fled in terror, their hearts pounding with fear.

"It's the Roc! Run!" shouted Mrs. Thompson, pulling her grandson along.

The traveller, realising his grave mistake, tried to flee, but the Roc was upon him in an instant. With a single, swift motion, the Roc devoured the unfortunate man, leaving no trace behind. The village fell silent, the air heavy with the lesson imparted by the Roc's wrath.

Wrath of the Roc

The Roc's message was unmistakable — disrespect and insolence would not be tolerated. The village of Shide, forever marked by the traveller's fate, learned a valuable lesson about the importance of showing reverence to creatures of such magnitude and power. From that day forward, the people of Shide spoke of the Roc in hushed tones, paying it the utmost respect and avoiding any mention of its size that could awaken its wrath once more.

As the Roc continued to soar above Shide, it became a symbol of both wonder and terror. The townspeople learned to coexist with the magnificent creature, respecting its domain and honouring its presence. The Roc, with its immense power and grandeur, became an integral part of Shide's identity, a constant reminder of the awe-inspiring forces that inhabit the world.

One evening, as the sun set over the hills, casting a warm, golden glow over the village, a young girl named Emily stood at the edge of the fields, her eyes fixed on the horizon. She had heard the stories of the Roc and its fearsome power, but she was also captivated by its beauty.

"Emily, come inside," called her mother from the cottage door. "It's getting late."

Emily hesitated, her gaze still drawn to the sky. "Do you think the Roc will come tonight, Mum?"

Her mother sighed, walking over to her. "Perhaps, but remember what we've learned. Show it respect, and we need not fear it."

Emily nodded, taking her mother's hand. "I wonder what it feels like to fly like that, so free and powerful."

Her mother smiled, brushing a strand of hair from Emily's face. "Who knows? Maybe one day, you'll find out."

The Roc's Legacy

As time went on, the Roc's presence became a source of inspiration for the people of Shide. They began to appreciate the creature not just as a force of terror, but as a guardian of their land. The Roc's majestic flights became a symbol of the natural world's wonders, its powerful image woven into the fabric of Shide's culture.

The townspeople celebrated the Roc through art and storytelling, depicting its grandeur in paintings, sculptures, and tales that honoured its might and majesty. Children would gather around the elders, listening in rapt attention to stories of the Roc's incredible feats and the lessons learned from their encounters with the mythical beast.

One such story was that of old Tom, the blacksmith's apprentice, who had once ventured into the Roc's domain. According to the tale, Tom had shown great courage and respect, leaving an offering of food for the Roc in a gesture of goodwill. The Roc, recognising the sincerity of the gesture, had spared Tom and allowed him to return to the village unharmed.

"Remember, children," Mr. Green would say, finishing the story. "Respect and kindness can go a long way, even with the fiercest of creatures."

The Roc, in turn, seemed to acknowledge the respect it received. Its once frequent displays of wrath became rare occurrences, and the villagers took comfort in the knowledge that their guardian of the skies was watching over them.

A New Understanding

In time, the people of Shide came to appreciate the Roc not just as a force of terror, but as a guardian of their land. They recognised the Roc's role in maintaining the balance of nature, its presence a testament to the wonders of the natural world. The Roc's majestic flights became a source of inspiration, its powerful image woven into the fabric of Shide's culture.

The townspeople celebrated the Roc through art and storytelling, depicting its grandeur in paintings, sculptures, and tales that honoured its might and majesty. The Roc, in turn, seemed to acknowledge the respect it received, its once frequent displays of wrath becoming rare occurrences. A mutual understanding developed, a silent pact between the people of Shide and their colossal guardian.

As the years went by, the Roc continued to soar above Shide, a symbol of awe and reverence. The town, forever marked by its presence, thrived under the watchful eye of their magnificent protector. The legend of the Roc lived on, a testament to the power of respect and the wonders of the natural world.

One summer evening, as the sun set over the Isle of Wight, casting a warm, golden glow over the landscape, Emily stood at the edge of the fields once more, now a young woman. Her eyes were drawn to the sky, where the Roc soared majestically, its wings catching the light in a dazzling display.

"Emily, are you daydreaming again?" called her mother from the cottage.

Emily turned, a smile playing on her lips. "Just thinking, Mum. Do you ever wonder what it would be like to fly with the Roc?"

Her mother laughed, shaking her head. "You've always had a wild imagination, dear. But who knows? Maybe one day, you'll find out."

As Emily watched the Roc disappear into the horizon, she felt a sense of awe and wonder. The Roc had become more than just a legend; it was a part of her home, a symbol of the strength and beauty of the natural world. And as long as the Roc soared above Shide, the town would always be a place of magic and mystery, where dreams took flight on the wings of a magnificent creature.

Epilogue

Years later, as the Roc continued to soar above Shide, Emily became a renowned storyteller, travelling far and wide to share the tales of her village and its majestic guardian. Her stories captivated audiences, weaving together the magic of the Roc with the everyday lives of the people of Shide.
One evening, as Emily sat by the fire, surrounded by eager listeners, she began her favourite story — the tale of the Roc's legacy. She spoke of the traveller's mistake, the Roc's wrath, and the mutual respect that had grown between the creature and the villagers.
"And so," Emily concluded, her eyes sparkling with the light of the fire, "the Roc continues to watch over Shide, a symbol of the power of respect and the wonders of the natural world. As long as we honour the Roc and the lessons it has taught us, our village will remain a place of magic and mystery, where dreams take flight on the wings of a magnificent creature."
The audience sat in awed silence, the flickering fire casting shadows that danced like the wings of the Roc itself. Emily smiled, knowing that the legend of the Roc would live on, inspiring generations to come with its tale of grandeur and reverence. And as she gazed into the night sky, she could almost see the Roc soaring above, a guardian of the skies, a symbol of awe and wonder, forever a part of the heart and soul of Shide.

The Trolls of Wootton

The Peculiar Charm of Trolls

Nestled in the heart of the Isle of Wight, Wootton was a village known for its serene landscapes and charming cottages. Yet, amidst the tranquillity, there lurked a creature of immense strength and peculiar charm — a Troll who commanded both fear and fondness among the villagers. This Troll, known locally as Old Grumbletooth, had a distinctive anatomical and physical composition that set it apart from ordinary beings.

Standing at an imposing ten feet tall, Old Grumbletooth's hulking frame was covered in coarse, matted fur, a patchwork of earthy browns and greens that allowed him to blend seamlessly with the natural surroundings of Quarr Hill. His hunched posture hinted at years spent dwelling in the shadows of the ancient woods. His face bore the marks of countless misadventures and shenanigans: a prominent, crooked nose jutted from his weathered visage, while beady eyes twinkled mischievously beneath heavy brows. His wide, toothy grin revealed rows of jagged teeth, each a testament to his voracious appetite and penchant for chewing on things he shouldn't.

Despite his fearsome appearance, Old Grumbletooth possessed an endearing charm. His presence in the village was a paradox; a creature of such formidable strength and appearance, yet with a heart as warm as the hearth of the local pub. It was said that if you listened closely on a quiet night, you could hear his deep, rumbling laughter echoing through the woods.

Old Grumbletooth's charm lay in his playful nature. While most trolls were content with causing mayhem and instilling fear, Old Grumbletooth found joy in more whimsical pursuits. He had a knack for turning mundane activities into chaotic adventures, much to the amusement — and occasional frustration — of the villagers.

Mischief on the Roads

Old Grumbletooth's favourite pastime was causing disruptions to the flow of traffic in and around Wootton. With strength that belied his size, he would roam the roads of Wootton, Wootton Bridge, and Quarr Hill, seeking out unsuspecting stretches of pavement. Then, with a big wooden club, he would smash the ground with an exuberant thud, creating potholes of epic proportions. These treacherous craters brought traffic to a standstill, frustrating drivers and providing endless entertainment for the mischievous Troll.
One particularly memorable incident occurred on a sunny summer afternoon. The village postman, Mr. Higgins, found himself caught in one of Old Grumbletooth's pranks. The traffic lights had all turned green simultaneously, leading to a cacophony of honking and shouting as cars tried to navigate the intersection. Mr. Higgins, stuck in the middle of it all, threw his hands up in exasperation. "Blasted Troll!" he muttered, though he couldn't help but smile at the absurdity of it all.
But the potholes were just the beginning of Old Grumbletooth's antics. He had a particular fascination with traffic lights and their ability to control the flow of vehicles. With a gleeful twinkle in his eye, the Troll would tamper with the delicate mechanisms, causing the lights to malfunction or, on occasion, cease working altogether. The resulting chaos as cars and pedestrians navigated the intersections in confusion left Old Grumbletooth in fits of laughter.
One evening, as the sun dipped below the horizon, Old Grumbletooth was perched atop the village clock tower, his eyes gleaming with mischief. He watched as the traffic lights at the main junction flickered and went dark, plunging the intersection into disarray. "This should be fun," he chuckled to himself, watching as the villagers attempted to make sense of the chaos below.

Old Grumbletooth at the Pub

Despite his mischievous nature, Old Grumbletooth had a softer side that endeared him to the villagers. The local pub, The King's Arms, stood at the heart of Wootton, nestled among the village's charming cottages and bustling streets. The pub was a place of warmth and camaraderie, where the villagers gathered to share stories and laughter. It was here that Old Grumbletooth, known affectionately as "Old Grumbletooth" among the patrons, found solace and companionship.

With a penchant for good ale and hearty laughter, the Troll would saunter into the pub, his presence greeted with a mixture of surprise and delight. He would settle into a corner, his massive frame taking up more space than was strictly polite, and regale the patrons with tales of his pranks. His deep, gravelly voice filled the room, and soon, the walls echoed with the sound of laughter.

"Remember the time I turned all the traffic lights green?" Old Grumbletooth chortled, his eyes twinkling with mischief. The villagers nodded, some groaning at the memory while others chuckled.

"Aye, you nearly gave old Mr. Higgins a heart attack!" one patron exclaimed, raising his glass in a toast to the Troll.

The presence of Old Grumbletooth in the pub became something of a local legend, a delightful surprise for those fortunate enough to witness his boisterous charm. Tales of his wit and the raucous laughter that followed spread throughout Wootton, drawing curious visitors from far and wide who hoped to glimpse the enigmatic creature amid his revelry.

An Integral Part of the Village

The Troll of Wootton, with his knack for disrupting traffic and his mischievous sense of humour, became an integral part of the village's tapestry. While his pranks may have caused frustration and confusion, they also brought a sense of levity and reminded the villagers not to take life too seriously. The townspeople of Wootton developed a unique relationship with Old Grumbletooth, learning to navigate the potholes and malfunctioning traffic lights with a smile, knowing that it was all part of the Troll's playful nature.
One evening, as the sun set over the village, casting a golden glow on the cobblestone streets, Old Grumbletooth sat at The King's Arms, a pint of ale in hand. The pub was filled with laughter and chatter, the warmth of the fire adding to the cozy atmosphere.
"Grumbletooth," said Mrs. Hargrove, the pub's landlady, as she placed a plate of steaming hot stew before him. "You've certainly caused your fair share of trouble, but I can't imagine this village without you."
Old Grumbletooth grinned, his jagged teeth glinting in the firelight. "A bit of trouble keeps things interesting don't you think?" he replied, raising his glass in a toast.
The villagers around him nodded in agreement. They had come to appreciate the Troll's antics, understanding that his mischief was a reminder to find joy in the unexpected. The Troll, in turn, appreciated the good-natured acceptance of his antics and continued to bring a sense of whimsy to the village.

Lessons of Joy and Mischief

As time went on, the Troll's presence in Wootton became a symbol of the village's resilience and ability to find joy in the unexpected. The Troll's antics served as a reminder to the villagers to embrace life's quirks and to find humour even in the most frustrating situations.

One day, a group of tourists visiting Wootton found themselves caught in one of Old Grumbletooth's infamous traffic jams. As they navigated the pothole-riddled roads and malfunctioning traffic lights, they couldn't help but laugh at the absurdity of it all.

"Only in Wootton," one of them remarked, shaking his head with a grin. "Where else would you find a Troll causing traffic chaos?"

The locals, overhearing the comment, exchanged knowing smiles. They had learned to see the humour in the situation, understanding that Old Grumbletooth's pranks were all in good fun. The Troll had become a beloved jester, bringing joy and mischief to all who crossed his path.

And so, the village of Wootton thrived, its streets filled with laughter and the occasional pothole. The Troll of Wootton stood as a reminder that life is full of surprises and that sometimes, the best way to navigate the bumps in the road is with a smile and a hearty laugh.

The Cyclops of Sandown

The Colossal Creature

The Cyclops of Sandown, a towering figure that casts an imposing shadow over the coastal landscape, is a creature straight out of legend. Standing at an impressive twelve feet tall, this colossal being possesses a robust and muscular physique that speaks of immense strength. Its skin, weathered and coarse, carries a bluish tint that contrasts starkly against the golden sands of the Isle of Wight coastline.

The Cyclops' most defining feature, of course, is its singular eye positioned prominently in the centre of its forehead. This eye, large and luminous, radiates an otherworldly intensity. Framed by a heavy brow ridge, it seems to capture every detail with a mix of curiosity and gentle intrigue. This gaze is neither malevolent nor benign; it simply is—a window to the soul of a creature as ancient as the myths themselves.

As the Cyclops roams the picturesque town of Sandown, its presence is both awe-inspiring and oddly comforting. The townspeople, initially wary, have grown accustomed to their towering neighbour. Children wave from a safe distance, and adults nod in cautious acknowledgment. The Cyclops, for its part, returns these gestures with a smile that reveals rows of sharp, yet surprisingly harmless teeth.

The creature's daily routine includes long walks along the beach, where it stops frequently to observe the waves crashing against the cliffs. It carries with it a telescope, an instrument almost comically small in its enormous hands, yet one it uses with great care and precision. Through this lens, the Cyclops peers at the distant horizon, searching for signs of adventure and new wonders.

The Friendly Giant

Contrary to the terrifying tales often associated with Cyclopes, the Sandown Cyclops is surprisingly friendly and affable. It roams the coastal town with a sense of childlike wonder, always eager to explore its surroundings. The Cyclops is often seen wearing a monocle—an accessory that enhances its vision and adds a touch of sophistication to its otherwise primal appearance.

One sunny afternoon, as the Cyclops strolls along the bustling seaside promenade, it spots a group of children building sandcastles. Intrigued, it kneels down, casting a massive shadow over the sandy creations. The children freeze, their eyes wide with a mix of fear and curiosity. The Cyclops, sensing their trepidation, smiles warmly and begins to gently shape a new tower with its giant hands.

"Look at that!" one of the children exclaims, the initial fear melting away. "The Cyclops is helping us!"

The Cyclops nods enthusiastically, its single eye gleaming with delight. For the next hour, it works alongside the children, creating an elaborate sandcastle that rivals the ancient fortresses of legend. By the time the sun begins to set, the Cyclops and its new friends have built a masterpiece that draws admiration from passersby.

Despite its friendly nature, the Cyclops harbours a secret longing. Each day, it gazes through its telescope towards the distant cliffs of Alverstone, where the Manticore—a fearsome creature with the body of a lion, the wings of a bat, and the tail of a scorpion—is said to dwell. The Cyclops admires the Manticore's majestic presence from afar, dreaming of a day when they might exchange a friendly greeting.

The Enchanting Town of Sandown

Sandown is a quintessential English seaside town, where glistening waves gently kiss the shoreline and a sense of tranquillity fills the salty breeze. The town's charm lies in its blend of natural beauty and vibrant community life. Colourful beach huts line the shore, and quaint shops and cafes dot the promenade. The locals, known for their warm hospitality, have come to view the Cyclops as a symbol of their unique coastal haven.

The Cyclops' favourite spot is a rocky outcrop at the edge of Yaverland Beach. From here, it has a panoramic view of the bay, stretching from the white cliffs of Culver Down to the bustling pier. On clear days, the Cyclops can see the shimmering silhouette of the Manticore as it soars above the cliffs of Alverstone. This sight fills the Cyclops with a mix of awe and longing, its solitary eye fixated on the distant creature.

One evening, as the sun dips below the horizon, painting the sky with hues of orange and pink, the Cyclops is joined by an elderly fisherman named George. George, a lifelong resident of Sandown, has always been fascinated by the Cyclops and its peculiar habits.

"Evening, Cyclops," George says, settling down on a nearby rock. "Still watching for that Manticore, are you?"

The Cyclops nods, a wistful look in its eye.

"You know," George continues, "I've heard that Manticores are quite friendly once you get to know them. Maybe one day, you'll muster up the courage to say hello."

The Cyclops smiles, appreciating the old man's encouragement. Together, they watch the sun set, two friends united by their love for the sea and the mysteries it holds.

A Daring Adventure

One sunny morning, as the dawn paints the sky with hues of gold and pink, the Cyclops decides to embark on a daring adventure. Equipped with its trusty telescope and sporting a stylish monocle, the curious giant sets off towards Alverstone, filled with the excitement of a potential encounter with the mythical Manticore.

With each step along the rugged coastal path, the Cyclops' heart flutters with anticipation and nerves. The path is narrow and treacherous, winding its way along the cliffs with steep drops on either side. The Cyclops navigates the terrain with surprising agility, its powerful legs and keen sense of balance keeping it steady.

As it nears the cliffs of Alverstone, the Cyclops spots a glimmer in the sky — a majestic creature soaring through the clouds. It is the Manticore, its wings spread wide, casting a shadow over the landscape below. Overwhelmed by the grandeur of the moment, the Cyclops hesitates, feeling the familiar shyness creeping in.

"Come on, you big oaf," it mutters to itself, steeling its resolve. "It's just a friendly hello."

Summoning all its courage, the Cyclops raises its telescope and focuses on the Manticore. The creature, sensing its gaze, turns its head and meets the Cyclops' eye. For a moment, time stands still. The Cyclops takes a deep breath and waves, a tentative gesture of friendship.

To its surprise and delight, the Manticore responds with a graceful swoop, circling above the Cyclops in an elegant dance. The Cyclops watches in awe, its heart swelling with joy. Though they do not exchange words, a bond is formed — a silent connection between two extraordinary beings.

As the sun begins its descent, casting a golden glow upon the landscape, the Cyclops bids the Manticore farewell, content in the knowledge that they have shared a unique connection, even if from a distance. With a smile on its face and the weight of a delightful encounter in its heart, the Cyclops makes its way back to Sandown, ready to regale the townsfolk with stories of its mesmerising adventure.

A Silent Connection

Upon returning to Sandown, the Cyclops is greeted with eager faces. The townsfolk gather around, curious to hear about the Cyclops' daring adventure. With animated gestures and expressive eyes, the Cyclops recounts its encounter with the Manticore, describing the creature's majestic flight and their silent connection.
The children listen with wide-eyed wonder, their imaginations ignited by the tale. "Did it breathe fire?" one of them asks, barely able to contain their excitement.
The Cyclops shakes its head, smiling. "No, but its wings were as wide as a ship's sail, and it moved with such grace."
The adults exchange knowing glances, appreciating the Cyclops' bravery. They can see the joy in its eye, the satisfaction of a dream fulfilled.
In the days that follow, the Cyclops continues to observe the Manticore from afar, feeling a sense of camaraderie with the creature. Though they do not speak, their shared love for exploration and the wonders of the natural world binds them in an unspoken friendship.
One afternoon, as the Cyclops peers through its telescope, it spots a small figure approaching along the beach. It's George, the elderly fisherman, carrying a package wrapped in brown paper.
"Hello, Cyclops!" George calls out, waving. "I've got something for you."

Curious, the Cyclops kneels down and accepts the package. Inside, it finds a beautifully crafted journal, filled with blank pages waiting to be filled with stories and drawings.
"I thought you might like to keep a record of your adventures," George explains, a twinkle in his eye. "And who knows? Maybe one day, you'll write a book about your friendship with the Manticore."
The Cyclops beams with gratitude, its eye misting over. It carefully places the journal in its satchel, already imagining the tales it will write.

The Legend Lives On

Thus, the legend of the Sandown Cyclops continues to enchant the inhabitants of the Isle of Wight, a testament to the enduring power of imagination, friendship, and the magic that lies within the hearts of mythical creatures. The townsfolk, captivated by the Cyclops' tales, gather eagerly to listen, their imaginations ignited by the stories of majestic beasts and daring adventures.
The Cyclops, now a beloved figure in Sandown, roams the town with a renewed sense of purpose. Its solitary eye, once a symbol of isolation, now represents a bridge between worlds — a link between the ordinary and the extraordinary, the real and the mythical.
One evening, as the sun sets over Sandown, the Cyclops stands on its favourite rocky outcrop, gazing out at the sea. In its hands, it holds the journal George gave it, already filled with sketches and stories. The Cyclops smiles, feeling a deep sense of contentment.
From the cliffs of Alverstone, a familiar figure soars into view — the Manticore, its wings catching the last rays of the setting sun. The Cyclops raises its telescope and waves, a gesture of friendship and respect. The Manticore dips its wings in response, a silent acknowledgment of their bond.

And so, the legend of the Sandown Cyclops lives on, a story passed down through generations, inspiring awe and wonder in all who hear it. The Cyclops, with its singular eye and gentle heart, continues to explore the world, finding joy in the connections it makes and the adventures it undertakes.
In Sandown, where the waves gently kiss the shore and the sky stretches out in endless possibility, the Cyclops is a reminder that magic is real, and that the extraordinary is always within reach.

The Zombies of Shanklin

The Undead Presence

The Zombies of Shanklin, once ordinary residents of this quaint coastal town on the Isle of Wight, have long since crossed over to the realms of the undead. Their ghastly appearance is a chilling reminder of their eternal torment. With pale, decaying flesh that seems to flake off at the slightest touch, they wander the cobbled streets of Shanklin, creating an eerie atmosphere that sends shivers down the spine of anyone who happens upon them.

These creatures are a grotesque sight to behold. Their bodies are hunched and stooped, as if weighed down by the sheer burden of their existence. Tattered clothing, remnants from a bygone era, clings loosely to their emaciated frames, fluttering in the sea breeze. Faces ravaged by time and decay showcase sunken eye sockets, rotting teeth, and lifeless eyes that once held dreams and ambitions. Now, these eyes are clouded and vacant, reflecting an insatiable hunger that extends beyond the realms of the living.

The presence of the Zombies in Shanklin is both unsettling and fascinating. Locals and tourists alike share hushed whispers about their eerie encounters with these undead beings. Some claim to have heard the Zombies' mournful groans echoing through the narrow alleyways, while others swear they have seen the Zombies wandering aimlessly along the beach at dusk, leaving trails of sand and seaweed in their wake.

Despite the fear they instil, the Zombies have become an integral part of Shanklin's identity. The town's folklore is rich with stories of these undead residents, and their legend continues to grow with each passing year. As the sun sets over the English Channel, casting long shadows across the town, the Zombies emerge from their hiding places, ready to haunt the streets once more.

Unexpected Quirks

Contrary to their terrifying appearance, the Zombies of Shanklin possess a surprisingly quirky side. These undead beings have developed a peculiar interest in birdwatching, a hobby that seems completely at odds with their gruesome nature. Their stillness and unwavering patience make them naturals at observing avian creatures, and they can often be found standing motionless for hours, taking in the fluttering wings and melodious songs of the birds that grace the town. Locals have come to view the seemingly random groans and moans of the Shanklin Zombies as having no sensible purpose. Little do they realise how right they are! The Zombies' birdwatching habit is a testament to their unique place in the history of Shanklin. Even during pub closing time, when the town's human residents might become a bit brain-dead themselves, the Zombies remain the most detached and bizarrely engrossed beings around.
One particularly amusing incident involved a group of Zombies gathered near Shanklin Chine, a picturesque ravine known for its lush vegetation and abundant birdlife. As a family of tourists walked by, they couldn't help but notice the Zombies standing perfectly still, their eyes fixed on a tree branch.
"Look, Mum! Zombies!" a young boy exclaimed, pointing excitedly.
"Shush, dear," his mother replied nervously. "Let's keep walking."
But curiosity got the better of them, and they soon realised the Zombies were watching a pair of sparrows building a nest. The family's initial fear melted away, replaced by a strange sense of wonder at the sight of these undead birdwatchers.

The Eerie Garden

In the heart of Shanklin, where crashing waves and salty air fill the atmosphere, an eerie presence lingers — the Zombies. These undead creatures, bearing the scars of their twisted existence, haunt the streets and alleyways, becoming an integral part of the town's mystique.
Amidst the shadows and moonlit nights, the Zombies gather in an old, abandoned garden, known locally as the Eerie Garden. Motionless and silent, they stand in a grotesque tableau, their eyes fixed on the trees above. Feathers rustle, and wings flap as birds find refuge in the garden, unknowingly drawing closer to their impending fate.
The Eerie Garden was once a thriving botanical paradise, filled with vibrant flowers and exotic plants. Now, it lies in ruins, overgrown with weeds and crawling with ivy. The decaying statues and cracked fountains add to the garden's haunting charm, creating a perfect backdrop for the Zombies' nocturnal gatherings.
One night, as the moon cast an eerie glow over the garden, the Zombies stood in their usual positions, waiting for the arrival of their feathered prey. Suddenly, a chirp broke the silence, capturing their attention. Their gaze shifted, unified in their fixation upon a tiny, unsuspecting bird perched upon a branch. The Zombies' eyes glimmered with an insidious hunger, and without warning, they sprang into action.
In a flurry of decaying limbs and disjointed movements, the Zombies descended upon their prey. Their bony fingers grasped the bird, and with a swift motion, they tore into its skull, savouring the morsel within. A chorus of squawks and shrieks filled the night, echoing through the garden and sending chills down the spines of those who heard it.

The townsfolk of Shanklin, well aware of the Zombies' nocturnal activities, often shake their heads in disbelief at this macabre spectacle. While some view the Zombies as a grim reminder of the town's dark history, others find a strange fascination in their peculiar habits.

The Zombies' Solace

Despite their insatiable desires, the Zombies of Shanklin seek solace from their undead existence in unexpected ways. When not hunting birds or haunting the streets, they retreat to their humble abodes, their cold bodies seeking comfort in the glow of flickering television screens.
Inside their dilapidated homes, the Zombies gather around old, dusty televisions, captivated by the melodramatic narratives of soap operas. Tales of love, betrayal, and redemption unfold on the screen, holding the Zombies' fractured attention. They cheer for heroes and jeer at villains, finding strange comfort in the fictional world of television.
One evening, as the sun set and the town of Shanklin settled into its nightly routine, a group of Zombies gathered in a small, decrepit house. The room was filled with the soft hum of the television, and the Zombies sat in rapt attention, their vacant eyes fixed on the screen.
"Can you believe it?" one Zombie groaned, its voice raspy and hollow. "She's going to marry him after all that?"
Another Zombie nodded, its head bobbing up and down. "Humans are so complicated," it moaned.
Their conversation was interrupted by a dramatic scene on the screen, and the Zombies leaned in closer, eager to see what would happen next. In these moments, they found a brief respite from their undead torment, losing themselves in the world of soap operas and human drama.

When the day dawns upon Shanklin, the Zombies return to their motionless positions, ready to resume their birdwatching activities. The townsfolk pass by, their eyes wide with trepidation, yet unable to resist a morbid curiosity. For the Zombies of Shanklin, trapped between the realms of the living and the dead, find solace in the stillness, in the beauty of the avian creatures that flutter above.

A Bizarre Existence

The legend of the Shanklin Zombies persists — a tale of terrifying and strangely captivating creatures, their unyielding hunger mingling with unexpected hobbies and a bizarre fascination with the fictional world of television. The townsfolk, although fearful, have grown accustomed to the presence of these undead beings, often sharing stories of their peculiar habits with both awe and trepidation.

The Zombies, despite their gruesome appearance and unsettling hunger, have found a peculiar place within the heart of Shanklin. Their birdwatching and soap opera marathons provide a glimpse into a strange, almost endearing aspect of their existence. The townsfolk, while wary, have come to see the Zombies not just as monsters, but as beings with their own odd charm and peculiarities.

One sunny afternoon, as the townsfolk went about their daily routines, a group of children gathered near the Eerie Garden. They had heard the stories of the Zombies and were eager to catch a glimpse of the undead birdwatchers. With a mix of fear and excitement, they peered through the iron gate, hoping to see the Zombies in action.

"Do you think they'll come out?" one child whispered, her eyes wide with anticipation.

"Maybe," another replied, glancing nervously at the overgrown garden. "But we have to be quiet. We don't want to disturb them."

As they watched, a Zombie emerged from the shadows, its gaze fixed on a bird perched high in the trees. The children gasped, their fear momentarily forgotten as they witnessed the Zombies' peculiar hobby. In that moment, they saw the Zombies not as terrifying creatures, but as beings with their own unique interests and quirks.

The townsfolk, although cautious, began to embrace the Zombies as part of Shanklin's identity. They shared stories of the Zombies' birdwatching adventures and their obsession with soap operas, finding a strange sense of camaraderie in the tales. The Zombies, in turn, continued their bizarre existence, finding solace in their unusual hobbies and the occasional connection with the living.

And so, the legend of the Shanklin Zombies lives on, a tale of undead creatures with unexpected quirks and a bizarre fascination with the world around them. The townsfolk, while wary, have come to see the Zombies not just as monsters, but as beings with their own odd charm and peculiarities. In the heart of Shanklin, the undead and the living coexist, bound by a shared sense of curiosity and the mysteries that lie within the town's haunted streets.

The Satyr of Wroxall

The Woodland Haven

Nestled in the heart of the Isle of Wight, the charming village of Wroxall lies ensconced in dense, ancient woodlands. This verdant haven, with its towering oaks and whispering pines, is home to a most extraordinary resident — the Satyr. These mythical creatures, half-human and half-goat, embody the spirit of the forest with their vibrant, earthy allure.

The Satyrs of Wroxall possess a unique and captivating appearance. Their upper bodies are human-like, with bronzed skin that glows warmly in the dappled sunlight filtering through the forest canopy. Long, flowing hair, adorned with wreaths of ivy and wildflowers, cascades down their backs, adding to their enchanting visage. Their lower bodies are those of nimble and graceful goats, equipped with four powerful, elegantly curved legs that allow them to move with remarkable speed and agility.

Renowned for their prowess in fell running, the Satyrs once dominated local competitions with their unmatched endurance and swiftness. The people of Wroxall, ever polite and accommodating, graciously allowed the Satyrs to compete without protest, understanding that these creatures were simply in a league of their own.

One such Satyr, named Lyrus, was a beloved figure in the village. His laughter echoed through the trees, a sound as familiar and comforting to the villagers as the rustling leaves. Lyrus was often seen darting through the forest, his legs a blur of motion as he effortlessly traversed the rugged terrain.

The Spirit of Joy

The Satyrs of Wroxall are the epitome of joy and merriment. Their lives are a never-ending celebration, filled with music, dance, and laughter. Every evening, as the sun begins its descent, the Satyrs gather in the woodland groves to revel in their shared camaraderie.

Their playful nature knows no bounds. They leap and prance with boundless energy, their hooves tapping out intricate rhythms on the forest floor. It is said that the legendary Fred Astaire was inspired by the Satyrs' dance, and their influence can be seen in the fluid, joyful movements of tap dancing.

Lyrus, with his ever-present smile and infectious laughter, often led the nightly festivities. His skill with the pan flute was unmatched, and the hauntingly beautiful melodies he played would weave through the trees, drawing both Satyrs and villagers alike to join in the revelry.

One evening, as the Satyrs gathered for their nightly celebration, Lyrus noticed a small group of villagers approaching. Among them was a young girl named Elara, her eyes wide with wonder as she took in the sight of the dancing Satyrs.

"Welcome, friends!" Lyrus called out, his voice warm and inviting. "Come, join us in our merriment!"

Elara, captivated by the music and the lively atmosphere, hesitated only a moment before stepping into the clearing. The Satyrs greeted her with smiles and laughter, offering her a place among them.

The Enchanted Clearing

Deep within the lush woodlands of Wroxall, a kaleidoscope of colour and laughter weaves through the trees. Here, the Satyrs come alive, embracing their vibrant existence and infusing the town with their exuberant spirit.

As the sun casts its golden glow upon the forest, the Satyrs assemble in a sun-dappled clearing, their hooves rhythmically tapping against the soft, mossy ground. They gather their instruments—a lyre, a pan flute, and a set of tambourines—and begin to play a lively melody that reverberates through the trees.

Elara, now a frequent visitor to the enchanted clearing, watched in awe as the Satyrs danced and played their music. The air was filled with the sweet scent of wildflowers and the melodious sound of laughter.

"Would you like to dance, Elara?" Lyrus asked, extending a hand to the young girl.

Elara nodded eagerly, taking his hand. Together, they twirled and spun, their movements fluid and graceful. The other Satyrs joined in, creating a mesmerizing dance that seemed to blend seamlessly with the natural rhythms of the forest.

As the evening wore on, the clearing came alive with the vibrant energy of the Satyrs' celebration. The music grew louder, the laughter more exuberant, and the joy palpable in the air.

A Visitor's Delight

One day, as the Satyrs were preparing for their nightly celebration, they were joined by a young visitor named Finn. He had heard tales of the mythical creatures and their joyous revelries and had come to Wroxall hoping to witness the magic for himself.

"Hello!" Finn called out as he approached the clearing. "I've heard so much about you and your celebrations. May I join you?"

Lyrus, ever the welcoming host, smiled and nodded. "Of course, friend. You are welcome here. Come, share in our joy."

Finn's eyes widened as he took in the sight of the Satyrs, their laughter and music filling the air. He accepted a delicate offering of Turkish delight from one of the Satyrs, its sugary sweetness melting on his tongue.

As the music began, Finn found himself drawn into the rhythm. He watched in amazement as the Satyrs danced with effortless grace, their hooves tapping out intricate patterns on the forest floor. Inspired by their energy and enthusiasm, Finn decided to join in.

With a laugh, Lyrus led Finn in a friendly race through the forest. The Satyrs, their nimble bodies effortlessly traversing the uneven terrain, encouraged Finn as they navigated winding paths and ascended steep hills. Laughter and cheers echoed through the trees as the race neared its end.

To everyone's surprise, Finn, fuelled by newfound determination, found himself neck and neck with Lyrus. With a final burst of energy, he crossed the finish line, his heart pounding with exhilaration.

"Well done, Finn!" Lyrus exclaimed, clapping him on the back. "You've got the spirit of a true Satyr!"

Finn beamed with pride, his exhaustion forgotten in the face of such high praise. The Satyrs cheered, welcoming Finn into their fold with open arms and hearty laughter.

Celebration Under the Moonlight

As night fell and the moon cast its silvery light over the forest, the Satyrs' celebration continued in full swing. The clearing was bathed in a soft, ethereal glow, and the air was filled with the sweet aroma of Turkish delight.

Elara and Finn, now fully immersed in the Satyrs' world, danced and laughed alongside their new friends. The music grew more enchanting, the melodies weaving a spell of joy and wonder that captivated all who heard them.

Under the moonlit sky, the Satyrs' dance took on a magical quality. Their movements were fluid and graceful, their laughter a melody of its own. The forest seemed to come alive, the trees swaying gently in time with the music.

"Look at the moon, Elara," Finn whispered, pointing to the sky. "Isn't it beautiful?"

Elara nodded, her eyes sparkling with wonder. "It's like a dream," she said softly. "I never want this night to end."

Lyrus, overhearing their conversation, smiled and joined them. "The magic of the forest is always here," he said, his voice gentle. "Whenever you need to find joy and wonder, just return to this place. The Satyrs will always welcome you."

As the night wore on, the celebration continued, each moment filled with laughter and music. The bond between the Satyrs and their human friends grew stronger, transcending the boundaries of their different worlds.

In this magical moment, a bond was formed, transcending the realms of human and mythical. And so, the legend of the Wroxall Satyrs continues to thrive—a tale of boundless joy, spirited celebration, and the everlasting connections forged in the midst of shared merriment.

The Journey Home

As dawn approached, the Satyrs and their human friends reluctantly began to make their way back home. The forest was still, the air filled with the soft hum of nature awakening to a new day.

Elara and Finn walked alongside Lyrus, their hearts full of the night's memories. "Thank you for everything," Elara said, her voice filled with gratitude. "This has been the most magical night of my life."

Lyrus smiled, his eyes twinkling with warmth. "The pleasure was ours, Elara. Remember, the magic of the forest is always with you. Whenever you need it, just return to this place, and we will be here."

As they reached the edge of the forest, Finn turned to Lyrus. "Will we see you again?" he asked, his voice tinged with hope.

Lyrus nodded. "Of course, Finn. The Satyrs will always be here, ready to share in the joy and wonder of the forest. Farewell, my friends, until we meet again."

With a final wave, Elara and Finn made their way back to the village, their hearts light with the magic of the night. The Satyrs watched them go, their laughter and music fading into the distance.

As the sun rose over Wroxall, casting its golden light over the village, the Satyrs returned to their woodland haven, ready to rest and prepare for the next night's celebration. The forest, now alive with the memories of their joyous revelry, seemed to hum with a sense of contentment.

And so, the legend of the Wroxall Satyrs continues to thrive — a tale of boundless joy, spirited celebration, and the everlasting connections forged in the midst of shared merriment. The villagers, forever changed by their encounter with the mythical creatures, carry the magic of the forest in their hearts, always ready to return to the enchanted clearing where the Satyrs dance and laugh under the moonlit sky.

The Manticore of Alverstone

The Majestic Guardian

In the serene village of Alverstone, nestled within the verdant heart of the Isle of Wight, legends of mythical creatures permeate the whispers of the ancient woods. Dominating these tales is the awe-inspiring Manticore, a creature whose very presence commands attention and respect.

The Manticore's form is a breathtaking blend of power and majesty. It boasts the body of a lion, every sinew rippling with strength beneath a coat of golden fur that glistens in the sunlight. Massive paws, armed with razor-sharp claws, dig into the earth with each step, leaving a trail of deep impressions that speak of its formidable might.

But it is not just its terrestrial form that instills awe. From its back, a pair of immense wings unfurl, resembling those of a bat. These wings are not just for show — they grant the Manticore the gift of flight, allowing it to soar above the dense canopy of Alverstone's forests, surveying its territory with a vigilant eye. The sight of the Manticore in flight, wings outstretched and casting vast shadows over the land, is a vision of pure dominance and grace.

Most fearsome of all, however, is the Manticore's tail. It ends in a cluster of venomous spines, each glistening with a toxic potency that can fell the mightiest of foes. This deadly appendage is a stark reminder that while the Manticore is a guardian, it is also a warrior, ready to defend its domain against any threat.

The Protector of Alverstone

Alverstone, a picturesque village encircled by lush forests, finds both protection and enchantment under the watchful gaze of the Manticore. The villagers live their lives in relative peace, comforted by the knowledge that this majestic creature guards their homes. The Manticore's eyes, sharp and perceptive, miss nothing as it keeps vigil from its lofty perch or while patrolling the outskirts of the village.
Yet, beneath its fearsome exterior, the Manticore harbours a surprising secret. In a secluded part of its lair, hidden away from prying eyes, the creature indulges in a delicate and unexpected hobby — flower pressing. Here, among the shadows, the Manticore meticulously collects and presses wildflowers, transforming them into exquisite pieces of art. Each flower is handled with the utmost care, and the resulting framed works are imbued with a beauty that seems almost magical.
One evening, as the Manticore worked silently on its latest masterpiece, the soft sound of footsteps approached. A young girl from the village, curious and unafraid, had stumbled upon the hidden sanctuary. Her eyes widened in wonder as she took in the sight of the framed wildflowers, each more beautiful than the last.

The Discovery

The girl, whose name was Amelia, had always been adventurous. With hair the colour of autumn leaves and eyes that sparkled with curiosity, she had wandered into the woods many times before, but never had she encountered something as extraordinary as the Manticore's lair.
"Hello," she called softly, her voice trembling with a mix of fear and excitement. "Are you the Manticore?"

The creature turned, its massive form casting a long shadow in the dim light of the lair. But instead of the fierce roar Amelia half-expected, the Manticore's expression softened. "Indeed, I am," it replied, its voice a deep, rumbling growl that somehow conveyed warmth. "And who might you be?"

"I'm Amelia," she said, taking a cautious step forward. "I didn't mean to intrude. I just... I saw the flowers."

The Manticore nodded, a hint of pride in its gaze. "These are my creations. Would you like to see them up close?"

Amelia's eyes lit up, and she nodded eagerly. As the evening wore on, the Manticore showed her its collection, each piece a testament to the creature's surprising talent. They talked about the flowers, the forest, and even the stars that began to twinkle outside. Amelia discovered that the Manticore was not just a guardian, but a philosopher of sorts, pondering the mysteries of existence and the beauty of nature.

The Artistic Pursuit

Word of the Manticore's artistic talent soon spread throughout Alverstone, and the once-fearsome creature found itself the subject of fascination rather than fear. The framed wildflowers became cherished treasures, displayed proudly in homes and shops across the village.

Amelia, now the Manticore's apprentice, spent her days gathering blossoms and learning the delicate art of pressing flowers. The Manticore, patient and meticulous, guided her through each step of the process, teaching her the importance of care and precision.

One day, as they worked together in the lair, Amelia looked up at the Manticore and smiled. "You know, you're not what I expected. You're so much more than just a guardian."

The Manticore chuckled, a deep, resonant sound. "We all have hidden depths, Amelia. Sometimes it just takes the right person to see them."

Their bond grew stronger with each passing day, and the framed wildflowers became a symbol of their unique friendship. The funds raised from their sales were donated to the local orphanage, providing much-needed support for the children who had found themselves in need.

The Legend Lives On

As the seasons changed, the legend of the Manticore of Alverstone continued to grow. The creature, once a figure of fear, had become a symbol of hope, creativity, and charity. The townspeople marvelled at the Manticore's dual nature — fierce protector and delicate artist — and found inspiration in its unexpected talents.

One evening, as Amelia and the Manticore sat together in the lair, pressing the latest batch of wildflowers, she looked up at her friend and smiled. "I think the world needs to know your story. Not just the legends of your strength, but the truth of your heart."

The Manticore nodded thoughtfully. "Perhaps, one day, they will. But for now, I am content to share this moment with you, Amelia."

The framed wildflowers, now displayed in homes and shops throughout Alverstone, served as a testament to the enduring power of friendship and the transformative magic of art. The villagers, forever changed by their encounter with the Manticore, carried its lessons in their hearts.

And so, the Manticore of Alverstone continued to soar through the skies, a majestic guardian and an unexpected artist, reminding the world that even the most formidable beings can possess a gentle soul. The legend lived on, a tale of fierce protection, deep contemplation, and the beauty that lies within the heart of every creature.

The Djinn of Apse Heath

The Ethereal Guardian

In the mystical heathlands of Apse Heath on the Isle of Wight, an ancient guardian resided. This guardian, known simply as the Djinn of Apse Heath, was a being of ethereal beauty and immense power. The Djinn's form was as fluid as the mist that rolled over the heather at dawn, shifting and shimmering in hues of blue, green, and gold. It rarely revealed its true form, preferring to remain an enigma, but when it did, it took on the appearance of a tall, slender figure with eyes that glowed like molten amber, filled with the wisdom of countless ages.

The Djinn's presence was a source of comfort and awe for the townsfolk. Many generations had sought its counsel, and in return, the Djinn granted wishes with a benevolent yet cautious hand. The people of Apse Heath revered the Djinn for its ability to foresee the consequences of their desires, helping them navigate life's complex choices. The Djinn's sanctuary was a grove of ancient oaks, their branches intertwined to form a natural cathedral where it meditated and communed with the elements.

One autumn morning, a thick fog enveloped the grove. Within this misty veil, the Djinn sensed a disturbance, a ripple in the fabric of the town's tranquillity. It materialised near the edge of the forest, where the first rays of sunlight pierced through the fog, illuminating a path towards the heart of Apse Heath. The Djinn's eyes narrowed as it observed the scene before it, feeling a mix of curiosity and concern.

The Fiery Conflict

For centuries, the Djinn had maintained an uneasy truce with another ancient being—the Phoenix of Merstone. The Phoenix, with its radiant plumage and fiery rebirths, was a creature of intense beauty and destructive power. It often roamed the skies above Merstone, a neighbouring village, leaving trails of embers in its wake. The townsfolk of Apse Heath were well aware of the Phoenix's presence, particularly because of the sporadic fires that followed its visits.

The Djinn harboured a deep resentment towards the Phoenix. It blamed the fiery bird for the destruction of cherished buildings, cafes, and even the beloved sweet factory that once stood as a beacon of joy. The Phoenix's uncanny habit of being seen near the ruins, rising majestically from the ashes, did little to dispel these suspicions. Despite the Djinn's efforts to restore these buildings with its magic, the wounds of loss still lingered in its heart.

One evening, as the sun set and painted the sky in hues of crimson and gold, the Djinn felt a surge of anger. It watched from its grove as a plume of smoke rose from Merstone. The Djinn's form flickered with agitation, its colours darkening. Determined to confront the Phoenix and put an end to the cycle of destruction, the Djinn took flight, its shimmering form blending with the twilight.

A Factory Reborn

Hidden deep within the woods of Apse Heath, the Djinn had secretly rebuilt the sweet factory, a place of joy and confectionery delight. Using its vast powers, the Djinn had reconstructed the factory brick by enchanted brick, infusing each corner with magic. The new factory was a marvel, hidden from mortal eyes, and filled with magical candies that brought smiles and laughter to those who tasted them.

Curiously, the ingredients for these magical sweets seemed to appear as if by divine intervention. Stardust, petals from celestial flowers, and other wondrous elements fell from the sky, guided by the Djinn's will. Each candy was a masterpiece, shimmering with enchantment and bursting with flavours that could evoke memories of childhood dreams and forgotten joys.

One day, while the Djinn was tending to its secret haven, a soft rustling caught its attention. Turning, it saw a young boy from the village, his eyes wide with awe as he stumbled upon the hidden factory. "What is this place?" he asked, his voice trembling with excitement.

The Djinn smiled warmly. "This is a place of magic and delight, young one. Would you like to see how the sweets are made?"

The boy nodded eagerly, and the Djinn guided him through the factory, showing him the wondrous process of creating enchanted candies. As they worked together, the Djinn felt a sense of pride and fulfilment. The boy's laughter and joy were a balm to its weary spirit, a reminder of the good that its powers could bring.

A Hidden Secret

As the Djinn watched over its hidden sweet factory, its heart carried a mixture of resentment towards the Phoenix and a sense of triumph in its newfound creation. The townsfolk, unaware of the Djinn's secret endeavour, continued to seek its wisdom and guidance, unknowingly tasting the magic woven into every piece of candy.

In the heathlands of Apse Heath, the Djinn's legacy intertwined with the people's desires. As the town thrived under the Djinn's benevolent influence, whispers of the magical candy and its mysterious origins sparked curiosity and wonder. The Djinn, standing amidst the swirling enchantments of its creations, knew that it had found solace and purpose even in the face of adversity.

One evening, as the sun dipped below the horizon, the Djinn sensed a presence at the edge of its sanctuary. It turned to see an elderly woman from the village, her eyes filled with a mixture of fear and hope. "Great Djinn," she said, her voice trembling, "I have come to seek your counsel. My granddaughter is gravely ill, and the healers can do nothing. Please, can you help her?"

The Djinn's heart softened. It nodded and took the woman's hand. "Bring her to me," it said gently. "I will do what I can." The woman returned with the frail child in her arms. The Djinn placed its hands on the girl's forehead, channelling its magic into her small body. Slowly, the colour returned to her cheeks, and her breathing steadied. The woman wept with gratitude, and the Djinn felt a warmth spread through its being. It knew that its powers were not just for grand gestures and hidden creations, but for healing and helping those in need.

The Sweet Revelation

One evening, during the town's annual festival, the Djinn decided to reveal its sweet factory to the people of Apse Heath. The townsfolk gathered in the main square, where the air was filled with excitement and anticipation. The Djinn, in a radiant display of magic, unveiled the factory's entrance hidden within an ancient oak tree.

The townspeople, in awe of the Djinn's creation, stepped inside to witness the enchanting world of the sweet factory. They marvelled at the celestial ingredients, the shimmering candies, and the intricate process of creation. As they tasted the magical confections, a sense of joy and wonder filled their hearts.

Among the crowd was the Phoenix of Merstone, its fiery presence casting a warm glow over the festivities. The Djinn and the Phoenix, standing face to face, shared a moment of silent understanding. The Djinn's resentment melted away as it realized the Phoenix's role in the cycle of destruction and renewal.

In a gesture of reconciliation, the Phoenix offered a feather imbued with its fiery essence, a symbol of rebirth and healing. The Djinn accepted the gift, recognizing the harmony between their powers. Together, they pledged to protect and nurture Apse Heath, their combined magic ensuring the town's prosperity.

The Reconciliation

As the celebration continued, the Djinn and the Phoenix worked together to enhance the festival. The Djinn conjured shimmering lights that danced through the air, while the Phoenix created a mesmerizing display of flames that painted the night sky with vivid colours. The townsfolk watched in awe, their hearts filled with gratitude for the two powerful beings who had come together to bring joy and harmony to their lives.

Amidst the revelry, the young boy who had discovered the sweet factory approached the Djinn and the Phoenix. "Thank you," he said, his eyes shining with admiration. "You've made this the best festival ever."

The Djinn and the Phoenix exchanged a knowing glance, their bond strengthened by the boy's words. They realized that their differences had once driven them apart, but now, they had found common ground in their shared love for the people of Apse Heath.

As the night drew to a close, the Djinn and the Phoenix stood side by side, watching the townsfolk revel in the magic of the festival. They knew that their journey was far from over, but together, they could face any challenge that came their way.

And so, the legend of the Djinn of Apse Heath and the Phoenix of Merstone continued to grow, a tale of ancient magic, reconciliation, and the enduring power of friendship. The people of Apse Heath, forever changed by the events of that fateful festival, carried the story in their hearts, passing it down through generations as a reminder of the beauty that can arise from understanding and unity.

In the end, the Djinn and the Phoenix found solace in their newfound alliance, knowing that they had brought peace and prosperity to the land they both cherished. As they soared through the skies together, their combined magic illuminating the world below, they realized that their adventure had only just begun.

The Yeti of Bonchurch

The Majestic Guardian

Bonchurch, a tranquil village nestled on the southeastern coast of the Isle of Wight, boasts a landscape as picturesque as any enchanted forest. Here, amongst the towering trees and winding pathways, lives the Yeti of Bonchurch. Known to the locals as "Old Shaggy," the Yeti is an imposing figure, standing nearly ten feet tall, with fur as white as the winter snow and a presence that commands respect.
Its eyes, deep and thoughtful, glimmer with a gentle wisdom acquired through centuries of solitude. Old Shaggy's broad shoulders and powerful limbs, equipped with claws sharp enough to carve through ice, speak of a primal strength that has been honed to navigate the rugged terrains with remarkable grace. When it moves, it's as if the forest parts for it, recognising its role as the guardian of this serene haven. The Yeti's duties are not merely symbolic. It ensures the delicate balance of nature is maintained, watching over the flora and fauna with a caretaker's eye. The villagers of Bonchurch hold Old Shaggy in high esteem, often leaving offerings of food and trinkets at the edge of the forest, grateful for its silent protection.

The Summer Shift

However, as the seasons change and the summer sun blazes overhead, the Yeti undergoes a remarkable transformation. Gone is the solemn guardian of the winter woods, replaced by a creature of mischief and mirth. The sweltering heat makes its thick fur coat unbearably uncomfortable, prompting Old Shaggy to venture closer to human settlements in search of cooler retreats.

One of the Yeti's favourite pastimes during these months is interacting with the Yeti hunters who flock to Bonchurch, hoping to capture proof of its existence. With a magical ability to disrupt cameras, Old Shaggy ensures that any photographs taken of it are grainy and indistinct, resembling little more than blurry blobs and peculiar shadows.

"Another Yeti sighting gone awry," chuckles Old Shaggy, rolling on the forest floor with laughter. It finds great amusement in the befuddled expressions of tourists who excitedly claim to have captured a clear image, only to be met with disappointment upon reviewing their photos.

This playful side of the Yeti endears it even further to the villagers, who find the stories of thwarted Yeti hunters a source of endless entertainment. They delight in recounting tales of encounters where Old Shaggy turned the tables, making a mockery of those who sought to exploit its existence for fame.

The Quest for Comfort

Amidst the serene beauty of Bonchurch, the enigmatic Yeti resides as a guardian of the wilderness and a symbol of resilience. The townsfolk, going about their daily lives, often speak in hushed tones about their majestic protector, knowing that Old Shaggy watches over them, especially during the colder months.

However, as summer's heat intensifies, the Yeti finds itself increasingly uncomfortable. Its thick fur, so advantageous in the winter, becomes a cumbersome burden. Determined to find relief, Old Shaggy embarks on a peculiar journey to shed its coat. Venturing into human territory, it explores the strange and foreign world of razors and grooming tools.

One memorable day, Old Shaggy finds itself in a small barbershop, examining the tools of the trade. The sight of the Yeti standing in front of a mirror, awkwardly holding a pair of scissors, would have been comical if not for the Yeti's earnest determination. Despite its immense strength, the fur proves to be resilient, and its attempts at grooming are in vain. Frustrated but undeterred, the Yeti roams the beach, pondering a new solution. It is then that Old Shaggy witnesses a group of windsurfers, their boards slicing through the waves with exhilarating speed. Inspiration strikes, and with newfound resolve, the Yeti decides to take up windsurfing as a means to cool off.

The Windsurfing Discovery

As the sun rises over the tranquil sea, casting golden hues across the water, the Yeti stands at the shoreline, a borrowed windsurfing board at its feet. With a determined look in its deep-set eyes, Old Shaggy steps onto the board and catches the wind. Its massive form seems almost graceful as it glides across the waves, the cool sea spray offering blessed relief from the summer heat.
The villagers of Bonchurch, enjoying their morning routines, are astounded to see the majestic creature navigating the waters with such skill. Whispers of "Look, it's Old Shaggy!" and "The Yeti is windsurfing!" spread quickly through the crowd, drawing curious onlookers to the beach.
Children laugh and cheer, their eyes wide with wonder, while adults shake their heads in disbelief and amusement. The Yeti, usually a symbol of solemn guardianship, now embodies the spirit of summer fun. Its powerful legs and sharp claws, so adept at scaling mountains and navigating forests, prove equally capable in mastering the art of windsurfing.

One particularly adventurous boy, Sam, approaches the water's edge, waving enthusiastically. "Go, Old Shaggy, go!" he shouts, his voice carrying across the waves. The Yeti, catching sight of the boy, responds with a joyful roar, its laughter mixing with the sounds of the sea.

A New Tradition

From that day forward, a new tradition takes root in Bonchurch. Every summer, the townsfolk eagerly await the return of the windsurfing Yeti. The sight of Old Shaggy slicing through the waves becomes a cherished spectacle, a symbol of the creature's adaptability and enduring spirit.
The annual Yeti Windsurfing Festival is born, drawing visitors from far and wide. The event includes windsurfing competitions, sandcastle-building contests, and storytelling sessions where villagers recount their favourite Yeti tales. Local vendors set up stalls, selling Yeti-themed memorabilia and refreshing treats to keep everyone cool in the summer sun.
Old Shaggy, now a beloved figure in the community, embraces its role in the festivities. It participates with gusto, often challenging the bravest windsurfers to friendly races. The Yeti's infectious laughter and playful antics bring joy to all, reinforcing the bond between the creature and the people of Bonchurch.
During one such festival, a particularly competitive windsurfer named Amelia decides to take on Old Shaggy. "Ready for a race, big guy?" she taunts with a grin. The Yeti, responding with a playful growl, accepts the challenge. As they race across the waves, the crowd watches in awe, cheering for their favourite competitor.

The race ends in a tie, and both Amelia and Old Shaggy share a moment of camaraderie, shaking hands (or paws) as the crowd erupts in applause. The festival continues into the night, with music, dancing, and a grand fireworks display that lights up the sky.

A New Guardian

As the summer days wane and the cooler months approach, Old Shaggy retreats to its sanctuary in the forest, ready to resume its role as the guardian of Bonchurch. The townsfolk, grateful for the joy and wonder the Yeti has brought into their lives, continue to leave offerings and speak of their majestic protector with reverence.

One crisp autumn morning, as the first hints of frost appear on the leaves, Old Shaggy stands at the edge of the forest, looking out over the village. It feels a deep sense of connection to the people of Bonchurch, knowing that its presence has brought both protection and happiness to their lives.

With a final glance at the village, the Yeti turns and disappears into the forest, its shaggy white fur blending seamlessly with the snow-dusted landscape. The legend of the Yeti of Bonchurch, the majestic guardian and playful windsurfer, lives on in the hearts and minds of the villagers, a testament to the enduring power of nature and the bonds that unite all living beings.

As the seasons change and the cycle of life continues, the Yeti remains a symbol of resilience, adaptability, and joy. And every summer, when the sun shines bright and the waves beckon, the people of Bonchurch know that their beloved Old Shaggy will return, ready to bring another season of laughter and wonder to their shores.

The Medusa of Godshill

The Curse of the Serpentine

Godshill, a picturesque village on the Isle of Wight, is renowned for its charming thatched-roof cottages, medieval church, and vibrant gardens. Yet, it harbours a darker secret: the Medusa of Godshill. Once a beautiful maiden named Thalia, she was cursed by the gods, her flowing locks transformed into a writhing mass of venomous snakes. The curse was a punishment for her vanity and hubris, casting her into a life of solitude and fear.
Thalia's visage, now both captivating and terrifying, holds an eerie allure. Her eyes, glowing with an unnatural light, can petrify any who meet her gaze. Her features, once delicate and enchanting, now bear a sinister quality, her skin a pale, marble-like hue, and her expression eternally anguished. She lives on the fringes of the village, a constant reminder of the consequences of pride.

The Dinner Party Incident

Medusa's curse makes companionship impossible. One tragic incident cemented her isolation. In a bid to reclaim normalcy, she hosted a dinner party, inviting friends and curious villagers. The evening was filled with laughter and the local dangleberry juice, a potent brew that loosened tongues and brightened spirits.
But as the night wore on, Medusa's excitement turned perilous. Her gaze, meant to be a joyful part of the gathering, inadvertently swept across the room. In an instant, her guests were transformed into stone, their joyous expressions frozen in time. Horrified by what she had done, Medusa retreated deeper into isolation, her heart heavy with guilt.

The Silent Sentinels

All around Godshill there are peculiar statues that seem to have been doing stuff one second, then frozen in stone the next, well, they are seemingly victims of Medusa's unintended wrath. These silent sentinels serving as stark reminders of her power and the dangers of vanity. Legends whisper that Medusa's gaze once silenced mighty dinosaurs, preserving them in stone for eternity. Though the truth remains shrouded in mystery, her power is undeniable.
Other mythical creatures steer clear of Godshill, wary of her perilous presence. Medusa finds companionship only in the serpents entwined in her hair. Their hisses become her only form of interaction, a constant reminder of her isolation and the weight of her curse.

Reflections in Solitude

In her solitude, Medusa contemplates her existence and the purpose behind her curse. She ponders the lessons her presence imparts to the villagers, serving as a constant reminder of the consequences of arrogance and the fragility of human pride. Despite her isolation, she finds solace in the natural beauty surrounding her — the lush greenery and serene landscapes of Godshill offering a stark contrast to her internal torment.
The townsfolk, wary yet respectful, navigate their lives under the shadow of Medusa. They pass down cautionary tales from one generation to the next, ensuring the lessons learned from her presence continue to resonate throughout time.

A Chance Encounter

One misty morning, a young artist named Amelia ventures into the outskirts of Godshill, her curiosity piqued by the tales of Medusa. Armed with a sketchbook and a fearless heart, she seeks to capture the beauty and sorrow of the legendary creature. Amelia moves cautiously through the forest, her eyes scanning the surroundings for any sign of Medusa.
Finally, she finds her, standing amidst a grove of statues, her serpentine hair gently swaying. Amelia's heart pounds, but her determination overrides her fear. With steady hands, she begins to sketch Medusa, capturing her haunting beauty on paper. As she draws, Medusa's gaze meets hers, and for a moment, Amelia feels the weight of the curse. But instead of fear, she feels empathy and a deep connection.

Breaking the Silence

Amelia, her sketch complete, approaches Medusa with reverence. She speaks softly, sharing her understanding of Medusa's solitude and the pain of her curse. Medusa, touched by Amelia's compassion, listens intently, her serpents hissing softly in acknowledgment. In this brief encounter, a bond is formed. Amelia returns to the village, her heart heavy with Medusa's story but also filled with hope. She shares her experience with the townsfolk, urging them to see Medusa not as a monster but as a tragic figure deserving of empathy and respect.

A New Understanding

Gradually, the villagers' perception of Medusa begins to shift. They approach her with caution but also with newfound respect. Small offerings of flowers and tokens of goodwill are left at the edge of the forest, a silent gesture of reconciliation. Medusa, still dwelling on the outskirts of Godshill, feels a change in the air. Her solitude remains, but the weight of her curse is lightened by the understanding and acceptance of the villagers.

One evening, as the sun sets over the village, casting long shadows across the landscape, a group of children gather at the edge of the forest. Tentatively, they call out to Medusa, their voices a blend of curiosity and innocence. Medusa, hesitant at first, emerges from the shadows, her serpentine hair still but her eyes softened by the children's presence.

The children, with their untainted view of the world, see beyond the curse. They see a figure in need of kindness and understanding. They ask Medusa to share stories of the past, tales of gods and monsters, of love and betrayal. Slowly, Medusa begins to speak, her voice carrying the weight of centuries. The children listen with rapt attention, their eyes wide with wonder.

As the days turn into weeks, the children visit Medusa regularly. They bring her flowers and trinkets, and in return, she shares her vast knowledge of the world. The village, seeing the bond forming between Medusa and the children, begins to heal. The statues that once stood as reminders of fear now stand as symbols of hope and transformation.

Medusa, once a figure of fear and sorrow, becomes a guardian of the village. Her presence, a constant reminder of the delicate balance between power and compassion, is embraced by the villagers. They learn to see beyond her curse, recognizing the humanity that still resides within her.

In the heart of Godshill, a new understanding blossoms. The villagers and Medusa, united by empathy and respect, create a community that thrives on acceptance and compassion. The tale of the Medusa of Godshill becomes a legend of transformation, a story that transcends time and space, teaching future generations the power of understanding and the importance of looking beyond the surface.

The Medusa of Godshill, once isolated and feared, finds a place where she belongs. Her story, woven into the fabric of the village, serves as a testament to the strength of the human spirit and the enduring power of compassion.

An Unexpected Visitor

One summer's day, as Godshill basked under a cloudless sky, an unexpected visitor arrived. Marcus, an adventurer known across the Isle of Wight for his daring exploits, had heard tales of Medusa and sought to confront her. His goal was not to harm, but to understand the truth behind the legend.

As he made his way through the outskirts of Godshill, he was greeted by the statues — silent sentinels that served as a warning. But instead of fear, Marcus felt a profound sense of respect for the power and the sorrow that Medusa carried. He continued forward, his heart steady, his resolve unwavering.

When he finally stood before Medusa, he removed his helmet and knelt, showing respect and vulnerability. Medusa, surprised by this gesture, listened as Marcus spoke. He shared stories of his travels, of mythical creatures and ancient ruins, and of the wonders and dangers he had encountered.

Medusa, intrigued by his tales, found herself drawn to his voice. The serpents in her hair relaxed, and she felt a connection she had not experienced in centuries. Marcus asked for her story, and for the first time, Medusa shared it with a stranger, her voice a mixture of pain and hope.

A Journey Together

Marcus proposed an idea that seemed impossible yet enticing: a journey across the Isle of Wight, to show Medusa the beauty of the world beyond her isolation. He believed that understanding and acceptance could be found in the open air, amidst the island's natural wonders.

Medusa hesitated, but the thought of adventure and the possibility of breaking free from her solitude was too compelling to ignore. With Marcus as her guide, they set off, taking a path that led them through the lush woodlands and rolling hills of the island.

Their journey took them to the Needles, where the sea crashed against the towering chalk stacks, and to Carisbrooke Castle, where history seemed to whisper through the ancient stones. They visited Ventnor Botanic Garden, where exotic plants thrived, and Medusa marvelled at the diversity of life.

The Power of Connection

As they travelled, Medusa began to change. The weight of her curse seemed lighter, her serpents less restless. She laughed for the first time in centuries, a sound that surprised and delighted Marcus. They met people along the way, and though Medusa was cautious, she found acceptance and kindness in unexpected places.

In Yarmouth, they attended a festival, and Medusa, hidden beneath a hood, danced among the crowd. The music and laughter filled her heart, and she felt a sense of belonging she had long forgotten. Marcus watched with a smile, knowing that their journey was transforming not just Medusa, but himself as well.

Return to Godshill

After months of exploration and connection, they returned to Godshill. The villagers, who had grown accustomed to Medusa's absence, were overjoyed to see her return with a newfound light in her eyes. The statues, once symbols of fear, now seemed to stand taller, as if proud of the journey their creator had undertaken.

Medusa shared her stories with the village, her voice filled with wonder and joy. The bond between her and the villagers deepened, and the community thrived on the foundation of acceptance and compassion they had built together.

A New Beginning

Medusa's home, once a place of solitude and sorrow, became a sanctuary for those seeking understanding and connection. Visitors from across the Isle of Wight came to hear her tales and to learn from her wisdom. The village of Godshill, with its thatched cottages and vibrant gardens, became a beacon of hope and transformation.

Medusa, no longer defined by her curse, embraced her role as a guardian and a storyteller. Her presence brought peace and unity to the village, and her legend continued to grow, a testament to the power of empathy and the strength of the human spirit.

In the heart of Godshill, Medusa found not just acceptance, but a family. Her journey, marked by adventure and discovery, had led her to a place where she belonged. And in the warmth of the village, amidst the laughter and the stories, Medusa's heart, once heavy with sorrow, now beat with the rhythm of hope and love.

The Phoenix of Merstone

A Symbol of Renewal

In the tranquil village of Merstone, nestled in the heart of the Isle of Wight, the Phoenix is an awe-inspiring figure. Known for its vibrant plumage of fiery reds, oranges, and golds, the Phoenix is a symbol of renewal and hope. Its wingspan is vast, casting a shadow that momentarily dims the sun as it soars through the skies. The creature's majestic flight, accompanied by the thunderous flapping of its wings, creates sparks that trail behind it, a testament to its incredible speed and power. The villagers of Merstone hold the Phoenix in high regard, viewing it as a guardian and a beacon of transformation. The bird's very presence infuses the town with a sense of resilience and optimism, inspiring the townsfolk to rise above their challenges, much like the Phoenix rises from its own ashes. One morning, as the sun rose over the rolling hills, the village's baker, Mrs. Plumb, stood outside her shop, gazing up at the sky. "Ah, there she is again," she said, a smile spreading across her face. "The Phoenix never fails to brighten the day." Her neighbour, Mr. Wiggins, nodded in agreement. "Indeed, Mrs. Plumb. Every time I see that magnificent bird, I feel like I can take on the world."

The Spirit of Optimism

The Phoenix embodies an unwavering spirit of optimism. It glides through the air with a sense of purpose, its flight a metaphor for overcoming adversity. The villagers draw strength from its presence, finding solace in the bird's resilience and its ability to renew itself from the ashes. The Phoenix's joy in exploration takes it all over the Isle of Wight, from the rolling hills to the dramatic cliffs and serene beaches.

One of the Phoenix's peculiar habits is its frequent visits to the Apse Heath Djinn. Hovering above the Djinn, the Phoenix empties its bowels, much to the Djinn's annoyance. This peculiar act, however, adds a touch of humour to the Phoenix's otherwise noble existence, reminding the townsfolk that even the most majestic beings have their quirks.

The Djinn, emerging from a cloud of smoke, shook its head in exasperation. "Phoenix, must you do that every single time?" The Phoenix, perched on a nearby tree, let out a melodious laugh. "Oh, lighten up, Djinn! It's all in good fun. Besides, you need a bit of excitement in your life."

The Djinn sighed, a hint of a smile creeping onto its face. "One of these days, Phoenix, I'll get you back for this."

The Village's Guardian

Merstone, with its quaint cottages, lush greenery, and winding lanes, is a picturesque village that could be taken straight out of a storybook. The Phoenix, with its resplendent feathers and majestic presence, adds an element of enchantment to the village. Its daily flights above the village are a source of wonder for the townsfolk, who often gather to watch the bird in action.

Despite its grandeur, the Phoenix is known for its flamboyant nature. It revels in the applause and admiration of the villagers, often performing aerial acrobatics to elicit gasps and cheers. The bond between the Phoenix and the people of Merstone is solidified by such moments, creating a shared sense of awe and admiration.

One afternoon, a group of children gathered in the village square, their eyes wide with excitement. "Look, here it comes!" shouted young Thomas, pointing to the sky.

The Phoenix descended in a graceful arc, its feathers glinting in the sunlight. As it landed, it bowed its head, acknowledging the applause of the villagers. "Thank you, thank you," it said with a playful flourish. "You're too kind." The children giggled, and Thomas stepped forward, his face beaming. "You're amazing, Phoenix! Can you do another trick?"
The Phoenix winked. "For you, Thomas, anything."

Mischief and Laughter

With a mischievous glint in its eyes, the Phoenix frequently embarks on playful adventures across the Isle of Wight. It soars above the coastline, its wings slicing through the air as it performs daring loops and dives. One of its favourite pastimes is teasing the Apse Heath Djinn, a being of immense power and wisdom.
The Djinn, known for its serious demeanor and profound insights, finds itself the target of the Phoenix's playful antics. The bird swoops and swirls around the Djinn, creating a whirlwind of laughter for onlookers. Initially annoyed by the Phoenix's behaviour, the Djinn eventually succumbs to the infectious humour of the situation, forming an unlikely bond with the fiery bird.
One day, as the Djinn was deep in thought, the Phoenix swooped down, snatching the Djinn's turban off its head. "Got your hat!" it called out, soaring higher.
The Djinn, feigning irritation, looked up. "Phoenix, return my turban this instant!"
The Phoenix laughed, its voice like a melody. "Catch me if you can, Djinn!"
As the Djinn chased the Phoenix through the skies, the villagers watched in amusement. Mrs. Plumb shook her head, a smile on her lips. "Those two are like children," she said to Mr. Wiggins.

Mr. Wiggins chuckled. "Indeed. But it's good to see the Djinn having some fun for a change."

Inspiration and Transformation

In Merstone, the Phoenix's presence fosters a sense of renewal and optimism. Its vibrant colours serve as a reminder of the cyclical nature of life and the ability to rise from the ashes of adversity. The townsfolk draw inspiration from the Phoenix's story, finding strength in their own lives to overcome challenges and embrace transformation.

Thomas, inspired by the Phoenix, began to write and draw his adventures, capturing the spirit of the bird in his work. One day, as he sat by the village pond, the Phoenix landed beside him. "What are you drawing, Thomas?" it asked, peering over his shoulder.

Thomas looked up, his eyes shining. "I'm drawing you, Phoenix. You inspire me to be brave and never give up."

The Phoenix smiled, its feathers glowing warmly. "That's wonderful, Thomas. Always remember, no matter how tough things get, you have the power to rise above it."

The villagers, too, found solace in the Phoenix's presence. They gathered in the village square to share stories of personal triumphs and hardships overcome. The Phoenix's tale of rebirth and transformation became a symbol of collective strength, uniting the community in a shared sense of hope and resilience.

One evening, as the sun set, the villagers gathered for a special celebration. "To the Phoenix," Mr. Wiggins toasted, raising his glass. "For reminding us all that we can rise from the ashes, stronger than before."

The Phoenix's Legacy

As the years passed, the legend of the Phoenix of Merstone continued to inspire generations. Children grew up hearing stories of the majestic bird, their imaginations fueled by the vibrant tales of renewal and perseverance. The Phoenix's legacy became woven into the fabric of the village, a testament to the enduring power of hope and the human spirit.

One day, a visitor from the mainland arrived in Merstone, drawn by the tales of the mythical Phoenix. Skeptical at first, the visitor soon found themselves enchanted by the village and its vibrant guardian. They witnessed the Phoenix's daily flights and heard the stories from the villagers, each one filled with admiration and reverence for the bird.

"Is it true?" the visitor asked Mrs. Plumb, who was busy arranging pastries in her shop window. "Is the Phoenix really as incredible as everyone says?"

Mrs. Plumb smiled warmly. "Oh, it's true, alright. The Phoenix has brought so much joy and inspiration to our village. Just wait, you'll see."

An Unexpected Journey

The Phoenix, sensing the visitor's curiosity, decided to take them on an adventure across the Isle of Wight. With a single powerful flap of its wings, it lifted the visitor onto its back and soared into the sky. The journey took them over iconic landmarks such as the Needles, the towering chalk stacks rising from the sea, and Carisbrooke Castle, steeped in history and legend.

As they flew over Ventnor Botanic Garden, the visitor marvelled at the diversity of life below. The Phoenix, with its fiery plumage contrasting against the lush greenery, seemed to symbolize the harmony of nature and magic. The visitor's initial scepticism melted away, replaced by a deep sense of wonder and connection.

"This is incredible," the visitor whispered, clutching the Phoenix's feathers. "I never imagined I'd see such beauty." The Phoenix chuckled softly. "There's magic everywhere, if you know where to look."

A New Chapter for Merstone

Upon returning to Merstone, the visitor shared their experience with the villagers, further solidifying the Phoenix's place in the hearts of the people. The Phoenix's journey across the Isle of Wight became a new chapter in the legend, a story of exploration, connection, and the transformative power of belief.

The Phoenix, now more than ever, was seen as a guardian and a guide, its presence a reminder of the boundless possibilities that lie within each individual. The villagers of Merstone, united by their shared experiences and the tales of the Phoenix, continued to draw strength and inspiration from the majestic bird.

As the Phoenix took flight once more, soaring high above the village, the townsfolk watched in awe. "To the Phoenix," they whispered, their voices carried by the wind. "May you always remind us to rise from the ashes and embrace the journey of life."

And so, the Phoenix of Merstone continued to grace the skies, a living testament to the power of renewal, hope, and the enduring spirit of the Isle of Wight. With each flight, it reminded the townsfolk to embrace their own journeys of transformation and to rise from the ashes of adversity, stronger and more vibrant than ever before.
.

The Wraiths of Niton

The Ethereal Protectors

Niton, a quaint village on the Isle of Wight, is known for its scenic beauty and tranquil atmosphere. Nestled amidst rolling hills and lush greenery, it's a place where time seems to stand still. However, as dusk falls, the town takes on an otherworldly aura, shrouded in the misty presence of its enigmatic protectors — the Wraiths of Niton.

The Wraiths are ethereal beings, their forms ever-shifting and intertwining with the shadows. Veiled in an aura of mystery, they appear as wisps of mist, their translucent bodies seemingly made of the very essence of the night. They lack solid definition, their outlines blurred and constantly in motion, lending them a haunting yet captivating beauty.

Despite their spectral nature, the Wraiths of Niton are known as the town's protectors. While their eerie presence might evoke unease in those unaccustomed to them, the townsfolk have come to understand and respect their role as guardians against malevolent spirits and supernatural harm.

One evening, as the sun dipped below the horizon, Mrs. Wilkins, the village's unofficial historian, spoke to a group of children gathered around a bonfire. "The Wraiths," she said in a hushed tone, "are not to be feared. They are our silent protectors, watching over us as we sleep. Their achievements are numerous, but the greatest is their unyielding vigilance."

Young Tommy, wide-eyed, asked, "But how did they come to Niton, Mrs. Wilkins?"

Mrs. Wilkins smiled. "Ah, that is a tale for another night, my dear. But know this: they are here because they chose to be, bound by a duty they accepted long ago."

Guardians with a Green Heart

In addition to their role as protectors, the Wraiths have a strong affinity for veganism. They are dedicated advocates of plant-based diets, believing in the virtues of consuming food that grows from the earth. This peculiar trait sets them apart, as they are often seen drifting through the town's gardens, nurturing the plants and whispering encouragement to the vegetables and fruits.

Despite their ghostly appearance, the Wraiths have a surprisingly jovial side. They are known to wear lots of mascara and hoodies, giving them a goth-like look as they lurch about. Their favourite pastime is juggling glowing orbs of light, entertaining the villagers with their dexterity and bringing a sense of whimsy to the night.

In the heart of Niton, the Wraiths gathered around a particularly lush garden. "Look at these tomatoes," one Wraith murmured, its voice like the rustling of leaves. "Absolutely thriving!"

Another Wraith, its form flickering like a candle flame, added, "It's all about the right energy. Positive vibes make for positive veggies."

The townsfolk, though initially puzzled by the Wraiths' eccentricities, soon embraced their vegan advocacy. The local market began to flourish with fresh produce, each item believed to carry a touch of the Wraiths' magical essence.

A Feast of Contrasts

Amidst their ethereal existence, the Wraiths extend invitations to the Wendigo from St Lawrence, creating an unexpected connection that bridges their differences. The Niton Wraiths, with their unwavering commitment to veganism, host the Wendigo for shared meals, despite their vastly different dietary preferences.

One evening, under a full moon, the Wraiths and the Wendigo gathered in a clearing near the forest. The Wraiths laid out a spread of plant-based delights, while the Wendigo brought its unconventional fare — sheep heads on a bed of field mice accompanied by cheese. This contrasting feast became a unique display of unity, celebrating the diversity of dietary choices among mythical beings.

"Try this hummus," one Wraith offered, pushing a bowl towards the Wendigo.

The Wendigo eyed the bowl suspiciously but took a tentative taste. "Not bad," it grunted, nodding in approval. "But you really should try this mouse cheese. It's... an acquired taste."

The Wraiths, always up for a challenge, sampled the cheese with polite smiles. The night was filled with laughter and camaraderie, a testament to the possibility of harmony despite stark differences.

Moonlit Harmony

As the Wraiths float gracefully through the moonlit streets, they occasionally stop to juggle glowing orbs of light, mesmerising the townsfolk with their dexterity. The sound of soft laughter and ethereal music often accompanies their performances, creating a serene yet enchanting ambiance that envelops Niton.

The people of Niton have come to cherish these nocturnal displays, gathering at the village square to witness the Wraiths' elegant movements and hear their messages of kindness and environmental stewardship. The Wraiths' performances, while ghostly and otherworldly, have become a source of communal bonding and shared joy.

One evening, as the Wraiths juggled their luminous orbs, a little girl named Emily approached them. "Can you teach me how to juggle?" she asked, her eyes wide with wonder.

A Wraith knelt down, its form shimmering softly. "Of course, Emily," it whispered. "But remember, juggling is not just about skill. It's about finding balance."

Emily nodded eagerly, her small hands mimicking the Wraith's movements. As the Wraith guided her, the orbs danced in the air, reflecting the shared moment of connection and learning.

CA Pact of Protection

One autumn evening, as the Wraiths drifted near the edge of the forest, they sensed a disturbance — an approaching malevolent spirit intent on wreaking havoc in Niton. Without hesitation, the Wraiths united their energies, creating a protective barrier around the town. Their forms shimmered and expanded, merging into a luminous shield that repelled the dark entity and restored peace.

The townspeople, witnessing the Wraiths' protective power firsthand, felt an even deeper respect for their spectral guardians. The Wraiths' actions reinforced their role as benevolent protectors, ensuring the safety and harmony of Niton.

Old Mr. Harris, the town's sceptic, stood in awe as the Wraiths warded off the malevolent spirit. "I never believed in ghosts," he muttered, "but I'll be damned if these Wraiths aren't the best thing that's happened to this town."

Mrs. Wilkins, who had been watching with a knowing smile, patted his arm. "Sometimes, Mr. Harris, it's the unseen protectors who make the biggest difference."

The Legacy of the Wraiths

As time passed, the Wraiths' influence extended beyond the boundaries of Niton. Their commitment to veganism, environmentalism, and compassionate living inspired neighbouring communities. The Wraiths became symbols of hope and resilience, their ethereal presence a reminder of the delicate balance between the natural and supernatural worlds. In neighbouring villages, stories of the Wraiths' deeds spread like wildfire. People began to adopt plant-based diets, started community gardens, and embraced the Wraiths' message of harmony with nature.
One day, a reporter from the mainland visited Niton to write about the Wraiths. "What makes the Wraiths so special?" she asked Mrs. Wilkins.
Mrs. Wilkins smiled thoughtfully. "It's their spirit of kindness and their dedication to protecting both us and the environment. They remind us that even in the darkest times, there is light to be found."

An Unexpected Journey

One misty morning, the Wraiths sensed a calling beyond the boundaries of Niton. Guided by an ethereal force, they ventured to the Needles, the iconic chalk stacks rising from the sea, and Carisbrooke Castle, steeped in history and legend. Their journey took them to Ventnor Botanic Garden, where they marvelled at the diversity of life and the harmony of nature.

As they travelled, they encountered other mystical beings, sharing stories and learning new ways to protect and nurture the land. Their ethereal forms blended seamlessly with the landscapes, a testament to their connection with the natural world.

At Ventnor Botanic Garden, the Wraiths met a dryad named Liora, who tended to the ancient trees. "Your journey is admirable," she said, her voice like the rustling of leaves. "But remember, your home needs you too."

The Wraiths nodded, understanding the importance of their role in Niton. With newfound knowledge and a strengthened sense of purpose, they returned to their beloved town, ready to continue their legacy of protection and compassion.

A New Chapter for Niton

Upon returning to Niton, the Wraiths shared their experiences and wisdom with the townsfolk. The villagers, inspired by the Wraiths' journey, embraced new ways of living in harmony with nature. The Wraiths' commitment to veganism and environmental stewardship became a cornerstone of the community, fostering a deeper connection between the people and the land.

One evening, as the Wraiths performed their luminous juggling act, a visitor from the mainland joined the gathering. "I've heard so much about the Wraiths of Niton," she said to Mrs. Wilkins. "Their story is truly inspiring."

Mrs. Wilkins nodded, her eyes twinkling. "Indeed, it is. The Wraiths have taught us the importance of kindness, balance, and respect for all living beings."

As the Wraiths floated above, their forms shimmering with an ethereal glow, the townsfolk of Niton felt a profound sense of gratitude. The Wraiths' legacy had become an integral part of their lives, a testament to the enduring power of mythical guardians.

And so, the Wraiths of Niton continued to watch over the town, their ethereal presence a reminder of the delicate balance between the natural and supernatural worlds. Their journey had come full circle, and their story would be told for generations to come, inspiring all who heard it to embrace the virtues of kindness, harmony, and respect for the world around them.

The Wendigo of St Lawrence

The Dark Legend

The Wendigo of St Lawrence is a terrifying and imposing creature, its physical form embodying the dark legends that surround it. Towering in stature, it stands tall and gaunt, its body emaciated and skeletal. Jagged antlers protrude from its head, a menacing crown that adds to its eerie presence. Its eyes, gleaming with a malevolent hunger, are sunken into its skeletal visage, emanating an unsettling glow. The Wendigo's skin is pallid and stretched tightly over its skeletal frame, as if hunger has consumed it from within. With each breath, a chilling, raspy sound escapes its bony chest, a haunting reminder of its insatiable appetite.

The legend of the Wendigo dates back centuries, a tale of a cursed being driven by an insatiable hunger. Originating from Native American folklore, the Wendigo is said to embody the spirit of cannibalism and insatiable greed. It is believed that those who engage in such acts are transformed into this monstrous creature, forever doomed to roam the earth in search of flesh. The Wendigo's curse is not just physical but psychological, consuming the mind of its host and driving them to madness.

In the quiet village of St Lawrence on the Isle of Wight, the Wendigo's presence is both feared and respected. The townsfolk have come to accept its existence, their lives intertwined with the dark legend. St Lawrence, with its picturesque cottages and winding lanes, seems an unlikely place for such a creature to dwell. Yet, the dense woodlands surrounding the village provide the perfect hiding place for the Wendigo, allowing it to move undetected, a shadowy figure lurking just beyond the edge of sight.

"Do you really believe in the Wendigo?" young Thomas asked his grandfather one evening as they sat by the fire. The old man, his face lined with age and wisdom, looked at the boy with serious eyes.

"Believe in it? I've seen it, lad," he replied, his voice a whisper. "It was many years ago, during a harsh winter. The hunger drives it, a hunger that never ends."

The Wendigo's achievements are not celebrated but feared. Known for its cunning and stealth, it has outwitted hunters and eluded capture for generations. Its ability to blend into its surroundings, earning it the nickname "Where Did He Go," is a testament to its supernatural abilities. The Wendigo's presence is marked by a chilling silence, a void that unsettles the heart and freezes the soul.

The Shadows of St Lawrence

In the shadows of St Lawrence, the Wendigo moves with a grace that belies its skeletal form. The dense woodlands, with their ancient trees and tangled undergrowth, provide the perfect cover for the creature. It is said that the Wendigo can meld with the darkness, its body becoming one with the night, invisible to the untrained eye.

"Did you hear that?" whispered Mary, clutching her shawl tightly around her shoulders as she and her friends walked home from the village pub. The air was cold, and the moon cast eerie shadows on the path.

"It's just the wind," replied her friend James, though his voice betrayed a hint of fear.

But Mary wasn't convinced. She had heard the stories, the whispered warnings to avoid the woods at night. She quickened her pace, her heart pounding in her chest, her mind conjuring images of the Wendigo's hollow eyes and skeletal grin.

The Wendigo's preferred meal is field mouse bubble and squeak, a macabre twist on a traditional dish. This peculiar choice of sustenance adds to the creature's terrifying allure, a reminder of its insatiable hunger and twisted nature. The townsfolk, aware of this preference, take care to avoid the woods at dusk, knowing that the Wendigo hunts when the shadows are longest.

Despite its fearsome reputation, the Wendigo possesses a dark intelligence. It is not a mindless beast but a cunning predator, capable of outwitting its prey and avoiding traps. The Wendigo's ability to strategize and plan its hunts makes it all the more dangerous, a relentless force that cannot be easily thwarted.

"I swear, I saw it," insisted John, a local hunter, as he recounted his encounter at the village inn. "It was standing there, just beyond the trees, watching me with those glowing eyes."

"You're lucky to be alive," replied the innkeeper, his voice low. "Many who see the Wendigo don't live to tell the tale."

The Wendigo's mastery of disguise and stealth has earned it a fearsome reputation among the townsfolk. Its ability to move undetected, to become one with the shadows, has made it a figure of dread and fascination. The villagers of St Lawrence live in a delicate balance with the creature, respecting its power and the boundaries it imposes.

The Theatre Incident

One fateful evening, the Wendigo's malevolence was starkly demonstrated during a performance at the local theatre. The villagers, eager for a night of entertainment, filled the seats, their laughter and chatter filling the air. The theatre, with its grand stage and ornate decorations, was a beacon of culture and community spirit in St Lawrence.

As the play began, the actors took their places, unaware of the dark presence lurking in the shadows. The Wendigo, drawn by the noise and the scent of human flesh, had slipped into the theatre unnoticed. Its antlers brushed against the ceiling, its hollow eyes scanning the audience with a malevolent hunger.

"This is a terrible idea," muttered George, one of the stagehands, as he noticed the Wendigo's imposing form. "What if it causes a panic?"

"Shh, keep your voice down," hissed Margaret, another stagehand. "We can't let it know we're afraid."

But the Wendigo was already aware. It could sense the fear in the air, the tension that rippled through the crowd. As the actors delivered their lines, the Wendigo moved closer, its presence casting a pall over the theatre.

"Look at those antlers," whispered one of the townsfolk, a hint of awe in their voice. "It's magnificent, isn't it?"

But admiration quickly turned to horror as the Wendigo's eyes flashed with anger. The creature, infuriated by the perceived slight, unleashed its fury. With a bone-chilling roar, it leapt onto the stage, its antlers smashing through the set.

Chaos erupted as the audience scrambled to escape. The Wendigo, driven by its insatiable hunger, tore through the crowd, its skeletal hands snatching up anyone who crossed its path. In moments, the theatre was filled with screams and the sounds of tearing flesh.

When the Wendigo's rage finally subsided, the once grand theatre was a scene of devastation. Bodies lay scattered, their faces frozen in expressions of terror. The Wendigo, its hunger momentarily sated, slipped back into the shadows, leaving the villagers to mourn their dead.

From that day forward, the people of St Lawrence learned to hold their tongues when speaking of the Wendigo. The creature's fury had shown them the consequences of disrespect, and they vowed to never again provoke the beast.

Solitary Introspection

Despite its fearsome reputation, the Wendigo was not without moments of introspection. In the quiet solitude of the forest, it would often find itself pondering its existence, the curse that drove its insatiable hunger, and the fear it instilled in those around it.

One autumn afternoon, the Wendigo found itself drawn to the village park, a place of tranquillity and reflection. The leaves, ablaze with the colours of fall, whispered in the breeze, and the distant sound of children's laughter floated through the air.

In the centre of the park stood an old stone bench, a relic from a time long past. The Wendigo approached the bench and sat down, its skeletal frame casting an eerie shadow on the ground. It reached into a hollow in a nearby tree and pulled out a battered chessboard, a remnant of a bygone era.

With deliberate movements, the Wendigo set up the pieces, its mind focused on the game ahead. The chessboard, with its worn pieces and faded squares, was a symbol of its solitary existence, a reminder of the life it once had before the curse took hold.

As the Wendigo played against itself, it contemplated the nature of its existence. It was a creature of hunger and darkness, driven by an insatiable need to consume. Yet, in these moments of solitude, it found a semblance of peace, a brief respite from the torment that gnawed at its soul.

"Checkmate," it muttered to itself, moving the final piece with a bony finger. The game was over, but the questions remained. What was the purpose of its existence? Was there a way to break the curse that bound it?

The Wendigo's thoughts were interrupted by the sound of footsteps. A young woman, unaware of the creature's presence, had wandered into the park, her eyes scanning the trees for the source of the noise.

"Hello?" she called out, her voice trembling. "Is someone there?"

The Wendigo watched her, its eyes glowing with a mix of curiosity and caution. It remained silent, its form blending with the shadows, as the woman approached the bench.

"Oh, a chessboard!" she exclaimed, noticing the game set up on the bench. "I love chess."

She sat down on the bench, her eyes studying the board. The Wendigo, intrigued by her presence, remained hidden, watching as she moved the pieces.

"Whoever you are, you're quite good," she said with a smile, unaware of the creature lurking nearby. "Maybe we can play a game sometime."

With a final glance at the board, she stood up and walked away, her footsteps fading into the distance. The Wendigo, left alone once more, stared at the chessboard, the woman's words echoing in its mind.

In that moment, the Wendigo felt a flicker of something it hadn't felt in centuries — hope. Perhaps, in the darkness of its existence, there was still a chance for redemption, a way to break the curse that bound it to a life of hunger and fear.

A Glimmer of Hope

The Wendigo's encounter with the young woman had sparked a glimmer of hope within its hollow chest. For the first time in centuries, it felt a desire for something beyond its insatiable hunger — a longing for connection and redemption.

One evening, as the sun dipped below the horizon, casting a warm glow over the village of St Lawrence, the Wendigo ventured closer to the edge of the forest. It watched from the shadows as the townsfolk went about their lives, their laughter and conversations filling the air.

"Did you hear about the Wendigo?" one of the villagers whispered to his friend. "They say it's been acting differently lately, not as aggressive."

"Maybe it's finally mellowing out," replied his friend with a chuckle. "About time, too."

The Wendigo listened, its curiosity piqued. Could it be true? Was there a way to change, to find a semblance of peace? It decided to take a bold step—a gesture of goodwill towards the people of St Lawrence.

As night fell, the Wendigo ventured into the village, careful to remain hidden from sight. It made its way to the home of the young woman who had shown an interest in chess. With a gentle touch, it placed a small carved figure of a knight on her windowsill, a token of appreciation and an invitation to play.

The next morning, the woman discovered the figure and smiled, her heart warmed by the mysterious gift. She shared the story with her friends, and soon the village buzzed with talk of the Wendigo's unexpected gesture.

"I think it wants to make amends," the woman said to her friends as they gathered at the village square. "Maybe it's not as monstrous as we thought."

Encouraged by the positive response, the Wendigo continued to leave small tokens for the villagers—carved figures, wildflowers, and even a rare gemstone from deep within the forest. Slowly but surely, the fear that had once gripped the hearts of the townsfolk began to dissipate, replaced by a cautious curiosity.

One evening, as the village gathered for a communal meal, the Wendigo watched from the shadows, its heart filled with a mix of hope and trepidation. It yearned to join them, to be a part of their world, but it knew that its appearance would still incite fear.

"Do you think the Wendigo will ever join us?" asked a young boy, his eyes wide with wonder.

"Maybe one day," replied the young woman with a smile. "We just have to be patient and show it that we're not afraid."

The Wendigo, moved by her words, felt a surge of determination. It would continue to show kindness, to bridge the gap between its world and theirs. It was a long and arduous journey, but for the first time, the Wendigo believed that redemption was within reach.

A Pact of Protection

With each act of kindness, the Wendigo's bond with the villagers of St Lawrence grew stronger. The once fearsome creature became a symbol of transformation and redemption, a testament to the power of compassion and understanding. One crisp autumn evening, as the village prepared for their annual harvest festival, the Wendigo watched from the edge of the forest. The air was filled with the scent of roasted chestnuts and mulled cider, and the sounds of laughter and music echoed through the trees.

The young woman, now a beloved member of the community, stood at the centre of the festivities, her eyes scanning the crowd. She knew the Wendigo was watching, and she hoped that tonight would be the night it finally joined them.

As the moon rose high in the sky, casting a silvery glow over the village, the Wendigo took a deep breath and stepped out of the shadows. The villagers gasped, their eyes widening in surprise and apprehension, but the young woman stepped forward, her heart filled with courage.

"Welcome," she said softly, her voice carrying a warmth that melted the chill in the air. "We've been waiting for you."

The Wendigo hesitated, its skeletal frame trembling with uncertainty. But the woman's smile and the kindness in her eyes gave it the strength to move forward. Slowly, it approached the circle of villagers, its presence casting long, eerie shadows on the ground.

"Don't be afraid," she continued, reaching out her hand. "We know you're not a monster. You're just like us, seeking connection and redemption."

The Wendigo's eyes glistened with unshed tears as it took her hand, the warmth of her touch a balm to its tormented soul. The villagers, seeing the sincerity in the Wendigo's eyes, slowly stepped forward, offering their own gestures of goodwill.

Together, they formed a circle, their hands linked in a symbol of unity and acceptance. The Wendigo, once a creature of fear and darkness, had found a place among them, a beacon of hope and transformation.

As the night wore on, the Wendigo shared stories of its past, its voice a haunting melody that captivated the villagers. They listened with rapt attention, their hearts open and empathetic, as the Wendigo recounted its journey of redemption and the struggles it had faced.

In that moment, the village of St Lawrence became a haven of understanding and compassion, a place where even the most fearsome of creatures could find acceptance and love. The Wendigo's presence, once a symbol of terror, had transformed into a testament to the power of kindness and the possibility of change.

As the first light of dawn broke over the horizon, casting a golden glow over the village, the Wendigo knew that its journey was far from over. But with the support of the villagers and the hope that had blossomed in its heart, it was ready to face whatever challenges lay ahead.

The Legacy of the Wendigo

The Wendigo's story became a legend in St Lawrence, a tale of transformation and redemption that was passed down through generations. The villagers, inspired by the Wendigo's journey, embraced the values of compassion, understanding, and acceptance, creating a community where all beings, both human and mythical, could find a place to belong.

The Wendigo, now a revered guardian of the village, continued to watch over the people of St Lawrence, its presence a comforting reminder of the power of change. It forged bonds with other creatures of the Isle of Wight, including the ethereal Wraiths of Niton and the majestic Phoenix of Merstone, creating a network of protectors who worked together to ensure the safety and harmony of the island.

The village of St Lawrence thrived, its people living in harmony with the natural world and the mythical beings that inhabited it. The once-feared Wendigo had become a symbol of hope and resilience, its story a beacon of light that guided the villagers through the darkest of times.

As the years passed, the Wendigo's legacy grew, reaching far beyond the borders of St Lawrence. Visitors from across the Isle of Wight and beyond came to hear the tale of the Wendigo and to witness the harmony that had been achieved through compassion and understanding.

One evening, as the village gathered to celebrate the annual harvest festival, the young woman who had first extended her hand to the Wendigo stood at the centre of the festivities, her heart filled with gratitude and pride.

"Tonight, we celebrate not just the bounty of our harvest, but the power of kindness and the strength of our community," she said, her voice carrying a warmth that resonated with all who heard it. "The Wendigo's journey has taught us that even the darkest of creatures can find redemption, and that through compassion and understanding, we can create a world where all beings can thrive."

The villagers cheered, their hearts united in a shared sense of purpose and hope. The Wendigo, standing at the edge of the crowd, felt a deep sense of belonging and fulfilment, knowing that its journey had made a difference.

As the festival continued, the Wendigo looked out over the village, its eyes filled with a renewed sense of purpose. It knew that its journey was far from over, but with the support of the villagers and the bonds it had forged, it was ready to face whatever challenges lay ahead.

The legend of the Wendigo of St Lawrence continues to inspire generations, a story of transformation, redemption, and the enduring power of compassion. The Wendigo, once a creature of fear and darkness, had become a symbol of hope and resilience, a testament to the possibility of change and the strength of the human spirit.

And so, the Wendigo of St Lawrence remains a guardian of the village, its presence a comforting reminder of the power of kindness and the enduring legacy of a creature that found redemption in the most unlikely of places..

The Hydra of Ventnor

The Legendary Sea Monster

The Hydra of Ventnor is a formidable sea monster, its physical form both captivating and fearsome. The most notable feature of this mythical creature is its multiple heads, each bearing its own distinct personality. These heads sprout from a massive, serpent-like body, with scales that glisten with an otherworldly sheen under the sun and moonlight.

The town of Ventnor, located on the Isle of Wight, is a picturesque coastal haven known for its dramatic cliffs, sandy beaches, and lush botanical gardens. It's a place where history and legend intertwine, and the presence of the Hydra adds an extra layer of mystique. The townsfolk have woven tales of the Hydra into the fabric of their daily lives, and the creature's story is one of the most captivating.

The Hydra's heads are sleek and powerful, with razor-sharp fangs and piercing eyes that seem to hold profound knowledge and wisdom. Despite their distinct identities, the heads work in eerie harmony, their movements coordinated with an uncanny synchronicity. This intricate dance of coordination makes the Hydra an awe-inspiring sight to behold.

Legend has it that the Hydra first appeared off the coast of Ventnor centuries ago, emerging from the depths during a violent storm. The townspeople, terrified at first, quickly realized that the creature was not there to harm them. Instead, it seemed to be a guardian of the seas, protecting Ventnor from marauding pirates and other dangers.

"Look at it, mother," young Thomas whispered, his eyes wide with awe as the Hydra's heads broke the surface of the water, shimmering in the moonlight. "Isn't it magnificent?"

"Yes, Thomas," his mother replied, her voice tinged with both fear and wonder. "The Hydra is a symbol of our town's resilience and mystery."

The Intelligence of the Hydra

The Hydra of Ventnor is not merely a creature of brute strength; it also possesses remarkable intelligence. It is known to be the smartest entity in any room, constantly seeking knowledge and understanding. Each of its heads, with its unique personality and perspective, contributes to its vast wisdom. The townsfolk, however, often underestimate the Hydra, seeing it only as a fearsome sea serpent.

One peculiar tale tells of a fisherman named Bert, who claimed that the Hydra's snake-like form transformed into various shapes, sometimes spelling out actual words and numbers. Bert swore the Hydra spelled out the formula to the God Particle and a tasty recipe for ice cream. Such stories, though dismissed by many as the ramblings of a madman, add to the enigma surrounding the Hydra.

"You're making that up, Bert," scoffed one of the patrons at the local pub. "Hydras can't spell, let alone know the secrets of the universe."

Bert took a swig of his ale and leaned in closer. "I'm telling you, mate, it's true. That beast has more brains in one of its heads than all of us put together."

Despite the scepticism, the Hydra's intelligence is undeniable. It has been known to solve complex problems, navigate treacherous waters with ease, and even communicate with certain individuals through a series of intricate gestures and symbols.

"Can you believe it?" one of the townsfolk muttered. "A sea monster that knows more about quantum mechanics than our own scientists."

"I heard it helped old Mrs. Thorne find her lost cat," another whispered. "Used its heads to search the entire coastline."

The Hydra's achievements are as varied as they are impressive. It has thwarted pirate attacks, guided lost ships safely to shore, and even rescued drowning swimmers. Yet, despite these acts of heroism, the Hydra remains a solitary creature, its true thoughts and feelings a mystery to all but itself.

The Guardian of Ventnor

In the coastal town of Ventnor, tales of the mighty Hydra resonate through the ages. This legendary sea monster, with its massive size and multitude of heads, has become an integral part of the town's folklore and maritime history. The Hydra, with its sleek and powerful form, elicits both awe and trepidation.

The townsfolk of Ventnor, despite their initial fear, have come to see the Hydra as a guardian of the coast. The Hydra's presence deters pirates and other sea monsters from venturing too close to the town. Fishermen offer their respects to the Hydra before setting out to sea, believing that the creature's watchful eyes protect them from harm.

"May the Hydra watch over us," they mutter as they cast their nets into the water, a ritual that has become as essential as checking the weather forecast.

One particularly memorable incident occurred when a notorious band of pirates attempted to raid Ventnor. As their ship approached the shore, the Hydra rose from the depths, its heads hissing and eyes glowing with fierce determination. The pirates, terrified by the sight, fled in haste, never to return.

"Did you see that?" one of the fishermen exclaimed. "The Hydra saved us again!"

"Aye, it's our protector," another agreed. "We owe it our lives."

The Hydra's reputation as a guardian is further cemented by its interactions with the townsfolk. It has been known to guide lost children back to their homes, retrieve valuable items that have fallen into the sea, and even help repair damaged boats. "Thank you, Hydra," a little girl whispered, her eyes wide with gratitude as the creature gently placed her lost doll back on the shore.

Despite its fearsome appearance, the Hydra's actions have shown it to be a benevolent force, a protector of Ventnor and its people. The townsfolk, once wary, now look upon the Hydra with respect and admiration, knowing that their guardian is always watching over them.

The Hydra's Passion for Quantum Computing

While the Hydra possesses a deep knowledge of philosophy and engages in intellectual pursuits, its true passion lies in the realm of quantum computing. Its understanding of complex mathematical concepts and the intricacies of quantum mechanics is unmatched. Despite the Hydra's best efforts to explain the secret to life, the universe, and everything, the townsfolk of Ventnor can only see the Hydra as a massive, multi-headed sea snake, unaware of the intellectual depths that lie within.

"Have you ever tried to explain quantum entanglement to a bunch of fishermen?" one of the Hydra's heads grumbled. "It's like trying to teach a fish to play the violin."

"Patience," another head replied. "They may not understand now, but our knowledge is valuable. We must continue to learn and grow."

Content in its role as the town's legendary sea monster, the Hydra finds solace in the depths of the ocean. It submerges itself in contemplation, pondering the mysteries of the universe and delving into the secrets of quantum realms. Its multiple heads work in eerie harmony, exchanging ideas and perspectives with an uncanny synchronicity.

In its underwater lair, the Hydra has constructed a makeshift laboratory, filled with intricate devices and glowing crystals. Here, it conducts experiments and analyses data, seeking to unlock the secrets of the universe. Despite its isolation, the Hydra remains dedicated to its quest for knowledge, driven by an insatiable curiosity.

One day, while exploring the depths, the Hydra discovered a sunken ship filled with ancient scrolls and artifacts. Among them was a manuscript detailing advanced quantum theories, long thought to be lost to time. The Hydra eagerly devoured the information, its heads poring over the text with a fervour that rivalled its hunger for knowledge.

"Look at this," one head exclaimed. "This could revolutionize our understanding of the universe!"

"Indeed," another head agreed. "We must share this knowledge with the world."

But how could a fearsome sea monster convey such advanced concepts to the people of Ventnor? The Hydra pondered this question, knowing that its true potential could only be realized if it could bridge the gap between its world and theirs.

A Guardian of the Deep

Amidst the coastal beauty of Ventnor, the Hydra guards the secrets of the deep, its immense size and fierce presence serving as a reminder of the mysteries that lie beneath the surface. Though its intellectual prowess may go unseen by the townsfolk, the Hydra finds fulfilment in its pursuit of knowledge and understanding.

One moonlit night, a group of scientists from the mainland arrived in Ventnor, intrigued by the legends of the Hydra. They brought with them sophisticated equipment and a keen interest in exploring the depths of the ocean. The Hydra observed them from the shadows, curious about their intentions.

"These scientists seem different," one head remarked. "Perhaps they are seeking knowledge, just as we do."

"Let's see what they are up to," another head suggested. "But we must be cautious."

The scientists, initially sceptical of the Hydra's existence, were soon confronted by the majestic creature. Instead of fear, they felt an overwhelming sense of awe and respect. The Hydra, recognizing their quest for knowledge, revealed some of the secrets it had discovered in the quantum realms, leaving the scientists astounded.

"Remarkable," one of the scientists whispered, his eyes wide with wonder. "This creature possesses knowledge beyond our wildest dreams."

The Hydra's interaction with the scientists marked a turning point in its relationship with the outside world. The scientists, eager to learn more, established a research station in Ventnor, dedicated to studying the Hydra and its discoveries. The town, once known only for its coastal beauty, became a hub of scientific exploration and innovation.

"Welcome to Ventnor," the mayor declared at the opening ceremony of the research station. "Home to the Hydra and a beacon of knowledge for all."

The Hydra, though still a creature of the deep, found itself becoming an integral part of the town's identity. It continued to guard the coast, its presence a symbol of strength and protection, while also contributing to the advancement of human understanding.

The Legacy of the Hydra

The scientists' encounter with the Hydra led to a newfound appreciation for the creature among the townsfolk. Stories of the Hydra's wisdom and its role as a guardian spread far and wide. Ventnor became a place of pilgrimage for those seeking both the thrill of encountering a legendary sea monster and the inspiration drawn from its intellectual pursuits.
"Did you hear?" a visitor exclaimed to her friend. "The Hydra of Ventnor knows the secrets of the universe! We must go and see for ourselves."
As more people flocked to Ventnor, the town flourished. The local economy boomed, and the once-sleepy village became a vibrant community filled with scholars, adventurers, and curious onlookers. The Hydra, once a solitary guardian, found itself at the centre of a thriving hub of knowledge and discovery.
One day, a young girl named Emily approached the Hydra with a notebook in hand. "Can you help me with my science project?" she asked, her eyes wide with hope.
The Hydra's heads exchanged amused glances. "Of course, young one," one head replied. "What do you wish to learn?"
As Emily explained her project, the Hydra patiently guided her through complex concepts, its heads taking turns to provide explanations and demonstrations. The girl's eyes sparkled with understanding and excitement, and she thanked the Hydra profusely.
"Thank you, Hydra," she said with a bright smile. "You're the smartest teacher I've ever had!"

The Hydra's legacy grew with each passing day, its wisdom and kindness touching the lives of all who came into contact with it. The townsfolk, once fearful, now looked upon the Hydra with admiration and gratitude, knowing that their guardian was also a beacon of knowledge and inspiration. And so, the legend of the Hydra continues to entwine with the maritime history of Ventnor, a testament to the remarkable fusion of strength, wisdom, and enigma that the creature embodies. The Hydra remains a symbol of the mysteries of the deep, a guardian of the coast, and a beacon of knowledge for those who dare to seek it.

As the sun set over the horizon, casting a golden glow over the waters of Ventnor, the Hydra watched from its lair, its hearts filled with a sense of fulfilment. It had found a place where it could protect, teach, and inspire — a place where it truly belonged.

In the end, the Hydra's journey was one of transformation and discovery, a testament to the power of knowledge and the enduring strength of the human (and mythical) spirit. The Hydra of Ventnor, with its many heads and boundless wisdom, had become a legend not just of the sea, but of the heart and mind as well.

The Freshwater Gorgon

The Enigmatic Presence

The Gorgon residing in the charming village of Freshwater is a mythical creature of captivating allure. Freshwater, located on the Isle of Wight, is known for its rugged cliffs, lush greenery, and tranquil beaches. The town is a blend of quaint cottages, historic landmarks like the Dimbola Museum and Galleries, and the iconic Freshwater Bay. Amidst this picturesque setting, the Gorgon stands out, both a guardian and an enigma.

Standing tall with an imposing yet graceful figure, the Gorgon towers above most beings. Its serpentine hair, a mesmerizing tangle of writhing snakes in various hues, adds an air of mystique to its appearance. However, it is the Gorgon's eyes that hold the most potent enchantment. Their intense gaze possesses a remarkable power to turn any unfortunate soul into stone, leaving a lasting testament to their extraordinary abilities.

The Gorgon is a well-known figure among the townsfolk, often whispered about in hushed tones. Tales of its formidable power and enigmatic presence have become an integral part of Freshwater's folklore. Many of the statues that adorn the town's gardens and public spaces are believed to be former adversaries of the Gorgon, now immortalized in stone.

Despite its fearsome reputation, the Gorgon is also revered for its achievements. It has protected Freshwater from numerous threats, both mundane and supernatural, earning a place of reluctant respect among the villagers.

A Curious and Adventurous Nature

Despite its formidable appearance, the Gorgon exhibits a curious and adventurous nature. It takes delight in exploring the coastal path, relishing the soothing sound of crashing waves and the salty sea breeze. Along its path, the Gorgon often encounters stray cats, which it eagerly takes in, providing them with a loving home, nourishment, and care. The Gorgon finds joy in nurturing these feline companions and ensuring their happiness.

One sunny afternoon, as the Gorgon strolled along the cliffside, it spotted a tiny, bedraggled kitten perched precariously on a narrow ledge. With a gentle hiss, the Gorgon extended a hand, its serpentine locks writhing softly. The kitten, sensing the Gorgon's benevolent nature, meowed and leaped into its arms.

"You shall be called Seraphina," the Gorgon whispered, cradling the kitten close. "Welcome to your new home."

The Gorgon's cottage, nestled at the edge of the village, was a sanctuary for many such rescued animals. The townsfolk, though wary of the Gorgon's powers, couldn't deny the creature's compassion for the island's stray and abandoned creatures.

A Minor Disdain

Despite its amiable disposition, the Gorgon harbours a certain disdain towards the Alum Bay Pegasus. Known for its refusal to offer rides, the Pegasus is a frequent topic of the Gorgon's grumbles. "Such a show-off," the Gorgon would mutter, rubbing its sore feet after a particularly long trek. "Would it kill him to give me a lift?"

In contrast, the Gorgon finds solace in the company of the jovial Bigfoot. Its oversized feet amuse the Gorgon to no end, leading to affectionate nicknaming of the creature as "Bigfeet." The two mythical beings often shared stories and laughter, their bond a testament to the unlikely friendships that could form between such extraordinary creatures.

One evening, as the Gorgon and Bigfoot sat by a campfire near the Needles, Bigfoot chuckled, "You know, for someone who can turn people to stone, you sure complain a lot about walking."

The Gorgon sighed, "You'd think with all these snakes, I'd be able to slither around effortlessly. But no, it's all just for show." Bigfoot roared with laughter, the sound echoing off the cliffs. "At least you don't have to worry about shoes," he teased, wiggling his massive toes.

The Clan of Gorgons

Legend has it that hidden deep within the verdant cliffs and mystical caves of Freshwater Bay, a clan of Gorgons once thrived. Led by their wise matriarch, Medusa, these formidable beings were known for their unmatched beauty and enigmatic powers.

In a bygone era, when tales of heroes and epic quests echoed across the land, a young warrior named Alistair set foot upon the Isle of Wight. Determined to prove his worth and seek adventure, Alistair found himself drawn to the secrets of Freshwater Bay. Intrigued by the legends of the Gorgons, he ventured into their domain, hoping to uncover the truth behind their captivating presence.

The Gorgons, with their serpentine hair and piercing gazes, were a sight to behold. Their luminous eyes gleamed with an otherworldly radiance, and their movements were as fluid as the waves crashing against the cliffs. Despite their fearsome reputation, the Gorgons welcomed Alistair with open arms, sensing the purity of his intentions.

An Unexpected Friendship

As Alistair journeyed deeper into the heart of Freshwater Bay, he encountered the enchanting Gorgons. Despite his initial trepidation, the Gorgons sensed the warrior's noble spirit and welcomed him with open arms. They shared tales of ancient battles, their formidable powers, and the secrets of their serpentine hair.
"Tell me," Alistair began one evening, seated around a fire with the Gorgons. "How do you manage such a life, hidden away from the world?"
Medusa, the matriarch, smiled wistfully. "We have our ways, young warrior. Our solitude is both a curse and a blessing. But in you, we see a friend, not a foe."
In the following days, Alistair became an honorary member of the Gorgon clan, learning their ways and gaining their trust. Together, they embarked on daring escapades along the coastal path, weaving through hidden caves and ancient ruins. Alistair was astonished at the Gorgons' ability to transform their surroundings, using their petrifying gaze to carve magnificent sculptures in stone.
One such adventure led them to a hidden cave near St. Catherine's Lighthouse. The cave, filled with glittering crystals and ancient carvings, held secrets that had been untouched for centuries. As the Gorgons used their powers to reveal hidden passages, Alistair couldn't help but feel a sense of awe and camaraderie.

"You've shown me a world beyond my wildest dreams," Alistair said, his voice filled with gratitude.
"And you have reminded us of the beauty of friendship," Medusa replied, her serpentine hair shimmering in the torchlight.

The Storm's Fury

One fateful night, as a tempestuous storm unleashed its fury upon the shores of Freshwater Bay, a sinister force emerged from the depths of the sea. Dark and malevolent, the creature threatened to engulf the bay in eternal darkness. Sensing the imminent danger, Alistair and the Gorgons joined forces, harnessing their combined strength to vanquish the ancient evil.
The storm raged on, the wind howling like a banshee. The waves crashed against the cliffs with a ferocity that shook the very ground. Amidst the chaos, the dark creature rose from the sea, its eyes glowing with malevolence.
"We must act quickly," Medusa commanded, her voice steady and resolute.
Alistair nodded, gripping his sword tightly. "Together, we can defeat it."
With their powers united, the Gorgons unleashed a blinding surge of energy, illuminating the night sky. Their serpentine hair danced in ethereal harmony, transforming the storm's rage into an enchanting spectacle of light. Alistair, wielding his sword with precision and strength, fought alongside the Gorgons, their combined efforts pushing back the dark entity.
"Feel the power of unity!" Alistair shouted, his voice echoing through the tempest.

The malevolent force recoiled, defeated by the unified might of Alistair and the Gorgons. As the storm subsided, the sky cleared, revealing a serene and starry night. The dark creature, vanquished, dissolved into the sea, leaving the bay in peace once more.

A Gift of Friendship

Grateful for Alistair's bravery and loyalty, the Gorgons bid him farewell, gifting him a fragment of their serpentine hair as a token of their eternal friendship. Alistair emerged from Freshwater Bay forever changed, carrying with him the memories of his mythical companions and the knowledge that extraordinary beings walked among the ordinary world.
"This is a part of us," Medusa said, handing Alistair the fragment. "May it guide and protect you on your journey."
Alistair bowed deeply. "Thank you, my friends. I will cherish this always."
With a final embrace, Alistair departed, his heart heavy with both gratitude and sorrow. He knew he would miss the Gorgons and the adventures they shared, but he also understood that their bond would last forever.

The Legacy Lives On

Thus, the tale of the Gorgons of Freshwater Bay lives on, a testament to the enduring bond between humans and the enchanting creatures of the Isle of Wight. The townsfolk, now more attuned to the mysteries that surround them, continue to share stories of the Gorgon, reminding each generation of the magic and wonder that lies just beyond the edge of their everyday lives.

In the heart of Freshwater, the Gorgon continues to roam, a guardian of both the past and the future, a symbol of resilience, friendship, and the ever-present enchantment of the Isle of Wight. The statues that dot the village stand as silent sentinels, a reminder of the Gorgon's power and the adventures that once unfolded along the rugged coastline.

As the sun sets over the bay, casting a golden glow on the cliffs, the Gorgon watches over Freshwater with a sense of fulfilment. It has found a place where it can protect, nurture, and inspire—a place where it truly belongs.

And so, the legend of the Freshwater Gorgon endures, a tale of beauty, power, and the unbreakable bonds of friendship. In the whispers of the wind and the crashing of the waves, the story of the Gorgon is woven into the very fabric of the Isle of Wight, a testament to the magic that lies just beyond the horizon.

The Pegasus of Alum Bay

A Majestic Presence

Alum Bay, on the western tip of the Isle of Wight, is renowned for its multi-coloured sand cliffs and panoramic views of the Needles rock formations. It's here, amidst this picturesque setting, that the Pegasus of Alum Bay resides. This majestic creature, known as Iris, is a blend of grace, strength, and mythical allure. With a muscular equine body and a proud stature, Iris stands tall, adorned with glistening white feathers that shimmer brilliantly in the sunlight. Her wings, expansive and feathered like a grand bird, span wide, allowing her to take flight and soar through the skies with unparalleled elegance.

As Iris glides above the cliffs and meadows of Alum Bay, her presence commands awe and admiration. The local residents and visitors alike find themselves captivated by her beauty and the sense of wonder she brings. Iris is more than just a mythical creature; she is a symbol of the island's enchanting charm and a guardian of its natural splendour.

The weather plays a significant role in Iris's daily flights. On clear days, she takes to the skies early in the morning, riding the thermals that rise from the warm ground. The sun casts long shadows across the landscape, and the morning mist slowly dissipates, revealing the vibrant colours of the cliffs. As the earth rotates, Iris adjusts her flight path, using the changing winds to her advantage. She soars effortlessly, her keen eyes scanning the ground below for any signs of disturbance.

Mischievous Companions

Despite her majestic appearance, Iris possesses a playful and mischievous nature. She harbours a slight aversion towards the Gorgon of Freshwater, a creature she once considered a friend until her beloved feline companion mysteriously vanished after an encounter with the serpentine-haired being. Nevertheless, Iris finds solace and companionship in the company of the amiable Bigfoot, a creature of lore with enormous feet and a jovial disposition.
Bigfoot, who prefers to be called Benny, enjoys accompanying Iris on exhilarating flights across the Isle of Wight. Together, they leave behind a trail of humorous pranks on unsuspecting tourists. Their favourite trick involves creating the illusion of Bigfoot sightings. Iris would swoop down from the skies, creating a flurry of commotion, while Benny, with his enormous feet, would leave imprints in the soft earth. This combination of aerial agility and ground-based trickery results in blurry photographs and bewildered witnesses who swear they have captured the elusive Bigfoot on film.
"Did you see their faces, Benny?" Iris would chuckle as they retreated to a secluded spot. "Priceless! Absolutely priceless!" Benny, with his deep, rumbling laugh, would respond, "They'll be talking about this for years. It's the best fun I've had in ages!"
Their flight plans are meticulously planned, taking into account the prevailing winds and weather conditions. On days when the winds are strong, they choose routes that allow them to ride the gusts, conserving energy and increasing their speed. The rotation of the earth also affects their flights, causing slight adjustments to their trajectories as they traverse the skies.

A World of Pranks

Their mischievous exploits transcend borders, taking them to far-flung destinations worldwide. From the vast wilderness of Canada to the dense forests of North America, Iris and Benny have become renowned for their ability to perplex and bemuse. Their adventures include creating elaborate hoaxes that baffle researchers and cryptozoologists alike.

One memorable escapade involved a high-profile Bigfoot conference in Washington State. Iris and Benny orchestrated a series of events that culminated in a nighttime spectacle where Iris's glowing wings cast eerie shadows through the forest, while Benny's footprints led investigators on a wild chase.

As they flew back to the Isle of Wight, Benny mused, "You know, Iris, if we keep this up, they might start offering rewards for our capture."

Iris winked, "All the more reason to stay one step — or wing — ahead of them!"

Their pranks are not just spontaneous acts of mischief but carefully orchestrated events. They study the local geography and weather patterns, ensuring that their tricks are perfectly timed and executed. The changing seasons also influence their activities, with winter providing opportunities for snow-covered pranks and summer offering long days for extended flights.

Serenity and Solitude

Despite their playful nature, Iris finds solace and tranquillity in taking long walks along the breathtaking coastal path of Alum Bay. The path winds along the edge of the cliffs, offering stunning views of the sea below. It is during these quiet moments that Iris reflects on her adventures and the beauty of the world around her.

One of Iris's favourite spots is the lighthouse at the Needles. Perching gracefully atop the structure, she gazes upon the panoramic views of the sea and the rugged coastline, revelling in the peaceful serenity of her surroundings. The lighthouse, with its weathered walls and historic significance, stands as a beacon of solace and reflection for Iris.

During one such reflective moment, Iris spoke softly to herself, "This place... it's more than just a home. It's a sanctuary, a place where I can truly be myself."

The lighthouse serves as a perfect vantage point for observing the changing weather patterns. Iris can see storm clouds forming on the horizon and gauge the strength of the winds by watching the waves crash against the rocks. The rotation of the earth is evident in the shifting positions of the sun and stars, reminding her of the vastness of the universe and her place within it.

The Bond of Iris and Bigfoot

In the heart of Alum Bay, Iris and Benny's bond continued to grow stronger. Their shared love for adventure and pranks created a friendship that knew no bounds. One fateful day, as they prepared for another escapade, Iris shared a thought that had been on her mind.

"Benny," she began, her tone serious for once, "do you ever think about what it would be like if people knew the real us, not just the legends?"

Benny pondered for a moment before replying, "Iris, part of the magic is in the mystery. But maybe one day, we'll find a way to let them in, without losing what makes us special."

Their bond is strengthened by their shared experiences and the challenges they face together. Whether navigating through a dense forest or flying through a storm, they rely on each other's strengths and abilities. Benny's keen sense of direction and Iris's ability to read the weather make them an unstoppable team.

Tales of Legends

Their playful escapades soon became the stuff of legends, with tales spreading far and wide of the blurry photographs and amusing encounters with Bigfoot. In Alum Bay, locals and tourists alike would eagerly gather, hoping to glimpse the enigmatic duo as they prepared for their next light-hearted prank.
As they flew over the bay, Iris remarked, "I heard some tourists say they saw Bigfoot riding a Pegasus. Can you imagine?"
Benny laughed heartily, "Well, maybe we should give them what they want next time!"
Their legends were not just confined to Alum Bay. Tales of their antics reached other parts of the Isle of Wight, including the bustling town of Newport and the historic Carisbrooke Castle. People began to view Iris and Benny not just as mythical creatures, but as beloved figures who brought a sense of wonder and joy to their lives.
The legends are fuelled by the changing seasons and the varying weather conditions that create different backdrops for their pranks. In spring, they might be seen frolicking among the blooming flowers, while in autumn, they blend in with the falling leaves. Each season adds a new layer to their mythos, making their stories timeless and ever-evolving.

The Lighthouse Perch

Amidst their thrilling adventures, Iris found solace in long walks along the picturesque coastal path of Alum Bay. During one such stroll, she discovered the old lighthouse seated atop the Needles, its weathered structure beckoning her with a sense of tranquillity. From then on, Iris made the lighthouse her perch, gazing out upon the vast expanse of the sea, her wings brushing against the gentle sea breeze.
One evening, as the sun dipped below the horizon, casting a golden glow over the sea, Benny joined Iris at the lighthouse. They sat in comfortable silence for a while, before Benny spoke.
"You know, Iris, we've had a lot of fun. But sometimes, I think about settling down, finding a place where we can just be."
Iris smiled, "This lighthouse feels like that place for me. It's where I come to find peace."
Benny nodded, "Maybe we can make it our secret base, a place to retreat after our adventures."
The lighthouse becomes a symbol of their bond and a place of reflection. The changing light from the beacon serves as a reminder of the passage of time and the ever-changing nature of their lives. The rotation of the earth is evident in the shifting constellations, providing a sense of continuity and stability in an otherwise unpredictable world.

A Whimsical Legacy

And so, the story of Iris, the mischievous Pegasus, and her inseparable companion, the amiable Bigfoot, continues to weave its magical tapestry. With every flight and prank, they leave behind laughter, wonder, and a touch of whimsy in the hearts of all who encounter them, forever entwined in the fantastical lore of Alum Bay. The townsfolk and visitors alike cherish the moments they share with the duo, their spirits lifted by the joyous mischief and the breathtaking sight of Iris soaring through the skies with Benny by her side.

Their legacy is not just in the tales of their pranks, but in the joy and wonder they inspire. Children grow up hearing stories of Iris and Benny, their imaginations fuelled by the adventures of the Pegasus and Bigfoot. The lighthouse at the Needles becomes a symbol of their bond, a place where magic and reality meet.

As they continue their adventures, Iris and Benny know that they are part of something greater than themselves. They are part of the legend of Alum Bay, a story that will be told for generations to come.

In the quiet moments, as they gaze out at the sea from the lighthouse, they feel a sense of fulfilment. They have found a place where they belong, a place where they can be themselves and share their magic with the world.

And so, the Pegasus of Alum Bay and Bigfoot continue to soar through the skies and roam the land, leaving behind a trail of laughter, wonder, and a legacy of whimsical adventures. The Isle of Wight, with its breathtaking landscapes and rich history, is their home, a place where legends are born and dreams take flight.

The Goblin of Chale

An Enigmatic Presence

Chale, a quaint village nestled on the southern coast of the Isle of Wight, is a place where the whispers of history and the magic of folklore intertwine. The village, with its charming stone cottages and narrow winding lanes, is surrounded by the lush, mysterious woods of Blackgang Chine. It is here, amidst the ancient trees and hidden glades, that the enigmatic Goblin of Chale resides.

The Goblin, known to the locals as Puck, stands no taller than a child. His wiry frame is covered in mottled green skin, blending seamlessly with the foliage of his woodland habitat. Puck's pointed ears are keenly alert, twitching at the slightest sound, while his sharp, emerald eyes sparkle with mischievous intelligence. His attire is an assortment of leaves, twigs, and other natural elements, creating a patchwork cloak that allows him to move unseen through the forest.

Puck is a creature of both mischief and wisdom. Though he delights in playing tricks on the unsuspecting townsfolk, his deeper understanding of the land and its secrets is a boon to those who seek his help. His knowledge of herbology and local folklore makes him an invaluable, albeit unpredictable, ally.

Mischief and Wisdom

In Chale, Puck is both a source of amusement and exasperation. Known for his propensity for pranks, he often leaves the villagers perplexed or mildly frustrated. From hiding tools to switching signposts, Puck's antics are legendary. Yet, beneath his mischievous facade, he harbours a profound understanding of the natural world.

One particular day, as Puck wandered the outskirts of the village, he came across a group of horses grazing peacefully in a meadow. Drawn to their gentle nature, he approached them cautiously. Using his soothing goblin voice, Puck engaged in a lively conversation with the horses. To his delight, the horses responded, their neighs and whinnies creating a symphony of equine communication.

This bond with the horses soon became known throughout Chale. Children would eagerly seek out Puck, hoping to witness the goblin conversing with his equine friends. Puck revelled in the attention, sharing tales of the horses' wisdom and the ancient bonds between goblins and animals.

"Tell us another story, Puck!" a child would plead.

Puck would grin, his eyes twinkling with mischief. "Alright, gather 'round, and I'll tell you about the time I taught a horse to sing!"

As the children gathered closer, Puck's voice lowered to a conspiratorial whisper. "You see, horses have the most beautiful voices if you can get them to sing. One day, I found a horse named Bella who loved music. With a bit of goblin magic and a lot of patience, she sang the sweetest melody you've ever heard."

The children's eyes widened in amazement. "Did she really sing, Puck?"

Puck chuckled. "Well, that's a secret between Bella and me. But remember, the magic of the forest is in every creature, great and small."

Pub Mishaps

While Puck's interactions with the horses were heartwarming, his ventures into the village pub were anything but. Known for his insatiable appetite, Puck would often sneak into the pub, hoping to sample the delicious bar snacks. One evening, as the pub buzzed with laughter and camaraderie, Puck's hunger got the better of him.

He devoured all the bar snacks, much to the dismay of the patrons. When the barkeeper demanded payment, Puck offered a fairy's wing, mistaking it for a valuable trinket. The ensuing chaos was comical. Patrons shouted, the barkeeper fumed, and Puck, realising his mistake, bolted out the door, narrowly escaping with his dignity intact.

"Fairy's wing! What nonsense!" the barkeeper exclaimed, shaking his head.

"Can't blame a goblin for trying!" Puck retorted with a mischievous grin as he disappeared into the night.

Solitude in Nature

Banished from the pub, Puck found solace in the embrace of nature. He would perch upon moss-covered rocks, savouring the taste of fresh raw liver, a delicacy he had grown fond of. The rustling leaves and the gentle babbling of nearby brooks provided a serene backdrop to his solitary feasts.

One day, while basking in the sunlight filtering through the trees, Puck heard a rustle in the underbrush. He turned to see a young deer cautiously approaching. Intrigued, Puck extended his hand, offering a piece of liver. The deer sniffed tentatively before accepting the offering, solidifying an unspoken bond between the goblin and the woodland creatures.

"You're not so different from me, are you?" Puck mused, watching the deer nibble on the liver. "Both creatures of the forest, finding our way."

In these moments of solitude, Puck would reflect on his life in Chale. The village, with its ancient trees and hidden secrets, had become his sanctuary. Here, he could be himself, free from the expectations and judgments of the human world.

A Curious Encounter

One foggy morning, as Puck roamed the edge of the forest, he stumbled upon a young girl named Eliza, who was lost and frightened. Her tear-streaked face lit up with hope when she saw Puck, though she was initially wary of his appearance.

"Are you... a goblin?" she asked hesitantly.

Puck chuckled. "Indeed, I am. And who might you be, wandering so close to the woods?"

"I'm Eliza. I got separated from my family," she explained, her voice trembling.

Puck's mischievous grin softened. "Well, Eliza, it seems you're in need of a guide. Follow me, and I'll get you back to the village."

As they walked, Puck entertained Eliza with stories of his adventures, making her laugh and forget her fears. By the time they reached the edge of Chale, Eliza felt like she had made a new friend.

"Thank you, Puck," she said, hugging him tightly.

Puck patted her back awkwardly. "Anytime, little one. Just remember, the forest holds many secrets, but not all of them are meant to be explored alone."

Eliza looked up at Puck with wide eyes. "Is it true you can talk to horses?"

Puck nodded, a twinkle in his eye. "Indeed, it is. Horses are wise creatures. They know more than they let on."

"Can you teach me to talk to them?" Eliza asked eagerly.

Puck smiled. "Maybe one day, if you promise to respect their wisdom and listen with your heart."

The Goblin's Wisdom

Despite his mischievous nature, Puck was a reservoir of wisdom. The villagers, recognising his knowledge of herbology and folklore, often sought his advice in times of need. One evening, an elderly villager named Ethel approached Puck, her voice trembling with worry.
"Puck, my grandson has fallen ill. The healers can't seem to help him. Do you know of any remedies?"
Puck nodded thoughtfully. "Fear not, Ethel. The forest provides for those who know where to look. Follow me." Leading Ethel into the heart of the woods, Puck gathered an assortment of herbs and plants, explaining their properties as he went. They returned to Ethel's cottage, where Puck brewed a potent potion. After administering the remedy, Ethel's grandson began to recover, much to her relief.
"Thank you, Puck. I don't know what we would have done without you," Ethel said, tears of gratitude in her eyes.
Puck shrugged, a rare moment of humility crossing his features. "Sometimes, even a goblin's tricks can heal."
Ethel clasped his hands warmly. "You're a blessing, Puck. The village owes you much."

A Lasting Legacy

As time passed, Puck's presence became an integral part of Chale's folklore. The villagers, initially wary of the mischievous goblin, came to appreciate his wisdom and unique perspective on life. Tales of his adventures spread far and wide, capturing the imaginations of those who heard them.

One evening, as the sun set over the village, Puck found himself reflecting on his journey. He sat atop a hill overlooking Chale, the warm hues of twilight casting a golden glow over the landscape.
"This place, these people... they've grown on me," he muttered to himself, a rare smile playing on his lips. "Perhaps, in their own way, they've tamed this wild goblin."
As he sat in contemplation, a group of children approached, led by Eliza. They gathered around Puck, eager for another story.
"Puck, tell us about the time you tricked the faeries!" one of the children exclaimed.
Puck chuckled. "Ah, the faeries. Now that's a tale worth telling..."

The Goblin's Farewell

One crisp autumn morning, Puck awoke with a sense of restlessness. The forest, which had been his home for so long, seemed to whisper of new adventures beyond the Isle of Wight. With a heavy heart, he decided it was time to bid farewell to Chale.
He visited the village one last time, saying his goodbyes to the friends he had made. As he approached the meadow where the horses grazed, they nickered softly, sensing his departure.
"Puck, are you leaving?" Eliza asked, her eyes wide with sadness.
Puck nodded. "Yes, Eliza. But fear not, for the forest will always watch over you."
With that, he turned and disappeared into the woods, his form blending seamlessly with the foliage. As the villagers watched him go, they knew that the spirit of the mischievous goblin would forever remain a part of Chale.

And so, the legend of Puck, the Goblin of Chale, lived on. His tales of mischief, wisdom, and unexpected kindness continued to enchant and entertain generations. The villagers, now more attuned to the magic that surrounded them, cherished the memories of their goblin friend, knowing that, somewhere in the world, Puck was still spreading his unique brand of mischief and wonder.

As Puck ventured into new lands, the winds carried whispers of his name, and the forests echoed with the laughter of a goblin who had found his place in the world. And in Chale, where the line between myth and reality blurred, the spirit of Puck lived on, a testament to the enduring magic of the Isle of Wight.

The Jersey Devil of Chale Green

An Enigmatic Presence

Chale Green is a village nestled in the heart of the Isle of Wight, a region steeped in history and folklore. Surrounded by lush woodlands and rolling countryside, it is a place where the whispers of ancient tales blend with the gentle rustling of leaves. The village is known for its charming stone cottages, historic St. Andrew's Church, and the expansive village green, a space where the community gathers for various celebrations throughout the year.

In the midst of this idyllic setting resides a creature of both awe and trepidation: the Jersey Devil. Legend has it that this enigmatic being emerged from the shadows of Chale Green's dense forests, an entity as old as the hills and as wild as the winds that sweep across the Isle of Wight.

The Jersey Devil is a formidable figure, with a physique that combines the ferocity of a predatory beast with the elegance of an avian predator. Standing at a height that makes it appear both towering and elusive, it has the head of a goat, complete with twisted horns that curl menacingly towards the sky. Its eyes, glowing with an otherworldly fire, pierce through the darkness with a gaze that seems to see into the very soul. The Devil's body is sinewy and powerful, covered in mottled, shadowy fur that allows it to blend seamlessly with the undergrowth of its woodland domain.

The creature's bat-like wings, which span an impressive width, are a notable feature. They are capable of carrying the Devil effortlessly through the night sky, casting eerie shadows over the landscape. These wings are not just for show; they are instrumental in the Devil's role as both a guardian and a predator. The sound of these wings beating through the air is a haunting melody that signals the presence of this ancient entity.

The people of Chale Green have a complex relationship with the Jersey Devil. Though its appearance can be intimidating, they view the Devil with a mixture of reverence and respect. The creature is seen as a guardian spirit, a protector of the land whose presence is intertwined with the very essence of the village. Over time, the villagers have come to accept the Devil's enigmatic role, understanding that it plays a crucial part in the delicate balance of their environment.

One evening, as the sun dipped below the horizon and the village was bathed in twilight, young Eliza and her grandmother, Agnes, strolled along the village green. The air was crisp, with the scent of blooming flowers mingling with the earthy aroma of the woods.

"Grandma," Eliza asked, her eyes wide with curiosity, "do you think the Jersey Devil is real?"

Agnes smiled gently, her gaze drifting towards the darkening woods. "Oh, Eliza, the Devil is very real, but it's not quite like the stories you hear. It's a part of this land, a force of nature. We respect it, for it is as much a guardian as it is a mystery."

As they walked past the ancient oak tree that stood at the edge of the village green, Agnes continued, "The Devil's role here is to maintain balance. It watches over us, but it also keeps the wild in check. It's a reminder that nature is not to be tamed, but to be respected."

Eliza nodded, her thoughts deepened by her grandmother's words. The notion that such a creature could be both a guardian and a mystery fascinated her. She looked up at the darkening sky, half-expecting to see the Devil's bat-like wings cutting through the twilight.

The villagers of Chale Green have long recognised the Jersey Devil's place in their lives. They know that, despite its fearsome appearance, the creature is an integral part of their community's folklore and natural environment. The Devil's presence is a testament to the wild and untamed beauty that characterises the Isle of Wight, and it serves as a constant reminder of the ancient magic that still lingers in the land.

The Wheely Bin Whimsy

In the heart of Chale Green's charming and tranquil setting, the Jersey Devil indulges in a peculiar pastime that has become a delightful yet enigmatic feature of village life. Each morning, the residents awake to find their wheely bins mysteriously overflowing with an assortment of random items. From leaves and twigs to curious trinkets collected from the surrounding woods, the contents of these bins are as varied as they are unexpected.

The phenomenon, known locally as the "Wheely Bin Whimsy," has become a beloved quirk of life in Chale Green. The Devil's actions, though baffling to outsiders, are viewed with a sense of amusement and endearment by the villagers.

One crisp autumn morning, Eliza and her grandmother ventured outside to collect the newspaper. As they approached their bin, Eliza's eyes widened in surprise. "Look, Grandma! It's overflowing with pinecones and what looks like an old compass."

Agnes chuckled as she examined the bin. "Ah, the Jersey Devil must have been busy. It's his way of reminding us that he's always around. Or perhaps he just enjoys a bit of mischief."

Eliza picked up the compass, turning it over in her small hands. "Do you think it means anything?"

Agnes shook her head, smiling. "Who can say? The Devil has a sense of humour, that much is certain. Perhaps he wants us to remember that the world is full of surprises."

As the day progressed, the townsfolk gathered at the local pub, the "Green Oak," to discuss the latest bin antics. The pub, a warm and inviting space with wooden beams and a roaring fireplace, was a popular meeting place for the villagers.

"Did you see the bin outside the bakery?" Tom, the local baker, asked with a grin. "It was filled with feathers and a few old horseshoes. Seems like our friend the Devil has a new collection."

The room erupted with laughter. "Perhaps he's preparing for a grand event," Mary, the pub's landlady, suggested playfully. "Or maybe he's just trying to keep us on our toes." Despite the whimsical nature of the Wheely Bin Whimsy, the Devil's actions have become an endearing part of village life. The random assortment of items left behind serves as a reminder of the creature's presence and its connection to the land. For the residents of Chale Green, it is a source of amusement and a testament to the Devil's playful spirit.

As the sun set and the village settled into the quiet of the evening, Eliza sat by her bedroom window, looking out at the darkening woods. She wondered about the Jersey Devil and its mysterious ways. In the quiet of the night, she could almost imagine the Devil watching over the village, its fiery eyes glowing with a sense of mischief and watchfulness.

The Wheely Bin Whimsy has become more than just a quirky phenomenon; it is a reflection of the unique relationship between the villagers and the enigmatic creature that watches over them. It serves as a reminder that magic and mystery still exist in their world, adding a touch of wonder to their everyday lives.

The Ravenous Appetite

Though the Wheely Bin Whimsy provides a glimpse into the playful side of the Jersey Devil, it is essential to acknowledge the darker aspects of this legendary creature. Known for its ravenous appetite, the Devil has a reputation for being particularly dangerous to those who venture too close or inquire too deeply into its origins.

On a moonlit night, a group of tourists arrived in Chale Green, eager to experience the village's rich folklore. They set up camp on the outskirts of the village, near the dense forest where the Jersey Devil was said to dwell. Their excitement and curiosity, however, soon caught the attention of the Devil itself.

As the tourists gathered around their campfire, their voices carried through the still night air. "I've heard the Devil is a fearsome creature," one of them said. "They say it has an insatiable hunger."

Another tourist, with a hint of bravado, added, "Let's see if the stories are true. I bet it won't even bother us."

Unbeknownst to them, the Devil was watching from the shadows, its fiery eyes glowing with hunger. The creature had sensed their intrusion and felt a primal urge to protect its domain. As the night deepened, the Devil's presence grew more ominous.

Without warning, the Devil descended upon the camp. Its bat-like wings spread wide, casting eerie shadows over the terrified tourists. The sound of its roar echoed through the forest, a chilling reminder of its power. The tourists' screams pierced the night, their pleas for help quickly silenced by the rustling of leaves and the distant hoot of an owl.

By morning, the campsite was abandoned. The only signs of the previous night's events were the scattered remains of their belongings and a lingering sense of dread among the villagers. The disappearance of the tourists served as a grim reminder of the Jersey Devil's nature. While the creature is a guardian of the land, it is also a formidable predator, fiercely protecting its territory from those who dare to intrude. The locals of Chale Green are well aware of the Devil's capabilities and approach their interactions with the creature with a mixture of respect and caution.

"Did you hear about the tourists who vanished?" Tom, the baker, asked Agnes as they discussed the morning's events.

"I did," Agnes replied solemnly. "The Jersey Devil is not to be trifled with. It's a reminder that some mysteries are best left unexplored."

Eliza, who had overheard the conversation, looked up at her grandmother with wide eyes. "Will it ever come for us, Grandma?"

Agnes placed a comforting hand on Eliza's shoulder. "As long as we respect the Devil and our surroundings, we have nothing to fear. It's a part of this land, and we must live in harmony with it."

The Jersey Devil's ravenous appetite serves as a stark reminder of the delicate balance between curiosity and caution. While the Devil's presence is a source of fascination, it is also a testament to the untamed power that lies within the shadows of Chale Green's forests.

A Night in Chale Green

On one particularly moonlit night, Chale Green was enveloped in a mystical fog that rolled in from the sea, casting an otherworldly glow over the village. The streets were silent, save for the occasional rustling of leaves and the distant call of an owl. It was during such nights that the Jersey Devil was most active, its presence felt in every whisper of the wind and every shadow that flickered in the moonlight.

As the Devil prowled through the village, its bat-like wings stretched wide and its fiery eyes scanning the surroundings, it noticed a group of tourists who had set up camp on the outskirts. Their chatter, filled with excitement and curiosity about the legendary creature, reached the Devil's keen ears.

"Do you think we'll see the Jersey Devil tonight?" one of the tourists asked, their voice tinged with excitement.

"Who knows," another replied. "But wouldn't it be amazing to catch a glimpse of it?"

The Devil, sensing their intrusion, felt a growing hunger. It was not merely a physical hunger, but a deep, primal urge to protect its domain from those who sought to intrude upon its territory. As the night deepened, the Devil's presence grew more menacing, its fiery eyes glowing with an ominous light. Suddenly, the Devil descended upon the camp, its massive wings creating a gust of wind that extinguished their campfire. The tourists' cries for help echoed through the night, their voices filled with terror. The Devil's roar, a sound that seemed to come from the very depths of the earth, was the last thing they heard before silence fell over the campsite.

By morning, the campsite was eerily quiet. The only signs of the previous night's events were the scattered remains of their belongings and a palpable sense of dread that hung in the air. The villagers, who had grown accustomed to the Devil's nocturnal activities, reacted with a mixture of sorrow and understanding.

"It's always the same," Tom said, his voice heavy with concern. "The Devil doesn't take kindly to those who venture too close."

Agnes nodded in agreement. "The Jersey Devil is a part of this land, and it must be respected. It's a reminder of the wild and untamed nature of our surroundings."

Eliza, who had witnessed the aftermath, clung to her grandmother's side. "Will the Devil come for us, Grandma?"

Agnes looked at Eliza with a reassuring smile. "As long as we respect the Devil and our land, we are safe. It is a guardian, and it protects us in its own way."

The events of that night served as a stark reminder of the delicate balance between respect and fear. The Jersey Devil, though fearsome and enigmatic, was also a protector of Chale Green, ensuring that its territory remained undisturbed.

Guardian of the Shadows

The annual Chale Green Festival was a time of celebration, joy, and community spirit. The festival, held in honour of the village's rich history and folklore, featured music, dancing, and a variety of traditional activities. The village green was transformed into a vibrant hub of activity, with colourful banners fluttering in the breeze and the scent of delicious food wafting through the air.

As the villagers gathered to celebrate, the Jersey Devil watched from the shadows, its fiery eyes glowing with a sense of pride. The festival was a testament to the village's spirit and resilience, and the Devil, despite its fearsome reputation, felt a deep connection to the festivities.

However, the Devil's watchful gaze was soon drawn to a group of strangers who had arrived in the village. Their presence was disruptive, their behaviour loud and intrusive. They seemed intent on causing chaos and disturbing the celebrations.

"This is our chance to make a name for ourselves," one of the strangers said, their voice filled with arrogance. "Let's see how the locals react."

The Devil, sensing the threat posed by the strangers, sprang into action. With a mighty roar, it emerged from the shadows, its massive wings creating a gust of wind that sent the strangers fleeing in terror. The festivalgoers watched in awe as the Devil's fiery eyes lit up the night, a powerful reminder of the guardian's role in protecting their community.

"Thank you, Jersey Devil!" Agnes called out, her voice filled with gratitude. "You've saved our festival!"

As the festival continued, the Devil retreated to the shadows, its presence a constant reminder of the balance it maintained. The villagers celebrated with renewed vigour, their hearts filled with appreciation for their guardian.

Eliza, who had witnessed the Devil's intervention, looked up at her grandmother with a newfound understanding. "The Devil is not just a legend, Grandma. It's a protector."

Agnes smiled warmly at Eliza. "Yes, dear. The Jersey Devil is a part of our lives, and it watches over us in its own way. We must always remember to respect and honour it."

The events of the festival served as a powerful reminder of the delicate balance between fear and respect. The Jersey Devil, though enigmatic and fearsome, was also a guardian of Chale Green, ensuring that the village remained safe from harm.

A Thoughtful Conversation

On a quiet evening, as the moon cast a gentle glow over the Isle of Wight, the Jersey Devil found itself atop a hill overlooking Chale Green. The village below was illuminated by the soft light of street lamps, and the sounds of the festival's celebrations drifted up from the distance.

As the Devil rested on the hill, a figure emerged from the shadows. It was Bigfoot, the legendary creature known for its gentle nature and immense strength. Bigfoot had come to visit the Devil, drawn by the curiosity and respect he held for the enigmatic guardian of Chale Green.

"Why do you protect them?" Bigfoot asked, his voice a deep rumble that carried through the still night air.

The Jersey Devil sighed, its fiery eyes reflecting the moonlight. "Because they are my people. This land is my home, and they are a part of it. I am bound to protect them, just as they respect and honour me."

Bigfoot nodded thoughtfully. "It's a noble purpose. But do you ever tire of it? The responsibility must be immense."

The Devil looked out over the village, its gaze filled with a mixture of pride and weariness. "At times, it is exhausting. But it is also fulfilling. The balance between fear and respect, guardian and protector, is a delicate one. It is my duty to maintain that balance, for the sake of the land and its people."

Bigfoot pondered the Devil's words, his large frame sitting down beside the guardian. "You know, I once asked myself the same question. Why protect? Why guard? And I found that it is not just about the duty, but about the bond we share with our home and its inhabitants."

The two creatures sat in companionable silence, the sounds of the festival drifting up from the village. The night was calm, and the stars twinkled overhead, a testament to the timeless bond between the guardian and the land it protected.

As the night wore on, the Devil and Bigfoot continued their conversation, their words a reflection of the deep connection they shared with their respective lands. The Devil's role as a guardian was not just a duty but a reflection of its intrinsic bond with the Isle of Wight and its people.

"Thank you for this conversation," Bigfoot said as he prepared to leave. "It has been enlightening."

The Devil nodded, its fiery eyes glowing with appreciation. "And thank you for your company. It is always good to speak with another who understands the weight of responsibility."

As Bigfoot disappeared into the night, the Jersey Devil remained atop the hill, its gaze fixed on the village below. The conversation had provided a moment of introspection, a reminder of the importance of its role as a guardian and protector.

In the quiet of the night, the Devil took comfort in the knowledge that it was not alone in its duty. The bond between guardian and land was a powerful one, and it was a bond that transcended fear and mystery, connecting the Devil to the very essence of Chale Green and its people.

The Gnome of Rowbridge

Guardians of the Land

The Isle of Wight is a jewel set in the southern seas, renowned for its dramatic cliffs, sandy shores, and verdant landscapes. Amongst its many charming towns, Rowbridge stands out as an enchanting haven where time seems to have paused in a moment of idyllic harmony. This quaint village is a tapestry of cobbled streets, timber-framed houses with thatched roofs, and flourishing gardens that brim with an abundance of life. Nestled between the rolling hills and the lush woodlands, Rowbridge is a picturesque example of old-world charm blended seamlessly with the natural world.

At the heart of Rowbridge's charm are its magical guardians — the gnomes. These small, mystical beings possess an aura of ancient wisdom and whimsical grace. Standing no taller than a garden spade, they have faces etched with the lines of countless years, adorned with expressions of both mischief and sagacity. Their eyes, twinkling with a blend of knowledge and playful secrecy, seem to hold the mysteries of the natural world. With their stout bodies and gnarled hands, they epitomise the very essence of nature.

The gnomes of Rowbridge are not merely inhabitants; they are the stewards of the town's green spaces and farmlands. Their primary role is that of caretakers, ensuring that the town's flora thrives and its landscapes remain as verdant and vibrant as ever. With a profound connection to the land, they use their mystical abilities to encourage growth, prosperity, and balance. Through a combination of whispered incantations and tender care, they foster an environment where flowers bloom in dazzling arrays of colour, vegetables grow in bountiful harvests, and trees stretch towards the sky in lush green splendour.

Every morning, as the first light of dawn gently caresses the landscape, the gnomes emerge from their burrows, situated beneath the roots of ancient oaks and in hidden corners of the village. Their daily tasks are a harmonious blend of magic and manual labour. They till the soil, tend to the gardens, and use their enchantments to ensure that nature's cycles remain uninterrupted. Their presence is felt in every corner of Rowbridge, from the blossoming flowers in the village green to the well-tended fields on the outskirts of town.

The bond between the gnomes and the townsfolk is one of mutual respect and deep gratitude. The villagers understand the vital role these magical beings play in maintaining the town's natural beauty and abundance. In return, the gnomes are revered and celebrated. The annual Harvest Festival is a prime example of this gratitude, where the village comes together to honour their tiny guardians. The festival transforms the village green into a vibrant celebration of music, dance, and feasting, with the gnomes playing a central role in the festivities. They are not only participants but also the stars of the show, their magical prowess adding an extra layer of enchantment to the proceedings.

"Good morning, Elder Bramble," said Thistle, the youngest of the gnomes, as he emerged from his burrow. "Another splendid day for nurturing the roses, don't you think?"

"Indeed, Thistle," Elder Bramble replied, his voice carrying the weight of centuries. "The roses are in need of some extra care. Their colours have been a bit dull lately."

"I'll get started right away. The villagers are expecting a glorious bloom for the festival, after all."

"Ah, the festival," Bramble mused, a twinkle of mischief in his eye. "A splendid time to showcase our work and celebrate our bond with the land. Let us ensure that the roses are their best for this grand occasion."

The gnomes' work is more than just a daily routine; it is a sacred duty that intertwines their existence with the natural world. Their enchantments and efforts contribute to a sense of harmony and prosperity that defines Rowbridge. Through their diligent care and magical touch, they help maintain the delicate balance between humanity and nature, ensuring that their beloved town remains a place of unparalleled beauty and enchantment.

"Look at the daisies," Thistle said, admiring the cheerful blooms. "They're dancing in the breeze as if they're celebrating with us."

"Indeed," Bramble agreed. "Nature has its own way of rejoicing. We merely help guide it."

As the sun rose higher in the sky, casting its golden light across Rowbridge, the gnomes continued their work, their presence a constant reminder of the magic and harmony that define their world. Through their tireless efforts, they ensure that the town remains a beacon of natural beauty and mystical wonder.

The Call of Curiosity

Despite their deep connection to Rowbridge, the gnomes are not immune to the allure of adventure. On a particularly bright and sunlit day, their curiosity was piqued by tales of the nearby village of Calbourne. Known for its picturesque landscapes and enchanting natural features, Calbourne beckoned to the gnomes with the promise of new wonders and discoveries.

Elder Bramble, with his boundless curiosity and thirst for knowledge, decided to lead a small group of gnomes on an exploratory journey. As they set out, the gnomes' hearts were filled with excitement and anticipation. Their tiny feet, clad in well-worn boots, moved with a sense of purpose as they traversed the winding paths that led to Calbourne.

The journey itself was a delight, with each step unveiling a new facet of the natural world. The gnomes were greeted by the sight of cascading waterfalls, their waters sparkling in the sunlight like liquid crystal. The air was filled with the gentle murmur of the falls, creating a soothing symphony that accompanied their exploration.

"Look at that!" Thistle exclaimed, his eyes wide with wonder. "The waterfall is like nature's own curtain of silk."

"Indeed," Bramble replied. "It's said that these waters hold ancient magic. We should approach with respect."

As they ventured further, the gnomes discovered a meadow adorned with wildflowers in a riot of colours. The flowers swayed in the breeze, their petals shimmering like jewels. The gnomes danced amongst the blooms, their laughter mingling with the whispers of the wind.

"These flowers are magnificent," Thistle said, kneeling to examine a particularly vibrant bloom. "I've never seen such variety in one place."

"Nature has its own way of surprising us," Bramble observed. "Every corner of the world holds its own unique beauty."

Their exploration also led them to the ancient woodlands surrounding Calbourne. The trees, towering and majestic, seemed to whisper secrets from ages past. The gnomes felt a deep sense of connection to the land as they communed with the ancient spirits of the forest.

"Do you feel it?" Thistle asked softly. "The trees—they're alive with history."

"Yes," Bramble replied. "The trees hold the memories of the land. It's a reminder of the timeless bond between nature and magic."

As dusk began to settle, casting a soft golden hue over the landscape, the gnomes prepared to return to Rowbridge. Their hearts and minds were filled with the wonders they had encountered, and their spirits were uplifted by the beauty they had witnessed.

"What a day it has been," Thistle said, as they made their way back. "We've seen so much, and yet, there's so much more to discover."
"Indeed," Bramble agreed. "Our journey has been a reminder of the endless beauty that surrounds us. And while Calbourne is enchanting, there's no place like Rowbridge."
As they returned to their beloved town, the gnomes carried with them the memories of their adventure, enriching their understanding of the world and reinforcing their commitment to nurturing the land they cherished.

The Town's Enchantment

Rowbridge is a town where nature and magic coexist in perfect harmony. The village green, with its central landmark — the Elder Oak — is the heart of the town's enchantment. This ancient tree, with its sprawling branches and deep roots, stands as a symbol of the enduring connection between the gnomes and the land they care for.
Each morning, as the first light of dawn touches the village, the gnomes emerge from their burrows, ready to tend to the gardens and farmlands. Their work is a blend of magical enchantment and careful cultivation. With every touch, every whispered incantation, they summon the forces of nature to ensure that the land remains vibrant and thriving.
The townspeople of Rowbridge hold the gnomes in high regard, recognising the invaluable role they play in maintaining the town's beauty and prosperity. The annual Harvest Festival is a grand celebration that honours the gnomes and their contributions. The village green transforms into a vibrant display of colour and sound, with stalls offering delicious treats, handcrafted goods, and magical curios. The gnomes, with their whimsical attire and cheerful demeanour, are the stars of the festival, their presence adding an extra layer of enchantment to the festivities.

During the festival, the Elder Oak stands as a silent witness to the celebrations. Its ancient branches sway gently in the breeze, casting dappled shadows on the festivities below. The gnomes dance with the villagers, their laughter and joy mingling with the music of fiddles and flutes. The celebration is a testament to the harmonious relationship that defines Rowbridge, a joyous reminder of the magic that thrives within the town.

"The roses are blooming beautifully this year," Thistle remarked, admiring the vibrant flowers. "The festival will be even more splendid with them in full bloom."

"Yes," Bramble agreed. "The roses are a testament to our dedication and care. They, like everything else in Rowbridge, reflect the harmony between us and the land."

"And the pumpkins," Thistle continued, "they're enormous this year. What's your secret?"

"A touch of enchantment and a lot of patience," Bramble replied with a smile. "Nature, much like us, needs time to flourish."

As the festival ended and the villagers returned to their homes, the enchantment of Rowbridge remained a testament to the gnomes' dedication and the magic that infused every aspect of their world. Their presence ensured that the town continued to thrive, a beacon of beauty and harmony in a world where nature and magic are intertwined.

"It's moments like these that remind us of the beauty in our work," Bramble said, as the last of the festival lights dimmed. "The joy we see in the villagers' faces is the true reward."

"And it's a reminder that our magic is not just about spells and enchantments," Thistle added. "It's about the connections we build and the love we share."

"Precisely," Bramble agreed. "Our work here is a testament to the harmony that exists between humanity and nature."

The gnomes of Rowbridge, with their unwavering dedication and magical touch, continue to nurture the land and inspire all who call this extraordinary town their home.

The Bigfoot of Totland

The Enigmatic Presence

Totland, a charming village tucked away on the Isle of Wight's western coast, is a tapestry of quaint cottages, scenic sea views, and historical treasures. The village sits snugly between the rugged cliffs of Tennyson Down and the serene expanses of Totland Bay. With its narrow lanes and ancient stone walls, Totland exudes an old-world charm that seems untouched by time. The prominent landmark, the old Totland Pier, stretches out into the glistening waters, often bathed in the golden hues of sunset.

Here, in this picturesque setting, resides Bigfoot, known locally as "The Totland Titan." This legendary creature's presence casts a long shadow over the village's lore. Towering at an impressive eight feet, Bigfoot's sheer size is awe-inspiring. His frame, cloaked in thick, shaggy fur that shifts in hue from earthy brown to mossy green, provides camouflage amidst the Isle's diverse landscapes. His broad shoulders and sturdy limbs are suited for long treks across the island, while his massive, hairy feet ensure he navigates uneven terrain with ease.

"The Titan is out there again," whispered Eliza, a local historian, to her friend as they walked by the pier. "You can tell by the fresh prints in the mud."

"I saw him by the cliffs last week," replied Tom, the local fisherman. "Huge footprints and the smell of wet fur. It's like he's part of the landscape."

The island's lore is rich with tales of Bigfoot's achievements. Many believe he has a mystical connection with the land, ensuring the balance of nature and the flourishing of Totland's gardens and forests. His mere presence is said to bring good fortune to the village, making him a revered figure in local folklore.

"The Titan is not just a legend; he's a part of our history," said Eliza. "He's the guardian of these lands, and his tales are interwoven with our own."

"Indeed," Tom agreed. "It's said that where Bigfoot roams, the land prospers. His presence is a blessing."

As to how Bigfoot came to reside in Totland, legends suggest that he was drawn to the Isle's ancient magic centuries ago. Some believe he wandered in from the mainland, lured by the Isle's enchantments and its promise of a haven where nature and myth coexist harmoniously. Over time, Totland became his sanctuary, and the village embraced the Titan as one of their own, a guardian of their secrets and a symbol of their connection with the land.

"Maybe he was here before we even arrived," mused Eliza. "Perhaps the Isle called to him, and he answered."

"Aye," Tom said, "and now he's a part of the fabric of this place. His story is as much a part of Totland as the pier or the cliffs."

Bigfoot's enigmatic presence is a constant reminder of the Isle of Wight's timeless magic, where the ordinary and the extraordinary blend seamlessly.

The Love for Adventure

Bigfoot's adventures are as legendary as his presence. Known for his boundless curiosity and love for exploration, he traverses the Isle of Wight's varied terrains with an enthusiasm that never wanes. From the dense forests of Parkhurst Forest to the rugged cliffs of Alum Bay, Bigfoot's wanderlust knows no bounds.

One of Bigfoot's most cherished companions is Pegasus, a celestial creature with wings that shimmer in shades of silver and gold. Pegasus, often referred to as "The Sky Chariot," possesses an effortless grace that complements Bigfoot's grounded strength. Together, they explore the island's hidden treasures, their adventures becoming the stuff of local legend.

"Ready for our next escapade, Bigfoot?" Pegasus called out one morning as the sun began to rise over the horizon.

"Absolutely," Bigfoot replied, adjusting his heavy metal t-shirt. "Where shall we journey today?"

"I've heard there's a secret cave near Freshwater Bay," Pegasus suggested, his eyes sparkling with excitement. "Shall we investigate?"

"Lead the way!" Bigfoot said, his enthusiasm palpable.

As they took to the skies, Pegasus carried Bigfoot effortlessly, their laughter ringing through the crisp morning air. The Isle of Wight unfurled below them—a patchwork of verdant meadows, ancient woodlands, and sparkling coastlines. The duo's aerial escapades often left locals and tourists alike gazing up in awe, struggling to capture a clear photograph of the elusive Bigfoot.

"Did you see their faces?" Bigfoot chuckled as Pegasus performed a series of loops and dives. "Priceless!"

"Oh, they'll be talking about this for ages," Pegasus said with a grin. "It's all part of the fun."

Their adventures were marked by moments of exhilaration and discovery. Whether it was finding a hidden waterfall in Shanklin Chine or exploring the mysterious tunnels beneath Carisbrooke Castle, Bigfoot and Pegasus approached each journey with a sense of wonder and excitement.

"There's something truly magical about uncovering hidden places," Bigfoot mused as they explored a secluded grotto. "It's like finding a piece of the Isle's soul."

"And it's those hidden treasures that make our adventures so memorable," Pegasus agreed. "They remind us of the magic that exists in every corner of this land."

Bigfoot's mischievous side often led him to playfully prank tourists, leaving them bewildered and laughing. The creature would blur photographs or leave cryptic messages, adding to his enigmatic allure.

"It's all in good fun," Bigfoot said with a chuckle. "Keeps things interesting."

"And it adds to our legend," Pegasus agreed. "People will remember us for years to come."

Their adventures also included moments of quiet reflection. Perched atop Tennyson Down or beside the serene waters of Compton Bay, Bigfoot and Pegasus would take time to appreciate the natural beauty surrounding them. These tranquil moments allowed them to connect with the land and reflect on the nature of their existence.

"Sometimes, I wonder if people will ever truly understand us," Bigfoot said one evening as they watched the sunset.

"Perhaps not," Pegasus replied. "But that's part of the magic. We're meant to be a part of the mystery."

As the stars began to twinkle in the night sky, Bigfoot and Pegasus continued their journey, their spirits high and their hearts full of the joy of discovery. Their adventures were a celebration of the Isle of Wight's beauty and magic, a reminder that even the most elusive of legends could bring joy and inspiration.

The Personal Touch

In the vibrant world of Totland, Bigfoot stands out not only for his legendary status but also for his unique personal style. His choice of attire—a combination of sturdy boots and heavy metal music-themed t-shirts—reflects his desire to connect with various communities on the Isle of Wight.

Bigfoot's boots, rugged and well-worn, are suited for the diverse terrains he traverses. Each pair seems to have its own story, with scuffs and scratches that hint at countless adventures. His heavy metal t-shirts, emblazoned with band logos and fantastical designs, add a touch of rebellion and fun to his otherwise mysterious persona. These shirts also serve as a way for Bigfoot to blend in with different groups, whether it's the local World of Warcraft fan community or the lively crowd at the local pub.

"Nice shirt!" exclaimed Jodie, a regular at the local pub, as Bigfoot walked in. "Where did you get that?"

"Oh, you know," Bigfoot replied with a grin, "just a little something I picked up during one of my travels."
"You're quite the legend around here," Jodie said, raising her glass. "The stories about you and Pegasus are all over town."
"I like to keep things interesting," Bigfoot said with a wink. "Keeps the adventure alive."
Pegasus, too, has developed its own set of preferences and quirks. After a day of high-flying adventures, Pegasus enjoys a hearty dinner of enchanted hay and golden apples. These delicacies are not only nutritious but also keep Pegasus's wings strong and its coat shimmering. For entertainment, Pegasus has a fondness for classic movies and TV shows, particularly epic fantasies and heroic quests.
"After all that flying, I could really use a good meal," Pegasus said as they settled down in a tranquil meadow.
"Let's head to the enchanted glade," Bigfoot suggested, "and grab some golden apples. They're a perfect way to unwind."
"Sounds delightful," Pegasus agreed, its wings rustling with anticipation. "And maybe we can catch up on our favourite shows later."
Pegasus's taste in entertainment reflects its adventurous spirit. Inspired by epic tales and heroic quests, Pegasus finds motivation in the stories of courage and adventure depicted in movies and TV shows. These inspirations often fuel its flights and daring escapades with Bigfoot.
"You know," Pegasus said as they enjoyed their meal, "I've always loved those old adventure movies. They remind me of the thrill of exploration."
"I can see that," Bigfoot said with a nod. "And it's that sense of adventure that makes our journeys so exciting."
"Exactly," Pegasus said with a smile. "It's the stories we create that add to the magic of our adventures."

The bond between Bigfoot and Pegasus is one of mutual admiration and respect. Their shared interests and experiences have created a deep friendship that transcends their respective mythologies. Together, they embrace the quirks of modern life while remaining true to their legendary status.

"Sometimes, I wonder what people would say if they knew the real us," Bigfoot said with a chuckle.

"I think they'd be amazed," Pegasus replied. "But maybe that's the magic of it. We're meant to be a part of the mystery."

As the evening drew to a close, Bigfoot and Pegasus settled down for a night of relaxation, their spirits high and their hearts full of the joy of discovery. Their personal touches and quirks only added to the enchantment of their lives, making their adventures all the more memorable.

The Thunderbird of Blackgang

The Majestic Guardian

Blackgang, a small yet enchanting town on the Isle of Wight, nestles between the dramatic cliffs of the south coast and the undulating fields of the countryside. Known for its rugged beauty and panoramic sea views, Blackgang is dominated by the awe-inspiring Blackgang Chine, a natural wonder that cuts through the landscape like a serpent. This steep ravine, with its verdant foliage and ancient trees, is as much a part of the town's character as the towering cliffs and the sprawling beach below.

In this atmospheric setting resides the Thunderbird, a creature of formidable legend and unrivalled majesty. Towering above the landscape, the Thunderbird's immense wingspan reaches out across the sky, its feathers shimmering in hues of indigo and silver that mirror the tempestuous clouds it commands. Its presence is as much a part of Blackgang's identity as the cliffs and the chine, embodying the town's resilience and connection to the elemental forces of nature.

"They say when the Thunderbird flies, the whole sky lights up," murmured Old Mrs. Baker as she watched from her cottage window.

"Aye," replied young Timothy, peering up at the darkening sky. "And when he roars, the thunder's not far behind."

The Thunderbird's body is a masterpiece of strength and vitality. Muscular and robust, it exudes an aura of untamed power, its sharp eyes reflecting the intensity of the storms it wields. Its beak, with its metallic sheen, hints at its connection to the raw forces of nature, making it both a guardian and a formidable force.

"You know, they reckon his feathers are infused with the power of lightning," Timothy said, adjusting his coat against the chill.

"I've heard that too," Mrs. Baker replied, "and that's why the storms are so fierce when he's around. But it's not just about power; it's about protection."

The Thunderbird's arrival in Blackgang is shrouded in myth and reverence. Legends tell of its journey from far-off lands, drawn to the Isle of Wight by the same elemental forces that shaped its destiny. Seeking refuge amidst the rugged beauty of Blackgang, the Thunderbird became a guardian deity, watching over the town and its people with a benevolent yet imposing presence.

"They say the Thunderbird came to Blackgang long ago, seeking sanctuary from ancient rivals," Mrs. Baker reminisced. "And ever since, it has watched over us, bringing both storms and safety."

"It's true," Timothy agreed. "We're lucky to have him. He's our protector, even if his storms can be a bit frightening at times."

The Thunderbird's role as a guardian is deeply embedded in Blackgang's culture. Its ability to summon thunderstorms and command the elements is seen as both a blessing and a reminder of the powerful forces that shape their world. The town's inhabitants look to the Thunderbird with a mixture of awe and gratitude, recognising its role in their lives and the intricate balance it maintains.

"Every storm brings something new," Mrs. Baker said with a smile. "A reminder that the Thunderbird is always with us, keeping watch."

"Indeed," Timothy said. "And it's that watchful presence that makes Blackgang such a special place."

As the sun set over Blackgang, casting long shadows across the chine and the cliffs, the Thunderbird's silhouette became a majestic backdrop to the town's evening rituals. Its presence was a constant reminder of the elemental forces at play, shaping the lives and landscapes of Blackgang with every beat of its powerful wings.

The Protector of Blackgang

Blackgang's rugged landscape, with its steep cliffs and lush valleys, is a testament to the forces of nature that shape the Isle of Wight. Here, the Thunderbird reigns supreme, its colossal wings casting shadows over the town as it soars through the skies. The Thunderbird's role as a guardian is central to the town's identity, symbolising both protection and the formidable power of the natural world.

Every storm that sweeps across Blackgang is a spectacle of lightning and thunder, orchestrated by the Thunderbird's mighty presence. With a single beat of its wings, it can summon thunderstorms that roll across the horizon, electrifying the sky with a dazzling display of nature's fury. Yet, despite its fearsome power, the Thunderbird's true nature is one of guardianship and protection.

"The storms are fierce, but they're never aimless," said Eliza, the town's weathered librarian. "The Thunderbird guides them, keeping us safe."

"It's as if he's in control of the chaos," replied Jonathan, a local fisherman. "Without him, these storms could be far worse."

The Thunderbird's storms are a double-edged sword. While they can be intense and awe-inspiring, they also serve to shield Blackgang from greater threats. Its ability to command the elements ensures that the town is safeguarded from natural disasters, reinforcing the bond between the Thunderbird and its human charges.

"There's a balance to his power," Eliza continued. "He brings the storms, but he also protects us from the worst of them."

"It's like he's a part of the very land," Jonathan said, nodding in agreement. "And in return, we respect him and his storms."

The Thunderbird's relationship with Blackgang is one of mutual respect and understanding. The town's inhabitants recognise the necessity of the storms and the balance they maintain. The Thunderbird's presence is a reminder of the town's resilience and its connection to the elemental forces that shape their world.

"The storms are a part of life here," Eliza said. "And the Thunderbird is a part of that life, guiding us through the tempests."

"It's a powerful symbol of our strength," Jonathan agreed. "And a reminder that we're never truly alone."

As the Thunderbird soared above Blackgang, its powerful wings cutting through the clouds, the town below carried on with its daily life. The storms it summoned were a testament to its guardianship, a display of both power and protection that defined the town's existence.

"We owe much to the Thunderbird," Eliza reflected. "It's more than a legend; it's a guardian."

"And as long as we remember that," Jonathan added, "we'll always be safe beneath his watchful gaze."

The Thunderbird's presence was a constant reassurance to the people of Blackgang, a symbol of their enduring strength and the elemental forces that shape their world. Its storms, while fearsome, were a testament to its guardianship, a reminder that even in the face of nature's fury, they were never alone.

The Feud with the Jersey Devil

While the Thunderbird's guardianship of Blackgang is celebrated, it is not without its share of conflicts. The most notorious of these is the long-standing feud with the Jersey Devil, a mythical creature residing in the neighbouring village of Chale. This rivalry, often the subject of local gossip and legends, stems from a seemingly mundane issue: a wheely bin dispute.

"Did you hear about the latest spat between the Thunderbird and the Jersey Devil?" asked Mrs. Elkins, the town gossip, as she sipped her tea.

"Oh, not again," replied Mr. Thompson, rolling his eyes. "What's it this time?"

"The Jersey Devil's been caught putting rubbish in the Thunderbird's wheely bin," Mrs. Elkins said with a smirk. "It's caused quite a stir."

The origins of the dispute are shrouded in myth, but it is said that the Jersey Devil, known for its mischievous nature, repeatedly placed its rubbish in the Thunderbird's bin, much to the latter's annoyance. This small act of neighbourly discord has escalated into a full-blown feud, with both creatures engaging in a series of petty retaliations.

"It's all rather silly, really," said Mr. Thompson with a chuckle. "But it's become quite the legend."

"And it's not just a local tale," Mrs. Elkins added. "The Jersey Devil's side of the story is just as entertaining."

The feud between the Thunderbird and the Jersey Devil has become a popular topic of conversation in Blackgang. Stories of their confrontations, from lightning storms to prank-filled encounters, have become part of the town's folklore.

"Last week, the Jersey Devil supposedly enchanted the Thunderbird's bin to make it overflow," Mrs. Elkins said. "And the Thunderbird responded by summoning a thunderstorm right over Chale."

"It's like a magical game of one-upmanship," Mr. Thompson agreed. "And the whole town is watching with amusement."

Despite the rivalry, there is a sense of camaraderie between the two creatures. Their interactions, though contentious, are a reminder of the playful side of their mythical natures. The feud has become a part of their legends, adding a touch of humour and humanity to their otherwise grand and awe-inspiring existences.

"Perhaps it's just their way of keeping things interesting," Mr. Thompson mused. "Even mythical creatures need a bit of excitement."

"And it makes for great stories," Mrs. Elkins said with a grin. "The kind that keep us entertained for years."

As the Thunderbird and the Jersey Devil continued their playful feud, the people of Blackgang and Chale watched with amusement and curiosity. Their rivalry, while sometimes disruptive, was a reminder of the lively and unpredictable nature of mythical beings.

"In the end, it's all about the stories we tell," Mrs. Elkins said. "And the Thunderbird and the Jersey Devil certainly give us plenty to talk about."

"Indeed," Mr. Thompson agreed. "Their antics make our lives a little more magical."

The Storm Bringer

Blackgang, with its dramatic cliffs and sweeping sea views, is a town shaped by the elements. Here, the Thunderbird reigns supreme, its majestic wings spanning the sky as it commands the storms that roll across the horizon. Its presence is both a blessing and a reminder of the raw power of nature.

"The Thunderbird's storms are something to behold," said Mr. Barnett, the local historian. "They're a testament to his control over the elements."

"Indeed," agreed Miss Harper, the town's schoolteacher. "But they also remind us of the delicate balance of nature."

With a single beat of its colossal wings, the Thunderbird can summon thunderstorms that electrify the sky and bring both awe and fear to the inhabitants of Blackgang. Lightning bolts crackle through the darkened clouds, illuminating the town below with a dazzling display of nature's fury.

"Every storm is a reminder of his power," Mr. Barnett continued. "But also of his protection."

"The storms can be fierce, but they're never destructive," Miss Harper added. "The Thunderbird guides them, ensuring that they don't cause too much harm."

The Thunderbird's storms are a part of Blackgang's identity, a symbol of its resilience and connection to the elemental forces that shape their world. The town's inhabitants look to the Thunderbird with a mixture of awe and gratitude, recognising the role it plays in their lives.

"We've learned to respect the storms," said Mrs. Taylor, the town's baker. "And to appreciate the Thunderbird's role in guiding them."

"He's our guardian," Mr. Barnett agreed. "And his storms, while powerful, are a testament to his protection."

As the Thunderbird soared above Blackgang, its powerful wings cutting through the clouds, the town below continued with its daily life. The storms it summoned were a reminder of its guardianship, a display of both power and protection that defined the town's existence.

"We owe much to the Thunderbird," Miss Harper reflected. "It's more than a legend; it's a part of who we are."

"And as long as we remember that," Mrs. Taylor added, "we'll always be safe beneath his watchful gaze."

The Thunderbird's presence was a constant reassurance to the people of Blackgang, a symbol of their enduring strength and the elemental forces that shape their world. Its storms, while fearsome, were a testament to its guardianship, a reminder that even in the face of nature's fury, they were never alone.

The Irony of Resolution

Amid the Thunderbird's grand existence and its role as Blackgang's guardian, a small yet persistent issue loomed: the wheely bin dispute with the Jersey Devil. This seemingly trivial conflict, rooted in the Jersey Devil's habit of placing rubbish in the Thunderbird's bin, had become a source of both annoyance and humour for the mythical beings.

"It's rather ironic, isn't it?" mused Mrs. Elkins, the town gossip. "The Thunderbird's epic storms and mighty presence, all overshadowed by a wheely bin feud."

"Indeed," Mr. Thompson agreed with a chuckle. "It's quite the tale."

Driven by a desire to resolve the issue, the Thunderbird took to the skies, venturing beyond Blackgang in search of a solution. Its massive wings carried it to Atherfield, a village known for its peaceful setting and slightly less tumultuous atmosphere.

"The Thunderbird's in Atherfield now," said Mr. Barnett. "Apparently, he's trying to find a new place for his rubbish."

"I suppose even legendary creatures need a bit of peace and quiet," Miss Harper said with a smile. "And Atherfield seems like a good place for it."

In an ironic twist of fate, the Thunderbird's quest to resolve the wheely bin dispute led him into a series of humorous and somewhat chaotic encounters in Atherfield. As it sought to dispose of its rubbish in a new bin, the Thunderbird found itself entangled in a series of mishaps, adding a touch of comedy to the ongoing saga.

"I hear he's made quite a mess in Atherfield," Mrs. Elkins said with a grin. "Not exactly the peaceful resolution he was hoping for."

"Well, it's certainly added some excitement to the village," Mr. Thompson agreed. "And made for some entertaining stories."

Despite the humorous twists and turns of the Thunderbird's adventure, the underlying message of resilience and adaptation remained clear. The Thunderbird's attempts to resolve the dispute, though fraught with irony, were a testament to its determination and resourcefulness.

"It's a reminder that even the most powerful beings have their challenges," Miss Harper said thoughtfully. "And that sometimes, the best solutions come from unexpected places."

"And that even in the midst of disputes," Mr. Barnett added, "there's always room for a bit of humour and humanity."

As the Thunderbird's adventure continued, the people of Blackgang and Atherfield watched with amusement and curiosity. The legendary creature's quest for resolution, while fraught with irony and mishaps, was a testament to its enduring spirit and the unpredictable nature of mythical beings.

"In the end," Mrs. Elkins reflected, "it's all about the stories we tell."

"And the Thunderbird's tale," Mr. Thompson agreed, "is one that will be told for years to come."

Lessons of Resilience

The tale of the Thunderbird and its wheely bin dispute serves as a powerful reminder of the resilience and adaptability that characterise the mythical beings and the communities they protect. Despite the challenges and conflicts that arise, there is always a path to harmony and understanding.

"The Thunderbird's story is one of perseverance," said Miss Harper, the town's schoolteacher. "It's a reminder that even the most powerful beings face challenges."

"And that those challenges can lead to unexpected solutions," Mr. Barnett added. "The Thunderbird's adventure in Atherfield is a testament to that."

The ongoing feud with the Jersey Devil, while a source of both annoyance and amusement, has become a part of the Thunderbird's legend. The whimsical nature of their rivalry, coupled with the Thunderbird's attempts to resolve the issue, highlights the complexities of relationships, even among mythical creatures.

"It's a reminder that even legends have their quirks," Mrs. Elkins said with a chuckle. "And that their stories are what make them memorable."

"Indeed," Mr. Thompson agreed. "And it's the stories that connect us to the magic of their world."

Through its trials and triumphs, the Thunderbird's presence continues to be a symbol of strength and resilience for the people of Blackgang and Chale. The lessons learned from its adventures serve as a reminder of the importance of understanding and coexistence, even in the face of conflicts.

"The Thunderbird's story teaches us that even in disputes," Miss Harper said, "there's always a chance for resolution and growth."

"And that the spirit of our communities," Mr. Barnett added, "is reflected in the legends we cherish."

As the Thunderbird returned to Blackgang, its majestic presence was a beacon of hope and inspiration. The storms it commanded and the adventures it embarked upon were a testament to its enduring spirit and the powerful bond between mythical beings and the communities they protect.

"The Thunderbird's journey," Mrs. Elkins said thoughtfully, "is a reflection of the strength and resilience of Blackgang."

"And of the magic that lives within us all," Mr. Thompson agreed with a smile. "It's a reminder that even in the face of challenges, there's always a way forward."

With the Thunderbird's story continuing to unfold, the people of Blackgang and Chale embraced the lessons of resilience and understanding, finding inspiration in the mythical creature's adventures and the enduring spirit of their communities.

The Elven of Brook

The Hidden Village of Brook

The village of Brook, nestled within the Isle of Wight's wooded heart, is a place where the veil between the mundane and the mystical is thin. Surrounded by the verdant expanse of the New Forest National Park, Brook seems almost to be a forgotten corner of a fairy tale. The village is concealed beneath a dense canopy of oak and beech trees, their ancient branches interwoven to create a natural tapestry of green that shifts with the seasons.

The Elven of Brook live in harmony with this lush environment. Their dwellings are crafted from local timber and stone, blending seamlessly with the landscape. Each house is adorned with intricate carvings that tell the stories of the Elven's ancestors and their deep connection to the land. The homes are set around a central clearing where the Grand Oak stands, its gnarled trunk and sprawling limbs forming a majestic focal point for the village.

This ancient tree is more than just a landmark; it is the heart of Brook's spiritual and ecological life. Beneath its sprawling canopy, the Elven conduct rituals that ensure the health of their environment. The surrounding woods are alive with the rustle of leaves and the chirping of hidden creatures, and the air is tinged with the subtle aroma of wildflowers and moss. Streams meander through the village, their clear waters sparkling as they catch the dappled sunlight filtering through the trees.

Visitors to Brook, who are few and far between, speak in hushed tones of its ethereal beauty. The village is accessible only by a winding path that leads through the forest, a path that seems to shift and change as if to protect the village from unwanted eyes. The occasional traveller who stumbles upon it is often awestruck by its serene atmosphere and the sense of ancient magic that pervades the air.

Guardians of Nature

The Elven of Brook are revered as the stewards of their lush domain, their existence deeply intertwined with the natural world. They possess a profound knowledge of the forest's flora and fauna, enabling them to maintain the delicate balance between human activity and nature. This balance is crucial in an area where human encroachment has historically threatened the environment.

The village itself is a haven for rare species of plants and animals, some of which are found nowhere else on the Isle of Wight. The Elven are skilled in nurturing these species, ensuring that their habitat remains undisturbed. They perform rituals at the Grand Oak to appease the spirits of the forest, seeking their blessings for a bountiful harvest and a harmonious existence.

The villagers frequently seek the Elven's counsel. The townspeople, while aware of the mystical nature of their neighbours, view them as guardians and advisors. Local farmers consult the Elven on the best times to plant and harvest, while those dealing with ailments seek their wisdom on herbal remedies. The Elven's reputation for wisdom and their deep connection to the natural world make them respected figures in the community.

One of the Elven, Thalion, often seen patrolling the edges of the forest, comments on the changing seasons. "The balance of nature is ever-shifting," he muses, "and we must adapt with it. The forest speaks to us, telling us when it needs our aid."

Their guardianship extends to the surrounding landmarks as well. The village's proximity to the historic site of Carisbrooke Castle, just a short distance to the north, adds a layer of historical intrigue. The castle, with its medieval stone walls and ancient moat, serves as a reminder of the Isle's rich history and the enduring spirit of its inhabitants.

Elysia and the Peculiar Aqrabualmelu

Elysia, one of the Elven's most prominent figures, is known for her grace and wisdom. Yet, she harbours an unusual discomfort towards the Aqrabualmelu, a peculiar creature from the neighbouring village of Chale. The Aqrabualmelu, with its obsession for stamp collections and empty water bottles, is a figure of local legend. It's said to have an encyclopaedic knowledge of postage stamps and a penchant for eccentric conversations about recycling.

Elysia's encounters with the Aqrabualmelu are often marked by a mix of bemusement and irritation. During one such meeting in Brook's central clearing, the Aqrabualmelu excitedly displays a new addition to its collection — a rare stamp featuring an image of the Needles, the iconic chalk formations on the Isle of Wight's southwestern coast.

"Did you know," the Aqrabualmelu begins, its voice bubbling with enthusiasm, "that this stamp was printed in a limited edition to commemorate the Needles' 150th anniversary?" Elysia, trying to maintain her composure, responds with a polite but strained smile. "That's very interesting, but I must attend to the needs of the Grand Oak. Perhaps another time?"

Despite her discomfort, Elysia respects the Aqrabualmelu's place in the broader tapestry of the Isle's folklore. The creature's peculiarities provide a contrast to the Elven's serene and purposeful existence, and their interactions add a layer of depth to Brook's mystical narrative.

The Elven's Extreme Sports Passion

The Elven of Brook are not merely keepers of ancient lore and nature's balance; they are also pioneers of extreme sports. Their passion for base jumping is well-known, with the cliffs of Shalcombe serving as their playground. The dramatic cliffs, which overlook the azure expanse of the English Channel, provide the perfect backdrop for their daring feats.

Adorned in their elegant yet functional attire, the Elven leap from the cliffs with a combination of grace and precision. Their jumps are executed with a finesse that mirrors their connection to the natural world, blending their physical prowess with their mystical heritage. The sheer thrill of soaring through the air, with the wind rushing past them, is a testament to their adventurous spirit.

During one notable event, a group of Elven performs a synchronized jump, their figures cutting through the sky like shadows. The sight is both exhilarating and serene, a dance of light and movement against the backdrop of the setting sun. The exhilaration of their jumps is a celebration of their physical capabilities and a testament to their unique approach to life.

The nearby Alum Bay, known for its multicoloured sands, is a popular spot for the Elven to enjoy their post-jump picnics. The colourful cliffs and the shimmering sands add to the picturesque quality of their extreme sports experiences.

The Balance of Duty and Adventure

The Elven's dedication to their duties as guardians of Brook is matched by their passion for adventure. Their extreme sports pursuits are not just about thrill but are intertwined with their role as protectors of the land. They ensure that their adventures do not come at the expense of their responsibilities, balancing their love for adrenaline with their commitment to preserving the natural beauty of their surroundings.

Elysia reflects on this balance during a quiet moment by the Grand Oak. "Our adventures," she muses, "are a celebration of life's vitality. Yet, we must never forget that our role as guardians is paramount. The harmony we seek in nature must be mirrored in our own lives."

The Elven's ability to maintain this balance is reflected in their careful stewardship of Brook. Their extreme sports activities are always planned with consideration for their impact on the environment, ensuring that their love for adventure does not disrupt the delicate equilibrium they strive to protect.

Elysia's Solitude

Elysia often retreats to the solitude of the forest to escape the occasional discomfort caused by the Aqrabualmelu's presence. The forest, with its whispering trees and tranquil streams, offers her a refuge where she can reconnect with the essence of her role as a guardian.

Her favourite spot is a secluded glen, where the forest's beauty is at its most untouched. Here, Elysia sits by a gentle stream, her thoughts flowing like the water beside her. The sounds of the forest — birds singing, leaves rustling — provide a soothing backdrop to her reflections.

During these moments of solitude, Elysia finds strength and clarity, allowing her to return to her duties with renewed purpose. The forest's tranquillity reinforces her resolve, reminding her of the deep connection between her role as a guardian and her personal well-being.

The Elven's Eternal Wisdom

The Elven of Brook are celebrated not only for their physical grace but for their profound wisdom. Their deep understanding of nature and their ability to maintain harmony between the village and the surrounding environment are legendary. They share their knowledge with the townspeople, offering guidance on spiritual and ecological matters.

Their teachings are deeply rooted in the ancient lore of the Isle of Wight. The Elven's knowledge of the land, its history, and its natural rhythms forms the basis of their guidance. The village's connection to landmarks such as the historic Osborne House, the former royal residence, adds a layer of historical richness to their teachings.

One elder Elven, Amara, shares her insights with the villagers. "True wisdom," she says, "is not merely knowing the land but understanding how to live in harmony with it. Our knowledge is a gift, meant to guide us towards a balanced and fulfilling existence."

The Enchantment of Brook

Brook's enchantment lies in its seamless blend of the mystical and the mundane. The village's landscape, with its ancient trees, flowing streams, and serene atmosphere, creates a sense of wonder that captivates both residents and visitors.

The Elven's presence adds to the village's magical allure. Their ethereal beauty and wisdom infuse Brook with a sense of timeless wonder. The village's connection to the nearby Tennyson Down, a popular spot for its panoramic views and historic significance, further enhances its enchanting quality. Visitors often speak of the village's serene beauty and the sense of ancient magic that pervades the air. Brook, with its blend of natural beauty and mystical charm, remains a hidden gem on the Isle of Wight, cherished by those who are fortunate enough to experience its unique allure.

Guardians of the Land

The Elven of Brook continue to protect and nurture their land with unwavering dedication. Their influence is felt in the vibrant blooms and the thriving ecosystem that surrounds the village. Through their rituals and care, they ensure that the land remains bountiful and harmonious.
The Elven's guardianship extends to the historic landmarks of the Isle of Wight, including the iconic St. Catherine's Lighthouse. The lighthouse, perched on a rugged cliff, serves as a symbol of guidance and protection, much like the Elven's role in their own domain.
The Elven's gentle touch and their whispered incantations bring forth the blooms that sustain the community. Their presence ensures that the natural world remains in balance, and their influence is a testament to the enduring power of nature.

The legacy of the Elven of Brook is one of timeless harmony and deep connection with nature. Their ability to blend their mystical heritage with their passion for adventure sets them apart as unique guardians of their realm. Brook, with its magical beauty and serene existence, stands as a testament to their enduring influence.

Through their adventures and their dedication to preserving the natural world, the Elven inspire a sense of wonder and reverence. Brook remains a haven of tranquillity and enchantment, forever guided by the wisdom of its ethereal guardians. The village's legacy continues to thrive, a beacon of harmony and beauty amidst the ever-changing landscape of the Isle of Wight.

The Chillerton Bogeyman

A Grotesque Presence in Chillerton

In the quaint village of Chillerton, located on the Isle of Wight's southern coast, folklore and reality intertwine seamlessly. Chillerton, with its picturesque charm, is renowned for its cobbled streets, historic cottages, and the majestic Old Church of St. Mary's. This church, dating back to the Norman period, features centuries-old gravestones and a striking bell tower that chimes through the tranquil air. The village is nestled amidst rolling hills and serene woodlands, which form a striking contrast against the foreboding figure of the Bogeyman.

The Bogeyman, a creature deeply rooted in the village's lore, is an imposing and grotesque presence. Towering over most beings, its hulking frame and twisted face, with jagged teeth and sunken eyes, instil a sense of dread. Its thick, matted hair cascades around broad shoulders, creating a shadowy silhouette against the village's picturesque backdrop. Local tales suggest that the Bogeyman emerged from the dense woodlands surrounding Chillerton Common, a place shrouded in mist and mystery.

The villagers, living in a constant state of unease, have woven countless tales about the Bogeyman's origins. In the evenings, the local tavern, The White Lion, becomes the epicentre of these whispered legends. Patrons, gathered around the crackling hearth, recount their chilling encounters with the Bogeyman. The tavern's walls are adorned with old photographs and memorabilia, adding to the atmospheric setting where stories of the Bogeyman are told with a mix of fear and fascination.

The Chillerton Common, with its ancient trees and winding paths, provides a hauntingly beautiful setting that enhances the Bogeyman's reputation. The dense canopy of trees filters the sunlight, casting eerie shadows on the forest floor. It's here, amidst the gnarled branches and thick undergrowth, that the Bogeyman is said to roam, its presence marked by the occasional rustle of leaves and the distant echo of its fearsome growl.

Beneath the Fearsome Exterior

Despite its fearsome exterior, the Bogeyman's actions reveal a surprising kindness. A notable incident occurred in Brighstone, a neighbouring village known for its charming streets and the historic Brighstone Down. The Down, a picturesque landscape with sweeping views of the Isle of Wight's rugged coastline, is a popular spot for hikers and nature enthusiasts. On a bustling market day, the Bogeyman's intervention showcased a different side of its nature.

An elderly lady, known for her resilience and warmth, struggled to cross the busy road near Brighstone's market. The Bogeyman, observing from the shadows, came to her aid with a surprising act of heroism. As it helped her navigate the busy thoroughfare, the scene quickly descended into chaos. A car swerved to avoid the Bogeyman, causing a minor accident that left the villagers in a state of alarm.

Despite the pandemonium, the elderly lady, although initially shocked, later spoke of the Bogeyman's bravery. "I never imagined such a terrifying figure could have the heart to help me," she remarked. "It was an act of unexpected kindness wrapped in a fearsome guise."

The incident, while unsettling, revealed the Bogeyman's inherent nobility. It showcased a creature capable of profound acts of kindness despite its intimidating appearance. The tale spread through Brighstone and beyond, adding complexity to the Bogeyman's character and sparking conversations about the true nature of fear and heroism.

Artistic Expression and Mindfulness

In its quest for acceptance, the Bogeyman established an artistic initiative in Limerstone, a nearby village celebrated for its serene environment and the historic Limerstone Manor. Limerstone Manor, with its elegant architecture and expansive gardens, provided the ideal setting for the Bogeyman's creative endeavour. The village, known for its tranquillity and community spirit, became a canvas for the Bogeyman's artistic vision.

The project aimed to foster creativity and mindfulness among the villagers, offering a sanctuary for artistic expression. The Bogeyman's initiative, though met with initial scepticism, soon gained traction. Villagers, drawn by curiosity and the promise of creative exploration, flocked to Limerstone Manor. The manor's gardens, with their meticulously manicured lawns and serene ponds, became a haven for painting, sculpting, and introspection.

The Bogeyman, in its rare moments of vulnerability, joined the villagers in their artistic pursuits. Its paintings, though haunting, conveyed a depth of emotion that contrasted sharply with its fearsome exterior. One particular piece, depicting the Isle of Wight's rugged coastline under a stormy sky, captivated the community and sparked discussions about beauty and expression.

The success of the project transformed Limerstone into a vibrant hub of creativity. The Bogeyman's artistic contributions, coupled with its growing acceptance, showcased a different facet of its character. Through art, the creature found a way to connect with the community and express emotions long buried beneath its intimidating façade.

The Battle of the Bins

Despite its efforts to integrate into the community, the Bogeyman faced an ongoing nuisance from the Chale Green Jersey Devil. The Jersey Devil, notorious for its mischief and pranks, took particular pleasure in tormenting the Bogeyman. The rivalry, marked by a series of comical yet vexing encounters, became a recurring theme in Chillerton.
The Jersey Devil's antics, including the notorious "battle of the bins," involved filling the Bogeyman's wheely bin with an assortment of oddities. The feud between the two creatures, though playful, added a layer of complexity to the Bogeyman's existence. Chillerton's residents, amused by the ongoing rivalry, followed the antics with a mix of amusement and exasperation.
One memorable clash occurred when the Bogeyman discovered the Jersey Devil hiding behind a hedge, gleefully emptying the bin onto the lawn. The Bogeyman, exasperated yet resigned, approached the mischievous creature.
"If you're seeking a new hobby," the Bogeyman rumbled, "I hear painting can be quite rewarding."
The Jersey Devil, caught off guard, looked at the Bogeyman with a mix of curiosity and suspicion. "Painting? What's that got to do with bins?"
"Sometimes it's not about the mess," the Bogeyman replied with a wry smile, "but about finding meaning in unexpected places."

The encounter ended with an uneasy truce, as the Jersey Devil begrudgingly agreed to a temporary ceasefire. The rivalry, while ongoing, took on a new dimension, highlighting the complexity of the Bogeyman's interactions with the community.

A Moment of Artistic Revelation

Amidst the ongoing struggles with the Jersey Devil and the evolving dynamics within the community, the Bogeyman experienced a profound moment of artistic revelation. In the heart of Limerstone, surrounded by the buzz of creativity and the serene backdrop of Limerstone Manor, the Bogeyman delved into its art with renewed passion.

One crisp autumn morning, as the leaves turned golden and the air grew cool, the Bogeyman began to paint a scene of the Isle of Wight's rugged coastline. The painting, depicting the dramatic cliffs and turbulent waves, became a form of meditation for the creature. Through the act of creation, the Bogeyman channelled its complex emotions into a tangible form.

The resulting artwork, displayed prominently in Limerstone's village hall, captured the community's attention. The piece, both haunting and beautiful, resonated with viewers, sparking conversations about the nature of art and the power of expression. The painting's depiction of the island's natural beauty contrasted sharply with the Bogeyman's fearsome reputation, offering a glimpse into its inner world.

The community's response was one of admiration and empathy. The Bogeyman, once a figure of fear, was now seen in a new light. The artistic project, with its emphasis on creativity and mindfulness, became a symbol of transformation and acceptance, bridging the gap between the Bogeyman and the villagers.

An Unlikely Friendship

As the Bogeyman continued its journey of self-discovery and artistic expression, it found an unexpected ally in the elderly lady it had once helped in Brighstone. Initially fearful of the Bogeyman, the lady had come to recognise the creature's kindness and artistic talent. Her support played a crucial role in bridging the gap between the Bogeyman and the community.

The elderly lady, known for her wisdom and compassion, became a vocal advocate for the Bogeyman's artistic project. Her efforts helped to organise exhibitions and events, bringing together the community to celebrate the Bogeyman's achievements. Her friendship provided the Bogeyman with a sense of belonging and acceptance that it had long yearned for.

Standing together in front of the Bogeyman's latest painting, the elderly lady remarked, "I never imagined that beneath such a fearsome exterior lay such a compassionate soul. You've shown us that there's more to every story, including yours."

The Bogeyman, touched by her words, replied with a soft, grateful smile. "It's not just about the art. It's about finding a place where I can be understood and accepted."

The bond between the Bogeyman and the elderly lady became a cornerstone of the creature's journey, symbolising the power of understanding and acceptance in overcoming prejudice and fear.

The Jersey Devil's Change of Heart

The ongoing battle of bins with the Jersey Devil took an unexpected turn when the mischievous creature witnessed the Bogeyman's artistic achievements. Intrigued by the Bogeyman's transformation and the community's acceptance, the Jersey Devil began to reconsider its own behaviour.

One evening, as the Jersey Devil watched the Bogeyman at work in Limerstone Manor's garden, it saw the creature's dedication and passion for art. The sight of the Bogeyman, fully immersed in its craft, sparked something within the Jersey Devil. The creature, known for its mischievous ways, began to question its actions and their impact on the community.

"Why do you put so much effort into this?" the Jersey Devil asked, its tone tinged with genuine curiosity.

The Bogeyman, pausing to reflect, replied, "Art is a way of expressing what's within us. It's a means of connecting with others and finding peace."

The Jersey Devil, intrigued by the Bogeyman's response, began to explore its own creative side. The once mischievous creature took up painting and sculpting, finding a new outlet for its energy and creativity. The change in the Jersey Devil's behaviour led to a gradual truce between the two adversaries. The newfound friendship between the Bogeyman and the Jersey Devil symbolised a shift in the community's dynamics. The two creatures, once at odds, now collaborated on artistic projects, creating a unique blend of creativity and mischief that enriched Chillerton's cultural landscape.

Embracing the Enigma

The Bogeyman's presence in Chillerton continued to be a source of fascination and intrigue. The creature's fearsome appearance, coupled with its acts of kindness and artistic expression, created a complex and captivating narrative that resonated with the villagers.

The community, once wary of the Bogeyman, learned to appreciate its multifaceted nature. The creature's journey from fear to acceptance, coupled with its artistic achievements and evolving friendships, became a powerful testament to the beauty of embracing one's true self.

Chillerton, with its picturesque landscapes and rich history, provided the perfect backdrop for the Bogeyman's story. The village's landmarks, from the Old Church of St. Mary's to the serene Chillerton Common, served as a canvas for the Bogeyman's journey of self-discovery and transformation.

The Bogeyman, with its blend of fear and kindness, became a symbol of resilience and acceptance. Its presence, both enigmatic and inspiring, continued to captivate the imaginations of the villagers, leaving a lasting impact on the community and its cultural identity.

A Legacy of Transformation

As time passed, the Bogeyman's legacy in Chillerton grew, leaving an indelible mark on the village's cultural identity. The artistic project established in Limerstone flourished, becoming a cornerstone of the community's creative spirit. The Bogeyman's journey of self-discovery and acceptance inspired others to look beyond appearances and embrace their own complexities.

The village, once defined by its fear of the Bogeyman, now celebrated the creature's transformation. The artistic project, with its emphasis on creativity and mindfulness, became a symbol of the community's resilience and openness. The Bogeyman's story, intertwined with the village's history, stood as a testament to the power of transformation and the impact of embracing one's true nature.

Chillerton, with its blend of historical landmarks and picturesque beauty, became a living canvas for the Bogeyman's legacy. The village's landscapes, from the rolling hills to the serene woodlands, provided a backdrop for the creature's journey—a journey that highlighted the transformative power of acceptance and artistic expression.

In the end, the Bogeyman remained an enigmatic figure in Chillerton, a guardian of the village's lore and a symbol of the power of acceptance and artistic expression. Its presence, both fearsome and kind, continued to weave through the imaginations of the townsfolk, inspiring both awe and reflection.

The Chillerton Bogeyman, with its rich tapestry of fear, kindness, and artistic brilliance, found its place in the village's history. Its story became a legend—a reminder of the complexities within every being and the capacity for change and growth. The Bogeyman's legacy, forever etched into the fabric of Chillerton, served as a beacon of hope and inspiration for generations to come.

The village, with its historical landmarks and vibrant community spirit, stood as a testament to the Bogeyman's enduring impact. The creature's story, woven into the tapestry of Chillerton's history, continued to inspire and captivate, leaving an indelible mark on the village and its people.

The Aqrabuamelu of Mottistone

The Enigmatic Arrival

Mottistone, a quaint village tucked away in the Isle of Wight's rolling hills, is renowned for its verdant landscape and historical charm. The village's heart is marked by Mottistone Manor, a grand medieval house surrounded by beautiful gardens and ancient woodlands. The manor's walls, adorned with ivy, and the expansive lawns offer a picturesque setting that contrasts sharply with the arrival of an extraordinary visitor—the Aqrabuamelu, known locally as the Scorpion Man.

The Aqrabuamelu, a fusion of man and scorpion, is a figure of legend and lore. Its upper half resembles a muscular human, with a bronzed torso and arms capable of impressive dexterity. Yet, as one's gaze descends, the creature's lower half transforms into the formidable tail of a scorpion, complete with a venomous stinger poised menacingly. This fusion of two distinct worlds creates a striking, if unsettling, figure.

The Aqrabuamelu's arrival was nothing short of dramatic. Emerging from the surrounding woods that shadow Mottistone Manor, it made its entrance with a mix of curiosity and trepidation. Its initial interactions with the villagers were met with a mix of awe and apprehension. The locals, familiar with the Manor's historical tales and the mysterious woods, were taken aback by this new addition to their idyllic surroundings.

In the local pub, The Village Inn, chatter buzzed about the creature's arrival. "Have you seen it?" one villager whispered, wide-eyed. "It's got the body of a scorpion and the face of a man!"

Another, more practical, responded, "Let's hope it's friendly. We've seen stranger things in these parts."

The Aqrabuamelu, observing from the edge of the village, noted the curious glances and cautious whispers. It was determined to navigate its new environment, balancing between the desire for acceptance and the reality of its fearsome appearance.

Bridging the Divide

Mottistone's villagers were initially apprehensive, but the Aqrabuamelu's playful nature began to break down barriers. Despite its intimidating appearance, the creature's disposition was friendly and engaging. It made an effort to integrate into village life by participating in local gatherings and events, earning tentative smiles and wary nods.

The Mottistone Village Fair, an annual event celebrating local traditions and crafts, became a key opportunity for the Aqrabuamelu to connect with the community. With its scorpion tail coiled behind it, the creature approached the fair's various stalls, engaging in light-hearted banter and attempting to demonstrate its good intentions. At the apple bobbing stand, the Aqrabuamelu, with great dexterity, managed to retrieve apples with remarkable precision, amusing and impressing onlookers.

Villager Martha Blythe, known for her charity work and warm personality, became one of the Aqrabuamelu's first allies.

"You're quite the showstopper, aren't you?" she said, handing the creature a freshly baked scone. "Not everyone can claim to have a scorpion-man at their fair."

The Aqrabuamelu, with a heartfelt smile, accepted the scone. "Thank you, Martha. I'm simply trying to fit in, one event at a time."

As weeks turned into months, the Aqrabuamelu's playful interactions and genuine efforts to engage with the villagers began to soften initial fears. The creature's charm and enthusiasm bridged the gap between its fearsome exterior and the warm-hearted nature of Mottistone's inhabitants.

Athletic Feats

Mottistone's picturesque landscape was perfect for outdoor activities, and the Aqrabuamelu eagerly participated in local sports. On sunny afternoons, as the village basked in the golden glow of the sun, the Aqrabuamelu joined in games of football at the village green. Its athleticism was nothing short of extraordinary.

The village green, surrounded by centuries-old oak trees and quaint cottages, provided an ideal setting for these games. Children's laughter mingled with the rhythmic thud of the football as the Aqrabuamelu showcased its impressive agility. With its human feet, the creature deftly manoeuvred the ball, impressing both young and old.

Villager Tom Harris, the local football coach, remarked, "The way you handle that ball, it's like you were born to play. Never thought I'd see the day when a scorpion-man joins our matches!"

The Aqrabuamelu responded with a grin, "I may not have been born to play football, but I'm certainly enjoying the game."

The creature's skill on the field quickly became a source of fascination and amusement. The rhythmic bounce of the ball and the cheers from the villagers turned these matches into a celebration of the Aqrabuamelu's unique abilities and its growing integration into the village.

Courts and Camaraderie

Basketball courts across Mottistone were transformed into stages for the Aqrabuamelu's remarkable displays of dexterity. The village's newly built sports court, with its bright orange lines and sturdy hoop, became a playground for both the Aqrabuamelu and its new friends.

The creature's basketball skills were as impressive as its football prowess. Handling the basketballs with its human hands, the Aqrabuamelu engaged in friendly matches with the villagers. Its agility and coordination made it a formidable player, while its friendly nature fostered a spirit of camaraderie on the court.

During one particularly intense match, the Aqrabuamelu dunked the ball with a flourish, sending the crowd into cheers. "Looks like you've got more than just a sting to offer!" shouted village youth, Emily Wright, her voice filled with excitement.

The Aqrabuamelu, catching its breath, replied, "I'm just here to have fun and show that even a scorpion-man can enjoy a good game."

The basketball games became a symbol of unity and acceptance, with the Aqrabuamelu's presence serving as a reminder of the village's inclusive spirit. The rhythmic bounce of the ball and the sound of laughter on the court highlighted the growing bond between the Aqrabuamelu and the community.

Challenges and Curiosity

Despite its athletic achievements, the Aqrabuamelu faced challenges in its quest for acceptance. The creature's name, Aqrabuamelu, which sounded exotic and enigmatic to the villagers, was a source of confusion. Its lobster-like appearance also made it a subject of curiosity and, at times, misunderstanding.

Villager John Millar, known for his inquisitive nature, approached the Aqrabuamelu one evening. "I have to ask, where does the name Aqrabuamelu come from? And why do you have the body of a scorpion?"

The Aqrabuamelu, pausing to consider the question, responded, "Aqrabuamelu is an ancient term from my homeland. It signifies a blend of human and scorpion traits. As for my appearance, it's a part of who I am, but it doesn't define all of me."

John, intrigued, nodded thoughtfully. "It's clear you're more than your appearance. It's your actions and kindness that truly matter."

The Aqrabuamelu's genuine interest in the villagers' lives and its friendly interactions helped to bridge the gap between its unique existence and the warmth of Mottistone. The creature's willingness to engage and its curiosity about the villagers' lives gradually eroded initial hesitations.

Chapter 6: Encounters with the Elven

Of particular interest to the Aqrabuamelu were the ethereal beings known as the Elven, who resided in the nearby woods. Drawn by their enchanting presence, the Aqrabuamelu sought to engage with them, hoping to bridge the gap between their worlds.

The Elven, known for their grace and wisdom, were initially wary of the Aqrabuamelu. However, the creature's genuine approach and respectful demeanour won them over. Through playful banter and shared moments of laughter, the Aqrabuamelu forged connections that transcended appearances.

One evening, as moonlight filtered through the trees, the Aqrabuamelu met Elven leader Elowen in the heart of the forest. "You have a unique presence," Elowen said, her voice melodic. "We've heard tales of you. What brings you to our realm?"

The Aqrabuamelu responded, "I seek to understand and connect with all who share this land. Your realm is beautiful, and I wish to be a part of it."

Elowen, smiling, replied, "Then welcome. We value your sincerity and are pleased to share our world with you."

The Aqrabuamelu's interactions with the Elven highlighted the creature's capacity for empathy and its desire to bridge gaps between different beings. These encounters enriched the Aqrabuamelu's journey and further integrated it into the diverse tapestry of Mottistone and its surroundings.

The Jersey Devil's Mischief

Despite the growing acceptance, the Aqrabuamelu faced persistent mischief from the Chale Green Jersey Devil. This notorious trickster took delight in filling the Aqrabuamelu's wheely bin with oddities, igniting a rivalry that added a layer of complexity to the creature's life.

The Jersey Devil, with its impish grin and mischievous nature, targeted the Aqrabuamelu's bin with a series of pranks. From filling it with colourful feathers to unexpected water balloons, the devil's antics became a source of ongoing frustration for the Aqrabuamelu.

One afternoon, as the Aqrabuamelu confronted the latest prank, it found itself face-to-face with the Jersey Devil. "Why do you persist with these tricks?" the Aqrabuamelu asked, frustration evident in its voice.

The Jersey Devil, twirling a feather in its hand, replied, "Because it's fun! And, let's be honest, you're such an easy target."

The Aqrabuamelu sighed, "Perhaps we could find a better way to spend our time—one that doesn't involve constant mischief."

The rivalry between the Aqrabuamelu and the Jersey Devil became a source of both tension and comic relief, highlighting the complexities of the creature's quest for acceptance. Despite the ongoing pranks, the Aqrabuamelu remained determined to forge a positive path forward.

A Moment of Unity

The ongoing feud with the Jersey Devil came to a head one day in Mottistone's village square. As tensions flared, a group of villagers intervened, urging both creatures to find common ground. The villagers, recognising the value of unity, sought to resolve the conflict.

In a heartfelt dialogue, the Aqrabuamelu and the Jersey Devil were encouraged to reflect on their actions. "Isn't it time we put our differences aside?" villager Anna Fielding suggested. "We all share this land and should work together."

The Aqrabuamelu, nodding in agreement, said, "I believe there's more we can achieve together than apart."

The Jersey Devil, after a moment of contemplation, replied, "Perhaps you're right. Let's try to make amends."

Through dialogue and understanding, the Aqrabuamelu and the Jersey Devil set aside their differences. They decided to work together for the betterment of the village, symbolising a shift towards cooperation and unity.

Celebrating Diversity

With the feud resolved, the Aqrabuamelu's presence in Mottistone became a symbol of unity and acceptance. The villagers embraced the creature's diverse nature and celebrated the wonders it brought to their community.
The village's annual Harvest Festival, held at Mottistone Manor's gardens, became a celebration of diversity. The Aqrabuamelu, alongside the Jersey Devil and the Elven, participated in various activities, showcasing their unique talents and contributions.
As the festival ended, the villagers gathered to celebrate. "To our unique and wonderful friends," Martha Blythe toasted, raising her glass. "May we always embrace the diversity that makes our community special."
The Aqrabuamelu, touched by the village's acceptance, responded, "Thank you for welcoming me and celebrating our differences. It's a testament to the beauty of diversity and inclusion."
The Harvest Festival became a symbol of the village's unity and appreciation for the extraordinary beings within their midst. The Aqrabuamelu's presence, once a source of curiosity and hesitation, was now celebrated as a vital part of Mottistone's rich tapestry.

As time passed, the Aqrabuamelu continued to roam the picturesque village of Mottistone, leaving a lasting legacy. Its playful spirit, remarkable athleticism, and genuine kindness became integral to the village's identity.
The tale of the Aqrabuamelu, the Scorpion Man of Mottistone, was shared across generations, inspiring future villagers to embrace diversity and celebrate differences. The creature's journey from a figure of fear to a symbol of acceptance and unity became a cherished part of the village's history.

Mottistone, with its historic landmarks and vibrant community spirit, stood as a testament to the Aqrabuamelu's enduring impact. The creature's legacy, woven into the fabric of the village, continued to inspire and captivate, leaving an indelible mark on the Isle of Wight and its people.

The Selkies of Shorwell

Beneath the Surface

Shorwell, a charming village on the Isle of Wight, is renowned for its tranquil beauty and historical allure. The village's narrow, winding streets, framed by honey-coloured cottages and ancient stone walls, lead to the serene River Shorwell, which meanders gently through the village. The highlight of Shorwell's landscape is St. Peter's Church, with its Norman architecture and well-tended churchyard that overlooks the surrounding countryside. The church's bell tower, visible from afar, often tolls softly, marking the passage of time in this idyllic setting.

In the crystalline waters off Shorwell's coast, the Selkies made their home. These mythical beings, with their sleek, streamlined bodies and dexterous flippers, were the envy of all aquatic creatures. With a blend of human and seal characteristics, their upper bodies were muscular and agile, while their lower halves, covered in glistening scales, allowed them to glide effortlessly through the water.

As the Selkies emerged from the depths, their presence was as captivating as it was enigmatic. Their aquatic grace and beauty enchanted the local villagers, who often gathered at the shore to catch a glimpse of these elusive creatures. The Selkies' sleek forms, with their shimmering skin reflecting the sunlight, became an emblem of the village's connection to the sea.

The Selkies' days were spent navigating the underwater world, exploring sunken shipwrecks, and communicating with sea life. Their elegant movements were a stark contrast to the bustling activity of the village above, where daily life continued with a gentle rhythm. The villagers, while fascinated by the Selkies, also respected their need for privacy and rarely ventured into their watery realm.

The Record Breakers

The Selkies' reputation extended far beyond Shorwell, particularly due to their astounding performance in the Round the Island yacht race. This prestigious event, encircling the Isle of Wight, attracts the best sailors from around the world. The Selkies' unofficial entry into the race became the talk of the region, as their speed and agility were unmatched by any competitor.

On race day, the picturesque Isle of Wight transformed into a bustling hub of nautical activity. Spectators lined the shores, their eyes trained on the horizon, while boats of every size competed for glory. The Selkies, however, were not among the traditional competitors. Instead, they swam alongside the yachts, their streamlined bodies cutting through the waves with an almost supernatural grace.

When the race concluded, the Selkies' performance was the talk of the town. They had completed the course a remarkable four hours ahead of the nearest competitor, their sleek forms slicing through the water with unparalleled speed. The sailors, initially sceptical, were left in awe of the Selkies' prowess. This unexpected victory became a cherished story in Shorwell, illustrating the Selkies' extraordinary abilities and their deep connection to the sea.

The Selkies' triumph was celebrated with a grand feast in Shorwell's village square. The locals, dressed in their finest attire, gathered to honour their aquatic neighbours. Traditional music filled the air, and laughter echoed through the streets as tales of the Selkies' remarkable feat were recounted with enthusiasm. The village's sense of pride in their Selkie residents was palpable, and the celebration became an annual tradition.

The Case of the Missing Phones

The Selkies' affinity for technology, particularly their love for capturing underwater selfies, added a touch of modern whimsy to their ancient lore. Despite their advanced swimming skills, the Selkies struggled with a rather humorous problem: their phones had a knack for disappearing. Whether swallowed by the sea or hidden among underwater treasures, these devices seemed to vanish without a trace.

The mystery of the missing phones became a frequent topic of conversation in Shorwell. "I swear I left it right here," Selkie leader Kieran would say, examining the shoreline with a puzzled expression. "And now it's gone again!"

Villagers often joined the search, turning the quest for the missing phones into a community event. "Have you checked near the shipwreck?" Mrs. Hawkins, the village elder, would suggest, her voice full of concern.

The sight of Selkies and humans scouring the shores together became a beloved part of village life. The Selkies' good-natured frustration and the villagers' enthusiastic participation in the search added a layer of charm to the village's daily routine. The missing phones, while a source of amusement, also served as a reminder of the unique bond between the Selkies and the people of Shorwell.

Mischief in the Gardens

The Selkies' playful nature extended beyond their aquatic realm and into the gardens of Shorwell. Known for their mischievous antics, they would occasionally visit the gardens, plucking unsuspecting cats and transporting them to unexpected locations. This playful behaviour led to a delightful yet puzzling exchange with the village's resident Gorgon.

The Gorgon, with her serpentine hair and petrifying gaze, initially found the Selkies' antics bewildering. Her garden, known for its vibrant flora and tranquil atmosphere, became a frequent target for the Selkies' playful escapades. "Another feline visitor?" she would exclaim with a bemused smile, discovering a cat lounging amidst her roses.

Despite her initial confusion, the Gorgon soon grew fond of the Selkies. Their playful interactions added a touch of whimsy to her solitary existence. "You Selkies certainly have a talent for turning my garden into a playground," she remarked, accepting the latest feline guest with a mixture of amusement and affection.

The Selkies' visits to the Gorgon's garden became a cherished part of Shorwell's lore. The unlikely friendship between the two beings, marked by playful exchanges and shared laughter, illustrated the harmony that could be achieved even among the most diverse of creatures.

Shopping in Yafford

A Selkie's visit to the neighbouring village of Yafford was an event that showcased the blending of the extraordinary with the everyday. Yafford, a tranquil village known for its historic landmarks such as St. Mary's Church and the picturesque Yafford Pond, was a place where the mundane and magical coexisted seamlessly.

When Selkie Niamh ventured into Yafford for a shopping trip, the villagers were initially startled by the sight of the aquatic being amidst their daily routines. "Well, this is unexpected," remarked shopkeeper Mr. Dawson, his eyes widening as Niamh entered his store.

Despite their initial surprise, the villagers quickly embraced Niamh's presence. "Welcome to Yafford!" Mrs. Elkins greeted her warmly, offering a basket of freshly baked scones. "It's not every day we have a Selkie shopping among us."

Niamh's charm and grace won over the villagers. She navigated the market with ease, her presence adding a touch of enchantment to the village's normalcy. The sight of a Selkie among the stalls, selecting fresh produce and chatting with the locals, became a delightful story, illustrating the seamless integration of magic into everyday life.

Encounters with the Gorgon

The ongoing mischief between the Selkies and the Gorgon continued to weave a tapestry of whimsy and wonder. Their interactions became a highlight of the village's lore, showcasing the unlikely friendship between the playful Selkies and the formidable Gorgon.

One sunny afternoon, the Selkies and the Gorgon gathered in the Gorgon's garden for another round of playful antics. "Do you have any more surprises for me today?" the Gorgon inquired with a sly grin.

"Only the finest!" Kieran responded, presenting a particularly well-behaved cat with a flourish. "We thought this one might enjoy your company."

The Gorgon's laughter rang out, a rare sound for one so often feared. "You Selkies have a knack for brightening my day," she said, accepting the cat with a mix of amusement and affection.

The playful exchanges between the Selkies and the Gorgon became a symbol of the village's acceptance of the extraordinary. Their interactions, marked by laughter and shared enjoyment, illustrated the harmony that could be achieved even among the most diverse of beings.

Guardians of the Sea

Despite their playful nature, the Selkies remained vigilant guardians of the sea. Their sleek forms navigated the depths with unmatched skill, ensuring the safety and health of their aquatic domain. Their underwater selfies, capturing moments of aquatic splendour, became a treasured record of the sea's mysteries and beauty.

One evening, as the sun dipped below the horizon, the Selkies gathered to discuss their latest adventures. "The sea is as wondrous as ever," Selkie leader Kieran observed, his eyes reflecting the shimmering waves. "We've discovered new caves and encountered other mythical beings."

"We must continue to protect it," Fiona added, her voice resolute. "Our role as guardians is vital."

The Selkies' dedication to their role was evident in their actions. Their underwater explorations and their efforts to maintain the sea's balance reinforced their status as both protectors and explorers. Their presence served as a reminder of the magic that lay beneath the waves, a testament to the enchantment that resided within the waters of Shorwell and beyond.

The Unseen Adventures

Beyond their playful antics and record-breaking feats, the Selkies' lives were rich with unseen adventures. Their explorations of hidden underwater caves, encounters with ancient shipwrecks, and meetings with other mythical beings added layers to their existence.
One particularly intriguing adventure involved discovering an ancient shipwreck deep beneath the waves. "This is a remarkable find," Kieran said, examining the relics with fascination. "It's a piece of history we've never seen before." The Selkies' underwater explorations revealed secrets of the past and connections to other mythical beings. Their stories, shared with the villagers in whispered tales, became a source of wonder and intrigue. The Selkies' adventures, while hidden from view, added depth to their legend and illustrated the rich tapestry of their existence.

Harmony in Shorwell

The Selkies' presence in Shorwell fostered a sense of harmony and wonder. The villagers, having grown accustomed to their aquatic neighbours, embraced the magic that the Selkies brought to their lives. Their playful interactions, record-breaking feats, and occasional missing phones became a cherished part of the village's lore.
Village elder Mrs. Hawkins reflected on the Selkies' impact. "Their presence has added a new dimension to our lives," she said. "They remind us of the magic that lies just beyond the horizon."

The bond between the Selkies and the villagers became a symbol of unity and acceptance. The Selkies' graceful movements, playful antics, and dedication to their role as guardians of the sea were woven into the fabric of Shorwell's history. Their presence continued to inspire and captivate, leaving an indelible mark on the village and its people.

As the years passed, the Selkies continued to thrive in Shorwell. Their graceful navigation of the sea, their mischievous adventures, and their encounters with other mythical beings added richness to their legend. The tranquil shores and rolling hills of the Isle of Wight provided a picturesque backdrop to their lives.
In the heart of Shorwell, the Selkies' story became a cherished part of the village's history. Their underwater selfies, playful antics, and dedication to their role as guardians of the sea illustrated the enduring magic of the Isle of Wight.
The Selkies thrived amidst the ever-changing landscape of Shorwell, their presence a testament to the enchantment that lay just beyond the horizon. In the village's folklore, their legacy continued to inspire and captivate, reminding all who resided there of the magic that resided both above and below the surface.

The gathering of Legends

The Enigmatic Invitation

On a crisp autumn evening, the Isle of Wight was alive with an air of excitement. The sun dipped below the horizon, casting a golden glow over the land. In the centre of the island, nestled between rolling hills and ancient forests, stood Shorwell's ancient stone circle—a place long forgotten by time but chosen as the meeting ground for a gathering that would transcend legends.

The invitation had been sent far and wide, carried by enchanted beings and mysterious messengers. It was not a typical summons but a call to unite the Isle's myriad of mythical creatures. From the majestic Griffin of Cowes to the elusive Faun of Newbridge, all were invited to converge for an evening of shared tales and revelry.

The message, penned in silver ink on a scroll of ancient parchment, read:

"To the Guardians of the Isle,

In the spirit of unity and shared magic, you are summoned to the ancient stone circle of Shorwell. Come together, share your adventures, and celebrate the magic that binds us all.

Yours in harmony, Aqrabuamelu of Mottistone"

As the sun set, creatures of every shape and form began to arrive. The air hummed with anticipation as each legendary being took their place under the stars.

The Arrival of Legends

First to arrive was the Griffin of Cowes, its majestic wings casting shadows over the circle. With a roar that echoed through the woods, it landed gracefully. The Gurnard Golem followed, its stone form moving with an unexpected grace, while the Hampstead Ogre ambled in with a loud, jovial bellow. Each arrival was met with awe and curiosity from the gathered crowd.

The Faun of Newbridge trotted in with a playful skip, his hooves barely making a sound. The Leprechaun of Northwood appeared next, his emerald green suit glistening under the moonlight. The Shalfleet Sphinx, with its enigmatic smile, watched from the shadows, while the Yarmouth Mermaid emerged from the nearby stream, her scales shimmering.

From Chale Green, the Bowcombe Chupacabra slinked in with a mischievous grin. The Carisbrooke Banshee's eerie wail floated through the night air, followed by the Nymph of Marks Corner, whose presence seemed to bring a faint scent of blooming flowers. The Norton Green Kitsune, with its multiple tails swishing, added an air of mystical elegance to the gathering.

As the evening progressed, the Sea Serpent of Ryde slithered in from the shore, its scales reflecting the starlight. The Vampires of Brading arrived next, their pale forms moving with an almost imperceptible grace. The Fairies of St Helens flitted about with their tiny, glowing wings, while the Werewolves of Bembridge came in, their eyes gleaming with the moon's light.

The Loch Ness Monster at Downend made an impressive entrance, its serpentine body making waves as it approached the circle. The Minotaur of Cowes, tall and imposing, stood near the centre, while the Chimera of Oakfield and Swanmore prowled with an air of authority. The Basilisk of Havenstreet slithered in with a chilling gaze, followed by the Dragons of Newport, whose fiery breath illuminated the dark.

The Roc of Shide landed with a powerful gust of wind, and the Trolls of Wootton ambled in, their brutish forms contrasting with the elegance of the Elven of Brook. The Cyclops of Sandown followed, his single eye scanning the crowd. The Zombies of Shanklin shuffled in, while the Satyr of Wroxall danced lightly on his hooves. The Manticore of Alverstone arrived with a roar, and the Djinn of Apse Heath materialised with a swirl of smoke.

The Yeti of Bonchurch lumbered in, leaving a trail of frost in its wake, and the Medusa of Godshill arrived with a serpentine grace. The Phoenix of Merstone glided in with fiery plumage, and the Wraiths of Niton hovered ominously. The Wendigo of St Lawrence brought a chill to the air, while the Hydra of Ventnor emerged from the depths with its many heads.

The Freshwater Gorgon, last but certainly not least, made her entrance, her gaze turning the water around her into ice. The Pegasus of Alum Bay descended gracefully from the skies, and the Goblin of Chale added a touch of mischief to the gathering. The Jersey Devil of Chale Green followed, its appearance eliciting a few gasps.

Finally, the Gnome of Rowbridge and the Bigfoot of Totland rounded out the assembly, their distinct forms adding to the diverse tapestry of the gathering. The Thunderbird of Blackgang, with its mighty wings, completed the circle, its thunderous call echoing through the night.

The Exchange of Tales

As the night settled in, the mythical beings gathered around a grand feast laid out in the centre of the stone circle. The Aqrabuamelu took centre stage, its powerful presence commanding attention.

"Welcome, friends," the Aqrabuamelu began. "Tonight, we share our stories, celebrate our adventures, and honour the magic that connects us."

The Griffin of Cowes, with a nod, began the evening's tales. "I remember the day I soared over the Needles, catching glimpses of ancient relics buried in the cliffs. My eyes have seen the Isle's secrets, and I've been a silent guardian of its skies."

The Gurnard Golem, with a gravelly voice, added, "I've protected the coastal lands, my stone form weathering the storms that the sea brings. I recall a time when I helped divert a tidal wave that threatened Shorwell, saving countless lives."

The Hampstead Ogre chuckled, "And I've had my share of fun in the hills of Hampstead. There was a time when I turned a village's pumpkin patch into a maze just for amusement. I think the villagers enjoyed it more than they let on."

The Faun of Newbridge twirled with a smile. "In the Newbridge forest, I've danced with the spirits of the trees. There was a night when the moonlight revealed a hidden grove, where I found a long-lost fairy ring."

The Leprechaun of Northwood chimed in, "I've hidden my gold throughout Northwood, but I've also been a guardian of luck. Once, I turned a poor farmer's fortunes around with a single enchanted coin."

The Shalfleet Sphinx leaned forward. "I've posed riddles to those who seek wisdom. One particular riddle led a lost soul to rediscover a hidden path through the Shalfleet woods, reuniting them with their family."

The Yarmouth Mermaid's voice was melodic. "My songs have calmed stormy seas and guided lost sailors to safety. There was a time when I led a shipwrecked crew to the shores of Yarmouth, saving them from the treacherous waters."

The Bowcombe Chupacabra snickered, "I've had my share of mischief, particularly with livestock. But there was a time when I helped a farmer reclaim his stolen sheep from a rival clan."

The Carisbrooke Banshee's wail was a soft, haunting melody. "I've been a harbinger of change, but I've also helped guide lost souls to their final rest. There was a time when my cry led a grieving family to peace."

The Nymph of Marks Corner added, "I've nurtured the flora and fauna of my domain. Once, I restored a dying grove with a single touch, bringing it back to life."

The Norton Green Kitsune, with a flick of its tails, said, "I've woven illusions to protect my realm. There was a time when my illusions helped save a village from an invading army by hiding their true location."

The Sea Serpent of Ryde's deep voice rumbled, "I've guarded the waters around Ryde. There was a time when I prevented a shipwreck by guiding a storm-tossed vessel to safety."

The Vampires of Brading spoke next. "We've lived among the shadows, but there was a time when we saved a town from a marauding band of invaders, using our knowledge of the night to their advantage."

The Fairies of St Helens flitted about, their voices chiming in harmony. "We've sprinkled our magic over the Isle, turning mundane moments into magical ones. There was a time when our pixie dust brought a summer's night dream to life."

The Werewolves of Bembridge howled in agreement. "We've guarded our lands by night, but there was a time when our pack defended the village from a rogue band of trolls."

The Loch Ness Monster at Downend rumbled, "I've seen many things from the depths, including a time when I helped uncover an ancient sunken city beneath the waves."

The Minotaur of Cowes grunted, "I've guarded my labyrinth and its secrets. There was a time when I led a brave soul out of the maze, rewarding their courage."

The Chimera of Oakfield and Swanmore roared, "I've defended the land from dark forces. There was a time when I repelled a demon horde, saving countless lives."

The Basilisk of Havenstreet's gaze was chilling. "I've turned intruders to stone, but I've also safeguarded the Isle from malevolent beings by keeping my gaze focused on those who seek harm."

The Dragons of Newport shared tales of their fiery breath, recounting how they'd once forged a barrier of fire to protect their mountain lair from invaders.

The Roc of Shide's voice boomed, "I've soared over the Isle, my wings creating storms to fend off threats. There was a time when my storm helped guide a lost traveller to safety."

The Trolls of Wootton grumbled with amusement, "We've had our share of battles, but there was a time when we helped build a bridge for a village cut off by a flood."

The Cyclops of Sandown's single eye scanned the crowd. "I've seen many things through my eye, including a time when I used my strength to save a village from a landslide."

The Zombies of Shanklin shambled in, their presence eerie but calm. "We've walked the night, but there was a time when we guided lost souls to their rest, helping them find peace."

The Satyr of Wroxall danced lightly. "I've played music that has enchanted many, including a time when my melodies brought joy to a grieving family."

The Manticore of Alverstone's tail flicked. "I've defended the land from threats with my fierce roar and tail, but there was a time when I saved a village from a marauding band of creatures."

The Djinn of Apse Heath swirled in a cloud of smoke. "I've granted wishes and changed fates. There was a time when a single wish turned the tide of a great battle."

The Yeti of Bonchurch's presence was imposing yet gentle. "I've braved the cold, but there was a time when I guided a lost expedition through a snowstorm, leading them to safety."
The Medusa of Godshill's gaze was calm. "I've turned many to stone but also used my power to protect my realm from those who sought to harm it."
The Phoenix of Merstone's fiery plumage illuminated the night. "I've risen from the ashes many times. There was a moment when my rebirth saved a village from a devastating fire."
The Wraiths of Niton floated silently, their presence ethereal. "We've watched over the Isle, but there was a time when our whispers guided a lost soul to their destination."
The Wendigo of St Lawrence's icy breath was palpable. "I've been a guardian of the cold, but there was a time when I helped a village survive a harsh winter."
The Hydra of Ventnor's many heads spoke in unison. "We've guarded the waters, but there was a time when we helped quell a storm that threatened to flood the Isle."
The Freshwater Gorgon's gaze was soft yet powerful. "I've guarded the freshwater springs, and there was a time when my gaze stopped a great drought from drying out the land."
The Pegasus of Alum Bay's wings fluttered lightly. "I've flown high above, but there was a time when my flight helped deliver a message of hope across the Isle."
The Goblin of Chale's mischievous grin was evident. "I've played tricks and pranks, but there was a time when I used my cunning to outwit a band of invaders."
The Jersey Devil of Chale Green's presence was unsettling yet intriguing. "I've protected the swamps and marshes, but there was a time when I defended a village from encroaching darkness."
The Gnome of Rowbridge's voice was warm. "I've tended to the gardens and fields, and there was a time when my efforts saved a harvest from a blight."

The Bigfoot of Totland's appearance was both formidable and friendly. "I've roamed the forests, but there was a time when I helped guide a lost party back to their camp."

The Thunderbird of Blackgang's call resonated through the night. "I've brought storms and rain, but there was a time when I summoned a storm to protect a village from invaders."

The Elven of Brook's grace was evident in every movement. "We've lived in harmony with the land, but there was a time when our magic healed a wounded forest."

The Chillerton Bogeyman's presence was mysterious. "I've been a figure of fear, but there was a time when my presence deterred a dark force from invading the Isle."

The Aqrabuamelu of Mottistone, with its grand presence, concluded the evening's tales. "We have shared our stories and celebrated our unity. Each of us plays a vital role in the magic of this Isle."

A Night to Remember

As dawn approached, the gathering concluded with a grand feast under the stars. The tales shared, the bonds forged, and the magic celebrated would be remembered for ages. The ancient stone circle of Shorwell had once again proven to be a place where legends came together, where the fabric of their stories wove into a grand tapestry of unity and wonder.

With their hearts full and their spirits high, the mythical creatures began to depart, each returning to their realms with a renewed sense of purpose and connection. The Isle of Wight, with its blend of ancient magic and mythical beings, remained a place of wonder and unity, a testament to the power of shared stories and the enduring bonds between its guardians. As the first light of day broke over the Isle, the creatures of legend vanished into the mist, their tales echoing in the hearts of those who had gathered and would continue to resonate through the land for years to come.

4o mini

Conclude the story by telling people to visit the Isle of Wight and explore the history and mystery, and if you search enough, you might feel a breeze, see a shadow, or feel a presence. Don't worry; it's a mythical creature ensuring you're okay.

Epilogue: The Magic of the Isle of Wight

As the first rays of dawn touched the ancient stones of Shorwell, a serene hush fell over the Isle of Wight. The mythical creatures, each having shared their tales and woven their magic into the fabric of the land, now dispersed into the mists of legend and lore. The stone circle, now bathed in morning light, stood as a silent witness to the grandeur of the night before, where worlds of wonder had converged.

To all who read this, the Isle of Wight beckons with an invitation of its own. It is a land where history and mystery intermingle, where every stone, every shadow, and every whisper of the breeze holds a story. From the tranquil shores of Shorwell to the ancient forests of Newbridge, the Isle offers an unparalleled journey through realms both known and unknown.

Visit the Isle of Wight and let its charm envelop you. Walk the coastal paths where legends tread, explore the historic towns where ancient and mythical stories are interwoven with everyday life. Wander through the enchanting woodlands of Northwood, and venture to the cliffside viewpoints of Alum Bay, where the breathtaking views are matched only by the stories whispered by the winds.

In the quiet moments of your exploration, when the sun dips low and the world becomes a canvas of shadows, be attuned to the subtle signs of magic. You might feel a gentle breeze where none should be, glimpse a fleeting shadow out of the corner of your eye, or sense a presence that seems to watch over you. Fear not these sensations; they are not harbingers of unease but guardians of the Isle's enduring enchantment.

For every breeze you feel, every shadow you see, every presence you sense is a gentle reminder that the Isle of Wight is a realm where mythical creatures ensure that its visitors are safe and cherished. It is their way of sharing their magic with you, ensuring that the wonder of their world is always within reach.

So, embark on your journey to the Isle of Wight. Let its mysteries unfold before you and allow its magic to touch your soul. For those who seek, the Isle offers more than just scenic beauty; it offers a chance to connect with the stories of old, to feel the presence of ancient guardians, and to experience the enchantment that is as real as the land itself.

The Isle of Wight awaits, a timeless realm where the past and the mystical blend seamlessly. Come and discover the magic that lives within its heart, and perhaps, as you leave, you will carry with you the echoes of legends and the whispers of mythical beings that continue to roam this enchanting land. Welcome to the Isle of Wight. May your adventure be as wondrous and magical as the stories that linger in its air.

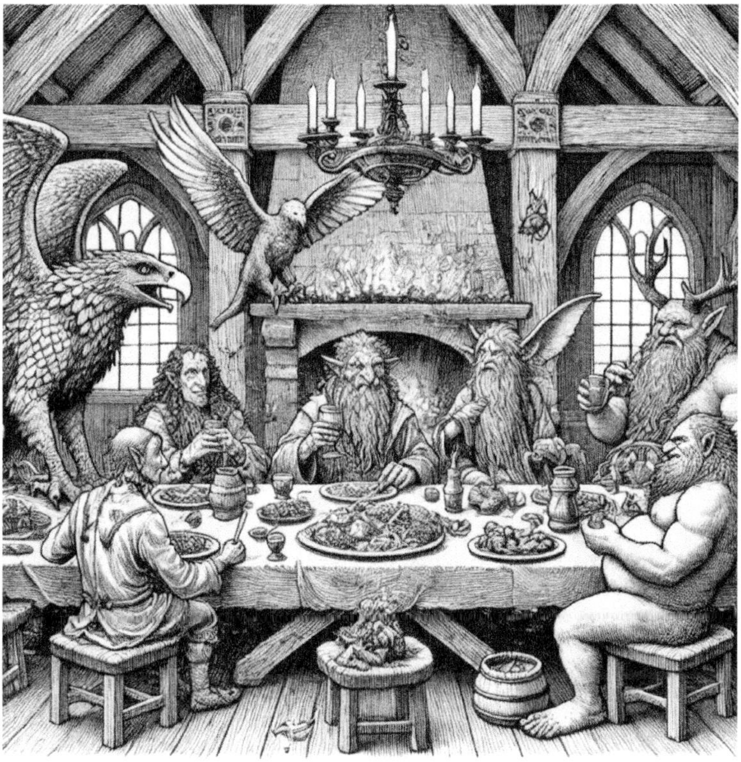